# BLACK BRIDGE

*Written by JOE O'HAGAN*

*The Bear and the Crow.*

# 1.

Lorcan was a faint silver outline in the moonlight, flitting in and out of shadow. Maeve lost him to the darkness. Rising panic gripped her as he failed to reappear, but abated as he again emerged into view, powering his way upwards. This pattern repeated itself with greater frequency as they left any semblance of civilization and light, ascending ever higher towards the top of Sliabh Dorcha. Maeve focused, needing to find out where Lorcan had been going, and she was determined to keep track of him. She just had to stay hidden.

Since starting back to school for their seventh, and final, year, he'd distanced himself from their friend group. He was practically estranged. Plus, for the last week she'd spotted him making his way past her house at the same time every night. *Midnight*. At first, she took no heed, after all, he was always out walking, but when it became a third and fourth time, she knew something had to be up. What possible reason did he have for late-night outings? It was most likely not good, and she hated that she felt compelled to involve herself. That was Maeve, ever the empath – maybe it was just curiosity or plain nosiness – but she was getting to the bottom of this.

She shivered, attempting to keep her breath shallow and silent, keen to not draw any unwanted attention from her prey, or anyone else who may be nearby. If her dad caught her he'd go into conniptions – she wasn't meant to be out of the house at this hour. But, then again, neither was Lorcan. He strode purposefully along the winding path and up the hill, hardly slowing down for the steep sections. Maybe he wasn't joking about running up the mountains every morning. She thought he'd been exaggerating or outright lying. Who in their right mind would put themselves through this on a daily basis? Maeve huffed, trying to keep pace as she pressed on, only slightly hyperventilating with the effort and vowing to renew her membership to the tiny village gym when she got the chance. A vow that was no doubt to be reneged on. To her great relief the ground levelled out, as did her ragged breathing, and she stayed off of the gravel path, treading carefully through the soft grass, damp and glistening with night air.

This was how they did it in the movies. They hid in tall grass, creeping on the periphery. It all seemed so unreal. The night. The moon. The cold. The whole situation. It was exciting and she felt like a predator. She felt lethal.

A clearing opened in the trees. Lorcan was heading towards the old ruined fort that sat perched atop the hill. Maeve guessed this is where he'd been leading them, but for the life of her couldn't figure out why. What could be here that was of such import he'd been sneaking out of his aunt's house and was dragging her into it? Even if he didn't realise he'd picked up a stalker. She half expected to see someone else there, maybe there was a drug deal going on? That might explain his behaviour lately, but he just didn't seem the type. And, anyway, where the hell would a person get drugs in a place like Droichead Dubh? A tiny border town that straddled the line between being in Northern Ireland and being a pedigree, purebred Republic of Ireland town. No man's land. The lack of true identity for the place was bad enough, but it was murderously difficult to get a good phone signal because of the territory dispute. It just wouldn't make good business sense for a drug cartel to set up shop here, everybody knew everybody, and she doubted any of them were into doing hardcore drug deals at ancient Irish ritual sites.

She watched him slink behind one of the monolithic standing stones that enshrined the crumbling central chamber. The black circular walls had long since lost their towering height to the aeons of erosion, but were still tall enough to hide a full-grown man in their bowels. A great, hungry, swallowing darkness. It was time to break cover. Without the trees to conceal her, Maeve moved more slowly, every footstep carefully placed, but was fairly sure that Lorcan was too focused on what he was doing to notice his clandestine follower. She froze as he stopped abruptly at the base of the fort. Had she been spotted? He carried on, more slowly this time, and her shoulders relaxed. Lorcan swivelled his head, appearing to examine the fort like he was expecting to see something or someone there. *Curiouser and curiouser.*

Maeve began to regret her tailing of him tonight. What if he was meeting a girl here – or a guy – or whatever? She didn't peg him for having secret romps under the light of the moon, and she certainly wouldn't want to intrude on that, but she'd come too far now. She was committed. Whatever was causing Lorcan to ignore them all, and making her feel like she'd been kicked to the curb for something unknown, she was going to find out. She just hoped it wasn't some weird sex fetish that she was stumbling on. In addition to being in no-man's-land, Droichead Dubh had a small but avid Pagan community at its heart. Maeve had no idea what they got up to, but there were rumours. The hypothetical drug deal would be preferable.

Lorcan disappeared behind the huge standing stones. This was her chance to get closer, there was no way he'd see her now, though Maeve's thumping heart might give the game away. Her rib cage rattled with every strained pump of her blood, pounding both from the climb and from the sheer anxiety of the situation. She took a few deep but silent breaths to calm down and, when the sound of rushing blood ceased in her ears, she could make out Lorcan's voice. Maeve listened for whoever he was talking to to reply, but only Lorcan could be heard calling out into the void, talking to himself.

She couldn't make out specifics from behind the stone, and so crept stealthily around it until she could parse what he was saying.

"...of course I do. I want nothing more, but I just don't

know how I'd do that."

Do what? What was he talking about? And why had he come to ruminate here? She was definitely going to have a talk with his aunt when this was over, Cara needed to hear about this. Maeve knew Lorcan was pretty messed up with everything that happened, but not *talking to yourself in ancient ruins in the dead of night* kind of messed up. It all felt a bit icky.

She didn't want to be here anymore – she'd found out what he'd been up to and was now feeling sorry for him. And if anything was 'icky', it was her spying on him. Maeve made to leave when a voice stopped her in her tracks. It wasn't Lorcan's voice. It was a new voice, another man's voice, or was he really at the point of changing his vocals to converse with himself?

"I've told you what you need to do, son. If you want to be with us again, you'll do it."

The voice rang older than Lorcan's, but it was thinner, like he couldn't quite get enough air into and out of his lungs. She didn't know why, but its timbre made Maeve's skin crawl, and she fought back a convulsive shudder. Nails on a chalkboard. A fork grinding a plate. She flexed her fingers painfully against the cold, aware of the sudden drop in temperature that seemed to leech warmth from her body.

"I do want to be with you daddy – you and mammy – but _"

"But nothing, now I don't want to see you here again unless -"

*Crack.* Maeve's stiff fingers rung through the still night air with a bony pop, halting the unknown's speech. *Shit!* She held still, hoping that they would just go back to talking and put the sound down to an errant animal. The approaching crunching footsteps said otherwise. She wheeled around to run down the hill again and failed to move. It wasn't just Maeve's fingers, her entire body was a block of ice. This wasn't just cold, it was something else, and her limbs were point-blank refusing to do as they were told. *Come on! Move! MOVE!* Despite the screaming in her head, she stayed put, as if held by some invisible icy demon.

The footsteps were here now. She turned her head just enough to watch Lorcan appear from behind the stone, his face half cast in shadow. His expression, manic. The look of a person caught doing something they really shouldn't be, and she feared what he was thinking, though she didn't have to guess. It was written all over his visage.

Lorcan stood stock still for a moment before lurching forward and reaching for Maeve's throat.

# 2.

Adrenaline surged through her veins, Maeve's arms shooting to intercept Lorcan's. The freezing ground met them as they fell in a frenzied tangle. His breaths came raggedly, unsteadily. He was unhinged. In amongst their scrambling Lorcan's hands found her throat and as he ably pinned her down. He was strong, and her reserves were draining. Fingers began to squeeze, and Maeve knew she didn't have long to manoeuvre herself out of this situation. As the pressure increased on her airway so did the intensity of Lorcan's mutterings. Through her gasped breaths she could just about make him out. *What did you see? How much did she hear? What did you see, Maeve!?* Over and over like a rhythmic chanting.

She searched for some string of words that might appease him. Opening her mouth to say something, anything, produced no sound. She had no breath to give. Clawing at his arms, she tried to pry them apart and get some air, but it wasn't working. He had a vice grip. Maeve knew she wasn't going to win. The sounds of their laboured breaths and the soft, shuffling of their feet on the grassy gravel scrambling for purchase filled the night. In the only move she could conceivably make, Maeve looked her attacker in the eye. If this was it, she was determined to face him. It immediately had an effect, like Lorcan only now realised what he was doing. His manic fury began to subside, leaving his body almost as quickly as it had possessed it. Fear streaked across his face as his grip lightened, and he violently shoved himself away from her, collapsing in a heap. Maeve rolled onto her side, gulping air and retching at the sudden influx of oxygen into her system. It was agony, but it was good.

Taking a moment, she gathered her thoughts. She didn't even want to look at Lorcan but, when she did, she saw that he had huddled up against the same stone she'd been hiding behind a moment prior. Head in hands and sobbing hard. She couldn't square this sight with the psycho who'd been throttling her just a moment earlier – almost. Maeve cleared her throat, making a few test sounds before attempting to speak again.

"What the hell is wrong with you? What was that?! Huh?!" She spat, keeping her distance.

"I'm sorry... I'm so sorry. You don't understand."

He didn't even have the balls to look up at her as he spoke. A spark of fury lit inside her. What the hell had he been thinking? She tightened her grip on that spark but felt it slipping away, fizzling itself out as she took him in. Lorcan shook as he cried into his sleeve, which was quickly becoming wet with tears and snot. He looked like a chastised toddler – he looked pathetic.

"What don't I understand?" She said, injecting a hard edge into her voice.

"I can't... you won't believe... you'll think I'm mad."

"It's a bit bloody late for that, Lorcan. So tell me what the hell is going on before I report you to the police. Or your aunt." She coughed out that last part.

"No! No, please, don't tell her about this!" He held out his hands in a '*stop!*' motion

"Then talk."

Lorcan's shoulders lifted and then dipped as a long breath trailed out, before tilting his head to look at Maeve. She could see the glittering paths his tears had carved out, winding down his face and framing his anguished expression. He really did look pathetic.

"How long were you there?" He whispered.

"Nope. Explain. I swear I will call the fucking police." Maeve snatched her phone out of her pocket and dialled the number, her thumb hovering over the ring button. She stared him down. He wasn't going to weasel out of this, she was getting an explanation now.

"Okay." He said, resigned, "But I'm not crazy."

Lorcan proceeded to recount the past few months in excruciating detail. His parent's sudden deaths. This she knew. Him moving in with his aunt, Cara. Again, this she knew. He'd better get to the point soon, she was losing patience with him and this all felt like a pity party to excuse his shitty behaviour. That's when things got weird.

"I started having these dreams. They were about my mam and dad and..." He stopped and looked at Maeve, as though probing for her reaction, "Well, they were more like nightmares. They'd start off normal enough – as normal as dreams can be anyway – but then it'd take a turn and my parents would be dead. They'd reach for me with their decayed hands and start dragging me down into the ground with them. I couldn't breathe, and I could almost smell the rot from the earth, and from them. I'd be dragged down and down and... they were vivid. And then I'd wake up, but I'd still be in the dream, and I'd wake up here." He indicated the fort with a hand wave.

"Okay, but nightmares don't explain this." Maeve too gestured to their current surroundings and her neck, which was beginning to ache as the adrenaline ran dry.

"I know. I'm getting there."

"Bad dreams I can handle. I've always had those. But these dreams... they didn't stop when I woke up, they carried on. Even during the day I saw things out of the corner of my eye, shapes. You know when you walk into a room and feel like something's there watching you, waiting for you? It was like that, except I knew there *was* something there. Someone." He was absentmindedly biting the calloused skin at the edge of his thumbnail as he spoke, "I told myself that it was just my mind playing tricks. Lack of sleep. Stress. Grief. The more I tried to ignore it, the more real it became and the more it took shape. I'd wake up in the middle of the night and there it was in the corner of the room, standing. Watching me. There was something familiar about it."

Lorcan's middle-distance stare told Maeve that he was reliving that scenario in his head all over again. This delusion was real to him.

"And then what?" She found the words had slipped past her lips despite her incredulity. It may have been a fantasy, but it was an intriguing fantasy.

"And then I saw it again, the next night, and the next night, and the next."

"Jesus. How long was this going on for?"

"A while."

"Is this why you got... strange? Why you cut us off?" There was pain in those words.

Lorcan nodded.

"You should have told us you were going through something. We might have been able to help you."

"As if any of you would believe me."

An uncomfortable silence befell the scene, amplified by the noiseless wind that rustled nearby trees.

"Why here? What's special about this place?" Maeve said, breaking the quiet.

"My dreams. As I said, I'd always appear here in them. I'm not even one-hundred percent sure I'd ever actually been to this fort before, but it was so clear. I looked at the shape, the figure, and I just knew that this is where I had to be. I was fed up with being followed, so I was being proactive and going to the source."

"I see." She tried to keep the disbelief at a minimum.

"Yeah, it sounds stupid. Imagine how I felt that first night, calling out to thin air for god knows how long. I was going to leave, it was bloody freezing, but then... I heard him. It was impossible, but I spoke to him, and I've *been* speaking to him ever since."

His near blue lips pulled into a weak smile. That was

well and good, but the cryptic bullshit had to stop.

"Who? Who are you speaking to?"

"My dad.

His smile suggested that this answer cleared up everything and there were no more questions to be asked, wrapping everything up in a neat bow. Sure, it explained him sneaking out and being exhausted in class, but it didn't explain that anger that she had witnessed earlier. He had very much lost his mind. In Maeve's opinion she wasn't dealing with a rational person. Still, he'd calmed down for now, so she would indulge him and get them both home safely.

"So that's who you were talking to when I arrived then? Your dad?"

"Yeah, that was him."

*Sure it was.* It wasn't just Lorcan putting on a voice.

"What about your mam? Have you seen her or talked with her?"

Lorcan hesitated at this and then said quieter, "No, not yet."

"I see." *Not yet?* Maeve didn't have much of a response. What could she say to that anyway?

She looked away from him, feeling awkward, and hugged herself. The thin material of her jacket wasn't doing much to retain body heat. Lorcan took note of this.

"It's cold. We should probably go." He said, raising himself in a smooth motion. He took a few big sniffs, wiped his face with his sleeve, and began to retrace his path down the hillside. Maeve followed cautiously, very aware of what happened last time Lorcan got too close to her. She was also very aware of how quickly his mood had changed. One minute he'd been crazed, the next he'd been outrageously vulnerable, the next oddly calm. What was she dealing with? She wasn't sure she'd ever truly known this boy. There was no chat as they descended and walked the unlit road to Maeve's house. Reaching the bottom of her garden, Lorcan turned to her, and she stopped a few metres short, not wanting to get too close.

His face was blank.

"I know what you must think, and I know you probably don't believe me." He said, failing to look her in the eye again.

Maeve said nothing. He was dead right, she didn't believe him. But maybe she did understand a little better now the depth of his grief and how much he was hurting. This was a damaged boy in front of her, and what little was left of her anger somewhat faded into the background. Her overriding feeling was concern for him.

"I'm sorry." He said, turning and beginning to walk back to his aunt's, "I'm so sorry."

She watched him. His shoulders tense, probably cringing from everything that just happened.

"I'm not going to call the police," She said, "and I won't tell your aunt. But you should talk to someone."

His shoulders sacked, and he continued on, disappearing into the darkness.

# 3.

The next school day was spent in a listless daze, and Maeve doubted that she'd learned anything at all. Mostly she focused her tenuous concentration on looking out for Lorcan who hadn't shown up. No surprise there. She was surprised she'd mustered enough energy to make it into class, but she wasn't one for bunking off. The lingering image of him looming over her, hands around her throat, kept replaying in her mind. Lucky for her it was snowing – unseasonably so – but it was a great excuse to wear a scarf, covering the bruises that had developed since last night. There were protests from her teachers about following uniform regulations, apart from Politics class, where she could pass it off as some lame protest about nonconformity.

Her friends kept nudging her throughout the day, bringing her back to the present. *Earth to Maeve, respond, I repeat, respond.* She'd force herself into the present moment, but the slideshow just started all over again. But it wasn't just the vision of the furious, maniacal Lorcan that swam through her mind, no, amongst the images sat a sad, pathetic Lorcan who was so clearly in pain. He suffered worse than he'd ever let on. That hit home.

It was true that ever since he'd arrived six months back, he'd been quiet and brooding. Maeve thought that this had been some affectation he'd adopted to seem aloof and to give off that *too cool for school* vibe that any new kid strives for. He'd attended class without much of a fuss, making few waves. After the first few days people sort of forgot about him, he blended in with the furniture. He joined no clubs and made zero effort to talk to any of his classmates. Droichead Dubh was a small town though, and news travels fast in small towns. Soon everyone knew that Lorcan was not just a broody loner, he was most probably in the throes of grief. According to the grapevine, Lorcan's parents had died horribly in an accident. Some said it was a boating incident, others a plane – there were rumours one or both of them had worked for some government organisation – but others insisted there was something more nefarious that had happened to them. Possibly involving Lorcan himself. Maeve doubted any of those rumours held any water, it was most likely a simple car accident without any of the spy drama tacked on. Occam's razor. Still, she could see that he was hurting despite the cool exterior, and she made it her mission to at least try to strike up an acquaintance with him. Easier said than done.

Getting more than a few words out of him was a Herculean feat, one worthy of myth. When it was time for them to pair off in Politics to debate a topic, she made a beeline for Lorcan every time, which was easy because no-one else wanted to work with him. They were less debates and more Maeve talking at a statue that would occasionally nod or grunt in her general direction until Mr. Dickson told them to stop. Once, she got him to agree that neoliberalism had polluted modern discourse on media.

"Yeah, I suppose they just wait and see what's popular and then, I don't know, repackage it and tell us they're woke or something. It's all bullshit really." He'd said.

That was it, the floodgates had opened and, slowly but surely, she broke down his thick walls. It started with a small trickle. She didn't have to kidnap him from his loner lunch table anymore, he came to her. When it was time to pair off in class, they found each other. They even lived in the same direction from school, so they would sometimes walk home together or to school in the morning. By the time the summer holidays rolled around they were more than acquaintances, they were friends, bona fide pals.

Not many people understood why she was making such an effort with him, when he clearly didn't seem to care. However, not many of them understood the pain of losing a parent at a young age. Maeve did. Her mother had died when she was eight and that pain, though it had faded, was still raw. She could barely imagine the pain of losing both parents so suddenly, no brothers or sisters there to help him through it. At least she'd had her dad. On top of that, Lorcan was thrust into a small, tightly-knit town where he knew virtually nobody. Damn right she was going to make an effort.

Over the course of the summer Lorcan began to loosen up, talking to the others in Maeve's group, though he kept them at arm's length. He became a bit of a staple member in their posse, no matter how standoffish he could be. He'd attend the parties, go to the movies – in Droichead Dubh's one and only tiny theatre – go to the beach and partake in their, oh so rebellious, underage drinking. When the pubs served you without asking for ID, could you really call it a rebellion? Maeve was proud of him for making the effort, and just a little proud of herself for helping another human being in need.

That's why it stung so much when they started back for the new school year, their final school year before being thrown out into a large world of academia or work. He dodged her messages, was silent in class, and she couldn't prove it, but she was sure that he was leaving his house at a different time so that he avoided having to walk with her to school. What had Maeve done? She didn't think she'd said anything bad or done anything particularly heinous. For a minute she entertained the thought that he was jealous that her and her other long-time friend, Oisin, had hooked up and got together, but Lorcan had never shown any interest in either of them. At least as far as she could tell. What was with the radio silence? That's why she'd followed him last night, and that's why what she'd seen had disturbed her so deeply. She was beyond worried for him.

The end of day bell rang and Maeve found Oisin at the front gate waiting for her. They hadn't had English today, so their contact had been limited, only speaking during lunch, and that was a big blur. He flashed her a smile, crooked and tinged with concern.

"Are you okay? You look knackered." He said, putting an arm around her.

"Oh yeah, I'm fine. I just couldn't seem to get to sleep last night."

"No Lorcan today?" He asked, scanning the crowd.

"No, I think he was sick. I messaged him, but he hasn't replied."

"Not like him to ignore a message." Oisin said with an ironic head tilt, as if his sarcastic tone needed to be reinforced.

"Yeah."

They walked to Maeve's house, huddled together the whole way. It was only October, but there was a biting chill that sliced through the town, hence the snow. Oisin talked, generally trying to keep the mood light as they ambled along. He was good like that. His house was in the opposite direction, but he'd told her time and again that he liked walking her home, despite her assertion that he didn't have to. According to him, he was glad of the exercise.

"You're sure you're okay?" He said as they stopped at her front door.

"I told you I'm fine, maybe it's a cold or something. I'm going to bed as soon as I get in."

"What about homework?" He said in mock horror.

"Fuck it."

Oisin dramatically gasped and laughed it off, kissing her goodbye. Maeve waited until he was out of sight, and they'd stopped waving before stepping inside. Her dad wasn't home yet, so she went straight to her room, flopping limbless on her bed. She checked her phone again – still no messages. Closing her eyes, fractals danced behind her lids as she felt the uneasy pull of unconsciousness draw her under.

\*     \*     \*     \*     \*     \*

Maeve's sleep was full of shapes. Dark, twisted shapes that made no sense, and she had the feeling of being dragged underwater, unable to breathe. Lorcan's hands slid around her neck again. She tried to cry out but choked as she looked upon his face, contorted in anger. But when she looked closer it wasn't his face, it was someone else, someone, something she didn't know. It leaned down to say something inaudible, sending a shiver racing down her spine. Cold emanating from its twisted mouth as a high voice brushed past her ear. Grinning, its grip tightened, crushing the breath from her.

Maeve shot up, gasping for air, her mind forcing itself awake. Hair and clothes stuck to sheets with films of sweat, and her scarf had somehow wound itself tighter. She wrenched it off, feeling relieved to be free of it for the first time today. Taking a beat to push the dreams down, she noticed it was just getting dark outside and her dad was due home soon. She changed into her pyjamas to at least keep up the appearance of normality. *Damn Lorcan and his nightmares!* They were like a contagion and now she had been infected.

She made her way to the bathroom to splash some water on her face. Wasn't that what people in the movies did when they were rudely awakened by bad dreams? The cold water felt refreshing for a second, and then it just felt like cold water. Wiping her face dry, she inspected the damage to her neck in the mirror. The bruising wasn't as bad as she had thought it might be. Good. Maybe a little make-up tomorrow instead of hiding under a scarf all day.

Maeve fixed her hair a little, trying in vain to tame the ginger frizz, it'd got wild during her restless nap. She re-entered her room whereupon she noticed her phone blinking with a notification light. Probably her dad saying he'd be home late and to order something from the chippy, at least she hoped it was – she was starving. Tapping the screen to life, she saw that it wasn't her dad. It was from Lorcan. Her fingers shook a little as she opened the message.

*Hey. Sorry about last night and everything. I don't want to do this over the phone, so can we talk tomorrow? After school? Sorry again.*

Sorry? That was all he had to say? It was progress, but really? No shit they needed to talk. That spark of anger Maeve had been harbouring toward him began flaring up. Lorcan was acting like this was a little tiff that needed to be brushed away. She composed and deleted multiple crude drafts of her message before simply replying.

*Yes.*

*   *   *   *   *   *

Maeve's stomach somersaulted every time Lorcan passed her in the corridor or crossed his path at lunch. She wanted nothing more than to talk to him. Partly to sort all of this out, partly to give him a piece of her mind. An increasingly big part of her wanted to punch him square in the jaw but she suppressed that urge, however difficult. She'd wait. That end-of-school bell couldn't come fast enough. At least he had deigned to make an appearance today. No doubt his aunt Cara had heard from the school about his absence yesterday, and she'd made sure he found his way this time. However, he was being his usual withdrawn self in English class and there wasn't much "talk" going to happen while they were attempting to decipher Chaucer.

Maeve waited outside Lorcan's Business Studies class, biding her time, and swooped in when she saw him.

"Just in case you try to do a runner." She said, grabbing him by the elbow.

They made their way through the crowd, roughly in some cases, out through the school gates and toward the town without saying a word. Maeve had already made her excuse to Oisin, saying that both she and Lorcan were going into town so that she could give him a good talking to for being such a bad friend, hopefully fixing their friendship in the process.

She wasn't lying, he just had no idea of the specifics they were to discuss. They had made it to the town centre before Lorcan broke the silence.

"So, uh, where are we going?"

"*You* are going to buy me a hot chocolate. It's the least you can do."

"I'm not sure if I have the change on me - "

Maeve shot him a death glare. A pretty intimidating one, judging by Lorcan's reaction.

"Maybe they'll take card." He muttered in response.

She ushered them into the local tea and coffee shop which was named *A Wee Tea.* A bit of a tourist trap during the summer months, when holidaymakers would come and stay in the nearby caravan parks. The decor was a little kitsch, but it did a killer hot chocolate, one with the melty marshmallows and whipped cream. They made their orders, saying their pleases and thank-yous. Lorcan was just having a simple tea with milk – and, yes, they did indeed take card. Maeve sipped at her hot chocolate, relishing the luxuriant warmth it brought as it journeyed down her gullet. She almost didn't notice Lorcan looking at her neck with a barely concealed grimace.

"I thought there might be bruising." He said into his cup.

"Make-up." She responded with an offhand gesture.

"Oh."

He broke her gaze, studying his cup instead, that was the safer place to look. Her intention had not been to make him suffer, but she was kind of enjoying considering what he had done to her. That was, until she saw him. For the first time in a while she really saw him. He was thinner than she remembered, his skin pale and papery with bones showing where they hadn't before. Dark rings encircled his eyes and bags were starting to develop. He looked as if he could keel over at any second. This wasn't the Lorcan she had hung out with, the Lorcan who had seemed to be healing over the summer holidays. What had happened between then and now for those wounds to have opened this much?

Concern rekindled, and she wasn't playing around anymore. Being with him here, she had imagined that they might be able to continue where they had left off, but something had shifted. She didn't know what it was yet, although something about Lorcan's life had gone out of balance, and he was stumbling, if not flat out falling, over the edge. She would kick herself if she didn't try to help him, however unequipped she might be. Maeve reached out a hand to his, struck by its iciness.

"You wanted to talk, so tell me what's *really* going on." She said.

"I did tell you." Lorcan continued to stare at his tea.

"Lorcan," She squeezed a little firmer, "I'm being serious."

"So am I. I know it sounds… weird, but I was, and I am, telling you the truth." He finally looked up at her, his eyes stony in their seriousness.

It was the cold light of day, and he was sticking to his story. Lorcan actually believed what he was saying, Maeve could see that. This poor boy was flapping in the wind, swept up in this delusion, and she couldn't think of anything that might ground him again.

"I think you need help, Lorcan. Maybe if you talked to Cara - "

"No!" He said, pulling away and drawing a look from the waitress, "You know that she'd freak out if she heard this."

"I'm kind of freaking out hearing about it, to be honest."

His eyes fell again, and she could sense that he was retreating back into that protective shell he'd built up. Lorcan had called Maeve here, and yet she was the one doing all the work. It was time to change tact.

"Alright, fine. So, you go up there every night to talk to your dad?" She said, casually sipping her hot chocolate.

"Not every night, but yeah, I talk to him."

*Mission success.* She'd re-engaged him.

"And what do you talk about?"

Lorcan explained to her that it wasn't all that weird when you thought about it a bit.

"People pray to God, or saints, or their relatives, or whoever every night. I just happen to have a… a direct line to the person I want to talk to. Or maybe, my dad has found a direct line to me. We just talk about normal things. Y'know, how school's going, how Cara is treating me, if I've made any friends, or met anyone." He darted a glance to Maeve and then the table, "Standard stuff."

"What does your dad say to you?"

"Huh? Oh, he mostly asks about me and how I'm doing. He does tell me how much he misses me. How much they both miss me." A tremor entered his voice, "And I've missed them. They were gone so suddenly, Maeve. Talking to him has made it a bit easier. You get it, right?"

She wanted to get it. She wanted to believe Lorcan's assertions that this was therapeutic or helpful in any way, but his ragged appearance told a different story.

"You said you haven't seen your mother yet?" She sidestepped.

"Yes, but my dad sends messages. From her."

"I see."

Lorcan had come to life throughout this tale, and there was a semblance of his former self in there somewhere, burning away under the ice. It was just being dragged down and drowned by whatever it was that was happening in his head. It would take some serious therapy or neurochemistry-altering drugs to even begin to fix what had been so clearly broken. Lorcan poured himself some more tea from his pot and visibly steeled himself.

"Maeve," He began solemnly, "I know you don't believe me."

She said nothing. He was right.

"But, I wanted to talk to you because I need you to know I'm not insane. I want you to -" He paused, struggling to find the words.

"Yes?"

"I want you to come with me. Tonight. To show you I'm not mad. That it's true."

She hadn't expected that. Taking a final sip from her hot chocolate, Maeve considered what he was saying. She wasn't sure that taking part in and enabling Lorcan's delusion was going to be of any help. In fact, she was sure that it would break him further, maybe even beyond repair. Having a second person there, however, might be the catalyst he needed to recognise reality. Setting her mug down, she made her decision, but she was going to set some ground rules.

"After what you did to me the other night?"

"God, I'm sorry, I'm so sorry about that. I was so scared." He practically recoiled under the table.

"You're not the one who almost died." She let that hang between them. Lorcan could say he was sorry all he liked, but Maeve was the one taking the risk. She was the one sticking her neck out to try and help him. She wondered if her mind was quite in one piece for even agreeing to speak with him.

"I don't know what to say."

"It can't happen again, Lorcan, I won't let it."

"I know. You'll understand if you come with me tonight." He wiped his red eyes with his sleeve and gave his nose a going over for good measure.

Maeve stared him down for a long moment. She was surprisingly good in these 'tough love' situations, and Lorcan definitely needed some right now. She empathised with his plight, God knows if she might have been the same way had she not had company in her own grief, but she couldn't sympathise with what he'd done to her. He needed help, not platitudes.

"Okay." She said plainly.

"Really?"

"Yes."

"Awesome! So I'll message you when I'm about to leave,

and we can meet up. Would that be okay?" There was genuine excitement about him. Before he floated away, Maeve had to bring him back to terra firma.

"That's okay but, Lorcan, if nothing happens tonight. If I go there and nothing, or no-one appears, we're going to get you professional help. Do you promise me that?"

His face froze for a second, weighing up his options. Maeve could see the wheels turning. She could practically hear his thoughts. *Accept reality or live out the fantasy a little longer?*

"Deal."

# 4.

Maeve crept down the stairs and into the kitchen, avoiding the creaky floorboards she'd mapped out in her mind for sneaking around in the dark. This wasn't her first rodeo. Lorcan had signalled his arrival by text and was waiting outside, while her dad was out cold for the night in his armchair before the telly. Tiptoeing to the cutlery drawer, she slid it open and removed a slender knife, running a finger along its edge. She hated feeling the need to take this precaution, but knew she must. Opening an inner pocket of her jacket, Maeve carefully stowed the knife and did a mock test of removing it quickly. If tonight was going to be *anything* like the last time, she was coming prepared. She was ready.

Lorcan waited at the bottom of her driveway. Seeing the same silvery outline she'd been observing the other night tensed her stomach. At least this time she didn't have to tail him. Resting her hand instinctively where she had easy access to the knife, Maeve told herself that she trusted him. But that didn't mean she trusted this other side of his personality, the side she had only limited interaction with. He nodded, and they set off at a brisk pace, it was all very businesslike.

The night was clear, though the moon was strangely dim. Their eyes had to adjust before they could confidently traverse the path. Like before, Lorcan bombed up the steeper bits, leaving Maeve lagging behind and panting while he waited for her to catch up. He was fit for being so sickly thin. Along the way they chatted about mundane things, trying to keep the tension at bay, but every so often Lorcan would go quiet, and her hairs would stand on end. He knew that his bubble was about to burst, and he'd be facing reality soon enough. No matter, she'd be there to help pick him up. God knows she knew what that felt like.

As they approached the clearing they slowed down and, upon seeing the ruins, Lorcan stopped. It was difficult to make out, but it looked like he was mouthing something. Before Maeve could catch it, he was off, forcing her to jog a few steps to keep pace. There was a stillness in the air around the fort. Like a microclimate sheltering the area, isolating it from the surrounding world. It was apart and they were alone here.

Together they entered the boundary of the standing stones and made their way to the centre of the fort. The quiet was intense, and Maeve was aware of the rhythmic rush of blood sounding in her head. She eyed Lorcan for any sudden movements, but he seemed too preoccupied with his big moment, twisting his head this way and that in searching movements before calling out softly. The suddenness of the noise cutting through the night caused Maeve to flinch.

"Dad, are you here? Daddy?"

There it was, 'daddy'. The use of the word struck her as oddly juvenile, but she let it slide. He seemed to be self-conscious enough as it was. She braced herself for the revelation that was incoming, and just hoped it wasn't going to be a violent one. Lorcan called out a few more times before going still. Waiting. Maeve waited with him, but she couldn't take much more of this, she'd played along with this charade, and it was time for it to end.

"Lorcan, I think you know he's not coming." She said.

"Shhh."

"Lorcan, come on-"

"Be quiet!" He hissed.

She was about to protest when a familiar feeling crept over her. It began at the top of her neck, running down her back until it washed over her entire body. It was the same numbing, iciness that had chilled her to her core last time. Was a localised temperature dip centred around this fort?

Her breath hung in the air clearly now, her hands stiffened and ached as she nervously flexed her fingers. Lorcan whirled around with what looked like a wide grin.

"He's here!" He said, looking into one dark corner of the fort.

Panic was taking a hold of Maeve. Even if it wasn't Lorcan's father, it might be some predator that preyed on vulnerable teens. What if that voice she'd heard last time really was this person's? They were in immediate danger. This had been a stupid idea. She grabbed for the concealed knife, but her body failed to respond just like last time. Something was preventing her movements, and she couldn't fathom what it might be. The awful, pained frost continued to spread through her cells. It was suffocating.

Unable to move, or do anything except whimper, Maeve followed Lorcan's eyeline to the shadowy corner. It was darker than its surroundings, as if a black hole had manifested itself in the middle of the ruins. Quickly she realised it wasn't a shadow, not really, it was a figure of a man. Shifting in the pale light, it didn't quite look anchored to the world. Stepping forward, footsteps making no sound, it revealed itself entirely. Nietsche's remark, 'when you gaze into the abyss, the abyss also gazes into you', came to mind. For that's what it was like looking directly at the thing. An unnatural abyss that formed from nowhere and everywhere all at once.

He wasn't lying. Lorcan was telling the truth, unless Maeve had fallen into the same psychosis, and they were having a shared hallucination. If it was a hallucination, it felt damn real. In the middle of it all she caught sight of Lorcan's face and plastered on it was the visage of pure delight. Seeing what he thought to be his deceased father, but also the smug, gleeful satisfaction that one gets when one is proven right, had wiped away his sombre exterior. Maeve regretted every decision that had led to this moment, wanting to be anywhere but in the presence of the shadow.

"See." Lorcan said without taking his eyes off of his

'father'. "I told you it was him."

Lorcan reached out a hand to the shadow in supplication, and it returned the gesture, but there were no defined fingers that Maeve could see as it enveloped his fingers. She froze all over again as it inclined its head toward her. There were no discernable features because, as far as she could tell in her petrified state, light didn't interact with it. It was a man shaped tear in the world. Releasing Lorcan from its grip, the black mass moved to her with silent intent, stopping within touching distance.

"This is her?" The thin, incorporeal voice she remembered sending chills through her had the same effect now.

"Yes, this is Maeve. She's the girl I've been telling you about. My friend."

"Maeve." It elongated the word, chewing the sound, "I'm so proud of you, son."

Lorcan looked like he would explode with happiness, not noticing the hell in which Maeve currently resided. The shadow advanced on her once again as it raised its hand to her arm. It was centimetres away now, and every instinct in Maeve was screaming for her to run away, or to grab the knife and slash at this thing. She couldn't do any of that. Instead, she closed her eyes as its grip encircled her wrist.

The sensation was unreal. It wasn't pain exactly, it was pain adjacent, and it felt like she would burn up, or shatter, or atomise into a trillion tiny particles all at once. Then it was over. The neurons in her brain ceased firing, her breathing returned to normal. Her cramped muscles gave way, and she collapsed forward in a heap – she wasn't frozen to the spot anymore. Revelling in the pain relief for a second, Maeve didn't dare open her eyes, not yet. She did, however, note a few different things. For one, the ground felt odd. It was warm and smooth, she could have sworn there'd been grass there a moment ago – very cold grass. And the smell. Before there hadn't been much of a smell, just the fresh scent of clear night air. Now there were a myriad of aromas invading her nasal cavity, and not all of them were pleasant. The most prominent sensation she had though, was an overwhelming sense of tiredness. If she didn't open her eyes soon, Maeve was sure that she'd fall asleep. So, she opened them.

Maybe she had fallen asleep and lapsed into a dream, for she didn't recognise any of this. Instead of the ruined fort, they were in a stone room with pristine walls that were untouched by erosion. It even had a roof. Lorcan lay on the floor, about where he'd been standing beforehand, but was hurriedly clambering to his feet like a kid on Christmas morning. He rushed to the figure in front of him, a man not much taller than he was, and hugged him fiercely, laughing and crying all at once. Another figure stepped from behind Maeve, brushing past her and leaving her on the floor. It approached Lorcan and the man, joining in on the jubilance. It was a woman.

Some sort of happy reunion was playing out in front of Maeve, a scene she was evidently not part of. She couldn't tell the time of day, there was a filter over the world, sepia toned and hyperreal. Focusing on anything in particular was impossible, and her head spun feverishly. She wanted to throw up.

The threesome stopped hugging long enough that Lorcan noticed she hadn't stood up yet. Untangling themselves, they talked hurriedly before a few more quick hugs and kisses. He rushed over to Maeve and attempted to haul her up by the shoulders. Failing, he hunkered down to her level and grabbed her shoulders.

"Maeve, thank you so much! Isn't this fantastic? Look!" He gestured to the man and woman behind him, "It's them, my parents! You made this happen!"

"I did?" Her mouth felt like a desert.

"You did!"

He pulled her into a tight embrace. There was a lot of hugging going on, but she still had no idea *what* exactly was going on. Somebody had better explain what the hell was happening right this second, or else – or else what? She couldn't even make the effort to threaten anyone, she was so drained. The two figures stood over her, but Maeve hadn't noticed them walking, so she craned her neck. They were smiling. Their faces were kind, the woman especially looked like Lorcan, but they too had that filtered, hyperreal quality. The woman crouched down beside them, glancing at Lorcan and then to Maeve.

"We'll be seeing you very soon." She said cryptically before reaching out and touching Maeve on the cheek.

An electric shock of cold and they were back at the fort. The real one. Maeve collapsed, the freezing ground sapping what little strength she had left. Lorcan laughed giddily beside her. He was sprawled out on his back, apparently unconcerned with the cold.

"You see!" He said through his laughter.

She said nothing.

"You see. I told you, they're here. They're not gone. I'm not alone." His words trailed off into a series of sobs, echoing off of the crumbling walls.

He was right. They weren't alone.

# 5.

Morning was firmly in its early hours by the time they made it back to her house. Lorcan had supported Maeve on his shoulders the entirety of the way, it was slow-going when you felt like death. They said their goodbyes, and she made her way into her house, taking care to make as little noise as possible. She barely had the energy to undress, never mind brush her teeth and slog through her nightly routine. She settled for just crawling under the covers.

As she lay wrapped in her cocoon, sleep aggressively gripping her, Maeve tried to process what had just happened. It was all very dreamy and surreal at the time, but now those images were taking on more solid forms. There's no way that Lorcan could have faked it unless he was some supernatural magician, which she highly doubted. So, had she really seen a couple of ghosts tonight? A real 'live', so to speak, pair of actual spirits? Pondering the implications of life and death, and what this could possibly mean for her own mortality and consciousness, she shut her eyes. Those were lofty thoughts, and her brain power was rapidly diminishing as it shut down for the night.

*    *    *    *    *    *

Her dad rudely awakened her the next morning from a black, dreamless sleep. Maeve had forgotten to set her alarm. She informed him that she wasn't fit for school that day, but was sick. It was rare for her to take days off school, being the type-A kind of student she was, so her dad accepted this and left for work after ringing the school's office. Sometimes there were perks to being a know-it-all.

The truth was she did feel terrible. Her body was profoundly weak, her head was swimming with the events of the previous night. She wanted to wrap herself up in her bed clothes again and block out the world, but she desperately needed the bathroom and so was forced to drag herself out of bed. In the bathroom mirror Maeve examined herself, going through her usual morning checks. She was shocked at how bad she looked. Having never been terribly vain, this was a big deal. Her whole body hunched over, her spine unable to properly support its weight, and her skin had a milky, translucent quality. She had always been pale, but this was a whole new level. On top of that, dark crescents had made a home under her eyes. She reminded herself of Lorcan. No wonder her dad had believed her without question.

Maybe should have cared more, but all she wanted was to go back to sleep, so that's what she did. Today was a duvet day. Life – and the afterlife – could wait.

\*      \*      \*      \*      \*      \*

When Lorcan left Maeve's home he'd intended to go straight to bed, and he did, but sleep was elusive and never came. He was wired. The past months had been spent fantasising about what had happened tonight. It was just as good – no, *better* – than he'd ever imagined it could be. He'd seen them, held them, his parents. They'd been torn from him, but they were in his life again! And they'd held him. That had been unbelievably nice.

He considered messaging Maeve, he needed someone to talk to, but she'd looked completely spent when they'd parted, so he thought better of it. He'd let her sleep. Instead, Lorcan spent the night looking through old photos of him and his parents, reading the occasional blog post about other people contacting deceased relatives. Skimming them now, he saw that they smacked of being completely fabricated, nothing like what had happened to him, his experience was the real deal.

Sunlight blossomed in the sky and his alarm went off, reminding that he was still in the real world, and it was time for his morning run. Reluctantly he put his running gear on and stepped out into the dewy morning air, his skin tingling with goosebumps. He never *wanted* to go for a run, but when he got part way into it, it was usually pleasant. His father had lectured him about taking care of his body, exercising and eating well. Even in death he was still looking out for him, in fact he was more fixated on Lorcan being healthy than ever. It was kind of hard to concentrate on exercise and nutrition when you were communing with the dead every other night, but now he felt renewed, buoyed up by what had happened. He felt alive.

He let the morning sun wash over him and imagined it cleansing him of his anxieties, feeling waves of relief, relaxation, and happiness rush through him. He pictured himself an ancient monk or guru atop a mountain, practising some sort of gratitude ritual to the sun god. He really was grateful. This was a perfect morning, and last night had been a perfect night.

He held onto that thought as he descended and jogged his way back to Cara's, grabbing a quick shower and whizzing through his morning routine. The mundanity of the day awaited him, and he was ready to face them head on. By the time Cara had roused herself and slumped into the kitchen, he was already on his second bowl of cereal and two more pieces of bread were toasting away.

"Morning. Hungry are we?" She said, rubbing her eye and looking more than a little bemused.

"Starving." Lorcan replied through a mouthful of milk and oats.

"You should have woken me, love, I'd have made you something. I thought you 'weren't a breakfast person'?" She made a beeline straight for the coffee press.

"As of today, I'm officially a breakfast person – and it's

fine." He finished off his cereal and grabbed his toast from the grill, slathering it in a thick coating of salted butter.

Cara studied him as he munched down on it. "You seem… good. I mean, you seem in a good mood this morning."

"Yep." Was all he could manage through the toast.

He could sense Cara examining him over the rim of her coffee mug. It was a little early to be engaging in critical thought and the caffeine was far from kicking in. She shrugged and went about making her own toast. Why question a good thing? She kissed Lorcan on the top of his head, ruffled his hair playfully and smiled at him.

It was a perfect morning.

# 6.

Maeve awoke from her stupor. She wasn't great, but she was doing better. *Progress.* Checking her phone, the time showed it to be early afternoon – she'd slept the morning away. Also waiting for her was a missed call from Oisin and a text, checking in on her.

*Sorry for the call, I was wondering where you were. Just heard you were sick today. Chaucer won't be the same without you. Feel better soon, miss you xx*

She dutifully sent a reply stating she missed him too and that she'd see him soon, but not to come over as she didn't want to get him sick. She really couldn't be seen like this. Her phone pinged with a new message, not from Oisin, but from Lorcan.

*Who'll be my partner today?*

That's right, if she were in school she'd be in Politics right about now. He must have been wondering where she was. Another ping.

*No matter, it's independent study today. No pairs. Lucky.*

He was in an oddly talkative mood. Clearly last night had taken a different toll on him. God, last night. It hit her all over again. The cold. The fear. The smells. That entity, Lorcan's father. And his mother. What had she meant when she said, 'We'll be seeing you soon'? She'd looked Maeve right in the eye, when she said that. Her innards twisted in a tight knot.

And another thing, Lorcan had said Maeve had "made this happen". How so? What was it she had done to reunite a boy with his dead parents' ghosts? Even thinking those words sounded ridiculous. The whole thing was ridiculous. But it *had* happened. Switching her phone to silent, she set it down. She didn't much feel like talking to him until she'd sifted through at least some of these thoughts.

*     *     *     *     *     *

Around four o'clock the doorbell rang. Neither she nor her dad were expecting a delivery and visitors were pretty rare, so when Maeve saw Lorcan standing on her porch, she was less than thrilled. He hadn't got the message, she didn't want to talk.

Opening the door wordlessly, she put on the best *yes?* expression she could muster in her current state. He beamed at her. He wasn't quite as wan looking as he had been before, there was actually a little colour in his skin, and he seemed – perky. He looked to be on some sort of stimulant, wide-eyed, almost vibrating with energy. Not that she knew what that was like, but she'd seen movies.

"Hi!" He said.

"Hi."

A moment of silence.

"I, uh, brought your homework for Politics." He handed her a page scrawled with notes.

"Thanks." She dropped it on the hallway table.

"I know you don't like to fall behind."

Another moment of silence.

"So, like -" Lorcan shuffled on the spot, huffing steamy clouds, "- can I come in and talk?"

"About?"

"About last night and what we need to do next."

Maeve looked at him incredulously, "What do we *need* to do next?"

"Well, I was thinking that when we go up again tonight we can - "

"Wait, wait, wait!" She held a hand to his face.

How the hell did he think that she wanted to go

back there tonight? First, she wasn't in any condition to go anywhere. Second, she had no idea how to process what on earth had happened last night. And third, she was pretty sure she was *never* going *anywhere* near that place again.

"But, Maeve, you said that if I proved it was real -"

"I said nothing! What I said was, if nothing happened then we'd get you some much-needed psychiatric help. Now, I don't know, maybe you need a fucking exorcist or something. I'm going nowhere." This was getting too much.

She swung the door to close it, but Lorcan held it ajar with one arm. She strained to shove it closed.

"Don't you dare." His face darkened. "Don't you *dare* take them away from me."

"Goodbye, Lorcan." She shouldered with all her weight, shutting it hard in his face.

Lorcan banged and raged at her from the other side. With every thump of the door, she felt her entire body jolt. His sudden anger was terrifying, this is what she'd been afraid of. Still bracing one arm against the door in a futile attempt to bolster its defences, set her phone to dial the police if it came to that. *Please go away. Please just leave.* Her body went stiff from the strain, but eventually the force of his blows waned and his white-hot rage turned to pleading. Scratching at the frame, he sobbed and begged Maeve to open up and talk to him. *How could she be so heartless? Didn't she have a shred of empathy? She'd come this far, was she going to abandon him now?* Tears stung the corner of her eyes, he knew what to say to make it hurt, she'd give him that. She fought the urge to undo the lock, imagining his emotional pain. Maeve knew that pain all too well, and he wouldn't drag her down with him. She'd already dragged herself out of that hole.

How long this stand-off lasted, she couldn't say, but the light had begun to dim, plunging them into a twilit haze.

"I'm sorry." His voice was hoarse from crying, "I'm sorry, please don't cut me off. I'll leave you alone for now."

His footsteps shuffled on her porch and faded down

the driveway with the muffled crunch of gravel. She finally broke. Running to her room, she closed the door and shut herself away. She'd dealt with these feelings long ago, but this situation, Lorcan, was wrenching them to the surface, opening old scar tissue to fresh pain. She wanted to hide from the world, to never come out again. For once, she had no idea what to do.

*    *    *    *    *    *

Maeve took the rest of the week off. She needed time to come to terms with her new reality, and the shift was taking its toll. Her fight with Lorcan had come at possibly the most inopportune moment, when she hadn't the mental capacity to grapple with a rapidly expanding world-view. Now, free from the distractions of school and socialising, she was able to begin wrestling these disparate thoughts into submission. Or, she tried to.

She was unable to completely rule out the possibility she may have had a mental break, stopping her from seeing things as they were. It didn't feel like that though. All the material she'd gathered on psychosis, breakdowns, or schizophrenia just didn't seem to apply to her experience. She was too lucid and rational about it all, at least in her own humble opinion, and there were no moments where it faded into fuzz. It was as clear and solid as any of here other memories, however sepia toned it might have been. That was as far as her self-diagnosis had got her.

She devoured article after article, post after post, about the afterlife and contacting the dead. She sifted through ghost hunting sites with clips of older TV shows where hack mediums pretended to commune with spirits trapped in our realm. None of them could encapsulate her experience – her's and Lorcan's. She even considered ordering an Ouija board online, stopping when she found out it was originally a popular children's game around the start of the twentieth century. It was *The Exorcist* that had popularised its demon-summoning image. Another dead end.

The rug was being pulled out from under Maeve, and she was faltering. She was usually the rational one, but there was nothing rational about this. She couldn't talk to her dad about this, he might think she was in the midst of a fever and rush her to the hospital for delusions. Maeve couldn't talk to Oisin about it either, he'd probably laugh at first, but she'd still end up in the hospital. The only person she could talk to... was Lorcan. They weren't exactly on speaking terms at the moment. Not yet anyway. He'd messaged a few times, apologies followed by assertive declarations that he was going to come over and force her to talk to him. He never did, but she half expected him to turn up one day like Stanley Kowalski and scream her name until she answered. She was eternally grateful that never happened.

Maeve existed for half a week in this paranormal research-driven state until Sunday, it was about time to get back to the land of the living, school beckoned tomorrow. She hadn't washed for a few days, and her dad was starting to throw hints that maybe she'd consider running a bar of soap over herself. She went through her normal Sunday routine: dinner, dessert, homework, shower – an extra long one –, skin routine and blow-dry. It brought her back to herself somewhat, she felt more grounded, more firm.

She meditatively dried her hair, realising Lorcan hadn't contacted her today. Usually there were at least a couple of messages laying unread by now. Maeve picked up her phone and scrolled through their conversation, dozens of unanswered messages stared back. A pang of guilt stabbed at her. Yes, he'd been an absolute shit the other day, but she could also tell that he was suffering greatly, and she did nothing to help him. Maybe Maeve hadn't been in the right state of mind but, still, she had made no effort.

Clicking on the text box, she began typing.

*Hey. Remember to do your politics homework? *smiley face**

An innocuous message to test the waters, Lorcan was forever 'forgetting' to do his homework. What it really said was, *Hey. Are you still looking to talk? Because I'm flailing here and don't know who to turn to. Or is that bridge burnt?*

She continued drying her hair, sneaking glances at her phone. Still no reply. Maeve set about completing her Sunday night ritual, watching crap TV with her dad. Game shows. Blooper shows. Inconsequential documentaries. She periodically checked her phone. Still nothing.

"Expecting something?" Her dad asked after she had checked it for the tenth time in five minutes.

"No, I was just talking to Oisin." She set it down and resisted the urge to pick it up every thirty seconds for the rest of the night.

Climbing into bed, Maeve set her alarm and turned over to go to sleep. Her phone finally pinged. She whipped around, snatching the phone from her bedside table to see a message from Lorcan.

*What? Me forget homework? Never! Oh, wait… OOPS!*

That was the start of it. Half the night was spent texting back and forth with Lorcan and when sleep had finally caught up with her, Maeve expected to be knackered when it came time for her alarm to go off. She wasn't. In fact, she felt good and when she met Lorcan who'd been waiting for her at the end of the driveway she felt even better. Their walk to school was more than a little awkward. The last time she had seen him, he'd been in a complete emotional state. Last night was the beginning of their reconciliation, but it was all still a little raw.

"At least it's a short week this week." He said after they'd lulled into a silence.

"What? Oh yeah, Halloween. I completely forgot."

"Yep, off for a week and a half. Cara says they take it pretty seriously here in Droichead Dubh."

It was true. They took all the old Celtic celebrations seriously here. There'd always been this underlying Irish pagan vibe running through the town, which reared its head most strongly during the summer and winter solstices and, of course, Halloween. Or *Samhain* as some older folk still referred to it. Every year Droichead Dubh went above and beyond, considering it was such a small place. Bonfires, costumes, storytelling, fireworks. This wasn't your commercialised "American" Halloween however, this was a celebration in the more traditional sense. The bonfires, costumes, and fireworks stemmed from the belief that fire and sounds deterred the mischievous spirits from harming you or your family, and the costumes helped you blend in with them. They made you one of the gang, so to speak. The veil between our world and the spirit world, sometimes referred to as the "Otherworld", was said to weaken around this time of year. Hence, all the scary costumes and fireworks. Now though, it was more of an excuse to get drunk and make a dick out of yourself, but some people in the town still took it to heart.

"So, are you dressing up?" Lorcan asked.

"I haven't dressed up since I was eleven, I don't really believe in all that sh-" Maeve had to stop herself because now she *did* believe in all that shite. Actually, she *knew* that at least some of it had to be real. Maybe not the costumes and fireworks, but there was some form of an "other" world, and she'd seen it.

"Well, I didn't believe in it until-" She trailed off.

"Indeed." Was all he said.

They arrived at the school gates. Maeve could see Oisin waiting for her at the front door, pretending not to be cold.

"I'll see you later." Lorcan said.

"Don't you want to come over and chat before class? There's still fifteen minutes."

"Nah, I'm just going to my form room." He threw a quick glance in Oisin's direction.

"Okay, well, I'll see you in Politics."

"See you in Politics." He said, turning to walk away.

"Please tell me you remembered your homework."

"I've got a free period, I'll do it then." He gave her a backhand wave and sauntered off in the direction of his class.

Oisin's eyes followed Lorcan even as Maeve approached, giving him an overdue hug.

"You two 'besties' again?" He said rather flatly.

"Ew, who talks like that?"

"I'm just hip to the lingo of the kids." He affected in a faux-fifties voice.

"Jesus, you're embarrassing. And, no, not 'besties' but I think he's coming around."

"Cool. Well, shall we?" He held out his arm for her to take, and they made their way inside as a mock old-timey couple. Even freezing, early mornings never dampened his spirit.

School came and went without much ado as everyone, including the teachers, was winding down for Halloween, and mostly talking about how drunk they were going to get. Party invites were doled out, and the staff were just looking forward to having a break from the pupils. Maeve would've joined in on all the fun, but she had other things on her mind.

Lorcan was nowhere to be seen for their walk home. She would have to make do with Oisin. They chatted about what parties they might go to, or if either of them were going to dress up. If so, should they get couples costumes or surprise each other? What if they dressed as the same thing?

"Yeah, it'd be awkward if we both went as Hulk or something."

"Why? Because I'd look stronger?" Maeve flexed a soft muscle.

"Hey! *Hulk strong!*" He said with a frown, in a low voice, picking Maeve up with a twirl.

He put her down again but kept a hold of her, planting a slow, affectionate kiss on her lips. He pulled away and looked at her in a way that only he did.

"You okay?"

"I am, why?" Maeve asked, her head still spinning.

"I don't know, you seem a little... off. Is everything alright?"

"It's fine, I think I'm still recovering from last week is all."

"Okay, well if you need to talk or anything -"

"I know." She kissed him again, preventing any further questioning.

The mood was light as they continued the walk to her house. They said their usual goodbyes and Maeve watched as he left.

"Hey!" Oisin shouted from the path, turning on his heels, "What about Bonnie and Clyde?" He made his hands finger guns.

"*Boy! What are you doin' with my mama's car*?" She shouted back in her best Texas accent. It wasn't a great accent.

"What?"

"It's a line from the mo- never mind! Clearly you've never seen it."

"I'll watch it!"

"It doesn't matter."

"I'll watch it!" He asserted, laughing as he moseyed down the road, making *pew-pew* noises with his finger guns and swaggering like a cowboy.

"Eejit." Maeve smiled to herself.

Opening the front door, kicked off her shoes and climbed the stairs to her room. There was no homework tonight, and she was at a bit of a loose end. What to do? She took out her phone and began typing.

*How's detention?*
**Riveting.**
*Should've done that homework when you had the chance!*
**Shoulda, coulda, woulda.**
*That'll teach you.*
**Hardly! What are you doing tonight?**
*Nothing, I think, why?*
**Do you want to come over for tea? Cara's making burritos**

*for the first time, and she could do with an extra test subject.*

It had been ages since she'd been to Lorcan's. It was almost starting to feel like they'd rewound the clock, and he was back to a facsimile of his former, non-edgy, self. She desperately wanted to talk about what had happened to them, but a little normalcy couldn't hurt in the meantime. Then they could get down to brass tacks.

*Sure, I'll be a rat in a maze for some free food.*

*    *    *    *    *    *

"Well, how are they?" Cara leaned back in her chair. She was trying and failing badly at affecting nonchalance.

"Awful." Lorcan said, "The worst thing you've ever made."

"Shit, I knew it. I shouldn't have tried them, I can never get rice right!" She threw her head back with arms in the air.

Lorcan laughed, grabbing her arm gently, "I'm joking, I'm joking. They're nice, you might even say they're perfectly edible."

"Thanks, chef Lorcan Ramsey." She lowered her head and shot him a playful glare, "What do you think, love?"

Maeve's mouth was full of rice, guacamole and corn tortilla, all she could manage was an enthusiastic nod, accompanied by, "*Mmph!*"

"Thank you! See, she knows how to be a good houseguest." Cara said, thrusting her burrito at Lorcan, sending a black bean flying in his direction.

Maeve had only really agreed to dinner because Cara was going to be there, she wasn't quite comfortable being alone with Lorcan in a closed room just yet. But now, in this setting, she found it hard to equate the Lorcan of their last encounter with this happy-go-lucky character. He seemed ordinary. It was all positively heart-warming. But she'd been fooled before.

They finished up their dinner, talked for a while about

the hardships of rolling burritos, and then Maeve made her exit. It was well and good coming over for dinner, but she didn't like to intrude on someone else's home too much. She was also afraid, taking into account recent interactions, the night could turn sour at any moment – best to leave while the getting was good. Cara and Lorcan stood in the doorway as Maeve stepped out into the rapidly cooling night air.

"Are you doing anything for Samhain?" Cara asked.

"Really?" Lorcan evidently disapproved of her terminology.

"That's what it's called!" She said, high-pitched. "We've been having this debate all weekend. What do you call it, Maeve?"

"Normally I'd call it 'Halloween' but I like the Idea of annoying him," She jabbed her finger at Lorcan, "so from now on it's Samhain."

"Good girl!" Cara smirked.

They small-talked a little more until Cara left the pair alone to say their goodbyes. The atmosphere was trending upwards on the awkwardness scale.

"So, one to ten, how were the burritos?" Lorcan said.

"Hmmm, a solid seven point five."

"Oof, she won't like that!"

"Why, it's a good score?"

"She's a perfectionist. A perfect ten or nada."

There was no eye contact to be had. They were circling the drain of their small talk and getting dangerously close to talking about the elephant in the room.

"Look, Lorcan, about the other day -"

"No."

"No?"

"I was way out of line. I don't even know how to apologise for that, you didn't deserve what happened. I was so... so... fucked. I'm sorry." He stared firmly at the ground.

Maeve just nodded. She understood where his outburst was coming from, but it was most certainly fucked.

"I've had time to digest what's been happening with me over the last couple of months, but you were thrown right into it. I was stupid to expect you to be okay with everything. To go along with it all. When you want to talk about it, we can." He leaned against the door frame, shooting her a contrite grimace.

"Okay, thanks." She turned away, "And I do want to talk about it, soon."

Stepping off of the porch and fully into the cold, Maeve pulled her jacket collar up around her neck against the wind.

"Seven point five?" He called after her.

"Round it up to eight!"

"You're harsh!"

He lingered in the doorway, watching her leave and giving a small, continuous wave. The rectangle of light narrowed as he shut the door and retreated into the house. Maeve sighed with relief. Her friend was still in there.

# 7.

"What did I tell you?" The shadow said.

Though shrouded in darkness, Lorcan could tell his father's face was twisted in fury. He had always done that whole, *I'm not angry at you, just disappointed* – thing that parents seem to love doing, but this was pure anger.

"I know, but she didn't want to. I don't think she'll come back." Lorcan choked through sobs, "I- I've tried talking to her, but she's not getting back to me." He hung his head.

His father stood silently, and for a long moment the boy's quiet snuffling and heavy breathing filled the still air of the ruined fort. Then his father knelt to his level, putting a hand on Lorcan's shoulder. The touch sent pangs of cold throughout his body, and he fought to repress a shiver.

"You want to see us again, yes?"

Lorcan nodded weakly, attempting to look into his father's obscured face.

"Then you know what you have to do." His grip tightened. Had he been flesh and bone, this may have been an affectionate gesture. Because of his current form, it felt like burning ice against his skin whenever his father touched him.

"What?" Lorcan managed, "What can I do?"

"Be smart. She's afraid of us – of you. She doesn't understand" He stood up, releasing Lorcan's shoulder. "Show her there's nothing to be afraid of. That we're just dying to see you – pun intended -" As 'punny', in death as he was in life, " - and she can help make it happen."

"*How* do I do that?" Lorcan practically begged on his knees.

His father pondered, "Tell her the truth. Honesty's the best policy, haven't I always said?"

"I don't think you've ever said that specifically."

"Regardless, there's two of us and two of you. That's how these things work. Help her to see that." He nodded, prompting Lorcan to nod back before he would continue, "And, when you do, you can see us whenever you like. As long as Maeve's there to help us. I'm sorry I got mad, it's just – there's so much that we want to show you on our side, if only you could be here with us."

Lorcan got to his feet, a resolve building in him. "Okay, I'll be back for you. The next you see me will be proper, I promise."

"That's good to hear. Please hurry, your mother misses you so much, and she loved seeing you." Something caught in his father's voice.

"I loved it too." Lorcan said through hot tears.

"I have to go. We miss you." His voice was fading, becoming as translucent as his body.

"I love you." Lorcan said quickly.

"And we love you."

He was gone, leaving Lorcan alone in the darkness.

# 8.

"I don't know, Lorcan, is it not a bit much at this point?" Maeve's tone was dubious.

"I swear, I wouldn't suggest it if I didn't think it was necessary."

"Fine, I'm going to have to trust you. There, what do you think?"

She opened her bedroom door, revealing her costume in all of its glory.

"Perfect. I told you to trust me about the chicken fillets. This is Bonnie and Clyde we're talking about, it has to be over the top."

"Yeah, maybe you're right. I do look ravishing." She examined herself in the mirror, pulling old Hollywood starlet faces and adjusting the fillets. "Thanks for helping. We agreed to go as Bonnie and Clyde, but said we'd surprise each other with the final costume."

"Gotta do something to keep the romance alive."

"*Why, boy, it never did die.*" In her Texas accent, the 'never' became 'neva'.

Strutting her stuff, she figured out how best to move in her new duds whilst getting used to being more top-heavy than usual. If she was dressing up, she was going to go all out and be in character the entire time, or until it stopped being fun. When she had tortured Lorcan into submission, forcing him to listen to the accent until she was satisfied with her performance, Maeve switched back to her normal clothes, and they made their way into the kitchen.

"Do you want a cup of tea?" She said, reaching into the

cupboard.

This was his reward for being subject to all the costume tweaking.

"Sure."

"What do you want? We've got normal tea, English breakfast, green tea, peppermint, camomile, honey, lemon, lemon and honey, ginger, lemon and ginger, raspberry, juniper, orange, aaannnddd hibiscus."

"Jeez, you like your teas."

"It's my dad, he's a fiend."

"Just tea will be fine."

"Okay… boring." She picked out a bag of lemon and ginger for herself.

They sat in a comfortable silence as the kettle heated, boiling to a whistle. Maeve poured their respective brews and waited for their teas to infuse and while they did, the room filled with the pleasant scents of spiced citrus and scorched tea leaves. It was a timeless moment, a moment she knew she'd remember, where Maeve enjoyed having her friend back in her life. They still had to have 'the talk' and it was coming on fast. In fact, it felt to her like the time had arrived. They both felt it.

"So -" She said, sipping her tea.

"So -" Lorcan replied as he blew gently at his steaming cup.

"I've been thinking about what happened. Well, that's probably an understatement." She began, "I'm still trying to figure out *what* happened."

Maeve looked searchingly at Lorcan's face for a reaction, but he was just listening intently. He gestured for her to continue.

"I mean, it's a lot to take in, and I'm not entirely sure what to think about it, or the way it made me feel. Can I ask, did you feel sick or anything?"

Lorcan considered for a moment, "It's hard to remember how I felt the first time I saw my dad. I was mostly happy, but I remember being dead tired afterwards. I think I slept for nearly a day."

"I see. I was shattered."

"You looked it." He took a tentative sip of his tea and blew again, "And I suppose I didn't help at all."

"Lorcan, you were upset, and I understand how -"

"No, Maeve, don't be making excuses for me. I was a dick and I shouldn't have done it. Now, what else would you like to know?"

Something had definitely changed about him. He exuded a more confident aura, his colour had returned and an air of calmness had developed that had never really been there to begin with.

"Okay then, let me ask you, what did you mean when you said that I had 'made this happen' when we saw your parents?" Her tone made her sound unsure whether that's who they had actually encountered.

From his expression, Lorcan had been expecting this question.

"You remembered that then?"

"Yeah, I kinda did."

"Alright," He set his cup down and centred himself, "here's the truth. According to my dad, Droichead Dubh lies on a bed of spiritual power, which is why the fort was built in the first place. That's what's let us connect with each other. The 'veil', as he calls it, is thinner here than in other locations."

Maeve recalled information she'd gathered from her recent research, how so many legends revolved around Ireland, the many similarities with other mythologies around the world. Perhaps they weren't mythologies. Why had an organisation like the Catholic Church taken such interest in a tiny island nation?

Lorcan elaborated, "There's a lot of power centred around here. Not just Droichead Dubh specifically, but it's one of the places of power in Ireland and the world. They were, or are, all connected to that other realm."

"Okay, but where do I come into the picture?"

"I'm getting there, don't worry." He knitted his brow, finding his place in the story, "The ancient Irish were aware of this connection, and were very careful to respect their dead, and lay them to rest properly. However, if someone had unfinished business, or were still connected strongly to something, they'd hold onto their ties to the living world. That's what happened with my parents, and why my dad is able to talk with me."

"Why just your dad?"

"Everything comes at a price, Maeve. The reason you felt drained? It takes a lot of energy for something to cross over into our world. Like when someone in a ghost movie talks about cold spots, or feeling drained, they're kind of alluding to the fact that the spirit is using energy from our world to make that connection. Most of the time it's pure bullshit or coincidence, but the phenomenon is based on truth." He took a long sip.

Maeve was astonished he was actually sitting here answering her questions coherently.

"So your dad was using you as a source of energy?"

"In a way, yes. Our connection is strong because we're related – and I'm a boy."

"What's that got to do with anything?"

"It's a spirit world thing, I guess. That's why my ma didn't appear to me until you showed up, I think."

"What, she was using my 'feminine energy'?" Maeve didn't really know how to feel about that.

"Don't worry, it's not like draining your 'life force' or something. You probably felt it as coldness or tiredness, right?"

"Yeah."

"That's why I said that you'd helped me see them both. You were the catalyst."

"So, did you just see me as a way to reunite with your parents?" She wasn't sure how she felt about that. 'Used' was probably the word.

"No!" Lorcan waved his hand, "No! Not at all. Sure, we

were friends before all this. Believe me, I wanted to tell you, but how do you tell someone you want them to come with you to a fort so that you can see your recently deceased mam and dad?"

"True." She admitted, "So when I followed you there that night, my presence gave your mam the chance to connect with the living world through the presence of another girl that was connected to you? Am I right?" The circle of life – or death.

"Pretty much, but -"

"But what?"

"That's not everything."

"There's more?"

Lorcan adjusted himself in his seat, "Apparently, the connection between my parents and I is so strong, with you providing the extra horsepower, we were able to cross over into their realm. Briefly."

So that's what Maeve had seen – another world. It had looked so filtered and hyperreal because it wasn't her world she had been looking upon, it wasn't even a world she was ever meant to see. Not until she had died, presumably.

"How is that possible?" Her brain was about to explode.

"You know all about it yourself, y'know, Samhain and the veil between worlds being weaker around this time of year."

"But that's just fairytales."

"Now you know they're not just stories. They're real."

Maeve's tea was all gone, and she stared into the empty cup. She was half expecting, and half hoping, that he would say it had all been some fever dream and to forget about it. Now it was crystallizing in her mind. She wasn't in Kansas anymore.

"So, what? You want me to go back there with you? To see your parents, I mean." She said after the buzzing in her head had become a mild background hum.

"That's the other thing." He had finished his tea too, "I don't want you to come with me again."

This shocked Maeve, she wasn't expecting that, "But, I thought you said -"

"I know what I said, but after seeing what it did to you, how you felt, I just couldn't put you through that again. I got used to it, and being around my dad doesn't affect me anymore, but I have no guarantee for you. It's far too much to ask."

Maeve had been struck silent. His face showed no trace of anger or resentment at this, it was a selfless decision.

"But, you'll not be able to see them again."

Lorcan nodded slowly to himself, "I'm fine with that."

"You are?"

"I am." The corner of his mouth twitched, "Maeve, how many people do you know get to speak to their loved ones after they're gone? I was lucky to get to speak to my dad – I was so lucky, and I didn't even realise it. I got greedy and wanted it all, I wanted my entire life back, to pretend like none of this had ever happened. I didn't care what I had to do or who I had to hurt, even if it was you. But enough's enough. If I can only speak to my dad, that is infinitely more than I deserve." Maeve could see tears prick at the corners of his eyes. "Besides, he can deliver a few messages between me and my ma, like a ghost-man Pat." He laughed softly, wiping his face.

Maeve had to wipe her face too between chuckles, 'ghost-man Pat' was a shit joke, but the tension had broken between them, and she couldn't help it. She reached out her hand to grab his.

"I'll do it. I'll help you see your parents."

Lorcan's smile dropped, "No, Maeve, I've said I'm fine with how things are."

"I know, but I want to help."

Pulling their hands apart, he stood, "No, I'm not letting you."

It was Maeve's turn to stand up, "Not *letting* me? It's not like you can stop me. And, besides, you dragged me into it without my permission and, what, now you're going to take it away? I think it's about time you started trusting me with this."

"I have to go, Cara's expecting me." Lorcan grabbed his

jacket, swung it on, and made for the front door. Maeve followed behind.

"So this is how it's going to be every time we have a conversation, is it? One of us ends up screaming at the other and running away?" She was furious. Who was *he* to tell *her* what *she* could or couldn't do? He'd been such a dick, and she'd been a fool for thinking she could help him. Unexpectedly he turned, pulling her tightly into a hug before she could react.

"I don't want that." He said, face pressed into her shoulder, "I don't want us to hate each other. I know you understand what it feels like, but I just can't let you get hurt."

He loosened the hug, placed both hands on her shoulders and kissed her cheek, "No." He said, vanishing onto the road.

Maeve spent the rest of the day in a daze. As night fell she sat on her bed, contemplating everything that had happened, everything he had told her. He was trying to protect her now, she knew that. But this was also the adventure of a lifetime. How could she ever turn back now when she knew she'd been to the afterlife, or the Otherworld, or whatever it was called? No bloody way was she going back to normal now.

She picked up her phone, sending one word to Lorcan.

*Yes.*

# 9.

The citizens of Droichead Dubh readied themselves for their yearly, Celtic inspired event. Maeve and Lorcan prepared for a trip. Despite his pushback, Maeve had convinced Lorcan that she was indeed going to accompany him to the 'Otherworld' – they'd settled on that name. He had acquiesced but made stipulations that they weren't just going to rush in like last time, they would map this out. There were lists of things they needed to bring: extra thick clothing to combat the cold, gel heat packs to provide them with additional warmth, sports drinks to restore electrolytes, protein bars for a pick-me-up, plasters, bandages, and disinfectant in case of injury. Were there bacteria or viruses in the Otherworld? Who knew, but best be safe.

"Are we missing anything? Have we left anything out?" Lorcan made some final checks before the mission-start.

"I don't think so, it's hard to tell. None of the guides online said anything about preparing for a trip to the spirit world." Maeve was packing her supplies in order of perceived importance, "We won't know what we've missed out until we need it."

"I suppose so." He zipped the backpack, "I'm all packed."

"Me too, let's get going."

Leaving Maeve's house, they took care not to alert her dad as they set out for their trek to the fort. The night was moonless, but Lorcan had walked the route enough that he barely had to use the torch. Navigating the perilously trip-hazard lined floor of the woods, they came to the clearing and paused. It was a different beast being here without natural lighting. Their eyes, having adjusted to the darkness made out the faintest, grainiest contours of the fort.

"You're sure?" Lorcan said.

His voice was sombre, like he'd weighed the full gravity of the situation, and they were about to pass the point of no return. Maeve imagined herself in a story, this was her time to accept the quest on offer.

"I am."

Wordlessly, and in perfect unison, they strode toward the fort. Lorcan pulled out his torch, the beam setting the ruins into stark contrast with the surrounding black landscape. It cast angular shadows and made the usually resolute, ancient stones warp and coil in the artificial light. Maeve's pulse fluttered, her fight or flight responses were starting to kick in. No surprise given that they were entering haunted ruins on a pitch black night. This was horror gold.

They stopped in the centre of the fort, Maeve giving her hands something to do by playing with her backpack strap. It was like standing on the precipice of a cliff, one more step, and they were over the edge, no going back.

"They call this place 'Dún Dubh', y'know." She said after a deep, shaky breath.

"Yeah?"

"Yeah. Droichead Dubh is Irish for 'black bridge' so this is 'black fort'."

"I never took Irish as a language in school."

"Well, now you know." She shrugged.

Maeve liked to talk when she was nervous, she supposed it was a sort of coping mechanism designed to displace the stress elsewhere, outside herself. And she was stressed. That gravity they had felt earlier weighed a ton now.

"I'm going to call them. Okay?" Lorcan said, clicking off his torch and plunging them into pure darkness. Maeve kept quiet, steeling herself for what was about to come.

Lorcan called out, first in whispers and then at normal speaking volume, which in the stillness felt absurdly loud.

There was an interminable moment of nothingness where time elongated, and his voice bounced from stone to stone. Something akin to relief filled her when nothing happened, but then she felt it. The recognisable coldness seeped into her, or rather, heat leached from her body, paying the toll for entry into another world. *Everything comes at a price*, she thought.

All at once, the sensation raced through her entire system. From her core, to the tips of her limbs, through every nerve was icy fire and, just as it had before, it stopped abruptly. Her body sagged, and her legs felt like they could give way, but Maeve remained standing this time round. She bent over, panting hard, it was still a wholly unpleasant experience. Lorcan hunched beside her, mirroring her actions, breathing heavily as if he'd been sprinting.

It occurred to Maeve that she could actually see Lorcan, it wasn't nearly as dark here. The walls of the chamber were lined with torches, not electric twenty-first century torches, but the wooden, oil-soaked rag kinds of torches. Her eyes tried to adjust, the world still had that odd sepia tone to it. She straightened herself up when the nausea had mostly abated.

Lorcan stretched his back, steadied himself, and immediately ran to the opposite side of the room. Maeve had failed to notice the figures entirely beforehand. They stood in a dark patch where the torchlight seemed to skip over, but now she could see them, and she could also see how happy Lorcan looked. How happy they all looked.

While Lorcan had his reunion, Maeve set about making herself a little more comfortable. Opening her backpack, she got out some of the gel heat packs, she'd packed them at the top, having a feeling they'd be necessary. She cracked them, starting the thermogenic reaction, and stuffed a couple against her torso with the smaller ones wedged in her gloves. It was a small relief, this world seemed to be draining her body heat every second, the heat packs were but a temporary measure. She wished she could do something about her feet, they felt stone-cold, but that was a problem for next time. She took a swig of her energy drink and zipped everything up again just in time for her presence to be acknowledged.

"Mammy, daddy, this is Maeve, who you met last time. Without her, we wouldn't have seen each other again." He led them over.

"Nice to see you, Maeve, you're a brave girl. Lorcan was just telling us what you did for him – for us." Lorcan's dad's voice hadn't that thin and insubstantial quality she'd heard in the living world. Maybe it had been a poor reception on their end.

"I really can't thank you enough." His mother began, "I didn't think we'd ever be a family again." She flew to Maeve with surprising speed, embracing her in a hug.

Maeve's body ignited with cold, and she reflexively shoved herself away, stumbling onto the floor in a shivering heap. Lorcan ran to her, taking heat packs from his own bag and stuffed them into her coat. His mother backed away, hands over her mouth, disgusted with herself.

"I'm sorry, pet, I'm so sorry! I forgot myself, I'm still learning." She gasped, unsure whether to reach out or stay put. She clenched her fists and remained where she was.

"Are you okay?" Lorcan said, "Do you need anything?"

"N- no." Maeve hugged herself, pressing the heat packs closer, "I'll be fine in a second. That feels good, thanks."

"You have to be more careful, mammy. I'm used to the cold, but she's not." He sounded like a teen should, annoyed at their parents.

"It was an accident." Maeve said, standing slowly and waving off Lorcan's help, "We're all learning, Mrs. Delaney."

"Thanks, pet, you can call me Bronach." She relaxed.

"Aiden." Lorcan's father chimed in, "No formalities in the afterlife."

She wondered if she had been naive having come here. Most definitely yes. A hug, an innocent gesture, had floored her. If just touching one of these spirits could do that, what was in store for them? She ate half a protein bar and took another swig of her energy drink, centering herself. She'd come this far.

"So, where to?" She said as brightly as she could but aware of the tiredness already setting in.

"You're okay?" Lorcan asked.

"Yes, I'm fine, stop asking me."

"I like her." Aiden said, "Very brave girl."

The pair escorted Lorcan and Maeve through a series of short hallways also lined with torches. It all had a morbidly gothic feel, the lighting, the architecture, but when they reached the main door of the home it was a different story. Maeve didn't know what she had expected. Maybe some peaceful rolling hills, a few huts, plumes of turf smoke, typical 'old Ireland' stuff, but *this* – this was something else.

A huge, ocular orb hung in the sky, way more massive than she'd ever seen the moon before. Its size was fascinating and frightening all at once. She ripped her eyes from it in order to take in the rest of the scene, which was lit by silvery-blue light. Maeve grew up on stories of the fairy world and Tír na nÓg, but nothing had ever come close to what lay in front of her now. From their vantage, expansive rolling fields dipped and peaked in impossibly fluidic ways. The surrounding mountains soared into the clouds so that their tops were obscured, looking like humongous walls built to enshrine the valley in which they were encased. Even the fort looked at least twice as high as it had been in their world – entropy had reversed, undoing centuries of erosion and pillaging.

Casting her eyes over the buildings dotting the landscape, she noticed the architecture. Not homogeneous in the slightest, she identified styles from multiple disparate eras. Not that she was some architect know-it-all, but she'd seen enough historical documentaries to know these buildings didn't belong together. There were huts that must have dated back centuries, if not millennia. Old stone buildings with an eclectic assortment of rock types held together by pressure tension and weak binding agents. She even noticed a little cottage with a thatched roof, puffing smoke from its adorable chimney. That matched her expectations at least.

Most striking of all, Maeve's attention fixed on a sight in the far distance. It appeared to be dozens of miles away, there was some strange optical effect going on with the atmosphere, but was clearly visible due to its sheer scale. A castle with walls that might as well have been features of the landscape, because no amount of manpower could ever construct something so magnificently, colossally beautiful. The stone glowed in the darkness, its sheer surface reflecting the moonlight, making the edifice stand out all the more. Within the walls she could make out two structures, a tower and a tree.

The tower was unlike any tower or skyscraper Maeve had ever seen, or even thought to imagine in the "real world". Like the castle walls encircling, it was a brilliant white, making it a beacon in the night. The scale was on another level. It brushed the clouds, not quite reaching, but it came close. Some of its levels seemed to poke out in strange ways, breaking the otherwise impressively clean silhouette, perhaps it was put together haphazardly. There was nothing like this back home.

Then there was the tree. At least, she guessed it was a tree, she could only see the spiralling grain of its trunk drilling into the clouds. It dwarfed the tower and might have even dwarfed the mountains on either side of it, there was no telling where it ended. For a second she thought she caught a glimpse of some branches hanging from the sky as the clouds undulated on wind currents.

They both stood dumbstruck, taking in the fantastical scene, doing slow three-sixty rotations as they looked this way and that. Catching each other's eye and smiled stupid, giddy smiles.

"Un-fucking-real." Maeve said eventually.

"You never told me about any of this." Lorcan turned to his parents.

They shrugged their shoulders, nonchalant, "You get used to it pretty quickly, and we had hopes that maybe someday you'd see it for yourself." Aiden said.

"And here you are – both of you." Bronach added.

A few more beats of awestruck silence passed.

"What is that?" Lorcan, pointed to the castle.

"That is the seat of the steward. He... he takes care of the land." Aiden replied.

"It's unbelievable." Lorcan lowered his arm, turning back to his parents, "Have you been there?"

"Not yet, we haven't exactly caught his attention." Laughed Bronach.

Aiden snorted, "Yet."

"We should go." Lorcan said.

His parents looked at one another as if to say, *this boy, eh? Incorrigible,* "Maybe next time." Aiden said.

Continuing to scan the landscape, wide-eyed and determined to take in every detail, Maeve began to recognise some of the land's features. They were definitely in the same place, geographically speaking, but everything was distorted. It was like someone had taken the topographical map and drawn it all wrong, plonking down buildings and landmarks that were never there. The mountains surrounding them were in fact large hills back in the living world that had now warped beyond recognition, however they were in the same basic pattern. The seaside could normally be made out pretty easily from where they were, but now the land stretched out into the distance, where glints from the water winked at them. The place had a dream-like quality, some undiscovered place that the ancients had always imagined being there but had never found.

A noise cut across the scene. A high-pitched squeal comparable to a horse whinny, followed by low, regular thrumming. Hoofbeats. What might animals look like in the Otherworld? Would they be stretched beyond recognition too? Or did they get to keep their appearance, like humans seemed to? The two humans she had seen so far anyway.

Maeve turned, about to ask that very question, when

she was suddenly aware of how cold she'd become. Her enthusiastic energy had abandoned her. Bronach noticed first, going to steady her but stopped, thinking better of it. At least she was learning from her mistakes.

"Maeve, are you okay, pet?" She said, her voice rife with concern.

"I'm – I just don't feel so good at the minute."

"She's still adjusting." Aiden said, abruptly turning to Lorcan, "That's probably enough for now, son."

A flare of indignation passed over his face, quickly replaced by concern when he saw how unsteady Maeve had become. Lorcan put an arm around her in an effort to keep her upright, with Aiden leading the way back into the fort. Bronach followed closely behind, fretting silently.

"I'm sorry, I was feeling fine and then – *bam*." Maeve croaked, struggling to breath with Lorcan's shoulder in her side.

"You're fine, it's not your fault." There was a hollow placation in his reply.

Reaching the chamber they had arrived through, Aiden reached out his hand, which hovered over Lorcan's shoulder.

"It was fantastic seeing you again, son. I can't believe how lucky we are to have you here." His warm expression exuded gratitude, "And you, young lady. Thank you for bringing our son back to us"

"Yes." Bronach said with teary eyes, "Thank you, love. I can't believe our luck, and we'll understand if you don't want to come back with how you're feeling."

Maeve raised her head at this, "No, I want to. We've only got started." She tried to put some strength into her words, "And, hey, I lasted a little longer this time. Only uphill from here." She might have been more convincing if her neck wasn't shaking from the effort.

"Time to go."

"Love you." Lorcan said.

"And we love you." His parents said in unison.

As the now familiar cold surged through her body, Maeve swore that she could hear that same high-pitched whinnying again.

She opened her eyes to the pitch dark of the "real" world. Lorcan's arm was still around her, and he escorted them out of the ruins.

"Come on, let's get you home."

\*       \*       \*       \*       \*       \*

Maeve lay awake, trying and failing to sleep. Physically exhausted as she was from their adventure, her mind wouldn't quit. It replayed the highlights of their escapades like a movie on repeat. She flipped the images over, examining them from every angle, scrutinising them down to the finest detail she could recall. It was magnificent!

Every image was super-bright and vividly real. Every remembered sensation could nearly be experienced all over again. Every feeling, every emotion, was cranked up to eleven. Her brain was lit up with the whole affair and firing on all cylinders. There was no way she'd be sleeping tonight.

Instead, Maeve did what she always did when she had become enthralled with a new topic, she researched. As she had told Lorcan, she had grown up on the tales of Fionn mac Cumhaill, King Lir, Cú Chulainn and a pantheon of other Irish legends that related to the Otherworld. After what she'd seen though, the descriptions in these stories seemed dull, tame, out of focus by comparison and not even close to being accurate depictions. She'd been to the source and witnessed the real, authentic epicentre of it all.

To be fair, the stories were target-tailored for a younger audience and, as such, didn't go into great depths. They could be finished in ten minutes flat, even if you took your time. Maeve forwent the hokey, mystic sites – they were mostly for the diaspora living in America anyway – diving deep into academic material, the serious stuff. Here she was getting some traction. These papers weren't dealing with the kid-friendly, touristy myths about the Giant's Causeway, no, they were dealing with the real stuff, the ancient stories before they'd been twisted by centuries of church appropriation.

A line of particular interest she followed led to tales and papers on the Tuatha Dé Danann. She'd heard the name thrown about before but had never learned much about them. They were basically an assortment of gods normally found in ancient cultures – your Zeuses, Freyas, Anubises, etc. Lugh, Áine and Mór-Ríoghain – the Morrígan –, respectively. Maeve had obviously never put stock in those tales being true, but her position on that was different now. If the Otherworld existed, and she'd been there, why *couldn't* these deities exist? Basic logic.

She read reams of pages documenting the exploits of the Tuatha Dé Danann. Earth-shattering wars that raged across the island of Ireland, their defence of Ireland from the sea-dwelling Fomhóraigh – Formorians as they became known – which may have had links to Norse mythology, or even the tale of Atlantis. Digging deeper, she read how they were slowly incorporated into religious myths as saints, or were demoted entirely to being mere mortal kings when the Catholic Church began their campaign to convert Ireland to Christianity. It didn't help that Ireland had a rich oral history, meaning few, if any, of these myths were written down until about six hundred years after they'd been assimilated by Christianity. She had to sift through a lot of that corrupted information to get to the truth.

Already riding a high from her world-hopping adventure, Maeve couldn't hold back laughter at the thought of seeing a real life (death?) god. She felt floaty, hysterical even at the prospect of communing with some divine being from ancient mythology. She doubted Lorcan had considered this, as he'd been too focused on seeing his parents, to look at the wider picture, but this had blown a hole in their world. Nothing would ever be the same.

Maeve lay back, allowing her mind to parse through her research and run the simulations of what it might be like to talk to Lugh or have dinner with the Morrígan. If Lugh was associated with the sun, did that mean he'd be literally scorching hot? Might the Morrígan show her the ways of divination? Or might she be bestowed with some sort of godly quest? She could only imagine for now. Soon, though, she might not have to.

*　　*　　*　　*　　*　　*

Lorcan watched Maeve slowly amble into her house. She was exhausted but hadn't been able to stop rambling the entire trek down the hillside. She talked his ear off about the implications of what they'd seen. Did everyone get to go to the Otherworld after they died? Was it just Irish people? What did this mean for organised religion on a global scale? Lorcan didn't really care about any of that crap, he was more concerned with when she'd feel well enough to go back.

That was twice now their visit had been cut short because she felt sick, necessitating a swift exit. He worried this might become a running theme. True, she'd lasted longer this time, but he resented the short amount of time that he got to spend with his parents. Maybe he could encourage her to take better care of herself. She could join him on his morning jogs and increase her physical health. That might help. Either way, she wasn't going to spoil everything.

He inhaled cold air, allowing himself to feel its cooling, calming effects, and exhaled a controlled stream of fog. It was fine. Maeve said that she was happy to go back when she felt better. That was more than he could hope for, and he made a bold decision to be patient. It was now a case of allowing her to climatise.

He walked along the deathly quiet road, throwing his gaze to the sky. There was a small parting in the clouds through which he could see a smattering of stars. He had to admit, Droichead Dubh's lack of light pollution made the countryside seem untouched, a little more magical.

Marvelling, he wondered if his parents stood under the same stars as he.

# 10.

Midday arrived and Maeve's dad burst in, announcing for the world to hear that it was indeed time to get up. Did he not know this was perfectly normal behaviour for a teenager and, scientifically speaking, teens needed more sleep than adults? She savoured those few sweet seconds after he'd vacated the room, allowing her brain to come to terms with the waking world. She sat up carefully and waited for the Otherworld pseudo-hangover to set in. It never came. Well, that was entirely true, she didn't feel one-hundred percent great, staying up until five in the morning would do that to a person, but she didn't feel awful. Maybe she was adjusting. Good to know.

Throwing aside her sheets, Maeve did a light hop out of bed. She felt jazzed from the previous night and her ruminations on the possible existence of gods. She waltzed into the kitchen and selected her tea, hibiscus today.

"How's things?" Her dad said, without taking his eyes off of his newspaper.

"Divine!" She said.

She chuckled inwardly at the joke alluding to her discoveries. An admittedly horrible joke that she would never repeat, but still, 'divine'. Who knew leading a double life could be so thrilling, and so funny? She settled at the table and checked her phone. A reminder popped up.

"Shit!" She said.

"Language."

"I'm meant to meet Oisin in a bit. Will you give me a lift, da?"

He continued to read his paper, his silence as good as a 'yes'.

*        *        *        *        *        *

"Sorry I'm late!" Maeve said, practically falling out of the car, "Thanks, dad, I'll see you later." Shutting the door, she ran to give Oisin a hug.

"I'm usually the late one. Have we swapped places? Am I the 'good one' in this relationship now?" He said, squeezing tightly.

"Yes, you'll have to take on all my organising and planning duties from now on."

He sighed, considering, "Can I be the 'bad one' again?"

"It was a short-lived reprieve, but sure."

"Phew, shall we?" He stuck out his arm for her to take, and they walked off together.

They had no grand plans, they were just hanging out, but Maeve was thankful her dad had woken her when he did. She and Oisin hadn't spent much time together since her "illness" the previous week. It was nice having a little downtime after all the craziness. Part of her wanted to spill the beans and tell him everything that had been happening, it would be nice to have a third party to talk to. She refrained, lest she look totally mad, and lest he try doing anything to stop her.

"So, where to? *A Wee Tea* for your hot chocolate?" Oisin suggested.

"Umm, no, how about we go mainstream for the day and get a pumpkin spiced latte or something?" Maeve was pretty sure the waitress there was a huge gossip and couldn't guarantee she'd keep quiet regarding the heated discussion she'd had with Lorcan last week. Nothing salacious, but it was better for no unnecessary questions to be raised.

"Eew, okay, you can get your pumpkin spiced shite. I think I'll just stick to a normal latte."

Their hot drinks left trails of fragrant steam behind

them as they walked. Droichead Dubh did go all out when it came time for celebrations. The whole place looked like a giant spider's lair, covered in cobwebs and skeletons hanging precariously from lampposts. Clerks were already dressed up and shop windows adorned with witches on brooms and every tiny café had punned names for all their food: *I-Scream-Sundaes, Rice "Creepies" Bun, Ham and Cheese Ghostie Toastie.* That last one puzzled her, what was 'ghostie' about the toastie? There was a palpable buzz of energy building for the holiday.

"You got your costume sorted?" Maeve asked, observing an unconvincing Frankenstein's monster serving customers as they passed by.

"It's not for a couple of days."

"You always leave everything to the last second."

Oisin was a terrible procrastinator when it came to stuff like this.

"Yes, oh-great-organiser, I've got everything sorted!" He narrowed his eyes James Dean style, "*This here's Miss Bonnie Parker. I'm Clyde Barrow. We rob banks.*" He said in his best Texan accent.

"You watched the movie?" She raised one sceptical eyebrow.

"Yeah, of course." He was about as convincing as the Frankenstein's Monster had been, "Oh alright, I watched some clips online."

"I knew it! But it's better than nothing, I suppose."

"We'll look great together."

"You just want to show off your damsel." Maeve swooned, hand on head.

"And? What's wrong with that?"

They called into most of the shops along their route, periodically escaping the cold, there weren't that many. Droichead Dubh was such a small town that they managed to lap it three times on their circuit before the sky started to dim, and they decided to call it a day.

As they walked home, Oisin filled her in on what she

had missed during her week off. Not much of consequence as it turned out, but it all seemed very important to him: who broke up with whom, who had said what, who hadn't chosen their university course yet. What were they ever going to do with their life? Maeve, despite being a top class student, was in the same boat. She'd thought she'd wanted to study political science but, in light of recent events, her mind was changing. Her trajectory had been nudged – no, smashed – off course, and now she had to either course correct or see where it led. She couldn't continue on as normal now, knowing what lay behind the curtain.

"Uuuh, hello?"

She had fallen into a daydream and missed a question, Oisin was waiting on a response.

"What?"

"Jeez." He rolled his eyes dramatically, "I said, are you going to the bonfire on Halloween?"

"You mean 'Samhain'?"

"Pagan."

"I'll take that as a compliment, and yes, as long as you are."

"Sure am." He paused, "Lorcan going?"

"Umm, I don't know, he hasn't said anything about it. Why?"

"Just wondering. You should ask him. Might be good to talk to him again."

"Sure, but I'll see what he says."

"Do that."

They soon reached her house, doing their usual over-the-top goodbye, but Maeve couldn't help notice the jaggedness that had entered the conversation at the mention of Lorcan's name. Was he jealous? She had never even considered that a possibility, however, when she thought about the last seven days she couldn't blame Oisin for thinking something was going on. Normally their couples' excursions would have been the highlight of her week, but it really was a minor footnote compared to what was going on. Instead of being genuinely enthused to see him, Maeve felt like she was *acting* enthused, waiting to get back to the real task at hand. She hoped he wouldn't be able to tell, but apparently acting was not her calling in life, and he'd sensed her off-ness.

She would have to figure out a solution. She couldn't exactly keep him at a distance forever, and something would eventually give. For now, there was a bonfire to plan for. Maeve pulled up Lorcan's name on her phone.

*Going to the big fire then?*

**You going?**

*Yeah. Costumes are mandatory BTW.*

**I'll slap on some eyeshadow and call myself a ghost.**

*Simple but effective, you're already pale enough.*

**Actually, I wanted to talk to you about Halloween.**

# 11.

The field undulated, bustling with what looked to be a majority of the residents of Droichead Dubh. All anticipating the veritable inferno of the bonfire, signalling that it was time for all hell to break loose. Every generation had turned up. Kids counted their takings from a productive evening of trick-or-treating, adults necked cider and whatever else they had to hand, students did the same, trying to remain surreptitious. Health and safety marshals patrolled the outskirts of the field, Maeve highly doubted they'd be doing much work seeing as most of them were already holding beer bottles, chatting amongst themselves and barely paying attention to the crowd. Small town logic.

It had been a dry October, but well-trodden parts of the field dissolved into a mucky mess. As such, Maeve had made some alterations to her costume, ditching the high heels in favour of more practical boots, and she'd taken up the hem of her dress. She was sure Bonnie would understand. Oisin had followed suit, except he'd swapped his dress shoes for trainers that didn't quite go with the rest of the aesthetic.

"This was all I could get." He said, appearing at her side and handing her a brown bottle.

She examined it, "Is it period accurate?"

"Not if we're talking about prohibition, but they still had beer back then. Now drink!" He tilted his head back, taking a gulp, "Maybe not this low calorie stuff though."

As far as Maeve could tell, everyone from school had turned up, some dressed, some not. They admired each other's costumes, made fun of unpopular pupils, and eyed their chosen targets for the night. She watched the scene dispassionately. They all spoke with heightened gesticulations, there was drama around every corner, and there were already miniature disputes afoot. It all had the feeling of an exquisitely rendered renaissance painting, but one that she wasn't particularly interested in looking at in detail. She took a long swill from her beer.

"Oh, look who it is." Oisin tapped her on the shoulder and pointed.

Lorcan had arrived with Cara in tow. He had stuck to his word and slapped on a bit of eyeshadow, his best attempt at a costume. Cara, on the other hand, had made an effort and was decked out in her full witchy gear. Hat, broomstick, cobwebs, the works. Lorcan looked around, scanning the throng. He quickly spotted them and turned to make his excuses to Cara, who was already off mingling with a crowd of people.

"She's feeling gregarious." He said flatly, shuffling his way over.

"I see you made a real effort." Maeve said.

"Yeah, well – you both look great."

"Do you want a beer?" Oisin asked, gesturing to the cooler behind them.

"Yeah, I'll partake." Lorcan grabbed himself a bottle.

It was pretty awkward at first. Having only really spoken to Maeve as of late, Lorcan's social skills were not up to par with how they used to be. Conversation was rough, and Oisin's usual amicable demeanour was tinged with an uncharacteristic sourness. Soon though, it was time to light the bonfire as the sun dipped below the horizon and darkness descended on the field. They could focus on the ceremony rather than each other. Small, handmade effigies were placed on the pile of wood, offerings to family spirits, wishes for the future, charms and wards for protecting households. Some were just meant as extra fuel for the fire. A figure approached the pile of wood with a lit torch, casting dancing orange light on the surrounding crowd, its flame swaying in the wind.

Maeve craned her neck to see who it was this year and stifled a laugh when she saw who it was, Mr. Dickson, their Politics teacher. Giggles and murmurs rippled through the students present, stopping as he began a well-rehearsed speech.

His voice carried over the crowd in a powerful, booming baritone, telling of the veils between worlds colliding, potentially evil spirits invading, hungry beings, children abducted in the dark of night. He waved and pointed his torch at the crowd as he spoke this, eyes wide and expressive. The whole thing was thoroughly dramatic and his Viking inspired costume, along with the warpaint added to the authenticity. It all felt appropriately ritualistic, so, when the torch touched wood, igniting with a bassy *VWOOMPH,* a raucous cheer went up from the crowd. Mr. Dickson spread his arms like a warlord at a feast. The party had officially begun.

A tribal mood took hold as attendees burst into dance around the fire, music started up and the drink flowed more freely. There was a mingling between generations that rarely happened as older members of the community were determined to show the young'uns 'how it was done'. The alcohol and the fire served to keep Maeve warm as the frenzy swept her into its fold. Even Lorcan was in a partying mood, joining for a couple of songs, bobbing stiff-armed to the beat. The crowd melded, becoming more disorganized and in the flitting about, Maeve had lost Oisin. Lorcan took this opportunity and led her to the edge of the horde, pulling her in close, so he didn't have to shout.

"So, what do you think?" He said.

"About what?"

"About what we spoke about. Are you up for it?" He stepped back, examining her.

"I don't know." She looked around, "This is pretty fun and people will notice we're gone."

"So?"

"So, I don't want to cause any problems."

"Think about it." His mouth was almost touching

Maeve's ear, "The Otherworld on Halloween. Who the hell can say they've done that? Nobody!"

She considered this for a moment. In the chaos of the party she had nearly reverted to her old self, the alcohol pulling her mind to the present moment and blurring both past and future. Lorcan's words had a sobering effect, her sense of adventure was stirring.

Maeve regarded the scene, what had seemed absorbing and fun thirty seconds ago now seemed quaint, trivial. She swung to Lorcan, nodding once. He was right, who the hell could say that they'd been to the Otherworld on Halloween? Nobody but them.

They slinked off with as little fuss as possible, walking hurriedly to Dún Dubh. If they timed it right, people might not even notice they'd been gone, the party would last into the wee hours of the morning and everyone was already pretty sloshed. Maeve was glad she'd switched out her footwear. Boots were much more appropriate for these steep slopes.

They reached the fort and made their way inside. It had lost a lot of its intimidation factor in all the excitement. They lacked the supplies they'd thought to bring last time, but maybe a belly full of beer would sustain them. She hoped so anyway. Reaching the centre, Lorcan inhaled as he prepared to call out and stopped short as nearby footsteps approached, zeroing in on their exact location.

"I fucking knew it!"

It was Oisin. What was he doing here? His phone torch was blinding, as he held it aloft, illuminating the pair. They froze as if caught in the midst of some sleazy act.

"I saw you two leave together. You think I'm a bloody eejit?"

Had he followed them all this way?

"Well?" He stepped closer, "Are you going to say anything?"

"Oisin -" Maeve had been caught, but not in the way that he imagined.

Lorcan remained silent.

"Jesus. Not even a decent excuse. Did you really think you wouldn't get found out? C'mon, we're going to talk." He grabbed Maeve's wrist, motioning her out of the ruins.

Lorcan grabbed her other arm and tugged. This looked bad, and she didn't know how to explain it away. Did she just go along with what Oisin thought was the case? That might be easier. Or, did she try to explain what had really been going on and risk a straitjacket? Would she even want to expose the Otherworld's existence? Honestly, all she wanted was to be somewhere far, far away from here. Desperately so.

"No, we have something important to do." Lorcan held her arm firmly.

She needed to be away from here.

"Important?" Oisin hissed, "Listen to me, you fucking shit -" The scenery shifted and his face dropped in a stunned disbelief.

Electricity raced across Maeve's skin, vision exploding with a sudden flickering, light as an icy prickle settled into her bones. They were in the Otherworld.

Lorcan hadn't called out and Maeve hadn't felt the same intense cold like she had before. There was no denying it, they'd crossed over into the Otherworld. How? How were they here? They looked around the torchlit chamber, but nobody had come to greet them. It was just Maeve, Lorcan - and Oisin.

"Lorcan, how did…?" She trailed off.

"I don't know, I didn't feel much this time. Did you?"

"No, nothing really."

"Mam, dad?" He called, barely above a whisper.

There was no response and the whole situation felt off kilter, which was saying something considering prior events. Oisin was transfixed by the room, stuck in a gaping, catatonic state. Wordlessly they started towards the doorway, Oisin groping at Maeve's arm for an explanation.

"I'll explain in a second but, for now you're going to have to follow me." She steadied her voice and guided him along. Maeve needed to see it again.

They stepped into the open. It was just as breathtaking as she remembered. The sheer mega-mountains piercing the clouds. The way the landscape surged and warped impossibly back in on itself, flecked with vaguely familiar landmarks. And, of course, the castle. She hadn't gotten time to take it all in last time. She flicked her head upwards. There they were, branches. Branches peeking through the clouds, belonging to an unfathomably titanic tree. She grinned at the absurdity of it all. So wrapped up in the scenery was Maeve that she forgot about Oisin until he let out a choking sound followed by promptly vomiting on the ground.

"What the hell! What did you do? Where are we? I don't understand." His voice was high and wild as he backed away, tripping and stumbling into the fort's solid stone wall. Maeve went to him and held him by the shoulders as he slumped to the ground.

"Oisin, Oisin, look at me. It's okay, you're alright." She'd snapped out of her wonderment, "Just breathe, and we'll explain everything, okay?"

"Did you - did you drug me? Did you fucking drug me or something? This isn't happening!" He shut his eyes.

Even compared to Maeve, he'd been thrown in at the deep end, she had at least been able to dip her toes in the water first before being shoved headlong in. It took him a full ten minutes to even begin to calm down, there was lots of head patting accompanied by soothing, shushing sounds along the way.

As well as they could, they caught him up on what had happened up until this point. Lorcan explained about his parents and how Maeve had become wrapped up in the situation. They omitted any details about unintended strangulation or emotional breakdowns, now was *not* the time for those complications. When it came to explaining their understanding of the Otherworld, Maeve did most of the talking, after all she was the one who'd done the hardcore research.

"So, yeah, we thought it'd be fun to pay a visit on Halloween. I'm sorry we didn't tell you, but I could hardly think where to start with something like this." Maeve said, apologetic, "Now you know."

Oisin had been quietly taking it all in, she braced herself for his response.

He swallowed, wiping a layer of panicked sweat from his forehead, "Y'know, I really don't appreciate the fact that neither of you trusted me with this. I don't see why I had to be left out." He shot that one at Maeve, "But - I understand at the same time. It's bloody crazy, and I probably wouldn't have believed you. No - I definitely wouldn't have believed you. So, we can deal with it when we get back." He stood up and properly took in the scene.

Maeve could hear how unsteady his voice was, it was still a lot to deal with. She was actually extremely impressed with how well he was carrying himself, even if he was struggling to hide his trembling.

"Is that why we were able to come across on our own?" He said after a moment.

"Is what?" Maeve was puzzled.

"Halloween, you just told me about the veils and the worlds colliding or whatever. Is it easier to cross tonight?"

"You might be onto something there." Lorcan said, having been silent for the past few minutes.

"Of course!" Maeve palmed her forehead in the age-old way of saying, *how did I not think of that!?*

"You're slipping, Maeve." Oisin said, "You're supposed to be the smart one." He let the comment hang, then winked.

Maybe they'd be alright after all.

The hill, situated as it was, gave them a good vantage point to examine the surrounding land. After a lengthy and heated debate, they decided that it would be prudent to conduct some basic reconnaissance. Oisin had argued for staying put, but where was the fun in that?

"I say we go to the castle." Maeve said. She was like a kid in a candy store.

"Okay, you're prepared to walk for miles and miles in an unknown, unexplored world on a Halloween night after you've had a few drinks?" Oisin reposted. He could be annoyingly practical when he wanted to be.

"It was just a suggestion."

"There's a few lights down there. How about that?" Lorcan offered.

They followed his eyeline. The location of the settlement was roughly analogous to their own town of Droichead Dubh back home, only far bigger and disordered in layout. There looked to be a celebration here too. Did the dead recognise Halloween? There was one way to find out.

"Seems like a good option. What do you think?" Maeve said, swivelling to Oisin.

His brow furrowed in concentration. He always appeared grumpy when he was considering something. She really had to hand it to him, Oisin had found out less than half an hour ago that a whole other world existed apart from their own, and he was keeping a level head, looking out for them - for her. She never did give him the credit he deserved.

"Okay, yeah, that seems reasonable."

At this Maeve turned, eager to get underway but felt a sharp tug on her arm from Oisin, "Any sign of trouble, or anything looks dangerous, you *swear* to me that you'll run away." His grip loosened, realising how tight it had been, "Please."

His face was grim. It was an expression that rarely adorned his features. Oisin acted like he didn't care about a lot of things, about most things, but when push came to shove he was so fiercely loyal and protective it could be frightening. She'd seen glimpses of it before, and she saw it clearly now. It reminded her of why she'd liked him so much in the first place. Maeve leant over and kissed him on the forehead, she would've gone for the lips, but was all too aware he had vomited not so long ago.

"Swear." She said, locking eyes with him.

They set off towards their new destination, planning the route as best they could from what they could see, which, apart from broad markers, wasn't a lot. However, the moon's light seemed to hang in the air regardless of whether it should have been blocked by a looming tree or not. It gave the night a sheen that was normally reserved for overly-stylised landscape paintings. Not only was it a mesmerizing effect, it was also pretty useful for navigating in the dark.

All around them vague buzzing noises emitted from the vegetation with periodic rustling that made Oisin jump, going on high alert for a few steps before returning to a general paranoia. Maeve could see that thick armour of his had some serious hairline cracks developing, threatening to spread and undermine that stoic demeanour. Sounds of merriment carried through the foliage, weaving over, under and around the group. It sounded like any other party, high and low voices whooping and hollering, music with discernible chord progressions, and the myriad of other sounds that came with a gathered mass of people. However, amongst the party's seemingly ordinary sonic landscape were sounds that didn't register to their ears as being normal. Piercing screeches, notes so bass-heavy that they couldn't possibly have been produced by a human, long, whining, lyrical cries. With each new sound, pangs of fear washed over Maeve - fear mixed with growing excitement.

The treeline stopped and so did they. Beyond, the moon laid in stark relief the diorama of the settlement. The buildings were an eclectic mix of structures from different periods, just as Maeve had noted from the hill. Now that she was seeing them up close, it was evident no planning had gone into the layout as the buildings faced this way and that, creating near cul-de-sacs where there shouldn't have been. Streets widened and narrowed at odd intervals, while some buildings even seemed to be joined together. Not in a regular semi-detached way, where there was a clear line denominating the separation of property. No, these houses looked almost fused together, they cannibalised one another. She noted a particularly peculiar example of two houses joined like this, a wooden one and a brick one. It was like someone had taken the smudge tool and went wild, the wood melded into the stone with no joins, it *became* the other house. Her head hurt even trying to conceive how that might work.

So focused was she on the housing situation in the Otherworld that she failed to notice both Lorcan and Oisin eyeing a figure making its way out of an older looking wooden house. A woman in a fine dress; she wore a hanging cloak off one shoulder, fastened with a large decorative brooch. Her wrists and neck were adorned with finely crafted gold jewellery. She looked straight out of a historical drama, or documentary series on ancient Ireland. The woman headed in the opposite direction of the trio, towards the commotion that was happening in the far off field.

"You can put your eyes back in your heads boys." Maeve whispered.

Oisin turned white, "Was she - was she a spirit? Or ghost, or whatever?"

"I suppose so, yeah."

He swallowed, "She looked so normal. Apart from the getup, like, but still -"

"If everyone's going to that celebration, maybe my parents are there." Lorcan said, stepping out of the tree line, barely paying them any mind.

"Lorcan!" Maeve hissed.

"What? We were heading there anyway, right?"

"We don't know what we're doing, we were only checking out the area."

"Well, I'm going to check it out." He set off down the road.

Before she could protest further Oisin burst out from cover and seized Lorcan from behind with a headlock. He talked quickly into Lorcan's ear at a volume Maeve couldn't make out. She gleaned from context that it was nasty stuff. Lorcan nodded, Oisin must have asked him a question, and they parted, both flushed red. The two boys stared each other down for a long moment before Oisin broke it off.

"We agreed before this, no going off on your own or putting us in danger. We have no idea what's happening here." He turned back to Lorcan, "So let's be careful, shall we?"

As a group this time they followed in the woman's footsteps, careful not to draw attention to themselves. They could see shadows in the distance heading to the same place, it was attracting a large crowd. Catching sight of herself in a darkened window, Maeve squeaked with alarm, forgetting she was in costume. When she thought about it, the older style might actually help them blend in. The same went for Oisin, apart from those very modern trainers, and for Lorcan, whose mascaraed eyes emphasised his already wan features.

Nobody spoke as they navigated the winding, sloping streets, giving Maeve time to take in the environment. This version of Droichead Dubh was more heavily populated and built up than the living version that was for sure. Generations upon generations living alongside and on top of one another in one area. Maybe that's why the land stretched and warped the way it did, it needed to accommodate the ever-growing influx of residents. Just one of her working hypotheses. Like unexpected houseguests on an overcrowded sofa, it was all a bit squashed, but they made room. She wondered if there were people in the Otherworld that could provide answers, like the undead version of a search engine, *enter soul query here.*

Lost on thought, it suddenly dawned on her that she might recognise some people here, older residents of the town who had passed away. Perhaps some of those nice old folks she'd been forced to volunteer with for the school's community programme. She froze, her stomach dropping when she realised who else she might run into. God, why had that never crossed her mind? She had never even considered the fact that her mother might be here. She looked at Lorcan, his grim determination, that desperate, longing look that occupied his eyes; she'd been there. Maeve was never going back, and she pushed those feelings down as hard and far as she could. That longing was years old, no way was it rearing its ugly head now, not here. If her mother did appear, would it be the mother of her childhood or - well, she'd cross that bridge if she had to. She hoped she didn't have to.

Running to catch up, Maeve rammed into Oisin's back as he halted dead in his tracks. Looking around his shoulder, Maeve saw why. They'd made it. There were hundreds, no, thousands of bodies gathering themselves in and around the confines of the field. Men, women and children of all ages and in a variety of garbs from the ages. She didn't recognise anyone, a small blessing, which allowed her to take in the scene as fully as she could, there wasn't one detail she wanted to miss.

Unblinkingly, she scanned the crowd and noticed not only men, women and children, but animals that looked far too sentient to be mere livestock or pets. Impossibly small people perched on shoulders, or hung onto loose clothing. Maeve could've sworn she saw someone with a pair of wings, but they disappeared behind a hulking mass of a man before she could get a closer look. Then there were the humanoid creatures. They were bipedal but their bodies and facial features were twisted so that they no longer resembled what she considered to be human.

It was all far too much to process in one go, letting her eyes defocus and drift over the crowd as a whole to take in its sheer queerness. Everyone was either making their way towards a central structure or had perched themselves along the side so that they could view it. There was a bonfire the size of a three-story structure, yet to be lit. On the platform in front of the structure stood a tall figure of a man. In one hand he held a flaming torch, with the other he gestured, silencing the onlookers; it was his time to speak. The standout feature of this man, even compared to all the sights Maeve had seen so far, was his lack of a head.

# 12.

The roaring of the gathered mass subsided to a low din as the headless figure's hand brought them to heel. The level of control he exerted so effortlessly over them was something to marvel at; he was of some import it seemed. Lowering his broad arm, he spoke, his voice ringing out true and clear. As loud as a sound system at a rock concert but as clean and precise as if he were standing next to them, it had the effect of sounding like his voice was being beamed directly into her brain.

"Welcome!" He boomed, "Welcome, my friends, to the quarter day festival of Samhain!"

A cheer went up from the crowd and just as quickly faded.

"Tonight we remember that life and death are ever connected as the barrier between worlds weakens. In years gone past our kind would wreak havoc on the living world and seek vengeance for perceived misdeeds, or long-held grudges." At this, jeers and laughter rose from parts of the crowd, but the headless man silenced them again with a quick, concise gesture. "Now - we exist in harmony under the High King, leaving life to the living and death to the dead. Tonight is a special night for it is the feast of Tara. Once every seven years the High King appoints to his council, one-hundred and fifty champions and a steward of Ireland."

There was shifting, whispering amongst groups, glances back and forth to the platform where the man stood. An uneasy, disgruntled anticipation.

"I am proud to inform you that I, William de Meath, have

been chosen as protector and watcher over these lands and its denizens as your steward!"

The cry was deafening. Maeve, Oisin and Lorcan actually had to cover their ears as the crowd exploded into pandemonium. Maeve's ears rang and her vision blurred, the sound assaulting them on all fronts and frequencies, from bone-rattling sub-bass booms to ear-splitting ultrasonic howls. Although it was hard to read the expressions of some of the gathered entities, she could see that not all of them were happy about the news. The jubilance was not unanimous.

"My friends!" He continued, "Troubled times await, you know of what I speak. We are once again on the precipice of change and our very ways threatened. We must all be aware of whom we follow and who we choose to defy. Your allegiance will define the fate of this land and its future. Nevertheless - tonight - rejoice!"

Cheer.

"Drink!"

Cheer.

"Let the living hear us and remember us!" This sent the crowd into a frenzy and the headless man plunged the torch into the pile of wood. There was a series of sharp cracks and booms as the wood ignited, splitting in the scorching heat as the white-orange light intensified, expanding into a giant plume. He stood on the platform, observing the chaos before he climbed off and descended into the mosh pit.

The celebration proceeded much as it had back home, though on a significantly grander scale. Alcohol. Dancing. Jostling. Alcohol. Fighting. Shouting. Joking. Alcohol. The dead sure could party hard. Probably, they didn't have to worry much considering they were most likely immune to dying from overconsumption. In the shifting throng, Maeve observed individuals more closely now that everyone was mingling. The tiny people who perched on other's shoulders looked like they might be - she couldn't believe she was thinking this - leprechauns. Seriously! Honest-to-god

Leprechauns. They were hopping from platform to platform, spilling drinks, knocking hats off heads and destroying intricate hairdos. Maeve couldn't help but smile.

She watched as another being changed its appearance, just like that, in front of an onlooking crowd. A circle of men surrounded it, ogling openly as it switched from a voluptuous, regally dressed woman to a scantily clad, equally voluptuous, redhead. They whooped and whistled, baying for more. Its mouth widened into a cheeky smirk, more than happy to oblige. Nude women performing for men wasn't exactly Maeve's thing, but the transformation was fascinating to watch, as were the men's reactions when it suddenly transformed into a rather large hairy gentleman with massive hanging (and hairy) genitals that almost brushed the floor. They booed and stuck out their tongues in disapproval, but it did surprisingly turn a few heads who hadn't been watching prior. The creature reverted to the form of a young man, clutching its stomach as he cackled and avoided a swipe from one of the spectators, dodging the attack nimbly.

"Aw, I was enjoying that!" Oisin said, earning a slap on the arm, "Ow!"

"Serves you right for looking at another naked woman."

"Did you see her - um, him - *it?* - transform? That was pretty cool!"

"Funny too."

She spun to see Lorcan on his tiptoes, straining to see over the crowd. She could guess what he was doing and who he was looking for.

"Do you think they're here?" She asked.

He continued his search and shrugged, "Don't know. Maybe we should look. In the crowd I mean."

They huddled together, agreeing that was probably a terrible idea. Maeve was quick to point out that it had just taken a single touch from Lorcan's mum to floor her, she wouldn't forget that in a hurry, and they didn't know what would happen if they went into an entire horde of spirits.

Begrudgingly, Lorcan acquiesced but insisted they stay on the fringes and keep looking for his parents.

Taking their positions, Maeve felt like a shy kid stood on the sideline of a cool party because they were too scared of being made fun of or, god forbid, having a good time. Still, she was transfixed by the unfolding scene, it was everything she'd hoped it would be, it was pure magic - maybe literally. She didn't know what it was and that enticed her all the more. Oisin looked entranced by it all, he was sweating profusely, and it wasn't exactly hot in the Otherworld. The stress was getting to him, and they might have to leave soon for his sake.

"I'd love a drink!" Oisin said, seeming to sense her worried stare.

"What do you think they have here?" She replied, "Maggoty Meade?"

"Meade's a Viking drink, we'd have to go to Valhalla for that. How about some delicious, golden Otherworld ale?"

"Sounds tasty."

As if on cue, a small inebriated man clocked them from the crowd and rushed over. All three stood alert, but he produced three bottles of what looked to be beer or stout, holding them out in front of him. They hesitated, looking from the bottles, to the man, to each other and back again. He inclined his head encouragingly and they each took a bottle, careful not to make physical contact. They gave a weak *cheers* motion, and he ran back into the throng.

Maeve examined her bottle. It was too dim to properly tell, but it appeared to be a dark beer or ale. She sniffed at the liquid. It *seemed* normal, in fact it smelled good. There was the usual yeasty smell of fermented hops, but she could also detect certain fruity notes with a warm butterscotch undertone. She impressed herself. With a sense of smell like that maybe she'd become an Otherworld beer and ale sommelier. She looked to the others, unsure of what to do but Lorcan was already drinking his.

"Jesus!" Oisin was horrified.

Lorcan swished the liquid around his mouth, tasting and swallowing with a satisfied *ahh!*

"Seems alright." He dived back in.

Maeve and Oisin waited a few minutes to test whether it would affect Lorcan negatively in any way and, when he appeared fine, Maeve swigged hers, followed by Oisin. As the liquid passed her lips and down her gullet, a curious cooling sensation coated her insides and was replaced by heat upon reaching her stomach. They all decided it was good beer, or ale, none of them could tell the difference, contrary to Maeve's excellent nasal abilities. It was certainly stronger than the stuff they were used to because, half a bottle in, they were all dancing along with the party goers at the edge. Even Oisin, who had been so careful, was dosey doe-ing and performing his best approximation of Irish dancing for groups of clapping party animals. What was in this stuff?

Enraptured by the moment, Maeve hadn't noticed Lorcan's absence. Her foggy brain worked to find him, spotting three figures in the shadow of one of the nearby huts. Were they his parents? She couldn't tell from here but grabbed Oisin and pulled his attention to Lorcan. His grin faded, and they sped towards him, not entirely steadily.

Upon closer inspection they were indeed Lorcan's parents, and they were giving him a hard time about something. As they neared Oisin stuck out a hand to stop Maeve. She remembered he had no idea who they were.

"It's okay. This is Aiden and this is Bronach." She gestured to them in turn, "They're Lorcan's mum and dad. And this is Oisin, my boyfriend." They looked just as tense as Oisin.

"They are?" He said with a look of bemusement.

"Yes."

"Oh… okay." Oisin said warily.

The intense suspicion faded from his eyes as he dropped his arm, everyone relaxed.

"Maeve!" Bronach said, "What are you doing here?"

"Well we -"

"That doesn't matter!" Aiden cut her off gruffly, "We need to get them out of here." He indicated to the ongoing soirée.

Maeve looked to the crowd and, sure enough, some of them were paying a little too much attention to their small group. The high she had been experiencing was threatening to turn into a crushing low.

"We weren't doing anything wrong, we just ended up here. I told you -"

"And I told you it doesn't matter." Aiden cut Lorcan off now, "Come on, let's get -"

A commotion erupted behind them as the crowd parted. There were people pointing in their direction, and barrelling through the crowd was the headless man. He may have been missing a crucial piece of anatomy, but he towered over most other people. There was that crushing low that had been looming over them since arriving, ready to drop.

"Run!" Aiden shouted.

The five of them took off at speed, bombing their way through the streets and winding alleys, retracing their steps. The laughter and merriment of the party goers that had been so inviting before, now sounded to Maeve's ears like the cries of an angry mod, out for blood. Their blood. Daring a glance back, she saw the armoured figure round a corner and gather a dark mist at his side. The mist shifted and solidified into a jet black horse that let out a piercing bellow as it reared onto its hind legs. Her gaze didn't linger long enough to see whether he mounted his steed, but thundering hoofbeats told her all she needed to know as they grew closer and more distinct. They had the advantage of narrow streets and sharp turns, but he wouldn't be long catching up.

Reaching the edge of the town, Aiden and Bronach led them into a thick part of the brush just in time for them to see the headless horseman fly past on his demon mount. He hadn't seen them.

"He'll have to follow the path. He's not as fast on foot

and his horse can't navigate the trees. We'll cut straight up the hillside." Aiden pointed.

"It knows where we're headed?" Oisin said, breathlessly.

"Yes, but we can get there first." Bronach reassured them.

There was no time to waste. They raced their way through the trees, tripping and pushing their way over and past thickets of leaves. Rays of moonlight pooled to guide them along, yet they still managed to trip over themselves at every turn, scrambling frantically back to their feet. At every out of place sound they'd pause, listening for any covert pursuers, and then shoot off at speed with Aiden spearheading the operation. Oisin kept a firm grip on Maeve's hand the entire way, refusing to let go even when she'd given little protesting tugs. She could flee on her own, thank you very much, but he was having none of it. Lorcan, on the other hand, was doing just fine as he deftly shadowed Aiden without issue. A pang of jealousy hit Maeve.

Arriving at Dún Dub, they stopped once again, making doubly sure they were alone. As they waited, she noticed all music had ceased from the Samhain gathering, replaced by horrid squealing and pained shrieks.

"What's happening?" She murmured.

"Never mind." Aiden sprinted for the entrance.

It may have been her pulse pounding in her ears, but Maeve imagined she could hear those hoofbeats nearing as they followed him into the central chamber.

"What is he?" Lorcan managed between gasps.

"We can't explain now." Aiden said.

"We'll explain next time, pet, we swear." Bronach said reaching out.

"Love you." Lorcan choked out too late.

They were back. The shocking, electric cold startled them into sobriety. All at once, they vomited sourly onto the ruins of the fort floor.

Thick clouds had rolled in, leaving the three in a stifling gloom as they recovered their breaths, working up the strength to speak. Though she could only see an indistinct outline of him, Maeve could tell Oisin was trembling, struggling to calm himself. She bit the bullet, inhaling sharply through her nose and broke the hush.

"So, that was -" She didn't know how to finish the sentence.

It was Lorcan who shuffled and stood.

"Yeah. It was."

He trudged out of the fort and into the clearing. Maeve heard him pacing and taking long, sustained breaths, as if practising some aggressive form of meditation. She and Oisin continued to marinate in the festering stillness between them. She couldn't help but mimic Lorcan's breathing, falling into a rhythm, and when her heart rate resembled something of a normal pace, she picked herself up and sidled over to Oisin. His hands shook, covered in a cold, clammy sweat.

"Are you alright?" She said.

"No." He replied, head buried in his arms.

Hugging him closer, she rubbed his back and shoulders, "I know, but we're okay. We made it out, and we'll be more careful from now on."

"From now on?" He raised his head, "You're planning to go back?"

"Well, yeah. Oisin, this is - this is completely outside of our understanding. Did you see everything? Wasn't it pretty wonderful? We just need to, y'know, do our research and prepare better."

Pulling away and pushing with his legs, he slid his back awkwardly up the wall until stood unsteadily.

"I can't believe you. Yeah, I saw it! I was nearly killed by it!." He shot back at her, leaving to join Lorcan in the clearing.

She understood his reaction, she'd had a similar one after all, but didn't he see the bigger picture? This was the adventure of a lifetime! What had happened tonight had only cemented that in her head. Yes, it was frightening and, yes, it felt dangerous (perilous even) but it was also exciting. It was like she'd fallen directly into one of the legends she'd been reading about. For the first time, Maeve felt as though she were part of something greater, and she wasn't about to turn her back on it because some of it might be scary. The best stories were always the ones where the heroes faced danger, but that's what made them great. She gathered herself and exited the fort.

The trio plodded down the hillside at a snail's pace. The bonfire was still flickering in the distance, wispy plumes of smoke rising from dying red embers. Tiny figures of people in the field ran about, still partying and keeping the fire going, no doubt the fire marshals were among them. They'd been part of that group not so long ago. Fast onsetting hangovers made the trek tedious, every step taking an extra effort to place properly whilst their stomachs and heads turned traitor on them.

Oisin surprised Maeve by still insisting on walking her home, she thought he'd be too mad for that. When they arrived Lorcan said his goodbyes and made off to his own house. He hadn't said anything, but she had a pretty good idea that tonight had not put him off, little could, Lorcan would be going back to the Otherworld. Oisin, on the other hand - he was a different story. She wondered if this was it for them, had their relationship reached its breaking point with lies and danger? He wasn't even looking at her as he leaned on the fence, he was gazing at some imaginary far-off point in the mountains.

"I've never been more scared than I was tonight." He said, frankly.

She joined him, leaning on the post and looking at that illusory point, "Yeah?"

"Mmhmm."

Maeve could think of a few times when she'd felt more frightened than tonight, even recently, but she'd let Oisin have this moment. It might be the last time they spoke as boyfriend and girlfriend.

"What were you thinking about?" He turned to her.

"When?"

"When we were running from that thing. What were you thinking?"

"I don't know, honestly. I suppose I wasn't thinking much, other than we needed to get out of there." He didn't respond, "What about you?"

Oisin returned his gaze to the ether, "I was thinking about you." That bored a hole of guilt right into Maeve's gut, "Every second I was thinking, *you have to protect her, you just have to, fuck everyone else just get her out.* That's what I was thinking."

There wasn't much of a comeback to that, Maeve was usually so good with those but no sound left her lips. Had she even once thought something along those lines? It was all so frantic. She must have! Although - she wasn't so sure. Oisin turned fully to her.

"I know where your head's at." He said, "You think I don't pay attention or notice things. I do." She was starting to realise that, "I can see that you think this is all some big game or adventure, and that it's all going to work out, and you'll be the hero or whatever. You're clever, Maeve, you're really damn clever, but you can be a bit thick sometimes."

She wished he'd just get on with it instead of leading her on this massive guilt trip. Her eyes were beginning to smart, and it was starting to feel a little too personal. Who was he calling 'thick'?

"Tonight was real. You could've died. Do you get that?" He widened his eyes so that the whites showed.

"Of course I get it." Her voice was small.

"I don't think you do." Oisin tried to laugh through it, but it came out sounding mocking, Maeve was losing her patience with this drawn out speech, "That's why -"

Here it was. What he'd been building up to. As she steeled herself for the inevitable she didn't feel sadness or despair - what surprised her was just how much she didn't want him to finish his speech. Just let it last a little longer, let *them* last a little longer.

"- you need me there with you." What? Had she heard him right? "To ground you and let you know when you're being a thicko."

She blinked, Oisin was just full of unexpected surprises. Flashing her one of his smiles, he pulled Maeve into a crushing hug, like he was afraid she'd disintegrate if he wasn't the one to hold her together.

"I will *never* let anything bad happen to you." He said into her collar.

She squeezed back with as much force as she could muster. His warmth was safe and reassuringly steady as the world was shifting around her. Maeve would let Oisin ground her.

"So, you're feckin' stuck with me." He pulled back, looking at her, "Is that okay?"

She kissed him on the forehead, "I love you." It was the first time she'd said that.

He returned the gesture, "And I love you."

# 13.

A distinct shift in the dynamics was occurring within the newly forming group. In the days that followed, Maeve shared research she'd been gathering on the Otherworld, reams of printed web pages and academic essays, along with excerpts from children's stories that, while dumbed down, might hold some useful information. Oisin made steps towards careful, practical considerations for their next trip.

"You've seriously never considered taking a weapon with you to this place? Neither of you?" He said, the shock and disapproval clear on his face.

"We were hardly thinking about murdering spirits all over again." Lorcan snorted.

"You're lucky I came onboard when I did, you're both eejits." He added 'weapons' to his growing list of supplies, "By the way. You mentioned 'heat packs' as one of the essentials. Why? It wasn't *that* cold."

"It was absolutely freezing the first few times." Maeve said, "Lorcan, maybe that could be one of your questions?"

"Sure."

Lorcan was being tasked with asking his parents pertinent questions. Up until now he'd just been excited to see them again and hadn't been focused on learning about the wider world, much to Oisin's (and Maeve's) annoyance. From what she'd seen, he wasn't the detail oriented sort, being more of a *travel to another world now, ask questions later* kind of person. It must be nice not to be constantly over analysing or sparing much thought for the wider implications of things, stumbling your way through life. She didn't much blame him. If Maeve had been contacted by her mother soon after she'd died, she dreaded to think of the lengths she'd have gone to hold onto that relationship. It's better they were a team now, if someone (i.e. Lorcan) overlooked a detail, someone else could pick up the slack.

As Lorcan wrote, Maeve could see that he was pressing a little too hard on the paper, almost tearing through it. His level of tension had shot up since their Samhain adventure. She wasn't sure if it was because of the events that had transpired, his parents yelling at him or whether it was Oisin's presence that set him on edge. She'd got the impression he had enjoyed it just being their secret. Maybe all of the above.

"Hey." She interjected as Oisin and Lorcan debated the usefulness of bringing money with them, "We've been doing a lot of planning, and we've still got a few days left until we go back to school."

"So?" Lorcan said.

"Sooo, why don't we do something? Cinema? Tonight?"

Droichead Dubh's only cinema was a pokey little picture house with one screen. Two if you counted the "VIP" section which consisted of a couple of worn armchairs and a free popcorn refill. It mostly screened reruns of classics or seasonal films because that's all they could afford to show. They didn't exactly have the funding to acquire the latest blockbusters seeing that the number of people in the town interested in that stuff could fill one showing - just about.

"Depends on what they're showing. That last one you dragged me to was a complete bore-fest." Oisin said.

"*Citizen Kane* is a classic!" She snorted.

"Yeah, a classic bore-fest. We get it, you loved your sled or whatever. Childhood innocence - blah, blah, blah." He was joking, hoping Maeve would take the bait. She loved classic movies and Oisin loved making fun of them.

"Orson Wells was a genius, you're just a Philistine."

"Does being a genius mean you have to be *so boring?*"

He was half hanging off of the table, mock falling asleep and Maeve hit him with a roll of papers to 'wake' him up.

"Okay, what are they showing?" He said, resigned to his fate.

Maeve did a quick search on her phone, *"Darby O'Gill and the Little People."*

"Classic!" Oisin said, his voice dripping with sarcasm.

"Oh, shush! What about you, Lorcan, what do you think?"

"Uum, I haven't seen it before, so okay." Lorcan looked afraid to say otherwise. He'd seen what she could do with a rolled up stack of papers.

*    *    *    *    *    *

They met outside the ambitiously named *Omniplex* where a small crowd had gathered and were making their way inside. They bought overpriced popcorn and drinks and found their seats in the small, sticky-floored auditorium. The cinema had been built before proper raked seating had become a thing, so having a good view was dependent on either being tall or not being seated behind a tall person. Luckily the showing wasn't packed, so they had their choice of seats, although they did have to ask one particularly spatially inept giant to move when he'd sat right in front of Maeve.

Despite his protestations, Maeve knew Oisin enjoyed this film. He told her he'd been terrified of the wailing banshee spirit as a young boy and, sure enough, she could feel his hand tighten around hers when it appeared on screen. They'd seen an actual demonic spirit, and he was cringing at this? The providence wasn't lost on Maeve that the cinema happened to be showing this particular film after all that had transpired between them. She couldn't help but wonder if they might encounter a real banshee at some point. Would she be an omen of death like the one in the film? Probably not. They were already finding so many discrepancies when it came to these legends, and nineteen-fifties Disney was hardly an authority when it came to Irish folklore.

"So, what'd you think?" Maeve said.

"Shite!" Oisin shouted quickly before Lorcan could answer.

"Liar. And thanks for giving me my hand back, I thought you were going to crush it there at one point. Was wee Oisin afraid?" She pronounced the 'r' in 'afraid' as a 'w' so that it sounded like baby-talk.

"Hey, she was freaky!" He shunted her shoulder. It was playful, but the nudge nearly sent her flying.

"Maybe if you're a five-year-old." She almost rugby tackled him but Oisin barely budged. He was annoyingly sturdy.

Lorcan watched them play fight, waiting for his chance to respond.

"Yeah, it was alright for an old film, I guess." He said during a gap in the flirtation, "I haven't been to the cinema in ages."

He had relaxed a little, but he was still wound way too tight for Maeve's liking. She needed to get him to open up in front of Oisin like he had with her and knew the perfect way to loosen someone's lips.

"Drink?" She said brightly.

*    *    *    *    *    *

Lorcan hadn't been a big drinker before being forcibly relocated to Droichead Dubh, given that he was underage and all. But it seemed that kids in small, rural Irish towns really had nothing much else to do. All summer long he'd battered his uninitiated liver into submission and had developed quite the taste for beer in the process, Droichead Dubh's poison of choice. Pubs here really didn't seem to care about the whole 'not serving drinks to minors' thing, they viewed that legislation as an optional guideline, best to let the kids decide for themselves.

They settled in a small corner booth in *Mc Donald's Pub*

away from the majority of the older clientele who tended to stare at Maeve, or any young woman that happened to grace their den. Oisin brought down three well-poured, fizzing beers and very carefully set them down. He didn't plan to relive the trauma of the time he'd spilled ten drinks at once, sending glass smashing all over the floor. That had been quite the cleanup and he'd yet to live it down.

"Do I get a toy with that?" Lorcan said, taking his beer from the tray.

"What?" Maeve said.

"Nothing - fast food joke."

"Ah, glad to see you can still make jokes." Oisin planted himself next to him.

"I don't get it." Maeve said, taking a long, pensive sip from her glass.

Lorcan was well aware this excursion was most likely an attempt to get him to open up and 'share with the group'. Maeve probably thought it was because Oisin had disturbed the dynamic duo relationship they had going before Halloween. His current caginess wasn't associated with Oisin. Well, it was and it wasn't. Despite the fact that he was cognisant of what she was doing, he appreciated the effort and rewarded them with a touch of sociability. He laughed and joked, and they talked about their plans for their next excursion, and it was all good fun. Really it was refreshing to talk about it in such light-hearted a manner, everything up until now had been dead serious, but Oisin had a way of bringing a level of joy to the proceedings. When he wasn't busy instilling caution and practicality.

"Do you think that shape-shifting thing will be there again?" Oisin asked, on his fourth beer.

"Watch it!" Maeve narrowed her eyes.

"I'm just saying, that was quite the show!"

They loved bickering and bantering, it was how they communicated. He also knew Oisin loved pushing her buttons because he loved Maeve's fiery side. It was one of her best

101

qualities. In all honesty, part of him was glad that Oisin had joined the group. Lorcan had always liked him, and he seemed like a decent guy with a level head. But what his parents had said stuck out like a splinter in his mind. He shot back to that night.

*     *     *     *     *     *

"How did you get here without us?" His father said, wrenching him away from the party, "And who is that other boy?" Lorcan really hated being scolded and had never taken it well.

"I don't know, we just came through." Lorcan was taken aback by how heated his parents were, his dad was practically pinning him to the wall.

"Lying won't help you here, Lorcan." His mother was using his name instead of 'pet', she was serious.

He tried to explain that they had come through accidentally, and they didn't know how, but his parents wouldn't accept that version of events. They were hell-bent on him having done something wrong or underhanded. Why was he always being blamed for something? When they couldn't get the 'truth' out of him, his father continued the interrogation.

"Do you know what you've done? Do you? You've brought a lot of unwanted attention to yourselves, and we might not be able to help. You're going to have to watch your backs. You've been noticed." A haunted look crossed his father's face.

"And that new boy," His mother said intensely, "we know nothing about him, can he be trusted?"

*     *     *     *     *     *

Maeve and Oisin had interrupted their little chat, followed by that headless guy. Is that what they had meant by unwanted attention? Everything happened so fast after that, so there was no time for questions. They'd been unceremoniously kicked out of the Otherworld, and he didn't know when, or if, they'd be welcomed back. He hadn't divulged any of this to the others, and it was beginning to weigh on his mind. The thought of not seeing his parents again sent rushes of panic through his mind every time he replayed what had happened. If he'd seemed tense, this was why.

From what he had gathered, Oisin could be trusted in so far as protecting Maeve. He'd made that abundantly clear when he'd got Lorcan in that headlock and said - what was it? Ah yes! He'd rip his fucking head off if he ever acted recklessly and put her in danger, knowingly or unknowingly. He'd vowed to send Lorcan to the Otherworld personally if that happened. Not the best way to reinitiate a former friendship but he'd got his point across. Maeve mattered to him and whether anything else did was up for debate.

When the situation called for it, Lorcan wasn't half bad at this whole socialising thing. He had a sardonic, arch sense of humour that, played to the right crowd, could elicit groans and ironic chuckles. Maeve and Oisin were the right crowd, they had brains and didn't just laugh at any old thing, even when half-cut on beer.

"Oh, I get it! *McDonald's Pub* - toy - happy meal!" Maeve said two and a half hours after the bad joke had been made.

"Seriously?" Lorcan shot streams of stinging beer bubbles from his nose.

"That's been pissing me off all night! I got it, finally!" She made sweeping gestures with her arms and threw her hands up as if to say *yeeesss, you may all bow to my genius mortals! Bow! I figured out the joke!*

"Right, that's it." Oisin turned to shout to the bartender, "Eamon! No more for this one!" He jabbed his thumb at Maeve.

Eamon hung his head grimly, "'tis a pity she be untamable on the ould drink!" He said in a wildly exaggerated old Irish accent. This wasn't the first time Maeve had been 'cut off', they'd played out this routine a good few times over the summer, and it was well rehearsed by now.

"Here, if I want more, I'll have more." Maeve's eyes became unfocused as she made a sound somewhere between a hiccup and a guttural burp, "I'll be right back." She walked urgently to the bathroom.

Leaving the pub, they stumbled and sang tunelessly as they used each other for balance. Droichead Dubh must have had more pubs per capita than any town on the planet because they passed at least a dozen groups on their way home doing the same, shooting over enthusiastic thumbs up their way and greetings of *what's the craic, big lad?* They didn't really want to know what the craic was, it was only polite to acknowledge another person's heroic levels of inebriation.

"Thanks for coming out tonight, Lorcan, it was so good to be friends again!" Maeve was at the 'feelings' stage of being drunk and emotional tears welled in her eyes.

"It was a pleasure, dude!" Oisin pulled him into a bear hug. Oisin was about the only person who'd ever called him 'dude'.

They said their prolonged, slurred goodbyes and Lorcan was alone again. Walking (staggering) down the road, he reflected on what his parents had said. Their words swam through his mind, twisting in on themselves, coalescing into dissonant, ugly thoughts. They'd have to watch their backs. What had they done? Oisin, could he be trusted? Could Maeve? They were in it for themselves, using him to explore the Otherworld. They'd leave him behind, like everyone else. Only he and his parents mattered. They'd all seemed so happy tonight.

He shook his head as if to clear those rancid thoughts stagnating from his mind and shuffle the good ones to the surface. It only served to make him dizzy, and he had to stick out his arms to steady himself. He paused, resting his head between his legs. When he rose again Lorcan swore he could see something, a figure in the distance. When he blinked to clear his vision it had gone. He knew what it meant. Message received. He *was* going to the Otherworld again, he needed to

- and he'd have to watch his back in the meantime. They all would.

# 14.

Maeve's phone buzzed incessantly, clattering itself against her bedside table and rudely awakening her. Who could be so callous? Didn't they have any concept of a hangover? Kicking the sweltering duvet aside, instantly regretting it as the chill air rapidly cooled her exposed skin, she checked who was vying for her attention. *The Weird sisters?* That's right, they'd made a group chat last night. The name was a reference to the Three Witches in Shakespeare's *Macbeth*. They'd read it last year in their English Literature class and been quoting it ever since, literary scholars that they were.

*Oisin: When shall we three meet again?*
*Lorcan: In Thunder, Lightning, or in Rain?*
*Oisin: When the Hurley-burley's done?*
*Lorcan: When the Battle's lost and won.*
*Maeve: STOP!!!*
*Oisin: Morning, cranky xx*
*Maeve: Lads, it's not even 9 o'clock*
*Oisin: I've been up since before 8*
*Lorcan: I've already been for my run*
*Maeve: You're both psychos!*
*Oisin: Back to my original point. When are we meeting up?*
*Maeve: Can't we just sleep? I'm dying!*
*Oisin: Nope! In all seriousness, we need to plan. You guys said you wanted to try again before we go back to school. We've got 3 days.*
*Lorcan: Meet up at mine this afternoon? Then we'll see.*
*Oisin: Sounds like a plan.*
*Oisin: ...*

*Oisin: Cranky? xx*
*Maeve: Fine! And don't call me that!*

Planning an adventure to the Otherworld in a group chat. Odd. Oisin, the one who was probably most against them going, was the one pushing it too. Even odder. He liked to be prepared though. He may have acted chaotic and as if he didn't have a care in the world but, underneath it all, he was a type-A pain in the ass when he needed to be; just like Maeve. She would've been all over this, but a throbbing headache wasn't conducive to critical thought. Maybe another hour in bed would sort that out.

That wasn't to be, because her phone kept buzzing.

*Oisin: No going back to sleep!*

Was that boy a mind reader?

*       *       *       *       *       *

So ecstatic was Cara that Lorcan was having friends over, she'd laid out a veritable smörgåsbord for them to nibble over. Maeve's last visit had caused quite the splash, and she'd been asking him when she'd get the chance to flex her aching culinary muscles again. Now was that time.

"Okay, so, here's some hummus for dipping." She said, leaning over the table and placing yet another platter down in front of the group.

"This isn't an all day thing." Lorcan said.

"I know, but try a bit of everything and see what you think. I'll leave you to it. Back in a bit." She flung on her coat and marched out of the house.

"Is she late for something?" Maeve asked.

"No Idea. She's lost it. I think she wants her own cooking show or something." Lorcan said, taking a bread stick and dipping it in the hummus, "Pretty tasty though."

They went through their preparations again, Oisin sure

did like to be thorough, and they agreed to make an attempt tomorrow night.

"Hold on," Oisin said, "Why does it have to be at night? Is that, like, a rule?"

"I don't know, I assumed it was some sort of witching hour thing." Lorcan said, shrugging.

Had he not questioned it?

"Why don't we go up there tomorrow morning? We'd have more time if we got in early."

"Sounds okay to me." Maeve was beaming, feeling revived after some fatty food.

Lorcan considered it for a moment and, finding no objection, nodded in agreement. There wasn't much more they could do at this stage, so they took the chance to sit back, chat and sample Cara's food platter. She was actually a great cook, Maeve couldn't get enough of the home-made crisps and her garlic mozzarella sticks. Crunching down on a hummus-coated carrot stick, Oisin looked like he was mulling something over, those concentration crinkles had formed on his brow.

"Lorcan," He said pointedly, "I know we've been planning to ask some questions of your parents."

"Yeah?" Lorcan was unsure where this was going.

"Maybe we should hold off on that, I don't want them to feel like we're grilling them or something. Y'know?" He reached for a handful of crisps.

"Umm, okay. I thought you wanted to know more."

"I do - we do, but let's just chill on that for now. I mean, I haven't even introduced myself to them properly yet, and I don't want to be like, '*hey, thanks for bringing me here, now answer my questions!*'"

"Fair enough." Said Lorcan, looking relieved that he didn't have to cross-examine his parents.

Maeve side-eyed Oisin, what was he up to?

They continued their feast with Cara returning from her excursion a while later, shopping bags in hand, which was their cue to leave. Maeve couldn't help but notice Oisin's quietude as they dandered back to her house.

"So," She started, "what was that?"

"Hmm? What was what?" He was playing dumb.

"Telling Lorcan not to ask the questions. We need to know more about this."

"Oh, that. I'm sure you know plenty already with all your internet research and -" He paused, picking his words carefully, "- and I want to hear what they have to say without prompting. Like, how we got there without their help."

"What if they don't say anything? What then?"

"Then they don't say anything." He sighed, "It's probably nothing, but I just think it's best we let them bring it up. That's all."

"If you say so."

The winter's sun hung low in the sky, amongst a gradient that went from red, to orange, to yellow and faded to a pale blue that seemed to stretch out to infinity. The calm before the storm. Tomorrow they'd be making the charge into another world, intrepid explorers going out of bounds on the map and trekking through heretofore undiscovered territory. She felt expansive, like she was at a crossroads with a million paths, and she had her pick of which one to take. What wonders lay ahead for them?

In her daydream, she hadn't noticed Oisin stop. He held her hand and spun her around gently to face him.

"You're sure?" His face was grave.

"About?"

"I'd be fine with not going. It's up to you, Maeve. You're sure you want to go tomorrow?"

"Do you not want to come?" She was taken aback by the sudden turnabout.

"That's not what I'm asking."

Maeve nodded, "Yes, I'm sure."

Oisin held her gaze. That moment seemed to elongate as he let her answer sink in fully.

"Okay." He said finally, pulling her in for a hug.

It wasn't one of his usual bone-crushing, bear hugs she'd gotten used to. Instead, he gently wrapped his arms around her, letting their bodies sink together, an island of warmth surrounded by the cooling dusk air. They didn't move again until the sky had noticeably dimmed. Tomorrow they'd make the leap together. Once more unto the breach.

# 15.

A thick layer of morning mist snaked over and down the hilltop as they stood at the foot of Dún Dubh. It felt like the beginning to a proper adventure, Maeve thought, shifting her weight from foot to foot, eager to get going. All at once, and without a word between them, they filed into the crumbled central chamber.

Lorcan nodded, a signal for *'ready?'.* Maeve and Oisin each gave an 'OK' sign with their thumbs and forefingers, and he called out. There was no response. He called out again. Still nothing. Again and again he called, and for half an hour they stood there, getting nowhere fast.

"Maybe they haven't woken up?" Oisin said. He sat on a rock sipping some hot coffee he'd brought in a flask, "Do they sleep?"

Lorcan shook his head, "I don't know. Like I said, I've only ever done this at night."

"We might be here a while then."

Mist lingered over and around the fort as the morning wore on, refusing to be burnt off by the rising sun. They got up, stretched, walked about the chamber, made small talk, exchanged ideas and information about the Otherworld, but they didn't leave each other's side. One of the rules they'd made was to stick together so that no-one could be left behind. They had to leave the chamber once so that Oisin could pee, coffee would do that to a person. Otherwise, the chamber was where they remained.

"Aaannnddd, that's two hours." Maeve said, checking her phone for the five-hundredth time.

"It was an experiment." Oisin sighed, "Maybe we should come back later."

"No." Said Lorcan, "They're not going to leave me - us here."

His eyes had gone wide with - what was that? Fury? Panic? Indignation? Maeve couldn't quite tell, but she knew that he wasn't about to leave until he got what he wanted.

"Okay, Lorcan, try it again." She relented

He did, his voice was clearer, more solid and more certain this time. It reverberated around the stone walls, bouncing from surface to surface as he repeated calls for his mam and dad. Maeve wasn't sure if it was her imagination, but his words seemed to be gaining traction, the air pressure was changing and the very daylight darkened in the fort. Oisin took Maeve's hand, fully on guard now, scanning in front and over his shoulder for any signs of someone or something.

A familiar dark shape caught Maeve's eye right in the centre of the chamber, and she reached out to grab Lorcan's hand. They were all going or none of them were. He didn't look at her, keeping his gaze focused on the forming void as if willing it into existence. Although she knew what she was witnessing this time, it didn't make it any easier to look at, there was something unnerving about the way light didn't seem to interact with it in any noticeable manner. Pain entered her hand and she realised that Oisin was gripping hard. He had never seen this before and for him, it must have been doubly unnerving. She gave him a reassuring squeeze back, as if that would help.

Continuing his rhythmic chanting, Lorcan stretched out his free hand to the shadow, and it mirrored the gesture. The grey daylight was replaced with a flash of painful white and then immediately dulled to the soft, flickering sepia of the Otherworld's chamber. She had been expecting the sensation, so the stabbing cold hadn't shocked Maeve, despite how unpleasant it still felt. Oisin, on the other hand, wasn't quite as prepared.

"Oh god!" He gasped and bent over, hands on his knees, "That was - give me a second."

Maeve rubbed his back, her own body quivering from the sudden loss of heat. Raising her eyes, she saw Aiden and Bronach standing together, a wry smile broke out over Aiden's face.

"Well? You rang?" He said to Lorcan, who wasn't running to hug them like last time.

"Come here, pet." Bronach said in a motherly tone, her arms outstretched, "We're sorry about last time. It was a mad rush."

It was an irresistible force. Lorcan dropped Maeve's hand and went to them. That peaceful look she'd seen before when they'd been reunited appeared again, he looked as if he never wanted that moment to end. When she touched Bronach before it had laid Maeve out on her ass, why was Lorcan okay to make so much contact with them? Family perks? There were so many questions she wanted answers to, but she remembered what Oisin had said, *let them bring it up.* She didn't know why he'd been so adamant about that, but she would indulge him for now. Eventually, however, they'd need some bloody answers rather than tripping over themselves in the dark.

The happy family separated and their attention turned towards the new boy, the elephant in the room, who was beginning to recover with the help of some well-placed heat packs.

"It's 'Oisin', isn't it?" Bronach said.

"Yes," Oisin straightened, "Mr and Mrs. Delaney. Thank you for bringing us here. It's nice to properly meet, unlike last time."

"Nice to meet you too, lad." Aiden said, a welcoming grin on his face.

Oisin stuck out his hand to shake but recalled what Maeve had told him and retracted the offer.

"Wise." Aiden winked and gestured to the exit.

As a group they made their way out of the fort and

into the clearing. Lorcan's parents seemed to be on the lookout for something, and they urged the trio to follow them into a thick patch of trees. Before it was obscured by a canopy of dense foliage, Maeve tried to take in the newly sunlit view of the Otherworld. How could it be *more* beautiful? There were so many little details that she hadn't noticed in the dark of night. The lines in fields denoting farmland like delineations on a hand-drawn map. The mountains were even more vast than they'd appeared before. The rays of the sun seemed to be made from solid matter as they penetrated gaps in the clouds, and - were those giant flying creatures? It was an all too brief reintroduction, but it was still incredible!

"What are we doing?" Lorcan protested.

His parents put their fingers in their lips as if to say, *keep it down child!*

"We want to show all you something." Aiden said in a hushed voice.

As quietly as they could, given the ground was covered in leaves and twigs, they trekked deeper into the woods. They were walking in the opposite direction of where the bonfire had been and the ground sloped downwards at steep angles. It didn't feel like they were heading towards civilization, they were heading into wilder territory. Maeve could sense Oisin's apprehension and, every so often, she'd look back to see him stony faced, alert, ready for action.

It wasn't a long walk, maybe twenty minutes, Maeve checked her phone for the time, but her screen was going haywire. Why did she think technology would behave normally here? It's not like they had a space program in the Otherworld for satellite GPS phone coordinates. Did they? *Sigh.* More questions.

The aromatic smell of peat filled Maeve's nose as the trees cleared, revealing where Lorcan's parents were taking them. There was a town, smaller than the other one they'd infiltrated, and it was more like what Maeve had initially expected upon first crossing over, more rustic and typically

"Irish" like the depictions on history textbooks that focussed almost exclusively on the Plantation and famine periods. It sat on a vast bog that stretched as far as they could see. The houses stood on raised stilts and boards that helped them stave off the inexorable pull of the sodden land, it made it look as if the buildings floated above the wet ground. Peculiar that land on either side of the mountains could be so drastically different but, even in the living world, Ireland's landscape was rife with contradictions. Though she doubted a bog like this had ever existed.

"Where are we?" Oisin asked.

"This," Aiden said, gesturing over the expanse, "is the real Otherworld."

He made off down the hill, not waiting for a response from the group. Maeve and Lorcan wasted no time in hurrying along, with Oisin taking a beat to process. As they descended, coming closer to the wet earth, the air became noticeably thicker. The humidity made it difficult to breathe, it was like inhaling a peaty soup, and it made all three of them regret packing heavy bags. The boardwalks connecting the houses and other buildings were made of thick knotted wood that stood sturdy as they tentatively tested their weights on them. The walkways were narrow, allowing two people at most to walk shoulder to shoulder. Aiden and Bronach led the way together, naturally, followed by Lorcan and Maeve with Oisin trailing behind, forever watching her back.

Venturing further into the town, Maeve noticed something. It wasn't the heterogeneous architecture, although that was noteworthy. And it wasn't that she was pretty sure she could see things writhing in the bog below them, best ignoring that. It was the fact that, apart from their group, she hadn't seen a single "person" since they'd entered the place. Oh sure, there were people-like things, but they were also very much *in*human. She was also pretty sure that these people-like creatures were beginning to notice them too, and it was becoming more unnerving as the seconds wore on.

A rakishly thin man turned to look over his shoulder as they passed, his eyes tracking them steadily, intently. He wasn't the only one who paid them undue attention. A woman, whose skin was quite literally sagging off of her bones, stood to attention as they passed. She leaned in for a disturbingly close examination of the new arrivals, the scent of death emanating from her every pore. Oisin urged Maeve on. A spotted horse on an entirely different walkway leered in their direction, following their path on the parallel boards opposite until it got distracted by a beckoning hand in a dark doorway. Morphing into a man, it made its way inside and sounds erupted that didn't bear thinking about. For once, Maeve didn't want to know. Oisin's hand on her back was meant to soothe, but she could feel the waves of anxiety emanating from him.

When an ominous creature about eight feet tall, with arms twice as long as they needed to be and a drooling snarl, stooped to inspect the group Bronach turned to face them.

"It's okay," She said calmly, "they're just curious." And continued walking.

All three of them kept their heads down and eyes averted as they were led along the snaking boards, eventually coming to a small cabin with rounded walls and a tall, pointed thatched roof. Ducking to enter, the room smelled heavily of burning peat along with other deep, earthy aromas; a pleasant contrast to the more unpleasant aromas they'd been subject to on their trip here. Aiden closed the door while Bronach went to work on the central fire, feeding it and filling a large teapot with water. Tea was a staple everywhere in Ireland it seemed, dead or otherwise. The hut was silent apart from the crackling of the now blazing fire and the muffled noises coming from outdoors. Maeve paid close attention to the sounds that slid by, guttural and animalistic. They were in a cage surrounded by hungry beasts of prey. Oisin's eyes flitted to the door whenever a shadow would pass by but ultimately no-one disturbed them.

Bronach took the pot from the fire, poured into five

roughly-made cups and handed them each one. She seemed fairly relaxed at least. Maeve let the steam from her cup waft over her face and felt the heat calm her nerves just a little. Bronach cleared her throat.

"Quite different from your previous experience here, no?"

They nodded in unison.

"We're sorry about last time," She reiterated, this time to the group, "I'm sure you can imagine that we were worried about you all, about your safety."

"I can imagine." Lorcan said curtly.

"We just didn't expect you to be there. Can I ask, how did you three end up at that celebration without us helping you cross over?" Aiden said, blowing on his tea.

"I already told you that, we don't know." Lorcan obviously still felt raw about his scolding.

It must have been a sore point for him, not to be believed.

"I know," Aiden held his hands up in a placating motion, "I want to hear it from your friends though. We didn't get a chance to speak to them."

Oisin spoke, "It's like Lorcan said, Mr. Delaney, we don't know. It was my first time being here, so I had *no* idea what was going on."

Aiden turned his attention to Maeve.

"Yeah, I really don't know what happened. One minute we were in the ruins, and then we were here. I'm not sure how else to describe it." Maeve shrugged and sipped on her tea.

*Let them bring it up. Let them bring it up.*

"And you saw nobody there?" Bronach said.

They all shook their heads. Aiden and Bronach continued with their line of inquiry. Had they talked to anyone? Had they seen anything unusual in the living world? Were they sure nothing was following them? There was a lot of questioning but no explaining on their part. Lorcan's parents were the cops, and they were the suspects keeping tight-lipped.

Except, they weren't lying, they actually had no information to offer the investigation. Eventually the couple sighed, resigned, or perhaps relieved, that the three of them were clueless.

"We're sorry for the barrage of questions. We don't mean to come across like we don't trust you." Lorcan snorted at his mum's words, "Of course we trust you." She placed a hand on his and squeezed gently.

"We need to make sure that we can talk openly. And we feel like we can now." Aiden added.

"How do you know that we're not lying?" Oisin said, "I mean, yeah, it makes sense we'd have no clue what happened - but how can you trust us, how do you *know*."

Maeve stared at him. Was he trying to get them kicked out and be stricken from the invite list?

"You're a sharp boy." Bronach smiled, "But, let's just say, when you cross over you get a bit of a 'sixth sense' for these things."

From his expression, Maeve could tell Oisin knew that was the only explanation he was getting for now, however unsatisfactory.

"Then *why* do you need to trust us?" Lorcan asked.

"Now, that's the question." Aiden clapped his hands, "Did you notice anything about the town?"

"Plenty of things." Oisin said.

"Okay, I'll be more specific. Did you notice anything about the people living here?"

Maeve cleared her throat, "I'm not sure if this is rude or not, but I didn't see any *people*. I mean, I saw a horse and that tall creature and everything -" Her voice faded away as Aiden and Bronach smiled politely like a couple who had taken offence but didn't want to point out their guest's obvious ignorance.

"I can see why you might think that they're not," Bronach began, "but, they *are* people despite how they might look. What do you know about this place, the Otherworld?"

Maeve looked to Oisin who nodded, giving her the 'OK',

they could share their knowledge "Well, I've read a lot online about it. The legends, the spirits and how the ancient Irish viewed it."

"I see, some of those stories aren't too far off from the truth, y'know. Tell me, did you recognise any of the *creatures* you saw out there?" Aiden said.

Maeve winced at how he emphasised the word 'creatures' but she played along.

"It's hard to say, seeing as I've only seen drawings of them, but at the party I think I saw some leprechauns." She glanced around to see if anyone was laughing, relieved when she saw they were listening intently, "I also think I might have seen a pooka. That shapeshifter, remember?" She clarified for Oisin who nodded, "There was a shapeshifter here too, although, I'm not sure, but that might have been a kelpie because it was a horse to start with."

"Very good!" Aiden said, "What about the elephant in the room?"

"The headless man?" Maeve asked.

"Indeed."

"Again, I've only read about this stuff. He looked like a dullahan, though."

"You've done your homework. But, I'm sure those books don't have all the details." Bronach said, pouring more tea into Maeve's cup, "Do you know how one becomes a dullahan?"

Now *this* was the kind of information they'd been hoping for.

# 16.

The thought of *becoming* a headless horseman, or dullahan, had never occurred to them. The atmosphere had shifted, sharpening as everyone focused, like they were gathered around a campfire and this was the story they'd been waiting for. The three exchanged glances between one another, ears perked.

"What do you mean?" Lorcan said.

"You heard his name?" Bronach looked at them in turn.

Their brows furrowed collectively, the dullahan had said his name when he'd made that speech but there was so much going on, and in the ensuing chaos his name wasn't all that important in the grand scheme of things.

"William du - ummm - I can't remember the surname." Maeve said, straining to pull the information from the recesses of her mind.

"William de Meath." Bronach volunteered, "He was a real person, so to speak, who lived in Ireland during the 14th Century."

Maeve hadn't expected the dullahan to be an actual human being. She'd just assumed he'd appeared out of the earth fully formed one day, kind of like how that black mist rose from the ground and became his horse. So, if he was a real historical figure, mustn't that then mean - ?

"What about the other people? The ones who don't look human?" Oisin beat her to the punch.

"You're a quick pair, I'll give you that." Bronach's eyes glinted in the dull light of the hut, fluttering between Maeve and Oisin, "I can see why you picked them to be your friends, pet."

*Picked?* An odd word choice.

Frustration was evident in Lorcan's body language. He'd been so focused on seeing his parents that he wasn't accustomed to questioning the Otherworld or its rules. In all, he was probably feeling dense right about now.

Aiden continued on unaware of, or perhaps purposely oblivious to his son's rising temper, "You're quite right, everyone you saw on your way here were once humans in life." He pointed in the general direction of the outside world.

"But -" Maeve couldn't think of a clever way of phrasing it, "- how?"

"Sit back, it's a mind bender." Bronach said, crossing her legs and settling in for a tale, "Lorcan, your dad and I died together and the events leading up to it are fuzzy at best. We were on our way somewhere and there was a crash or fall or - I don't know, it was all out of the blue. But, when it was over, we woke up in this blank space, and it felt like we had to make some sort of choice. I don't know how else to describe it. Either we move on into the unknown or hang on. Let me tell you it wasn't much of a choice, our last thoughts were of you, and we just couldn't leave you on your own."

Her eyes began to gloss over, and she stroked Lorcan's face once before gathering herself and resuming the story.

"So, remain we did, we had a duty of care to our son, a strong purpose and sense of who we were as parents. We basically remained intact, I'm sure you saw people like that at the party? People who looked 'normal' so to speak. That doesn't happen for everybody, some people don't remain so - recognisable."

"Like William?" Lorcan asked.

"Yes, like William."

"How did he end up as a dullahan?"

"This is what we're still trying to work out ourselves. We're relative newcomers too." Bronach indicated to Aiden, "But we have some ideas. Basically, what we think is that some people have a strong sense of self, like your dad and I, and they cross over to the Otherworld and persist as themselves without many, if any, changes. However, there are some people that might identify more heavily with a concept, or goal outside themselves, or they might skew further into certain personality traits. Those people, we believe, are then reborn in the Otherworld as one of many 'creatures' that reflect what they were in life."

Bronach took a long sip of her tea, letting them think on what she'd said for a few seconds. It was a lot to take in. Did those rules apply to everyone in the Otherworld? Every person, every creature, every god? Maeve's fears from earlier were abating, there was so much more to learn.

"So, let me see." Oisin began, rubbing his chin, "Say an extremely deceptive person was reborn here, they might be one of those shapeshifters? They could look like anybody?"

"Mmmhmm, they might have been very adaptive too. William de Meath, for example, was a man with a strong sense of justice. His mother, Petronilla, was the first woman in Ireland to be burned at the stake on the charge of witchcraft. William spent his life maintaining his mother's innocence, campaigning and insisting she was framed by the real witch, Alice Kyteler and *her* son William Outlaw."

"Funny that both men had the same name, the William who supposedly framed Petronilla and the William who defended her." Maeve mused.

"Until rather recently, sons were often named after their fathers." Aiden said with a rueful smile.

Maeve put her hand over her mouth in a silent gasp, "So, the William that framed Petronilla was de Meath's father?"

Aiden, giving a soft chuckle, nodded for Bronach to go ahead with the story.

"Yes, Petronilla *de Meath* was Alice's maidservant, but she was also her son's lover, it was all a big scandal back in the day, so we've heard. Young William had to grow up hearing how his mother was a dirty witch and deserved her fate, but something inside him rejected that. He was certain, absolutely certain, that she had been set up by Alice and his father. That idea lit a fire within him, and he carried an iron sense of indignant justice all throughout his life. He even gave up his father's surname in favour of his mother's. That 'sense of justice' carried over into his afterlife. Hence, he became judge, jury and executioner - a dullahan, one of the fiercest beings in Irish legend and the Otherworld."

Maeve's head reeled with this information. She was fascinated with the idea of someone actually becoming a being of myth but, if that was so, how did the myth begin?

"What came first then?" Maeve blurted out, "I mean, did people always turn into dullahans and leprechauns? Is that how the legends got started in the first place?"

Bronach's eyes narrowed on Maeve, one corner of her mouth curling into a smirk, "It took us a while to come up with that question ourselves and you just -" She snapped her fingers, "- impressive. But to answer your question, or not I suppose, we don't know. It's a chicken and egg kind of thing. We are working under some assumptions though." She held up her fingers and counted them off, "The living world and the Otherworld didn't develop in isolation, they influenced each other. The strength of a person's will, perception, or you could say consciousness, has a massive effect on their continued existence after death. And the worlds were always meant to interact, but are not being allowed to at the moment."

"William, he said that the living world used to be tortured by the beings here." Lorcan said, "So, is he stopping it?"

"He's not the only one but, yes, he's certainly one of the factors that's preventing the worlds from connecting."

"But if the living world was being tortured, is it not a good thing that he's doing?"

"That's his version of events." Aiden interjected, "The ancient Irish lived in tandem with the Otherworld, like two nations on friendly terms, with open borders. So many great heroes are said to have ventured to and spent their entire lives here. The natural state is for the worlds to be intertwined."

Maeve contemplated this. The living and the dead world connected. How would that work, and would death even mean anything, or would it be like transitioning from one phase of your life to the other? A lot of ancient cultures spoke of reincarnation and cycles of rebirth. Maybe this is what they were referring to.

"Why was he after us then?" Oisin said, "What was he going to do?"

There he was, asking the relevant questions again. Aiden and Bronach looked at each other and grimaced slightly.

"He wasn't happy to hear that certain spirits, meaning us, were smuggling live humans into 'his' territory." Aiden said, "So, he wasn't necessarily only after you, he was after us too."

"Why would you risk it?" Lorcan said, "Was it just for me?" There was hopeful longing in that question.

Bronach smiled and cocked her head, "Of course, pet, we'd risk anything for you but -" She paused and took a breath, "it's become bigger than us."

"What do you mean?"

Aiden put his hand on Lorcan's shoulder, "We want to see the worlds united again so that families like ours don't have to be ripped apart due to some accident. To answer your question, Oisin, William de Meath was really after us because - we're part of the revolution."

Revolution.

The word seemed far-off, abstract. They hadn't expected to fall headlong into an afterlife political conflict, they suspected there may have been shenanigans to be had, hijinks and running after ghosts, that sort of thing. But overthrowing an entire system? This was more adventure than Maeve had been bargaining for. She could see that Oisin was gearing up for another question but, before the words passed his lips, there was an urgent series of knocks on the door. They all snapped their heads in the direction of the noise.

"He's coming!" A gruff voice said from the other side.

Both Aiden and Bronach shot up from their seats. Bronach put the fire out and began whirling around the hut, taking the cups they'd been using and hiding them in little cubbies. Aiden gripped Lorcan by the shoulders and hauled him to his feet, motioning the others to get up as well.

"I thought we'd have more time, they must have spotted or followed us somehow." He said, checking everything was in order.

In a hurried whirlwind of activity the trio threw their backpacks on, fixing their belongings, so they were ready to go at a moment's notice, while Aiden and Bronach disposed of any evidence that suggested guests had ever been present. When the hut was in order, they were ushered outside and back onto the narrow walkways. The other residents bustled about as well, preparing for some imminent, unwelcome arrival. Doors slammed shut, shopkeepers packed frantically and Maeve saw someone throw an object into a deeper part of the bog, checking to make sure it sunk. The kelpie she'd watched enter the hut earlier burst through the doors and leap from the walkway, turning into a huge black bird and flew off towards the ocean, creating turbulence with its massive wings. What a sight.

"Where should we go?" Bronach said as Aiden shut their door.

"If they were watching us, they'll be coming from the hill." He pointed in the direction they'd entered the town, "Maybe we'd be better going through the -" He stopped and swivelled to the group, "We're going to make our way through the bog, but you're going to have to listen to me and follow *every* instruction. Understand?"

Maeve didn't know what was so dangerous about the bog, causing Aiden's eyes to bug, but it couldn't be worse than a certain headless someone she guessed was headed their way. She thought of the last time she'd seen him, summoning that sinister black mist to his side. What if he'd caught them? She wasn't about to find out. The bog it was.

"Understood." Maeve said.

The others followed suit and made towards the edge of the town, where the wooden paths ended and the marsh began in earnest. Aiden led the way on a winding patch of firmer ground that meandered out into the distance. The town disappeared behind them as they walked further out, swallowed by a thick mist that clung close to the wetlands. Aiden stopped, making some test steps, checking if the ground could take their weights. They had to double back more than once and take alternate routes, the peat turning to mush beneath them. As they advanced they came across more and more dead ends until they could go no further.

"Shite." He said under his breath, "I didn't want to do this." He looked at Bronach, who herself had donned a mask of anxiety ever since he'd mentioned the swamp, "This is where it gets tricky folks."

He made them retrace their steps and take a path they'd previously dismissed. This one was much more slender than the former and tapered in such a way that they had to proceed single file. Maeve was so laser focused on maintaining her balance that she hardly noticed when their squelching footsteps were no longer the only sounds that filled the stagnant air. Hidden, wreathed in fog, were what sounded like moans and sloshing water. Aiden held up a hand and turned to them.

"This is where you *need* to listen to me." He was deadly serious now and spoke in a hushed voice, "Ahead of us are what they call 'scáthanna'. All you need to know for now is to pay them no mind. They'll leave you alone if you leave them alone."

"So don't touch them?" Lorcan said.

"Yes, but I mean 'ignore' in an even wider sense. Don't look at them directly, don't talk to them, don't even let your thoughts dwell on them individually."

"Don't think about them? How does that work? Aren't

we thinking about them right now?" Oisin whispered. Maeve could tell those cracks were beginning to appear again, his tone gave him away.

"Yes, right now we're thinking about them in a broad sense." Aiden made a round gesture with his hands, "What I'm telling you is to not focus your attention on one or more of them in a fixed way." He steepled his fingers, "Keep your thoughts clear and concentrate on our goal to get out of the bog, and we'll be fine. It's okay to speak but try not to raise your voice. Any questions?"

They were all far too tense to speak, never mind asking questions. Maeve took slow controlled breaths, setting her mind to getting out of the waterlogged land and onto firmer ground. She didn't think it would be so difficult to keep that as her focus, seeing that was all she wanted at that moment. They pressed on slowly and the sounds that had been muffled in the thick air became more clear-cut as new forms slid into view.

Maeve had to fight not to look at anything directly, she tried to let her peripheral vision work out what was surrounding them. From what she could see there were people in the marsh, some were stuck fast, but others were traipsing through the mud limblessly or were altogether still. As they moved they let out rattling breaths or moans that sounded as if they're lungs were dried out wheezing husks. Every so often her hind brain unconsciously turned her head towards these threatening shadows and Maeve had to snap back to the path in front. She had to think about anything else. What did she have for breakfast yesterday? Had she done all the assigned homework for Monday morning? There was one shambling directly to her right. She counted back from one-hundred and then again in different multiples. Was it looking at her?

Aiden halted up front, holding his arms out to the side. His head was dipped to the ground, he too was using his peripheral vision.

"There's something in front of us." He said evenly, "There's enough space to go around it but watch your footing.

Only think about where you need to step, and you'll be fine."

They set off again. Maeve just imitated Lorcan's footsteps, that was a good focal point, and she ignored the rising sound of rattling breaths in front of her. The sloshing of the water and the stench of rot. His footsteps stopped. Aiden hadn't signalled so what was happening? She drew her gaze up Lorcan's back and saw a dark, thin limb wrapping around his wrist. It had noticed him, its breathing becoming quicker and more laboured as it reached out another arm. It moved in slow motion as every bone and tendon creaked to life in its emaciated frame.

Out of the side of her eyes Maeve felt heads swivel in their direction. What had been quite background noise before became a cacophony of lamenting groans surrounding them. She stared hard at the ground and thought about the moss beneath her feet.

Little shockwaves rippled through the water as putrefying fleshy legs waded nearer.

She thought of the structure of the moss's cells, and how lichens grow well in marshy conditions, and how bogs are a great hotbed of life, creating their own ecosystems, and how things fall into bogs and get preserved - like bodies.

Like the bodies that were drawing nearer and nearer. She could see them now, their wrinkled, withered skin, clinging to their bones, and heads with just bumps and grooves where their features should be. A cold hand began to worm its way around her ankle from a torso half buried in muck, tugging at her leg, its grip like iron.

Maeve's mind was on fire, she would have to make a break for it, but something brushed past her. It was Bronach. She stepped cleanly around Maeve, in front of Lorcan and cupped his face.

"Lorcan, love." She said calmly but firmly, "I'm going to need you to look me in the eye. Just think of my voice, that's all I want you to focus on - my voice." Bronach repeated this over and over at a measured, hypnotic pace.

Maeve guessed it wasn't just for Lorcan's benefit, she was providing an anchor point for them all. Like a guided meditation, Maeve sank into Bronach's voice, allowing it to become her world. The limb dropped from Lorcan's arm and from Maeve's ankle, and they proceeded on through the bog as the soft patter from Bronach persisted, cutting through the low whining. Gradually the land became less sodden, turning to grass and gravel. Each of them dropped to their knees or sat back on their hunkers, their legs giving out.

Maeve let out an exhausted sob, being on edge so intensely for so long left her body a wreck, along with her mind. She looked to Oisin whose face gave nothing away, he reached into his backpack, pulled out a bottle of water and downed it. Lorcan sat with his head in his hands, he seemed like he was about to pass out. His parents comforted him while sneaking glances over their shoulders, clearly eager to get going.

"What were they?" Oisin asked, putting the used bottle back in his bag and standing.

Aiden spoke, "We told you about what it's like after you die. About the choice you have to make to remain or move on into the unknown. Those were people who chose to stay but, in doing so, lacked the strength to survive."

"What do you mean?" He was demanding now.

"This place alters you. No matter how intact you might be, there's always something a little off. Something that's simply lost in the transition between life and death. If you're lucky, like us, it might just be a memory here or there and that's that. But, like the scáthanna, or 'shades', you just saw - that process continues to chip away at until you are no longer *you*."

"What did they want?" Lorcan raised his head to look at his parents.

"They sensed us and wanted a piece of what we have, a piece of our lives, or memories, or personalities, and we gave them power, feeding them by acknowledging their existence directly. If they'd got a hold of you, you'd be drained of everything. That's what was going to happen back there, but you were so brave and did so well. I'm proud of you." Bronach kissed Lorcan on his cheek, "Maeve and Oisin too, well done. We still have to get you out of here though."

They began their approach towards Dún Dubh from a steep, rocky hill that gave way underfoot, and they had to catch themselves every few steps. It was killer on their already tired thighs. Approaching the target with caution they stopped to check their surroundings, but upon entering the treeline it provided them some cover. Being further away from the swamp the air was cleaner, and they didn't have to strain for breath quite so hard. Maeve's nerves began to ease up, and she repeated Bronach's mantra-like performance in her head, it didn't have quite the same effect a second time round. Lorcan had other concerns.

"Since when did you two become revolutionaries?" He asked abruptly.

"We always supported the underdog, Lorcan. The people in that village aren't exactly the top of the food chain." Bronach answered, clearing a log with a graceful hop.

"Yeah, you gave to charity, but it's a pretty big leap from that to what you're doing now." Was he angry with them? It sounded that way.

"Like I said earlier," Aiden interjected, "this place changes you. You're mum and I might have made small efforts in our lives, but in our deaths we feel like we can make a big difference here. That village, our village, is full of outcasts from this place who want a return to the old ways and, without them, we may not have seen each other again. William de Meath wants to stop that entirely," He paused for emphasis, "and we think that's worth opposing."

He made a compelling argument and Maeve found herself starting to agree with him. If that's how the two worlds were created and meant to exist, who were William and his ilk to say otherwise? If he had his way, she'd never have seen all this and might have just spent her life in an ignorant daze.

Now she was awake, and she thought she might be ready to fight. Would Oisin join her if she did? Now wasn't exactly the time to be talking about joining a guerilla army, however, they had to get back to their own world and gather their thoughts.

As they made their final approach it was Maeve who stopped.

"What is it?" Oisin said, taking her hand.

She whipped around and said sharply, "Hooves!"

The low, furiously fast rumble of hoofbeats was becoming more audible, and they redoubled their efforts in clambering over fallen trees and through thorny bushes. Maeve caught a branch to the face, scratching her cheek, but that was nothing compared to what she imagined de Meath might do if he caught up with them. Oisin urged her along, he was a good runner, and she still needed a lot of work. Lorcan was an impressive sight, all those mornings running up mountains really paid off, he leaped over thick roots and stones like it was nothing. That small pang of jealousy re-emerged. In fact, he looked calm, it was one of the few times he didn't have some sort of pained expression on his face or undue tension in his body. She could see now the determination in him and the weirdly powerful inner drive that shone through occasionally. Just as quickly, she saw the forest floor come to meet her, she'd tripped and her arms sprawled in front of her. Oisin heaved her up, looking over her head in horror.

"He's here!" He shouted.

Maeve heard the screeching neigh of de Meath's steed and shot forward, she wasn't looking back this time. She knew what awaited her. They were nearly there, she could make it. Her legs pumped, her lungs were burning, her heart pounding, but nothing was stopping her from reaching that fort. Luckily the trees were slowing him down, it must have been hard to manoeuvre such a huge beast through such densely packed woods.

They burst out into the clearing and charged their way

towards the chamber, they didn't even have to think about where they were going, their instincts guiding them through the narrow corridors. They gathered together and held each other's hands. Bronach and Aiden outstretched their arms.

"Ready?" They said together.

"Ready." The three of them replied.

"Love you." Lorcan added.

"We love you."

Then a flash of white and the sting of ice to their cores. They each in turn stumbled to a wall. The effort of a sustained sprint coupled with the sudden chill sent them reeling, their bodies not knowing whether they wanted to be hot or cold. Maeve didn't notice initially, but it was raining heavily. She pulled up her hood and, after catching their breath, together made their way into the trees to find a dry-ish place to sit.

They unpacked a late lunch of protein bars and sports drinks, consuming them in silence. The rain pelted off of the leaves, a constant stream of white noise filling in for a dialogue between them. There was something to be said about the calming effect of rain, it was no wonder people fell asleep to its soundtrack. Just as wordlessly they packed up. It was like they were shell shocked after coming back from the war, except this war hadn't even started yet.

Standing to leave, they caught each other's eyes. Something odd happened, Maeve had no idea where it came from, but they began to laugh. Starting as a small chuckle that circled the group once, it got stronger with every lap. They were on their hands and knees pounding the ground, Maeve thought she'd pass out if she didn't stop soon. Lorcan was on his side, legs buckled, laughing so hard that no sound came out. Oisin's face was slick with rain and tears, roaring. What the hell was so funny? By the time they'd finished with their hysterics, Maeve's stomach muscles were painfully cramped and her throat was raw, but the endorphins were helping elevate their collective mood. Tension had been building all day long, like a rubber band and then - *snap!* They needed that.

After shakily making their way down from the soaked hillside, their legs were like jelly after all the running, they were recovered enough to formulate some chat. In general, they agreed it'd be best to sleep before deciding what to do next. It was after five before Maeve got into her house, it had been a long day, and she just wanted to veg out. Her mind had other plans though. Although they'd decided to wait, Maeve couldn't help but send a message, Oisin had made her an admin in their group chat after all. She went into the chat settings, changing the group name from *The Weird Sisters* to *Vive la Révolution.*

# 17.

Retreading the same points again and again, Maeve felt like they were getting nowhere fast. They tried to keep the conversation at a whisper, but it was starting to spill over onto nearby tables in the study hall with her growing exasperation at Oisin.

"*Vive la Révolution?*" He sneered.

"It's just a name. I'm not saying that we join ranks with the spirits or whatever, I just mean that we shouldn't let this guy, de Meath, stop us from visiting, and helping Lorcan see Aiden and Bronach." She repeated for the millionth time in the past week.

"And how are we going to do that? We're not getting involved in this! End of." He said with an air of finality.

Maeve frowned, "*You're* not." She muttered.

"Maeve!"

That made people stare and the librarian, Ms. Murphy, gave them a loud, hissing *ssshhhh!* Oisin threw up his hand in apology and lowered his voice.

"What's that supposed to mean?"

"This is important to Lorcan, and we can't let him down."

"What, you're going to get yourself embroiled in a war because Lorcan wants to see his mammy and daddy?" He snorted, "Come on, I'm not fucking thick."

"Huh?"

"Just admit it!"

"Admit what?" She knew what he was getting at and she'd made it abundantly clear before that there was nothing going on between her and Lorcan. Did he really have to play that card?

"Admit that you have this idea that life here just isn't all that exciting, it isn't enough, and this is your way of finding some 'purpose'. You're head's in the clouds, and you think that this is your *Narnia* moment. You think I don't know how your head works by now, oh 'Chosen One'?"

Okay, she didn't know what he was getting at. Maeve hadn't thought about it like that, but now that he'd laid it out on the table she took a second to reflect. Was he right? Did she have some 'Chosen One' complex? She'd consider it later, not about to let Oisin have the last word.

"It's not my *Narnia*, it's nothing like *Narnia* anyway -"

"You're right there! This is far more dangerous. We could have died in that bog, did you see those things? And that guy, de Meath, seems hell-fucking-bent on getting us any time we're there." He'd given up pretending to do homework.

"We'll be more careful, we'll plan -"

"We did plan. We spent a lot of time planning, and it didn't matter, we were still caught out."

"But now we have more information about what he is and what he wants. We can plan around that! Plus, I've been reading up about dullahans online and how we might be able to protect ourselves." She slid a sheet of printed paper over to Oisin.

Unfolding it, he scanned the contents, frowning as he studied what she'd cobbled together, "Gold? You think gold will work?"

"It might, it's like a lot of those mythical creatures, like silver for werewolves. Precious metals seem to hold some power, maybe it's the purity or something?" She scribbled on her English homework as he read.

"And you trust online resources? Where'd you get this from?" He handed the paper back.

"Different sites. It's better than nothing, they've been pretty helpful so far."

"And you trust them?"

Hadn't she already answered this? "What? I just -"

"Aiden and Bronach. You trust them?" Oisin closed his books and stared at her.

"Why wouldn't I?" She stopped writing, staring back.

"I'm just asking. Do you?"

"Where is this coming from? What have they done to make me not trust them?"

"I'm asking you a really simple question, Maeve, do you trust Lorcan's parents?" He leaned forward, elbows on the table, arms folded.

"Yes." She said plainly, "They welcomed us into their house - well, hut - and trusted us with a lot of very sensitive information."

"Except for our Halloween arrival."

"It's probably because it was the veils between the worlds getting weaker thing. Remember?" Maeve offered.

"That was *our* explanation. They didn't even try to help us understand." He was really off on one.

"You love all this conspiracy theory shite, don't you?" It was Maeve's turn to go off on one, "Aiden and Bronach have no reason to invite us in, they could stop us from crossing over if they wanted, and they saved us twice! So why don't you trust them?"

"I didn't say that."

"Well, do you trust them?"

Oisin opened his book and began reading over his homework that was due in fifteen minutes, "I don't know yet."

They worked without speaking for the next while, Oisin frantically writing paragraphs, shaking out cramps in his hand. He hadn't got a detention yet this year, but one more missed assignment would tarnish that record.

"So, when are you going back?" He kept writing.

"I don't know yet." She could see him smirking.

"Well, do keep me informed." He said packing his books and rising, "I'd hate to miss another adventure with Aslan and the White Witch. 'Vive la Révolution' and whatnot."

"I told you, it's not like *Narnia!*" She threw a pen at him.

"Alright, alright. See you at lunch?" He leant over the table to kiss her, eliciting 'ooooohhhs' from the adjacent tables.

"See you then." She smiled.

The bell rang and Oisin jogged out of the study hall. What had he meant, *did she trust them*? He was so suspicious of people sometimes, so protective of her. They'd done nothing to earn her mistrust, or his; just give it time and he'd see that. The question rolled around in her mind again. Did she trust them? Of course, she did! There was no reason not to.

# 18.

Lorcan regarded the wall of pictures Cara had curated in her hallway. It was a tapestry, a lifetime's worth of photographs that spanned more than seventy years from her parent's, Lorcan's grandparents, younger days right up until near present day, a picture of Lorcan with Oisin and Maeve at the beach. He smiled at that memory, it seemed like another version of him, one broken but healing. He wasn't too sure what he was now. Fixed? Partially-healed? Or, was he still broken?

His gaze came to rest on a picture of him and his parents, taken a year before they died. They had been visiting Cara at the time, a short summer getaway, so the photo was taken in her back garden. The mountain dominated the background, reminding him of the sense of peace when he climbed and was able to loom over the landscape too. That wasn't his focus though, no, he looked at his parent's faces. There they were, grinning and solidly real. Of course, Lorcan looked bored in that frozen moment in time, but he was a teenager, he was supposed to be bored with his parents. He let out a little laugh, which came out more like a small whine, and traced the frame with his finger.

A sound from the front door, a key turning in the lock. Cara was back from town. Drying his eyes to make sure it didn't look like he'd been crying, again, he went to greet her.

"Hey, need any help there?" He said, observing her struggle with her bags.

"Aw, fanks love!" She said in a faux cockney accent, a bad one at that.

Cara was always doing those kinds of things, accents,

small flourishes, everything seemed performative. Failed actress perhaps? Maybe she had just spent too much time living alone and didn't quite know how to interact like a normal human being. He took a few of her bags and helped her into the kitchen.

"Jeez, what did you buy, bowling balls?" He grunted, hauling them onto the counter.

"Close. Melons, for a starter tonight."

"Melons? Plural?" What could two people want with multiple melons?

"There was a sale on! Maybe you could ask your friends over again if there's too much? We could have a dinner party."

Ah, her plan became clear. More test subjects.

They unpacked everything and Cara put a brew of coffee on. A perk to her being a foodie was that she often had a range of grounds and an expensive looking coffee machine. She made a mean Americano! Slumping onto individual armchairs, they waited for their brews to cool enough to drink. This had become somewhat of a ritual lately and Lorcan could tell that she was starting to enjoy his company since he'd brightened up, not just amicably tolerating his angst. Now was as good a time as any to start probing.

"Cara?" He began.

"Mmhmm?"

"Did my mam and dad strike you as the 'activist' types?"

"What, like, animals rights or something?"

"I suppose so, yeah. Were they ever involved in anything like that?"

She sipped her coffee, still too hot, and she burnt her lip, "I'm not sure. They were always saying they donated to different causes, and anytime your da had a drink he'd go on these political rants about fairness and equality, and worker's rights, and how 'the system' was keeping us down. He was like that even when we were growing up. Peace dude!" She threw up the peace sign as she finished.

"What about mam?"

"Aye, she agreed with him. They were both advocates you might say, although she refrained from the sweeping political statements when we were having a drink - thankfully. She was a good laugh. Why do you ask?"

"I don't know, I was wondering is all. Politics homework, y'know?" He shrugged.

"I thought you were joining the socialist party, comrade!" She said, raising her coffee to toast like a beer.

He laughed, "No, no, I'm not quite that radical yet. I just wanted to know if they would've joined - revolutions." He threw the word out casually.

"Who knows," Cara was shrugging now, "maybe in the right time or place, or another life. Jesus, this coffee's hot!" She'd burned her tongue this time.

She'd also hit the nail on the head. Maybe in another life - another world.

# 19.

Sitting on Lorcan's bed, they fanned their gathered notes out. Cara thought they were planning some mid-week group project for school, little did she know they were planning yet another trip to the Otherworld and a potential uprising.

"There's precedent for ancient civilizations having contact with another world, and also being connected to one another because of that." Maeve said, pointing to a sheet.

"And you say *I'm* into conspiracy theories?" Oisin raised an eyebrow.

"Ha-ha. Look, I'm just saying that there's a lot of parallels between these belief systems," She was in full swing, indicating notes on various ancient religions, "and I'm not the only one to notice this. There've been loads of writings on it if either of you would pick up a book or do a simple web search."

She shuffled around papers on the bed until she came to the one she was looking for. With an *ah-ha!* she unfolded it for the other two to read. It was a map of Central Europe with a red line that snaked its way from one end to the other.

"This," Maeve pointed to the line, "is the Danube river. It's one of the most significant rivers historically in Europe, and the site of many battles as well as bloodshed. It's also been connected with countless mythologies and legends over the years."

"I didn't realise we were getting a history lesson." Lorcan said. Oisin gave him a high-five for that one.

"Anyway, there's this Romanian legend or folk tale," She continued, "that tells of a white monastery with nine white monks, or priests, that resided on a holy white island. That island was located at the end of the Danube river and was also part of Greek legend. Apollo's sun was said to rise from there and Achilles, the great hero, was said to be buried there!" She was laying down these revelations, but the boys weren't picking them up.

"I'm sorry, but what does this have to do with what we're doing?" Lorcan looked genuinely confused.

"Okay, I'll make it clearer. You've heard of the goddess 'Danu'?" Both Oisin and Lorcan shook their heads. No wonder they were both confused, they'd not looked at any of the links she'd sent, were they relying on her for everything? "Well, now you've heard of her, does the name ring any bells?" Nothing. "Maybe it sounds kind of like a river I just bloody mentioned?"

"Ah! Danube." The penny dropped for Oisin, "What's the relevance?"

Maeve sighed, "The *relevance* is that all of these cultures are intertwined in their beliefs, the fact that Ireland has a goddess named Danu, that can be interpreted as Dana. It's not a big leap to say that 'Dianna' the Roman goddess could be a derivative of that. Even the idea of a mother goddess with multiple facets to her personality - light and dark, life and death, earth and sky - shows commonalities among different regions and cultures. They may have been drawing on the same source, i.e. the Otherworld." She realised she'd forgotten to take a breath and inhaled a huge gulp of air. It made her look more than a little manic.

The boys stared at her, blinking, silent, until Oisin stirred, "You should've picked pyramids. They're structures that cross cultures around the world. Like the Egyptians and Mayans."

"Aren't those alien spaceships though?" Lorcan said.

"Yeah, I watched that on one of those shows. What if the Otherworld is actually a portal to an alien dimension? That'd be cool!"

"I give up!" Maeve rolled off the bed, dejected.

"Wait!" Oisin said, taking her hand, "We're just messing

with you. Obviously it's all fascinating how these cultures are connected, and you might really be on to something. I'm just not seeing your point. You sound really smart with all this research and notes but what are you trying to say?"

He knew fine rightly what she was trying to say, he wasn't that stupid, but she'd spell it out if he wanted.

"I'm saying it's not fair that there are certain powerful people in the Otherworld who've chosen to cut us off. Who've chosen to part families, like Lorcan's, when they could easily still be together. It's like we used to all be connected by this thing, and now we're separated for no good reason, other than someone says so. I'm saying I want to fight!" She'd made herself tear up for maximum impact, pretending like that speech had been made up on the fly, and she hadn't rehearsed it even a little.

"So, you want to bring the worlds together, like the United Nations or something?" Lorcan said.

"In a manner of speaking."

"I knew it." Oisin said, "You do have a 'Chosen One' saviour complex." He didn't seem as snarky this time.

Cara interrupted, calling up from the kitchen, "Folks! Come on down, it's melon and Parma ham time!"

"Joy of joys. Where does she even get Parma ham around here?" Lorcan rolled his eyes.

"We'll talk about your big ideas after dinner." Oisin said, pecking her on the lips.

It wasn't a flat 'no'.

*       *       *       *       *       *

Negotiations continued throughout the week with Oisin finally adopting a 'wait and see' approach to their involvement in foreign affairs. Maeve could be persistent when she needed to be.

"We need to hear both sides of the argument." He stated as they walked home on a Friday afternoon, "Besides we've got real life to worry about too, have you even done your uni application yet?"

"I'll get around to it. We've still plenty of time." Maeve retorted, "I've got a bit of a better idea about what I'd like to do now."

They didn't have much time until the applications were due, sure you could apply late, but then you ran the risk of not getting a place at all. That meant another year in Droichead Dubh where little happens. At least, that's what she'd thought before recent developments. Now she wasn't sure whether she wanted to leave the town ever, not if this is where she had the chance to access and explore an entire other world. Could university offer her that?

"What about you, Lorcan? Decided what you're going to do?" She said, deflecting the focus from herself.

"Uuumm, not yet. I don't know what I want to apply for, I've been kinda distracted to be fair." He probably hadn't even looked at a prospectus.

As they walked and talked they kept their eyes fixed to the ground. It had been raining the previous night, the freezing cold weather had coated the ground in thin layers of ice, making each step a hazardous unknown. It was yet to snow this year, but there was a persistent chill wind and it'd probably roll in soon. They hadn't yet decided when they'd be paying their next visit, and it was beginning to play on Maeve's mind.

"So -" She began, but was interrupted by Oisin.

"My parents are away next weekend." He stepped over an inconspicuous bit of slippery tarmac, "Actually they're away from Thursday until Monday, some anniversary thing I think. If you wanted we could take a trip to the Otherworld then? You could stay over too if that'd be alright?"

"Sure yeah!" Maeve snapped up the offer, "What do you think, Lorcan?"

"Yeah, why not. The sooner, the better. It'll be a shorter walk back to the house for you two afterwards anyway." He popped his collar against the cold.

"I meant you too, eejit. Our little group just isn't complete without the moody one." Oisin said, only half-joking about the 'eejit' comment, "You can come stay over, there's even a spare bed."

"Oh, okay." Lorcan tried to play it off but was visibly happy to be included.

Maeve was glad to see them getting on well after their rocky start. She'd thought she was going to have to be the peacemaker of the group, but luckily Lorcan was happy enough to follow Oisin's lead. He was certainly a good planner and could think clearly in stressful situations, something Maeve and Lorcan had yet to prove capable of - yet. It was a learning curve!

They conversed more easily with the logistics sorted, and made other plans for the weekend, normal, more recognisable teenager plans. Another trip to the cinema was arranged, much to Oisin's dismay. He did like the idea of being able to get drunk and critique it afterwards, however. Lorcan even invited Maeve for an early morning run to get her ready for her night of drinking. She claimed that she'd consider it, but it most definitely would not be happening, Saturday mornings were made for lie-ins.

"Honestly, it's not that bad when you get used to it. I don't even think about getting up early anymore." Lorcan said.

"How early do you wake up?" Maeve asked.

"About six usually." He said it as if that was the done thing.

She stared at him, mouth open, "Six? On a weekend? What the f-" Her legs came out from under her, she was falling on her ass.

"Gotcha!" Oisin hooked his arms under hers, "Black ice." He casually lifted her back up, "Maybe you should go for a run, it might improve your balance. That's the second time I've had to rescue you."

She stuck out her tongue, he returned the gesture with

that big crooked grin of his.

"Fine! I'll go, but does it have to be six? How about nine?" She was getting a taste for negotiating.

"I'll give you a ring in the morning, whatever will be, will be." Lorcan winked.

She'd have to work on getting better deals.

# 20.

Their week passed largely uneventful. Maeve had made strides towards a drastic lifestyle change, going for a whole two runs with Lorcan. It was a stretch to call them 'runs' since they consisted of her jogging a few steps until she needed to stop and breathe, Lorcan trying to look sympathetic but ultimately just being impatient. She walked to school and she'd had to run in the Otherworld, she thought that had set her up to handle a little run. Alas, a walk was easy and the latter had been a life or death situation. Her legs ached the whole next day, but it was a start.

As for the sleepover, Maeve's dad categorically refused to let her stay over at Oisin's house without his parents there. She hadn't told him they'd be away, but it was hard to hide anything in a small town, and he was, quote, "not going to let my daughter stay over at her 'fancy boy's' house, so they can get up to God knows what!" *Fancy boy*? Had he time-travelled back to the turn of the century? Even when she'd told him Lorcan would be there too, she was met with a cocked eye, and he went back to reading his newspaper. That was a no-go then.

Regardless they pressed ahead with their Otherworld plans for Saturday morning under the pretence of a group hiking picnic. Thankfully Cara could back Maeve up, her dad actually phoned to confirm that she wasn't just trying to be alone with Oisin all day. Was this him exercising his last vestiges of control before she'd be let loose at university? Lorcan agreed to pick her up on Saturday morning to show everything was above board, and they were off. Freedom!

Oisin met them at the foot of the hill, and they hiked up

together. Maybe it was her imagination, but it felt like an easier climb this time. This fitness thing was serious business. It was another cloudy morning, the sun rising later and later into the day as winter tightened its grip. The sky had only begun to lighten by the time they reached Dún Dubh. Like before, they were left hanging, Lorcan had to call out over the course of an hour. They'd all brought some warm drinks with them this time, learning from their experience. Again, there was a point when his words began to feel more solid, the boundaries between the worlds thinned and the burgeoning daylight dimmed around them. The white-hot cold of the Otherworld struck out, and they were across.

The formalities were followed, Lorcan looked happy as ever to see his parents, having gotten over the moodiness of last time, and Oisin was coping better with the unpleasantness of inter-world travel. They carefully made their way out of the fort, into the cover of foliage. So far so good. What did the Otherworld have in store this time?

"There's a meeting starting soon discussing the struggle, they're held fairly regularly. We'd like you to come along and hear what the people are fighting for, and what they have to go up against." Aiden explained, "What do you say?"

They exchanged glances between themselves and unanimously agreed. *This* is what it had in store, and this is what Maeve had been hoping for. They followed Aiden and Bronach along the same path they'd been led previously to the boggy town, being consciously inconspicuous and vigilant as they walked. When it came into view, even from a distance, Maeve could see that a large portion of the town was gathering in one building. It was a huge wooden structure with thick beams that elevated it above the surrounding properties, and a large spire rose from its centre, reminding her of a church. That must have been their equivalent of a town hall.

There was a lot of hubbub about town as they shuffled along the narrow walkways, taking care to avoid any contact with the residents. Maeve didn't want a repeat of what had happened on her early trips and Oisin needed no excuse to be more on edge than he already was. The thick fog that hung oppressively in the air, coupled with the mountains that walled off one side of the settlement, and the growing crowd made the town feel claustrophobic. She was no military expert but saw that fortifications had been made in the form of barriers, weapons were laid in strategic locations and - were those ballistas? New additions since their last visit.

The entrance was packed with bodies shuffling and making their way inside. As they approached, Aiden and Bronach whispered in a few ears and the throng began to part. Were they that important? Or, were special provisions being made for their unique presence? Finding a spot towards the back of the large, open room, they stood on a bench overlooking the scene. It was like the celebration of Samhain except everyone looked a lot less human, and there were sounds Maeve hadn't heard even back then. This was more feral, making the hairs on the back of her neck stand on end.

They weren't the only observers, eyes and heads swivelled towards them too, hungrily curious. Their inhuman faces made expressions unreadable, and she avoided eye contact, choosing instead to rest her gaze on the empty podium at the head of the hall. The murmuring died down though, as a confident figure strode to it, spreading out their long, sinuous arms, hushing the floor in a similar manner to de Meath. Their face was sharp and everything about them looked elongated, like they'd been stretched on a rack. Despite being at the back of the crowd, Maeve could make out their empty, milk-white eyes and blue-black veins underneath their all too pale skin.

"Welcome friends!" Its thin lips pulled back to reveal a nasty set of teeth that looked too big for its head, and when it spoke its jaw hinged open like a snake, "Thank you all for attending today. I'm sure you're eager to hear about the new developments we've had with regard to our old companion, William de Meath!"

Jeering erupted from the crowd as insults were hurled and the pale figure waited for them to calm down enough to be heard.

"Dear William appears to be stepping up his efforts in hunting down anyone thought to be conspiring against his regime of tyranny. He's segregated us and is now hunting the very citizens of our town. We have with us today, someone who has been on the receiving end of this hunt. He may be new to the cause, but he is fast becoming one of our greatest allies." Its thin voice carried over the mumbles and shuffling of the people gathered before it, themselves wondering who this mystery person was, "I give you , Aiden Delaney!" It thrust out a pointy hand in their direction.

The entire room turned to look at them. There was a burst of noise, whooping, hollering, and some of them even seeming to erupt in fits of laughter. What could be so funny about Aiden speaking? Maybe it was the fact that they were the only ones in the room that looked any way 'normal'. Aiden stepped down from the bench and began to walk through the horde. As he passed, people tugged at him, screaming with amusement and cheering him on. It might have looked terrifying, but he didn't seem perturbed at all, in fact, he pushed back and joked with the masses like some sort of celebrity. Was he popular? Maeve looked to Lorcan, whose face was frozen in confused shock with his mouth half open. Oisin, however, scowled at the scene playing out, staring unblinkingly at the podium where Aiden was now taking his place. He spread out his arms like the speaker before him, although it didn't look nearly as commanding with an ordinary human arm span. The commotion died to a mild bustling, and he began.

"Thank you, friends!" His voice was surprisingly powerful and commanding, "And thank you to Abar for letting me take the stand today." That got another round of cheers, "It is as he said. William de Meath has been taking measures to increase his stranglehold on this beautiful land. It was but two weeks ago, you may remember, that he personally entered this town. Not to help, not even as a passing visit - no. I'm sorry to say that he came for me and my family." He inclined his head towards them which drew more glances from the gathering.

"You see, William doesn't want news getting round that the barrier between our worlds has been weakening! We've all felt it! Some of you may have heard that myself and my lovely wife, Bronach," Cheers and wolf whistles, "have recently been able to bring my son, who is still very much alive, through the veil and into the Otherworld."

This set them off. People got to their feet, decrying the action and more eyes locked on their small group, who were now huddled against the back wall, leaning and straining to get a look at the freak show.

"It's true!" Aiden boomed over the noise, "Lorcan!"

He motioned for Lorcan to join him on stage, but Lorcan looked as if he might have a heart attack if he was forced to go up there. Bronach whispered something in his ear and he unsteadily stood down off of the bench, walking slowly to the podium. Everyone knew what to do, parting, making sure not to touch him, but that didn't stop some of them from getting awfully close. A queer silence spread as he took his place. Everyone was paying attention now.

"You can see it, can't you? My wife and I were able to defy de Meath and reunite with our boy, and now he's here with us, in the flesh. I know you've only welcomed us very recently, but I feel confident in saying this is a positive step in what we've been fighting for." In contrast to the cheering and jeering beforehand, a respectful clap resounded, "We're honoured to be here, and we're honoured to be fighting this fight with you, restoring balance between worlds. To a brighter future!" The applause rose in volume as more joined, "To Abar! And to the revolution!"

Again, the hall exploded in a fanfare of noise with Lorcan looking incredibly uncomfortable, but Aiden could be seen uttering words of encouragement to him. Maeve noticed

Oisin clapping half-heartedly out of the corner of her eye.

"That was a good speech." He said without intonation and continued to stare ahead.

Abar took to the stage after the racket abated, inviting others to speak. Maeve had never been to a meeting or rally like this before. She felt their longing to return to the old ways as more members got up to say their piece. Why shouldn't they be reunited with a world that was taken from them? Now more than ever, she was convinced she wanted to help them and didn't feel much need to hear what de Meath's supporters had to say. She was a convert.

The meeting ended with a final rallying call and the hall began to clear in amongst a lot of back slapping and over-loud talking. Aiden and Lorcan managed to squirm their way to the bench; Bronach couldn't have looked prouder of the pair. She gave Lorcan a big full-bodied hug, pulling him close. Maeve marvelled once more at how they were able to touch each other so freely. Could they control it to an extent? Oisin continued to be a blank slate.

"So, what did you think?" Aiden said, beaming at them.

"Wow! Just wow!" Maeve was blown away by the sheer spectacle of it all.

Lorcan beamed too, she could see that he was in a daze after what had just happened, but it looked like a happy daze. He just kept looking at his dad and grinning. Aiden looked to Oisin for comment.

"It was certainly interesting to hear what people had to say. They responded well to the new star here." He nodded to Lorcan, who flushed red.

"They did! And why wouldn't they, it's miraculous you're all here!" Bronach said, squeezing Lorcan more.

"Indeed." Said Oisin, checking his analogue watch, "Maeve."

She looked at the time, it was mid-afternoon and she'd told her dad she'd be back soon, "Shite!" She said, "I'm really sorry, but I have to be back home."

"It's okay, we can take you back. Do you have five minutes to spare for the scenic route?"

She would be five minutes late.

"Sure!"

They started back out of the town, feeling the fog lift from them as they did. It really tended to stick to them, weighing on their clothes unlike normal fog back home. Instead of taking them directly into the trees like they had been, Aiden and Bronach followed the treeline as it inclined its way up the hill. This gave them a clear view of the surrounding area. Maeve was yet to get tired of that view.

The November sun hung low in the sky, bathing the land in a soft wintry light that made it feel all the more magical. She couldn't wait to explore it when they got the chance. Maeve knew now the spectacular castle surrounding the gargantuan tree belonged to de Meath, but still, it didn't diminish either structure's beauty. She needed to go there eventually, clandestinely or otherwise. Maybe when this revolution was over she'd be able to freely explore it.

The scenic route ended up eating over ten minutes of their time, but its beauty was more than worth a bit of a bollocking from her dad. They made their final approach to the Otherworld's version of Dún Dubh, letting the golden light bathe them in its gentle heated rays, and prepared to head back to normalcy. They all stopped dead in their tracks when an unexpected rustle sounded above them.

A masked shadow leapt from a tree branch, diving straight for Lorcan with a vicious looking knife aimed at the nape of his neck. It was all happening in slow motion, but Maeve couldn't do anything to stop it, her body just wasn't fast enough. Bronach's was. She pulled Lorcan out of the way in time but received a deep gash to her upper arm in return. They both reeled away from the attacker who re-centred themselves for another strike.

This time it was Oisin who intervened, grabbing the figure's wrist and wrenched it hard, causing them to drop the weapon. It was a momentary victory because, almost as quickly, Oisin was struggling to hold himself up and was easily pinned to the ground. The assailant removed their mask, revealing the face of a young woman which was grotesquely transforming. Her nose and mouth protruded, growing more fearsome as the visage of a wolf began to take shape. Its muzzle snapped at Oisin's face viciously, and with every passing moment edged closer to his throat. Maeve didn't even remember grabbing for the knife, but it was in her hand now. Before she could do anything, Aiden had stepped in.

He shoved his arm between the wolf's head and Oisin's face, taking major damage to his arm. Blood sprayed on Oisin's very pale, drained face but almost immediately evaporated when it made contact. Having sacrificed one arm, Aiden used the other to wrangle the beast into a firm chokehold, and he held fast. It thrashed about in a frenzy but stopped when Maeve held the knife centimetres from its belly. She was ready to do what she had to. Defeated, the wolf's snout began to retreat back into it's skull and the girl's face returned. She glowered at them, but there was no point in fighting back now.

"Name!" Aiden demanded.

The girl remained silent. He tightened his hold.

"Name!"

"William de Meath sends his regards." She wheezed out.

Her right hand began to stretch out into sharp points until each finger was like a knife. Maeve tensed to attack, but Aiden pulled at the girl's neck until there was a loud crack, and she ceased moving. No-one spoke. They just stared at the body before them before turning their attention to the treeline, readying themselves for imminent assault. A strained moment passed as they waited, but once they were satisfied that they were alone again, it was time to check the wounded.

Lorcan was fine, Bronach had taken the brunt of the damage there, and she fashioned a bandage out of fabric from her shirt. Aiden's arm looked bad, the skin was mangled and the girl's wolf teeth had stripped parts of right to the bone. He winced when he moved but insisted he was fine and seemed more concerned with Oisin, who was sitting up, breathing deeply like he was about to throw up.

"I'm okay." He said unconvincingly, "I suppose I shouldn't have touched her but what else was I going to do?" He slowly stood, looking at Aiden and Bronach, "Thank you. I mean it, I'd probably be joining you here if you hadn't saved me."

They smiled at him, "Of course, pet, you're practically family now that you're one of Lorcan's friends." Bronach said as she wrapped Aiden's arm.

"I appreciate that." Oisin nodded.

They shakily entered the chamber as the sun made its steady, inevitable journey towards the horizon, the shadows lengthening around them. Standing in the central chamber once again, Aiden and Bronach looked to the group and hesitated.

"What is it?" Lorcan said.

Aiden closed his eyes and opened them again slowly, a grave manner had overtaken him, "We need you all to be watchful. This attack just proved that you're a target now, all of you. We can help protect you here but back home, in your world - we can't do much. So, please do whatever you can to be safe."

"We're so sorry for dragging you into this." Bronach rubbed at her eyes, "We were so selfish wanting to see you again, Lorcan, that we never even considered the risks." Tears streaked her face.

Maeve wasn't so good in these situations and could rarely say anything beyond meaningless platitudes. She was close to saying 'there, there' when Oisin took a small step forward.

"It's okay, Aiden, Bronach, from the start we knew that this was dangerous, and we didn't exactly run screaming away. We'll take care of ourselves." He looked drained, but there was a renewed strength in his words.

"Thank you." Bronach said, drying her cheeks.

They reached out their hands.

"Love you." Lorcan said.

"And we love you." They replied but Maeve felt that they were beginning to extend that sentiment to the entire group. It was a warm feeling.

That feeling almost counteracted the usual shock of being thrust back into their own world. Almost. They took some time to gather themselves, replenishing some electrolytes, before setting off back down the hillside in the fading light. Maeve's phone was awash with angry texts from her dad, and missed phone calls wondering where she was and why she hadn't replied. Apparently she was grounded for a couple of weeks but wasn't too worried about that, he never stuck to those punishments, and she was nearly eighteen. A little too old to be 'grounded'.

Ensuring Oisin was fit enough to walk, he thought they were fussing too much, they set off back home. Although they'd just survived what should've been a harrowing, traumatic experience, that's not how they felt. It was like they had just lived through their own movie scene or passage from a book. Hating herself for thinking this, Maeve wondered if this was how the Pevensie's would feel if *Narnia* was indeed a real place. She would *not* be telling Oisin she'd been pondering that, there would never be an end to the teasing.

Much to his dismay, she ordered Oisin home when he'd insisted on walking to Maeve's first. He needed sleep, and she could talk to him later anyway - if her dad didn't confiscate her phone that was. He reluctantly shuffled away, she could hear him muttering, and left them to dander home themselves. Lorcan and Maeve recounted the events of today, already it was as if it had all happened an age ago. The stuff of legends. They'd had enough excitement to fill a lifetime, and they were already anticipating their next foray. They giddily parted with their new catchphrase, *vive la révolution.* Time to face the music.

The bollocking from her dad wasn't so bad, he was more

the silent treatment type once he'd gotten over the yelling. Maeve estimated she'd be back on normal speaking terms with him by tomorrow afternoon. The rest of her evening was a typical Saturday night, they ordered takeaway, watched TV. She messaged Oisin, he hadn't replied yet, but if he felt even a fraction of the tiredness she'd experienced on her early trips to the Otherword she was happy to let him rest. She was getting tired herself and went to bed, mulling over their next adventure.

*    *    *    *    *    *

Maeve's dreams were filled with dark shadows that reached and called out to her, no, they screamed at her. Right in her face, clawing and shrieking. It was unbearable, and it was only getting louder, and louder. She sat bolt upright in her bed, wide awake, coming to the realisation that the keening was not of her dreams. It was very real and very close.

# 21.

The splitting sound filled her ears, cutting right to the centre of her being. Maeve clasped her hands over her head in an effort to block it out, but it was no good, it didn't do anything to drown out the cry. Her stomach clenched and she felt physically ill. What was this? She thought her dad might burst in at any moment to find out what was going on, but he didn't, how could he possibly sleep through it? Despite the unbelievable volume the noise wasn't coming from her room. It was coming from outside.

Rain pelted the windows, creating hundreds of rivulets obscuring the view better than any darkness. Maeve threw open the window and let the rain beat against her skin, barely feeling it as she strained her eyes in the gloom. Even through wind and rain, the mournful crying carried perfectly. It was pained; a lament for a lost loved one. Old memories of her own loss were dredged up involuntarily. She winced at the reminder and, gritting her teeth, shoved them aside. She couldn't stand this much more. Tracking the source of the sound, Maeve began to see something take shape in the distance as her sight adjusted. It was a woman.

Seemingly unaffected by the raging storm, her clothes flowed gracefully about her, and she fixed something at her shoulder. No, she was stroking at her hair. All the while standing in place and unleashing the most awful wail she had ever heard. What did she want, and how was it possible to produce such a sound? Every modulation in the woman's voice sent stabs of worry through Maeve as her brain slowly began to comprehend what it was she was witnessing. A banshee.

The realisation hit Maeve, her breath catching in her throat. Now she really felt sick. Banshees by themselves were not evil spirits, or even harmful, from what she'd read, but they did bring with them omens of ill fortune or death. They were like an early warning system that predicted doom. Why had she come to Maeve though?

She watched as the banshee clutched at her chest and folded, as if in tremendous pain, letting out an intense, agonised wail. Oisin! It was warning her about Oisin. She didn't know how, but Maeve knew something had happened or was about to happen to him. She lunged for her phone and fumbled until it was dialling his number. It rang until the voicemail picked it up. She tried again, and then again, but no answer. She left a voice message for him to call her back and sent a text saying the same thing. This was no use, she had to go to him.

Not caring if she woke her dad or the entire town, Maeve flew about her room, throwing on her clothes and dashed downstairs. As she slipped her shoes on she phoned Lorcan, who groggily answered the phone, obviously he hadn't been woken by the lament. She tried to explain what was going on but ended with, "Oisin's now!", and rushed out into the rain. She was instantly soaked but didn't notice in the slightest, pelting herself down the road as fast as her legs could carry her. The keening followed her as she ran, a reminder that this was no time to slow down. She pushed herself harder than she ever had, her lungs and heart working overtime.

In amongst the banshee's wailing there was another sound that began to creep up on her out of the darkness, a familiar voice.

"Maeve!" Lorcan shouted, cycling hard towards her, his headlight bobbing frantically side to side, "Get on."

He wasn't wasting any time asking what the hell was going on, he had shown up to help, and she had never been so glad to see him. Swinging her leg over the back wheel, she settled before yelling at him to hurry. Lorcan's legs pumped into action, his hands white-knuckled with effort. Oisin's house was downhill from hers, and they picked up a lot of speed, darting dangerously fast along the skinny lanes. It was the middle of the night, cars weren't going to be an issue.

At last Oisin's house came into view, the main hallway light was on, so he was up. Lorcan pedalled harder, even with the racket in her ears Maeve could hear he was breathing heavily. They came to a skidding halt at his front garden and, leaping off the bike, Maeve sprinted through the main door that lay open to the elements. This only served to send her panic into overdrive.

There was movement in the living room, she burst in to see an excruciatingly thin man looming over Oisin as he struggled fruitlessly under the skeletal grip. The man expended no effort in holding him in place, and failed to acknowledge Maeve's presence in the house. Oisin strained, looking over the man's shoulder.

"Maeve! Get out, I don't know what he wants!"

Aiden and Bronach had warned them this would happen. Had de Meath sent this thing here to kill them? Lorcan ran in then, rushing to yank at the man's arms, having zero effect. The man's bony frame may have suggested a lack of strength, but he stood rooted to the spot unperturbed by the two boys, she doubted a car could move him, so what chance did they have? She took stock of her surroundings, looking for something to hit him with but could find nothing. Unless she could distract him with a throw pillow. She darted to the kitchen, grabbing a knife and stopped. Would this do *anything* to him?

Maeve needed to slow down, she'd only waste more time with failed solutions. The knife probably wouldn't affect the man unless it was weak to stainless steel. If only they had a silver or gold knife lying about, that might do something, but she had never heard his mother mention anything about a cutlery collection. Then it hit her, she'd been reading about how to deal with different mythical beings, like the dullahan.

This obviously wasn't a dullahan, thankfully, but what was it? A moment like this required her to put theory into action. Breathing, Maeve forced her mind to concentrate, it was a special feat considering the myriad of distractions, and she went through the list. Okay, he was tall, extremely thin, but he didn't seem to be harming them (yet), just harassing Oisin badly. What in the hell was he?

She made a grab for the bread bin, pulled out a sliced white loaf and raced into the living waving the slices in front of the skeletal man's face. This got his attention. Result!

"Here! This is what you want, right? Food?" Her voice was shaking but it was working.

The man let go of Oisin's arm and, with the same hand, took the bread. He inclined his head slightly towards Maeve and made his way back out into the wet night, grumbling incoherently as he left. They all collapsed in relief. Oisin was crumpled on the floor breathing and whimpering.

"Bread?" He managed, "He wanted bloody bread?"

"He was a 'fear gorta' or 'hungry man'. He'll accept food or money as payment for leaving you alone."

"Jesus!" Lorcan said, slumping onto the couch, "Thank fuck you read a lot. Maybe we should too."

"Finally! It took this to make you realise?" Maeve staggered her way through the hall to the door.

The man was nowhere to be seen, and it registered with her that the banshee's wailing had stopped. She let out a sigh and a small, grateful sob. It had frightened her like nothing else had before, but it was a friendly warning.

"Thank you." She whispered, closing the door.

She'd have to explain everything to the boys now, and they'd probably have to stay the night. When her dad found out there'd be another grounding session. Lorcan was studying Oisin's hand when she made her way back into the living room. They were both hunched over, looking puzzled and more than a little concerned.

"What is it?" She said.

Oisin held up his hand. There was a black mark on it that had spread over his palm, forming a rough circle. It looked like it had been drawn on crudely with a marker.

"I'm not sure." Oisin replied, walking swiftly to the kitchen.

Maeve followed him as he went to the sink and began washing his hands furiously, trying to rub the mark off with hot water and dish soap. When that failed he grabbed a brush and set about violently scrubbing.

"Stop!" Maeve said, grabbing at the brush, "You'll peel your skin off!"

"It has to come off!" He shook her loose and continued, "It needs washed."

"What is it?" She shouted at him, but there was no answer, "Oisin! What is that mark?"

He whirled around to face her, "I don't know! I don't fucking know what it is! That's why it needs to come off!" He turned back to face the sink, dug into his palm a few times and stopped.

Hurt at the outburst but more concerned for him, Maeve turned off the hot water. He had rubbed his skin raw, tearing his hand up, but still the mark remained. Blood streamed from his wound into the sink and his shoulders began to tremble.

"I don't know what it is. What any of it is." He said quietly.

Maeve pulled him in close to her, stroking his head soothingly.

"It's okay," She crooned, "we'll find out, and we'll sort it. Yeah? We'll go back tomorrow, and we'll ask Aiden and Bronach if it's anything, and then we'll fix it." She wished it could be as simple as she'd made it sound.

Oisin buried his head in her shoulder and, saying nothing, let her comfort him. It had finally caught up with him, all that effort he'd poured into being brave and keeping it together must have been taxing. He grabbed at her sodden top, staining it with blood, and wept. Now it was Maeve's turn to keep it together for him. She'd fix this. Whatever this thing was, she'd fix it.

# 22.

A series of bangs at the front door woke them as morning sunlight streamed in through the living room bay window. Lorcan watched Maeve shoot up and cringe when she spotted her dad coming to forcibly collect her. In fairness, she'd left in the middle of the night without saying a word. He must have had a good idea of where she'd gone, he'd driven straight to Oisin's when he saw her empty bed.

She tried to come up with some cockamamie excuse about the storm, and Oisin needing help from both her and Lorcan to get the electricity running. He wasn't buying it, instead giving her the ultimate guilt trip.

"Maeve, you know I worry about you - you're the only lady in my life that matters. Especially after your mother." Oh god, he'd pulled the mother card.

Whether he did it on purpose or not, it appeared to make her feel awful, and she agreed to stay grounded. They had a quick conspiratorial meeting before she was hauled off to solitary confinement, with Lorcan arranging that he and Oisin would go together to see if they could gather intel on what had happened. Oisin was uncharacteristically quiet throughout this, last night's events playing on his mind. Lorcan suggested that they go to Cara's house first, she may not think it weird he was gone because of his morning excursions.

He was right. Plus, she was happy that he had 'run into' Oisin while they were out, and she fixed them a slap-up Sunday breakfast.

"Did you hurt your hand?" She pointed to the crude bandage he'd fashioned.

"Oh, yeah. Scratched my palm up pretty good falling on the icy roads." He replied, sipping on his coffee.

"Awk, sure, easy done. Do yous want any sandwiches made up for your walk this afternoon?"

"No, thanks, you're alright. We won't be going for a long one today." Lorcan said.

It was good Oisin hadn't been left to stew on his own. He looked shaken, rightly so. He'd had some unknown creature break into his house, probably sent to kill him, and now there was the matter of this marking. After they'd wolfed down their breakfast, Lorcan more enthusiastically than Oisin, it was time to go get some answers.

The cold had really set in from last night and the frozen rain glittered in the morning light. It gave the landscape a preserved, pristine look that contrasted with how tainted and rotten they felt internally. Neither of them had gotten much rest, but Oisin looked done.

"Is it worth it?" He said after a long silence.

"Sorry?" Lorcan said.

"The Otherworld, seeing your parents again. Is it worth all this - shite?"

Lorcan didn't know quite how to respond to that, so he answered as honestly as he could, "I - I don't know. I mean, it's amazing to see them again. You have no idea how much I missed them before -"

He paused.

"*But?*" Oisin prompted.

"But, I don't like putting you or Maeve in danger. I didn't know we'd get caught up in any of this, and I didn't think she'd be so into it." They both had to laugh at that, "If you had've told me all this beforehand - well, honestly, I probably still would've done it. That's how much I missed them, and how messed up my head was. Maybe still is." No point in lying.

"I see."

They crested a small hill before Oisin spoke again.

"I remember when Maeve lost her mum. It was before

we'd ever properly started speaking or hanging out, but she was in my class, so I remember what she was like." He looked ahead of him as he spoke, accessing some deep memory, "She went from this happy little girl to a quiet, morose kid who spoke to no-one for ages. She must have been devastated."

"Yeah, I know how she felt." Lorcan said.

"I know you do, and I think that's why she was so onboard with this whole thing. She knew how you felt, and she wanted to help. Now though, she's found some sort of 'cause' to fight for. The 'revolution'. Maeve probably thinks she's going to unite the worlds and end death as we know it or something. That'd be just like her to do something so crazy."

Lorcan wasn't sure where this might be going.

"She understands your pain, but I don't. I don't know what it's like to lose a parent, I've never even had an aunt or uncle die, so I can't begin to approximate the pain. I suppose I'm pretty charmed that way." He didn't look charmed right now, "What I do know is if I could spare Maeve from feeling that pain ever again, I would do it in a heartbeat, so I kind of get why she's doing it for you." He smiled at Lorcan.

"Thanks." Lorcan smiled back, "And thanks for helping as well. I don't know where we'd be without you. Dead probably."

Oisin chuckled, "Probably. Here's my 'but' though -" He got serious, "If anything does happen to her, you'll wish you'd never gotten her involved in all this. I'm happy to go along with everything for now, but if it becomes anything more than a *thrilling adventure* then I'm pulling it. And -" He sighed, "if anything happens to me just please promise me that you'll take care of her. Promise me that you won't drag her into more danger if I kick it."

"What? You're going to be -"

"Just promise me!" Oisin stopped, staring at Lorcan with an intense sincerity.

Lorcan was taken aback but managed to say, "I - of course, I promise."

"Good."

"You're blowing this way out of proportion though. You'll see."

They resumed walking. He wasn't sure where this was coming from. Was Oisin really so worried about that mark, or that they'd seriously become involved with the revolution? He didn't think Maeve had been saying those things in earnest, believing it to be excited posturing. It wasn't *their* world after all.

"You know I'm coming back to haunt you if you don't keep your promise." Oisin said, letting the tension drop, "I'm totally going to do that. You'll never sleep again."

Like Maeve's dad, he too was a master of the guilt trip, and he definitely didn't want Oisin's ghost torturing him for eternity. They soon arrived at Dún Dubh. It didn't take long to get a response this time, their world warping into the Otherworld. Taking a second to shake off the cold, Lorcan noticed his parents looking more tense than usual, sporting bandages where the wolf had wounded them.

"Boys, what has you back so quickly?" Bronach said frantically, "Is everything alright?"

"Not really, mam. Oisin was attacked last night."

"What!? Are you hurt?" She examined him from a safe distance.

"I'm okay, I wasn't hurt, just freaked out." Oisin reassured her.

"Was it one of de Meath's people?" Lorcan said.

"It most likely was. We didn't want this to happen." Aiden admitted, "But we're glad you're okay."

"Who was it?" Bronach asked.

"We're not sure *who* it was, but Maeve seemed to think it was a 'fear gorta'." Lorcan was unsure if he was remembering right.

Their eyes widened, exchanging a worried look between them.

"What happened?"

They relayed the whole story. There'd been a knock at the door, and when Oisin answered it, thinking it might be either Maeve or Lorcan in trouble, the fear gorta pushed his way inside and attacked him. There was no way he was able to fight it off, but fortunately Lorcan and Maeve had arrived in time to help.

"It's a good thing that girl is so smart." Aiden said when they told them about Maeve's bread rescue.

"That she is." Oisin agreed.

Bronach knitted her eyebrows together, clearing her throat, "So, you're hand, Oisin. Can I see it?"

He winced and began to unwrap his bandage. In the stillness of the chamber the action felt grave and important. Although the skin of his palm had been torn up by panicked scrubbing, the black mark was still clearly visible. Oisin didn't seem to want to look.

"I've never seen one before." She said.

"What is it?" Oisin asked, his head turned away.

"It's a curse mark." Aiden said, "The fear gorta leaves them if you refuse his wishes."

"But Maeve gave him what he wanted." Lorcan interjected.

"It wasn't Maeve's door he knocked on, it was Oisin's. I'm really sorry lad." Aiden rubbed at his mouth.

"What does it mean?" Oisin's voice was steel.

"It's a curse, so it could mean any number of things." Bronach hesitated, "But, mostly they bring misfortune and - death."

Oisin's face drained of all colour except for the area around his eyes which was quickly turning red.

"Is there a way to, I don't know, break the curse?" Lorcan said, a touch of desperation in his tone.

"We'll ask, love, don't worry. We know a lot of clever people here, and I'm sure they've heard something."

Oisin didn't look convinced.

Lorcan hugged his parents, careful not to disturb the

BLACK BRIDGE

wrappings on their wounds. It was only a flying visit, they had work to do with regard to the mark and methods of removing it. Before sending them back his parents had one last pearl of wisdom.

"Boys, you're connected to this world now but that connection goes both ways. Take care back there. If we hear any word about your situation, we'll send you a signal." He nodded to Lorcan.

They said their final goodbyes, and they were back in the land of the living. Maybe it was because they hadn't spent much time on the other side, but neither of them felt the effects much. Oisin didn't look reassured in the slightest. Lorcan tried to dispel his fears by reassuring him that his parents were on it as they climbed down. There was nothing to worry about.

They reached the point where they had to part ways. Oisin locked eyes with him.

"You say nothing to Maeve, I'll tell her what happened. It's better she hears it from me, okay?" He was stipulating rather than asking.

Lorcan nodded, "Yeah, sure."

"You promise me? What you said earlier, you promise?"

"About Maeve? I do."

Oisin softened, turning to leave. Lorcan stood rooted to the spot, watching him carefully pick his steps on the icy road.

"You'll be fine though!" He called after him.

Oisin didn't turn around but gave him a small backhand wave.

*    *    *    *    *    *

"A bit of bad luck doesn't sound too awful." Maeve said as they passed the school's gates.

Oisin hadn't told her the full story then? Lorcan didn't see it as his place at the minute to be the bearer of bad news - or the harbinger of death as it were. He didn't want her to worry

169

unnecessarily. If they could lift the curse and prevent anything from happening in the first place, then there was no need to worry.

"Yeah, we just need to be careful. No handling sharp objects for me." Oisin said, casual as you like, waving his bandaged hand about.

"Do you think your parents will get back to you soon?" Maeve asked Lorcan.

"I'm not sure, but they seemed to think someone would be able to help. So, hopefully." He'd become pretty adept at lying by omission over the past while, it was no big strain on his conscience to do so.

"I'll do some research tonight and see about lifting curses anyway, might as well get a head start."

"When do you find time to do homework? Or study? Or - do university applications?" Oisin sounded genuinely perplexed.

"Give over about those applications! I'll get around to it." That came out a little more harsh that Lorcan thought she meant it, "Here, are you going for a run this evening?"

"Um, I wasn't planning to, why?" Lorcan said.

"Are you planning to now? I might as well get fit for any potential *running for our lives* we have to do."

"Sure, couldn't hurt."

It seemed an odd request, especially from Maeve, who practically had to be dragged out of bed in the mornings. Almost literally. Lorcan wondered what she was up to.

\*       \*       \*       \*       \*       \*

The path was pitch black by the time they reached the summit, clip-on torches illuminating their breath, creating huge, diffuse clouds with tiny wisps of steam rising from their arms. Maeve was breathing hard, but she was doing better than she had been on their previous treks, she didn't even stop to throw up this time.

"Not too bad." She said, taking a gulp from her water bottle.

"You'll be sprinting up in no time."

They turned their torches off, looking out over the dark scenery. The sky was a deep purply-blue that provided little contrast with the black silhouette of the land. Lights twinkled in houses, cars were tiny wind-up toys, people were invisible from this vantage point. There was a special kind of peacefulness and stillness about looking over somewhere wreathed in night from up on high. Like nothing much mattered; you were apart from it all, observing dispassionately.

"It's nice, isn't it?" She said.

"Mmhmm."

"Everything seems so insignificant from here."

She took another drink from her bottle and put it away. They stayed like that for a long moment. Lorcan knew that she hadn't come here to make small talk, or to enjoy the view, but he would let her bring whatever it was up in her own time.

"Is that really what your parents said?" And there it was, the reason she'd wanted to get him alone, "That it was just some bad luck, nothing more serious?"

She turned towards him, her features obscured by the gloom, the faint light from Droichead Dubh was unable to touch them here.

"Yes. That's really what they said." He wasn't about to tattle on Oisin, that wasn't his job.

"Really? So there's nothing to be worried about?" She didn't sound overly convinced, "You'd tell me, wouldn't you, Lorcan?"

He shifted into his best 'believe me' voice, "I would, Maeve. There's nothing to worry about, and my parents sounded sure they could help us to fix it. We'll have him back to normal soon." It sounded convincing.

She looked back to the lights below them, "Thanks, I just needed to hear that from you without Oisin around. I'm not sure if he would honestly tell me something like that, he's too concerned with 'protecting' me."

"Nah, he'd tell you." He was doubling down on the lies now, "He's just stressed from the whole ordeal."

"Yeah, it's a stressful time for us all. But still, I'm glad I'm a part of it. It's an amazing thing," Lorcan could hear her mood lift, "even when we're running for our lives."

Business concluded, they began the gravelly descent. Upon reaching the bottom, Maeve hugged Lorcan and thanked him again for being honest with her. This stung a little, but he rolled with it nonetheless. He began a gentle jog home, stopping halfway as a dark figure crossed his path. He couldn't blame the drink this time, it was really there. It raised an arm in the direction of Dún Dubh. He supposed that was the signal.

# 23.

Stifling a yawn, the cold seeping into Maeve's bones from Dún Dubh's freezing stone floor. They'd waited for her dad to fall into a deep sleep before sneaking her out of the house. This was an urgent matter and couldn't be postponed until the weekend, despite Oisin's insistence that sleep and school were just as important. Yeah, right. Both he and Lorcan had told Maeve that there wasn't anything major to worry about with the mark, but her gut said otherwise, and they were going to sort it out sooner rather than later.

Lorcan had barely uttered a syllable when they were transported, Aiden and Bronach had been anticipating them. The transfer from world to world was becoming more seamless, they hadn't felt the stabbing freeze so viscerally that time, in fact the cold back in the living world had been more draining.

"We've found someone with answers," Bronach said, there was an eagerness about her, "but we have a bit of a journey ahead of us, and we've got a couple of friends to aid us. Are you ready?"

The three of them didn't even have to look at each other before nodding, this is what they'd come to do. Outside they found their new companions waiting; a young man with a sword strapped to his belt, he looked perfectly ordinary apart from one distinctive feature. He possessed a singular eye right in the centre of his forehead. It was difficult not to stare, but Maeve managed to rip her gaze away to take in their other new addition. A tall, wiry woman with grey skin and long, talon-like fingers. It didn't appear she needed a sword, she was a weapon unto herself.

"These are friends of ours and part of the cause, they're here to protect us tonight." Aiden pointed to Bronach's sliced shoulder and his own wrapped arm, still healing from their last fight, "Lea," He said gesturing to the tall woman, "and Bal." Now to the young man.

They both inclined their heads, saying nothing. Without another word they set off, not wanting to delay any more than they had to. In contrast to the frigid conditions they had come from, the Otherworld's night was positively temperate, leaving Maeve to question whether the seasons here worked differently, or if they had the same type of weather system at all. Come to think of it, they hadn't encountered rain yet, which was rather unusual coming from Ireland, on which any given day there was a fifty-fifty chance it would pour down.

They made their way through a copse of trees, coming to a monumental cliff face with a thin, jagged crack that looked to run all the way to the top and out of their sight. The crescent moon picked out specular highlights on the surface, making the crack a silvery scar in the dark rock. Lea led the way, easily fitting herself between the small gap in the monstrous mountainside despite her tall frame. They followed her lead with Bal taking the rear.

The passage was barely shoulder width at its widest, containing parts where they had to turn their bodies and sidle along, shuffling in single file. If it weren't for Lea it would have been impossible to see, but she had done something to make one of her hands glow, giving off a faint bluish light that kept them from feeling completely trapped. Up ahead, Maeve could make out a long vertical line in the darkness, the exit. With one last push, the passage narrowed so much Maeve had to suck herself in and give a massive heave, they were out of the gloom.

They stepped out into a swampy glade, the Otherworld's geography was all over the place. Maeve was sure a location like this didn't exist back home, maybe once upon a time but not now. Lea's glowing hand made the shadows around them stretch and slither all over, vines and branches catching the light, creating the illusion of movement. She shook her hand and the glow went with it, leaving their path illuminated by the shafts of moonlight breaking through the overhead cover.

As they walked the wet earth compacted beneath them, their footsteps mushy and awkward. For a swamp it was eerily quiet. There were no crickets or frogs chirping like she had heard in so many movies where a protagonist had stumbled into an exotic environment. There was the occasional bird squawking in the distance, but that only served to break up the uneven rhythm of their march. Lea's footsteps, however, didn't make a sound as she stepped carefully over fallen branches, vines and under hanging moss with an ease that made Maeve both enraptured and envious. Not of her freakish proportions, but her graceful, almost dance-like movements through the challenging terrain. She was a ghost moving serenely through the forest, leaving no disturbance in her wake. Within that relaxed demeanour, though, there was a keen alertness as her head darted to either side, ever watching. Obviously picking up things beyond what Maeve's dull human senses could perceive. Lea would stop, hold her hand out in front of her, Maeve observed her lips moving as she did this, and then after a few seconds she would start walking again.

"Is she a witch or something?" Oisin whispered into Maeve's ear.

Lea snapped her head back at him. Evidently, whatever she was, her hearing was impeccable. He fell back into line and didn't talk for the rest of their trek that took them deeper into the swampy territory. They had to be coming up on their destination soon, it was getting trickier to walk, and they couldn't keep going forever. Thankfully this was the case. The branches and vines thinned out to form a glade amongst the trees.

In the centre stood a wooden cabin similar to the

buildings surrounding Aiden and Bronach's hut. It looked to be an old construction, centuries old, but well maintained. Smoke rose from a fire within, causing the windows to radiate warm, orange light. With the moonbeams filling the clearing and their peculiar surroundings, it gave the spot a fairytale-ish quality of the Grimm kind. Maeve just hoped the house wasn't crafted from gingerbread.

As they approached the cabin, Lea's edgy vigilance fell away, allowing Maeve to relax as well. Before they got to the front step the door opened to a hooded figure, standing semi-silhouetted in the fire glow.

"I see you've brought some friends with you." They said in a smooth voice, waving a hand over the group.

"It's good to see you again, Florence, we've come to seek your help and advice." Lea replied, her voice was surprisingly sweet, completely at odds with her appearance.

Florence gestured for them to enter, stepping aside as they gathered in the surprisingly spacious room. It was teeming with various jars, bowls and crystals, things hung from the ceiling, some inanimate and others that used to be animated. Maeve ducked under what looked like a dried out relative of one of the birds she'd heard squawking earlier. The air in the cabin was richly spiced with smells that Maeve could scarcely begin to identify; they weren't unpleasant, but she was happy to let the source of the odours remain a mystery for the time being. Florence sat on a stool close to the fire as the rest of them procured their own sitting space.

She pulled her hood down, revealing herself to be much younger than Maeve had anticipated, late twenties early thirties at most. Her white skin and red hair made a striking combination in conjunction with the patterns of licking flames illuminating her petite features.

"So, how can I help or advise?" She said, businesslike.

Lea gave the floor to Bronach, "Thank you for meeting us, Florence. We've come about a curse mark."

"Oh?" She leaned forward.

"Yes, a fear gorta placed it on young Oisin here, we presume it was sent by William de Meath." Florence fixed her gaze on Oisin who blushed, failing to meet her eyes, "We want to know if there is a way to remove it."

Florence gave a sniff, "Oh, there's always a way to remove these things. It just depends on what price you're willing to pay. Hand please." She stuck her palm out to Oisin.

He looked to Bronach, then Maeve and slowly extended his bandaged hand. In one deft movement Florence undid the wrappings, tutting.

"This won't do. Did you maul your own hand?" She reached into her robe and pulled out a small jar of what looked to be salve. Whispering a few words, she began rubbing it firmly into his palm. His face twitched as she pressed into the scratches, and he convulsed in pain as an effervescent fizzing emanated from the salve. He tried pulling away, but she held him effortlessly in place. Was everyone in the Otherworld ridiculously strong? Maeve and Lorcan stood to their feet but, just as quickly as he had started, Oisin stopped squirming and was looking in astonishment at his palm. Florence wiped the excess off with a small cloth, revealing perfectly healed skin. They sat themselves back down, aghast at what they had just witnessed.

"There. Now I can get a much better look."

She tilted his palm towards the fire, bringing the black mark into stark relief. Lea and Bal leaned in to get a look at it. It was the first time Maeve had gotten time to study it properly. In the fire light it almost seemed to writhe on his skin, little thin tendrils following the tributary lines in his hand.

"Hmmm, yes." Florence said languidly, "I see - quite nasty." Her nose was almost touching his palm at this point.

"Well, can you help us?" Bronach said, anxiety evident in her voice.

Florence sat back in her seat, "I'm afraid this is far beyond my capabilities. It's a powerfully set curse."

Oisin slumped and Bronach let out a shaky sigh, "I was

afraid you'd say that." Her eyes were beginning to glisten.

Their reactions confirmed what Maeve had been suspecting, the 'bad luck' from this mark was far more serious than Oisin had been letting on. Had Lorcan known it too? She looked over to his face, but he wasn't looking up to meet her. That said it all.

"Now, now." Florence interrupted their ruminations, "I said it was far beyond *my* capabilities, I didn't say there was nothing that couldn't be done."

"What can we do?" Aiden said urgently.

She looked into the fire, "Tell me, what do you know of Sliabh Laoch?"

The ensuing silence was all the answer she needed.

Sliabh Laoch, Florence explained, was a legendary mountain that housed the greatest heroes in Irish History. Its name literally translated to 'Hero's Mountain'. Normally Maeve would have been more than happy to hear some history, but she was impatient for Florence to get to the part where they could help Oisin. She'd have to exercise some patience because it didn't look like this woman was in any rush to get through her preamble.

"At Sliabh Laoch's summit, there sits the resting chamber of one of Ireand's greatest legends, Fionn mac Cumhaill, surrounded by his loyal warriors. It is in this chamber where you will find what you need to rid Oisin of his predicament. Fionn was said to have never died, but remains sleeping and ready to spring into action should Ireland ever be in need."

If it was a Snow White kind of situation, which one of them would have to do the kissing?

"So, we find this Fionn guy, and we wake him up?" Lorcan interrupted Florence.

She stared at him, narrowed her eyes and then gave him a nasty smirk, "*This Fionn guy*, is not your goal. You are seeking one of his most trusted allies, his Fianna. I can do nothing for your friend here but one of their weapons can, the Gáe Dearg, belonging to Diarmuid Ua Duibhne. Fionn's greatest betrayer and greatest protector."

"Okay," Oisin began, "So how do we get the 'Gáe Dearg' and what does it look like?"

"It's in the name." Maeve said, "It means 'red spear'."

"Quite right, child" Florence inclined her head, "As for *how* you obtain the spear…" She looked to Lea.

"Sliabh Laoch is nearly impossible to get to from here." Lea said, "In years gone by it would have been simple, but now it's a treacherous journey. Especially for you." She looked to the three of them, her eyes hard and frank.

They looked back at her, hoping she would offer something else or elaborate a little, but that was it. Was this what they had come here for? To be told that they just had to live with it, or die with it? No, that wouldn't be the ending.

"Then we'll go there." Maeve said.

"You'll die." Lea replied.

"You said it was *nearly* impossible, which implies there's a chance that we can make it. Just tell us how, and we'll get there."

"It's very brave of you to volunteer your life and the lives of your comrades but -"

"She's not volunteering anything." Lorcan said, "We're more than willing to go - I'm more than willing to help."

"As heart-warming as it is to see the youth so eager to throw their lives away for a good cause, there is another method for getting to Sliabh Laoch." Florence said, cutting through the heightened emotions.

She sat back, almost lounging off the stool, clearly this was just another day for her; no high stakes. It didn't look like she got visitors very often, but she wasn't intimidated by their foreign presence.

"Now, I don't know the specifics of it, but I'm assuming you've entered this world through a place of power?" She scanned their faces.

Had they?

"The fort, Dún Dubh." Lorcan answered Florence.

"Ah, so that's how they sneaked you in. Clever." She looked to Aiden and Bronach, "You might have gathered then that Dún Dubh might not be the only entryway into the Otherworld, there are others scattered about."

She got up and sauntered to one of her many shelves, pulled down a rolled up piece of parchment paper and laid it out on her workbench. It was a map of Ireland, at least that's what Maeve assumed it to be. The general shape was there, but there were bulges that didn't correlate to anywhere she knew and the proportions were way off. There were points on the map indicating where these entry points were. It was like Lorcan had alluded to when he'd first told her of the Otherworld, and what she'd inferred from her own research; there were other ways of getting through the barrier, other places. She would feel vindicated if it wasn't such a serious matter and if she didn't feel so lied to by her so-called friends.

Florence ran her slender finger along the map, settling on a point located on the west coast of the island.

"Here is where you'll need to go. You'll need to find the corresponding location in your world and cross over from there."

They examined where she had indicated, "That looks like Sligo." Maeve said.

"That's where the mountain is said to be in the legends." Bronach chimed in, looking over their shoulders, "Although no-one has been for years."

Okay, they had an idea about where they needed to go, but there was one massive, gaping hole in that plan.

"How do we cross over?" Maeve asked.

Florence was one step ahead. She held out her empty palm and passed her other hand over it in a flowing motion. No longer was it empty. The firelight glinted off of a small blade that looked to be made of green glass, and of simple construction with unassuming dimensions. There were small symbols etched into the handle that Maeve couldn't identify, but they looked like ancient Celtic writings. Florence then produced a matching leather sheath, slotting the dagger into it.

"This is your key back to our world but, be warned, it is a one time key. It will get you here and back, and then it will return to me." She handed the dagger to Lorcan, "When at a place of power plunge the dagger into the air in front of you, and it will stick like you've torn into the very fabric of the world. Use it to create a tear in the veil and step through. Do the same when you want to come back. Understand?"

He nodded and took the dagger, tucking it into his coat pocket. Florence rolled her parchment back up and placed it onto the shelf. There didn't seem much more to say. They all stood, Lea handing her something as payment, Maeve didn't see what it was exactly, but she thought she caught a faint tonal ringing from it. Saying their goodbyes, they stepped out into the night.

"One more thing." Florence called after them, "Do not linger on the mountain. Fionn and his fianna may sleep, but restless creatures roam its hidden paths."

With that the cabin's orange glow faded back into the darkness, and they entered the thick overgrowth of the swamp.

Bal led the way this time, he hadn't said a single word during this whole trip, it was like he wanted to go as unnoticed as possible. Arriving at the split in the cliff face again, Maeve squeezed herself into the narrow gap, following his lead. Lea reignited her hand with the blue-ish light, helping them avoid jutting rocks at head level.

They made quick progress through the pass; it always felt shorter retreading already-walked paths. Maeve thought she might have imagined it, but she could have sworn a tremor moved through the mountain. Only lasted an instant, she put it down to her tired body and mind. But there it was again, it was unlikely she'd imagined it a second time, and she wasn't the only one who'd felt it. Bal stopped moving.

"Quiet." Lea hissed urgently, scrubbing out the light.

They froze, as still and quiet as they could, trapped in the blackness between mountains. The tremor intensified in severity until it became an audible rumbling through the rock and stone around them. Was this an earthquake? If so, would they be buried here, never to be found? She thought of their families and how they'd be left wondering what had happened to them back in the living world. Would their bodies even rot here, or would they be preserved and entombed? As the noise rose, Maeve began to realise that the rumbling was not coming from the rock or ground, not all of it anyway. There was an organic origin to that sound.

The moon shone through in a tiny crack of light above them. However, it was being broken up by a shape moving across it. Something huge. Something that was almost the size of the mountain itself. It wound across the craggy line of light, it's body testing and turning as it shook the very earth beneath. Dust fell around them and the movement dislodged loose rocks and pebbles. The gap was so small that any larger rock would have become stuck on its descent towards their craniums.

As it passed the shaking quietened and stillness returned to the mountain. Maeve let out a cough she'd been holding in as she cleared dust from her lungs, and they continued to creep along the passage more hastily than before. Exiting back into the open they searched for the source of the disruption, but there was nothing to be seen. The only evidence was a layer of dust and a few scattered boulders that had evidently plummeted from high up, seeing as they were coated in snow and ice. One of the boulders had managed to fall on a tree, snapping it clean in half. Perhaps they were lucky they'd been inside the mountain when it journeyed past.

They set off at a brisk pace, not wanting to encounter whatever that was. Even Bal had a look of concern, as far as she could tell from his single eye, although he remained mute. Returning to Dún Dubh without incident, Bal and Lea stood watch as they entered.

"We'll do our part to help on this end in any way we can." Aiden assured them.

"We'll see if we can dig up the name of the place you need to go, it wasn't on Florence's map." Bronach added.

"Thanks." Oisin said.

To Maeve, he didn't sound overly thankful.

The chamber vanished around them, and they were back in the open air. Maeve steadied herself against one of the crumbling walls, breathing hard. It was still a difficult feeling to get used to. Oisin ambled over to check on her, but she pulled away.

"What's wro-"

"Don't even!" She said, "Don't you even - bad luck? Is that what it is? Because they made it sound an awful lot worse, and you knew it!"

Oisin didn't say a word. Maeve didn't want to hear it anyway.

"You know what, I'm bloody done with both of you. Until you wise up and start trusting me and treating me like an adult, and not some child you have to protect."

"You lied to me about all this, remember?" Oisin retorted.

"Yeah! I thought we were past all that! That we were all in this together? If we start lying now, where do we stop? This is life or death - literally!"

Maeve spun on her heels and marched out into the clearing. She could hear them both running after her.

"Maeve, wait!" Oisin cried.

"What? What is it?" She turned, standing on her tiptoes to match his height.

"I - I just wanted to -"

"Treat me like a wee girl? Guess what, Oisin, I can handle it. I've been handling it, and I'm going to handle it. Don't follow me."

With that she stormed down the hillside and power

walked to her house, creeping in without disturbing her dad. As far as he was concerned she'd been there all night. Her alarm went off not long after she'd climbed into bed. Good, she probably wouldn't have been able to sleep anyway.

*     *     *     *     *     *

Their subsequent team gatherings were conducted with the utmost professionalism. Maeve distanced herself from the two boys, treating it all like some board meeting that she couldn't wait to get away from. Lorcan watched her eyes light up every time they discussed exploring a new part of the Otherworld; she was still very much engaged in the endeavour. Not a bit of him doubted that she'd go through hell and back to cure Oisin, but the cold shoulder was very much in effect. *Note to self, don't get involved in another couple's lies,* he thought as the awkward atmosphere flared when Oisin asked if she'd like to do anything after the meeting.

"Can't, sorry, I'm still grounded." She said.

"It's been over a week."

"What can I say, he doesn't trust me." With that she left the study hall.

It was just Lorcan and Oisin now. Actually, it had been mostly just the two of them for a solid week now. Whatever negative effects it was having on their group dynamic, Maeve's absence meant the two boys had started to bond. They were almost friends.

"I didn't think she could hold a grudge like that." Oisin sighed, turning back to their crudely drawn map of Sligo.

"I'm sure she'll cool down, I think it's a combination of things really." Lorcan marked off another possible monument they could hit in their quest for the place of power.

"Oh? What?"

"Think about it, wouldn't you be super pissed if she lied to your face about being in imminent danger of dying?"

"Thanks." Oisin said with a look that read *'really?'*.

"I just meant to say, you'd want to know, and the fact that she didn't feel comfortable telling you would show a real lack of trust on her part. I can imagine you in particular taking that badly. And because I joined in on it after we went to the Otherworld alone, it looked pretty shady. Like we were taking away her agency or something after she'd helped so much."

Oisin stared at the map blankly, "Good summary. I don't think I'd act like that but - ugh, I don't know." He said frustrated, "When did you become so adept at reading social situations?"

"I've always been good at reading them. Just not responding to them." Lately, however, Lorcan was becoming more practised and was starting to master the craft.

In their subsequent meetings they agreed that they couldn't go to Sligo until their Christmas break, which was fast approaching. In the meantime Oisin would have to look over his shoulder and triple check every time he crossed the road. Misfortune could come in many forms. They also set up an hourly messaging system so that they knew he was alright even if they were apart. Overkill? They didn't think so. These were supernatural forces they were dealing with here. By Friday, they had the plan in place and had cleared a New Year's getaway with all of their respective families; they'd even booked a B&B in a central location that would allow them to drive to the various sites. They would strike out radially and see if they couldn't find a new way into the Otherworld.

"Are we done?" Maeve said, standing. It looked like *she* was done.

"I guess, but it's the weekend, want to do anything tonight?" Oisin suggested again.

"Can't."

"Grounded?"

"Yep."

"Tomorrow?"

"Can't." She grabbed her books and shoved them in her bag, "Anyway, make sure to message me, okay? I worry when you forget."

Her face softened for just a moment, rehardening when she remembered to be angry. Lorcan wondered when she'd let it go. She had a lot of pride, he'd give her that.

"I'll remember." He gave her a smile and waved goodbye.

She returned the wave and almost returned the smile before walking away.

Oisin looked depressed. That was the only way Lorcan could think of describing that expression on his face and slump in his body. The wear was beginning to show in the rings that were forming under his eyes. They packed their papers away, no point in lingering if there were no more plans to be made.

"Lorcan?" Oisin said before they parted, "Can I ask you a favour?"

*     *     *     *     *     *

Lorcan walked back to Cara's alone. It had been a while since he'd been to Dún Dubh on his own. It felt way too lonely without the others. Taking out his phone, he grinned as he typed.

*Mission accomplished. They agreed, all set!*

The reply came back a few seconds later, he must have been waiting for that all night.

**OMG! Thanks dude!**

Lorcan still wasn't accustomed to being called 'dude' but there were worse names he could think of. At least now this might help their group get back into their groove, and he could continue playing happy family. Win-win.

# 24.

Maeve packed the necessities for their trip to the Otherworld, Lorcan had received word from his parents that they must come on a particular date, and that date happened to fall towards the start of their Christmas holidays. Maeve still had some shopping to do, but there was still a few days to go, so she could spare the time. Oisin had been very specific about what type of things she should bring, it looked like the contents of a picnic basket. Flask? Check. Sandwiches? Check. Binoculars? Check. Maybe it was a picnic with a side of birdwatching. She'd find out soon enough.

Oisin waited at her gate by himself. Apparently Lorcan had gone on ahead and was waiting for them up there. Who knew why, they were fond of not filling her in on the pertinent details.

They made awkward small talk as they walked in the predawn murk. Maeve knew that she was being a little harsh on the boys, particularly Oisin, but that lie had hurt. It was bloody serious, she needed to know these things and if they weren't going to keep her in the loop, she'd keep them at a safe distance. There was a powerful urge to just say that she was sorry, and they could go back to being normal, but what did she have to be sorry for? She didn't recall them apologising. A powerful but short urge.

They summited the hill, it was pretty easy going now as she'd kept up her running (by herself). They went to the chamber but Lorcan was nowhere to be seen. She glanced around to Oisin, confused. He smiled apologetically.

"Sorry, Maeve. Just one more white lie."

He took her hand, the world spun around her, and suddenly they faced Bronach and Aiden. What the hell was going on?

"We'll leave you two alone." Bronach said wryly, before she and Aiden walked out and left them alone.

Maeve only had time to look confuddled before Oisin said, "Come on, this is time sensitive."

He pulled her gently towards the exit. She snapped her hand away a little harder than she meant to, "It's okay." She said, "I can walk on my own."

Oisin shrugged, and she followed him out of the fort. They made their way along a ridge to the side of Dún Dubh until they'd reached an open hillside that overlooked the landscape below. Maeve could see people had gathered in the valley and were chattering excitedly, their voices carried like murmurs on the wind.

"What's going on?" She asked, but Oisin had started unpacking and laying things out.

She did so too, all the time wondering what he was up to and what he had planned. With their blankets laid out they sat down, and he unscrewed a flask.

"Cuppa?" He poured a cup of hot tea, handing it to her, "There, we're all set to watch it."

"Watch what?" She snapped, smelling the notes of ginger and citrus from her steaming mug.

Oisin pointed to the crowd below. A man stood on a small mound not much taller than himself, elevating him above the rest. Shirtless from the waist up, his muscular torso was decorated in an intricate array of criss-crossing, richly coloured tattoos. In one hand he held a long spear with a glowing, golden head in the shape of a leaf blade. As he took his place, the persistent chattering died, and he began speaking. Maeve failed to comprehend what he was saying, guessing it must be some form of ancient Irish; she doubted that most of the gathering understood it either. The words, however, sounded powerful and his voice rang throughout the hills as he spoke, she recognised intrinsically that this was an important ritual.

The man let out a cry and the congregation followed suit, their bass, tenor and alto notes melding into one cohesive choir. He heaved the spear above his head and turned his back on them. Taking aim, and with an almighty throw, the spear hurtled its ways towards the horizon. The speed was unreal as it glimmered across the land like a golden bullet from a high-powered rifle. It shimmered out of view, exploding in a flash mere seconds later, and the first hints of the sun's rays began to slink their way over the scenery. The beams reached slowly to the dark corners of mountains and trees, bathing the world in its golden brilliance. The tattooed man threw his arms out, inviting the sun's warmth to wash over him. As it did, he and his congregation began to sing a song that, all at once, sounded triumphant and mournful.

Their voices ebbed and flowed with the lines of the tune, crescendoing and diminishing. Maeve closed her eyes, allowing the melody to create whatever images it wanted behind her eyelids. She didn't need to understand what they were saying, it guided her on a journey through the darkness, and the slow inexorable ending of life as it weaved its tale. Every beginning has an end; the thesis of the piece. The last verse lifted her up, filling her mind with a light and hope she'd never experienced from music before. This ceremony marked a beginning. She opened her eyes as the final notes faded, the valley falling back into natural silence as the gathering allowed the morning heat to envelop them. Tears traced cooling paths down Maeve's cheeks; she allowed them to remain.

"Thank you." She said, taking the first sip of her tea, "That was beautiful."

"It's the Winter Solstice. They're celebrating the turning of the days, a return to lighter times. I thought you'd like it." Tears shone on his cheeks too.

They let the scene play out below them. Some of the

people continued to bask in the sunlight, while others talked amongst themselves, and others still made their way out of the valley. Oisin topped up their cups.

"I'm sorry." He said eventually.

"I know you are." She didn't sound reproachful or hurt, Maeve was just glad they were having this conversation - and this moment, "How come you didn't tell me?"

"It's like you said, I wasn't trusting you enough to handle it... and I suppose I just wanted it to be less serious than it was, y'know?"

"I do. We're in this together though, and I need to know everything that's going on, otherwise I can't help you."

Oisin nodded solemnly, looking out onto the horizon, "I was scared. No, I *am* scared." Maeve could hear a quiver in his voice, "I'm fucking terrified, Maeve. I've spent the past two months being terrified of everything and pretending I'm not."

This wasn't like his breakdown in the kitchen, this was Oisin opening up to her at last. The armour was coming off. She put an arm around him, resting her head on his shoulder.

"You think I'm not scared?" She said, "It's okay to be human."

"Yeah, but you're brave."

"No I'm not."

"Okay, you're psychotic then."

"You've got me there."

They sat there together, allowing the rising sun to melt away the lingering cold, along with any negative feelings they'd been harbouring.

"Who thought this'd be such a great place for a picnic." Maeve said munching on one of the sandwiches she had made.

"I know, you could say it's *out of this world*." Oisin waggled his eyebrows.

"Oh my god, stop!" She managed through a mouthful of bread and ham.

"You know you missed the cringe." He said, "Serious question though." He set his tea and sandwiches down, turning his body towards her, "Why are you dragging your feet on the university applications?"

Maeve sighed an exasperated sigh. This again?

"Why are you asking me this? You've got yours all sorted out, so you should be happy enough. I'll get mine sorted when I feel like it." There was much to add beyond that.

Oisin dipped his head and looked away, "Alright, full disclosure - I haven't done mine yet."

"Huh? I thought you'd applied to architecture in a few places. What, did you get rejected?"

"You can't get rejected if you don't apply. I was waiting for you to make your choices so that -"

Though warm light illuminated his face, Maeve saw it wasn't the sun that was making him red.

""So that' what?" She prompted.

"I could know which university I should pick." He was looking anywhere but her face.

"What? You were going to make that choice based on where I went?"

"I can do Architecture anywhere, it's not an uncommon degree. I just wanted to do it wherever you'd be."

She looked at Oisin then, the candidness and embarrassment only serving to make him more adorable. Had he really been waiting on Maeve to make her choice? She saw now why he'd been pressing the issue, wanting to know where he was headed as well.

"You can't make life decisions based on what someone else wants to do. Especially not at our age." She said, placing her hand on his.

"I know." He leaned on his elbow, "It's just, we're a team, now more than ever, and we should be together. Who else am I going to talk to about being cursed by a spirit from the Otherworld with? That's not the best introduction at uni, is it?"

"I don't know, I hear you artsy kids are pretty damn weird."

"I'd be more worried if they believed me." The corners of his mouth turned up, "So, what about it, are you going to apply?"

"We'll see." She said, kissing him.

"Let me know." Oisin took a big bite of the sandwich, screwing up his face, "Ever heard of butter?" He took a gulp of tea.

"You are so annoying."

They sat until the crowd had dissipated and their picnic had all but gone. Aiden and Bronach were waiting for them back at the fort, ready to send them home. They must have been watching the ritual nearby.

"Did you enjoy it?" Bronach asked.

"It was amazing." Maeve said, "Thanks for letting us see it."

"This is your world now too." Aiden said.

They walked to the central chamber, bracing for the cold that would inevitably rack their bodies. The murkiness of the interior was in stark contrast to the brilliant light that streamed into the parapet windows above

"You're all ready for your trip to Sligo after Christmas?" Bronach said.

"Huh?" Maeve didn't remember telling them anything about their trip.

"Oh, Lorcan told us when he was here helping us organise the viewing for you. He's very hopeful."

"Yeah, we're all set." Maeve nodded.

Aiden and Bronach stood there as if waiting for more details, but neither Maeve nor Oisin volunteered any more information.

"Okay, well, enjoy your trip. We've never been to that part, so we can't help much." Bronach said after a beat.

"We will, and thanks for your help so far." Oisin said, giving them a small bow in lieu of a handshake.

They were back in the living world in an instant, shivering and rubbing their arms to create some friction heat.

They didn't have the luxury of sunlight here, it was cloudy and tiny dew drops clung to every available surface. Funny how the afterlife seemed far more vibrant and alive most of the time.

"Plans?" Oisin said as they started downwards.

"I have to get some Christmas presents, so I'm going shopping in town."

"I'll tag along, if that's okay?"

"Fine by me."

Oisin's was one of the presents she still had to get, but that could wait. She was happy to be spending time with him again.

# 25.

Lorcan awoke to excited knocking on his bedroom door. What time was it? The door swung open, hallway light spilling into his dark room. Cara wore a red and green themed dressing gown and was covering her eyes.

"Wakey, wakey! Santa's been to see us! I want you down in two minutes."

She backed out of the doorway, banging straight into the frame.

"You don't have to cover your eyes, I'm decent." Lorcan groaned.

"I don't know what young men get up to, but I'm not walking in on anything I don't want to see." She felt her way out of the room and left him to get ready.

The holiday season was the perfect time for Cara. It allowed her to be flamboyant and over the top without seeming weird, she could just call it "holiday cheer" and people would accept it. She didn't go overboard and turn her house into a light show, they were in the country, so what would be the point in that? No, she settled for wearing antlers when out shopping and dressing in kitsch knitted jumpers with garish colour combos. It was fine, she claimed, all the kids were doing it. The kids were not doing it.

Lorcan lumbered down the stairs and into the kitchen. Cara had prepared a breakfast of smoked salmon, eggs and toast. It was a bit much for first thing in the morning but, he had to admit, it was pretty delicious. After they'd imbibed their Christmas breakfast, it was time to open some presents. Sitting next to the tree, Cara handed him gifts to unwrap, she had a particular order that they had to be opened in.

There wasn't a cornucopia of gifts for him, he wasn't exactly a well established member of the community yet, but there were a few. He opened a box with a card attached:

*To Lorcan,*

*Maeve wanted to give you a shoebox full of exotic teas because she knows your tastes are basic, but I talked her out of it. Please take this gift as permission to call at her house and wake her at 6am EVERY MORNING, she'll thank you in the long run.*

*Yours sincerely and forever,*

*Oisin*

*xoxoxo*

Lorcan sniggered as he read the first message. Underneath it was another:

*My dearest Lorcan,*

*Thou must disregard the above transcription, 'tis but the ravings of a lunatic. One hopes you enjoy yonder contents of this package, and get goodly use from these fine… ummmm, runners. I can't write like this anymore! Feck what Oisin wrote, you wake me at 6am every morning, and you'll live to regret it!*

*Merry Xmas!*

*Your correspondent,*

*Maeve*

*xxxxx*

Lorcan tore the brightly coloured paper to reveal a shoebox. Maeve and Oisin had pooled their money to buy him a joint present, a pair of trail running shoes. They were a good pair too, his size and everything. He didn't recall ever telling them his shoe size, but Maeve had subtle ways of extracting information, or maybe she'd made an educated guess. Who knew.

The next few presents were the usual parade of socks, aftershave and the autobiography of whatever celebrity had released their tragic life story, that you just 'had to read', in time to cash in on the Christmas rush. Cara had bought him a designer hiking jacket that truly looked and felt good to wear. The soft faux fur collar would certainly be warm on those cold mornings or nights, and the discreet reflective strips would help if he ever fell and got stuck on an outcropping in need of a search and rescue team. Cara was ever morbid in her practicality.

"Thanks! I really like it, it's just what I needed. I'm sure Maeve will be jealous." He said enthusiastically.

Lorcan always had a hard time sounding genuinely grateful for things, so he put extra effort into making sure people knew he appreciated their gifts. He thought it sounded terribly fake, but Cara was smiling and clapping her hands together, relieved he liked the jacket. When she opened his present, a wooden plaque with the Delaney coat of arms on it, plus a framed certificate to hang on the wall, she gasped. Being into family history it seemed like something she would go for. It was a typically over the top reaction from her, but it was enjoyable seeing her so animated over the gift.

That was all of the presents unwrapped, now for the cleanup. He picked up the scraps of paper lying everywhere and saw Cara lean behind the sofa to grab something. She emerged with an envelope, holding it out for Lorcan to take.

"What's this?" He said.

"An invisibility cloak." She raised a sarcastic eyebrow, "Open it and see."

He took the envelope and flipped it open. There was a typed letter inside, no - it was a bank statement in his name. He looked at the balance, it was his turn to gasp.

"Cara - are you - is this right?"

"It is. I managed to sell your parents' house and I thought it only right that the money go to their son." She explained, "I took my seller's commission of course, but you deserve it. This way, you can choose what you want to do with your life. Go to uni, take a gap year and travel. Just don't be spending it on drink, drugs and rock'n'roll, okay?"

He stared blankly and then gave Cara the biggest hug he could muster. He found it hard to verbalise, but perhaps this might communicate how he felt. It seemed to work, she squeezed back and there was a catch in her throat when she spoke.

"You're welcome, pet."

# 26.

Lorcan slid into the back seat of the car with Maeve taking her place as the front passenger. Oisin was busy assuring his dad that he would indeed take care on the road and there'd be no drink-driving or speeding. He was the only one out of the three that had a driver's licence, and the responsible air to convince his parents that their car would be safe with them.

"What do you need all those tools for?" His dad inquired.

"Fishing, da! I told you, me and Lorcan are going to do a bit of fishing while we're down there. I'll see you when we get back." He said, closing the boot and making his way to the front of the car.

His mum embraced him, giving him a quick peck on the cheek.

"Be careful, love, and watch your hand okay?" She said, indicating to his bandage.

"I will." He climbed into the driver's seat and keyed the ignition, the car thrummed to life, but his dad knocked on the window.

Oisin sighed and rolled it down, allowing his dad to lean on the car door and stick his head in, "I just wanted to say, enjoy your trip, be responsible. And, you," He pointed to Maeve, "take care of these two hallions, alright?"

Maeve grimaced exaggeratedly, "That's a tall order! But, I'll try."

"There's a good girl, see you all in a few days!"

With that, Oisin rolled up the window, switched on the radio, the news anchor's voice blaring out.

*Unrest continues as droughts sweep Northern Africa and the surrounding Mediterranean region. The Egyptian president had this to say -*

"Ugh, that's the millionth time I've heard that this week."

Oisin tuned away from the news to a more upbeat music station, and they set off on their road trip. It wasn't like the road trip montages that Lorcan had seen in movies so often, with a bunch of American teenagers going on a cross-country voyage. This was more following backroads and dual carriageways, with a couple of stops to pee and a snack break thrown in. Still, they tried to make the most of it. They cycled through a couple of different playlists and stopped for a few photos. The further south they went, the sunnier it seemed to become despite the small size of the island. The change of scenery helped them forget about what they had actually set out to do until they neared their destination, then it began to feel more like work again.

They arrived at the B&B after losing their way on some country lanes, phone signals had cut out and none of them were particularly skilled navigators. Greeting them were a couple of men who were 'so happy' to see them in a way that only people dedicated to maintaining their good reviews online can be happy to see someone. They showed the trio their rooms, Lorcan had his own whilst Maeve and Oisin shared a room, separate beds of course. All the usual awkward jokes were made that one makes when staying in another couple's house, they received their breakfast timetables and little maps to local points of interest. They already knew where they would be going, thank you very much.

By the time they got settled and unpacked everything they wanted to unpack, it was just past midday. Lorcan knocked on Maeve and Oisin's door, they probably weren't doing anything, but he didn't want to assume. Oisin answered, already dressed and ready for adventure, Maeve appeared behind him looking just as eager to go. Rushing to the car, they punched the first address into their map.

"Let's go!" Maeve said, pointing like a general commanding the troops.

Lorcan felt the glass knife concealed by his jacket's inner pocket, he hoped they didn't have any security searches at these places. There'd be a lot of explaining.

He needn't have worried, their first destination was a castle that would normally have been filled with tourists. Hardly desolate, but it was cold and people were probably recovering from the Christmas boozing or getting ready for some New Year's boozing. It didn't have quite the right vibe to them, however, they found a private spot without any cameras watching and Lorcan took out the knife. He waved it around in the air with vague stabbing motions. If there were security cameras it would look like he was doing some uncoordinated martial arts kata. He felt dumb waving it about, to no avail. He was unsure what he was supposed to feel, but they agreed that this location was a bust. Onto the next sightseeing spot.

They hit up two more tourist attractions which were both flops. It might have been their imagination, but they felt like they had become attuned to the feeling of a place of power, having spent time at Dún Dubh and in the Otherworld. These locations just weren't cutting the mustard

"It's too commercial." Lorcan said over dinner.

They had called into a pub for some homely food after an unsuccessful first day. He hadn't expected to hit the bullseye right away, but it would've been nice.

"I feel like we need to get out of the city and into the rural areas, like back home."

"I agree." Oisin said, stuffing his mouth with a mammoth piece of fried fish.

"Okay, we'll start looking at castles and forts in the country tomorrow. There's plenty to choose from." Maeve searched on her phone.

That filled Lorcan with mixed emotions. On the one hand, they had plenty of options, on the other, plenty more opportunities to strike out. Would they come close to hitting upon the right spot?

His fears were well-founded when they had another failure of a day and were no further along in finding their way into the Otherworld. It seemed that even the rural sites weren't suitable locations for the worlds to intersect. What were the prerequisites? They'd come here under the pretence of a holiday, it was anything but. They all slumped to bed that night defeated. Lorcan hoped that tomorrow might bring about more fruitful results - the sinking feeling in his gut told him otherwise.

*    *    *    *    *    *

"I think we're going about this all wrong." Maeve said over breakfast.

Apparently she'd been struggling to sleep and had a brainwave in her knackered state. Lorcan was open to any suggestion at this point.

"Sliabh Laoch means 'Hero's Mountain', yeah? Well then, instead of looking for an entryway into the Otherworld through tombs or castles, why not go straight to the source?"

"You want us to climb up a bunch of mountains?" Lorcan snorted.

It wasn't that it was a bad idea, he was just in a bad mood from their so-far unproductive trip. Oisin had been strangely quiet throughout their time here.

"Nope." She whipped out her phone, "I want us to climb one mountain. If I'm right, this'll be *the* mountain."

She turned her screen, showing Lorcan an online article about a mountain called Benbulbin. He recognised the shape from pictures they'd found when booking their B&B. A unique landmark when contrasted with the surrounding geography, Benbulbin stuck up like it had thrust itself straight out of the flat plains on either side of it. It sported a remarkably flat top, as if sliced off neatly with a huge blade, covered in grass with precariously steep, jagged sides. In actuality its shape was as a result of glacier erosion during the ice age, but it was a striking feature nonetheless.

"It's cool looking but what makes it '*the* mountain'?" Lorcan handed the phone back.

Maeve reclined, a smug confidence spreading over her face, "I was doing some reading about famous mountains in Sligo and, of course, up pops Benbulbin. I thought, '*okay, this looks cool, I'll give it a read*' and, wouldn't you know it, Benbulbin is said to be the resting place of none other than Diarmuid ua Duibhne." She tucked her phone away triumphantly.

"Not bad." Lorcan said.

He had to admit, it was handy having someone so dedicated to research in the group. It was the best lead they'd come across so far. What was there to lose? Other than a bit of time walking.

"So, how long's the walk up?" He took a gulp of orange juice.

"Three and a half hours."

Lorcan almost did a spit take.

"Do we have the time?" He said, half-choking.

"What choice do we have?" Oisin said, speaking up for the first time this morning, "We've only got today and tonight. We're going home tomorrow, and this is the closest we've got to an actual lead."

He was right. Plus, it'd give Lorcan a good excuse to try out the trail shoes they'd bought him. They finished up their breakfast and drove to Benbulbin. The weather had made a turn from being pleasantly chilly yet sunny, to overcast with an icy wind that sent jerks of random shivers through them periodically. The mountain was as impressive as the pictures had suggested, but the summit was covered by a layer of thick, grey-white cloud today. Oisin parked up and they planned their route. Most likely they'd be passing other hikers along the way, but would need enough alone time to try out the knife; another potential bump in the road. As they readied to set off

Oisin stopped them, opening the car boot, he rifled through some folded blankets.

"Here."

He held out a switch knife and an extendable baton to Maeve and Lorcan.

"Really?" Lorcan said, "What are we going to do with those?"

"What does it look like?" Oisin nudged them towards the pair.

"It's better than nothing I suppose. I brought a gold ring, in case we needed it for repelling something, and I've got a snack bar if we encounter another fear gorta. Good thinking." Maeve took the switch knife and kissed Oisin.

Lorcan shook his head, taking the baton. What, were they going to bash one of the spirits to death? They'd been unable to do a single thing to the creature that broke into Oisin's house, so what was this flimsy baton going to do? Would he even have the presence of mind to do anything when the time came? When they had been attacked by the shapeshifting she-wolf, he had been pushed aside by his mother and sat on the sidelines. He doubted next time would be any different.

"Okay, let's go." Oisin said, tucking a small axe into his backpack.

The hike was moderately difficult, it would have been fairly easy had it been a dry day, but the dampness of the clouds, coupled with rolling mist made the rocks and grass slippery to walk on. He'd have to properly thank them for buying him a quality pair of shoes, they made otherwise tricky sections manageable. Pints were on him after this.

As they ascended higher into the clouds it was like walking into the Otherworld step by step. The mountain itself hummed with energy, they could sense that they were on the right track this time. Lorcan recalled one of Maeve's lectures on all the mountains worshipped by ancient cultures: Mount Olympus, Mount Fuji, the Sinai Mountains and so on. Whether this was the right one or not, mountains as a whole seemed to be hotbeds of spiritual energy.

They passed hikers making their pilgrimages before the clock struck midnight and a new year began. Awkwardly they would acknowledge each other as the groups passed with small nods and waves, and quick non-committal exchanges of, *"How're you doing?"*, *"That's some weather, eh?"*, *"What about ye?"* before moving on. Stopping for a water break, they took in the view. Clouds cleared at irregular intervals, allowing them to see the surrounding flatlands. Green stretched out beneath them right to the sea and golden rays peaked through the clouds, creating tiny patches of sunlit earth. This was a relief from the monotony of grey they'd been experiencing but, inevitably, another cloud would roll in and swallow them up, and they'd be back to trudging.

After a particularly unrelenting incline they reached the summit. There were a few tourists taking photos which Lorcan didn't see much point in, there was no scenery to be seen other than the drab greyish backdrop. After the tourists had left they took out the knife. Almost immediately Lorcan sensed something, he could tell that they'd found it. Maeve had done good. Every swish with the knife felt like he was moving his hand through water. Testing a few thrusting motions in different directions, he followed the path of most resistance until the knife stuck. It literally stuck in midair. On a whim he let go and watched it float, fixed in place. They gathered around the knife to observe it, and then he yanked it out of whatever it had lodged itself into. Checking once more to see if they were alone, Lorcan raised the knife above his head and stabbed, reverse grip, into the world itself. He pulled the knife downwards, ripping open a seam right before their eyes.

They stepped back to witness their handiwork in its full glory. It was as if they were looking at a high resolution display floating on invisible wires, and it was showing some nature documentary about a far off land. Compared to the grey clouds, the brightly lit landscape of the Otherworld looked extremely appealing. Oisin stepped forward, already having drawn his axe from his bag. When did he do that? Maeve followed him, lifting her feet over the rim of the portal and cautious not to touch the sides, who knew how sharp or dull those edges might be; better safe than sorry. Lorcan gave one last look to make sure no-one was watching and then slipped through.

Squinting at the sudden influx of light, his vision adjusted, and he was greeted with an awe-inspiring sight. The Benbulbin of the Otherworld was much, much taller than its counterpart in their world. They were twice, maybe three times as high as they had been. Oisin and Maeve had dared walk to the edge, looking out over the expanse of the sea. It had been farther away before, but now they stood at the precipice of a massive cliff with a violently crashing sea beneath, waves at least a dozen metres high. The smell of fresh, salty air filled their noses, each of them taking a moment to breathe it in.

Lorcan turned to find the scar he'd inflicted on the world had healed. He also found something else that hadn't been there before. Accompanying them on the summit was an enormous circular burial mound that towered over them. Its walls were constructed with massive, heavy interlocking patterns of stone and, unlike the rest of the mountain, its top was covered in overgrown grasses and trees. The entrance was a long wedge cut out of the circle, leading to a tall thin door, beyond which they could see only darkness.

"I was right." Maeve said.

Oisin passed between them, his axe readied, and strode towards the structure.

# 27.

As they approached, it became clear just how monumental this place was. It was like a small mountain unto itself. Lorcan recalled some drawings he'd seen. Turtles stacked on top of more turtles, carrying the world on their backs. It was turtles all the way down. He gripped the baton in his pocket, he didn't think it would do much if the mountain turned out to be a living entity, but it made him feel a little better. A warm current of air blew along the entrance as they crept into the cut-out passageway, the walls enveloping them on either side. A musty smell emanated from inside, the smell of years gone by with old, long forgotten, decay. Some deep part of Lorcan's brain told him to run, that this was not a place he wanted to enter, ignoring his built-in warning signals he carried on. There was no turning back now.

They flanked the towering entrance at either side, Oisin giving them a small hand sign like they were part of a military strike team. Taking out their torches, they stepped carefully over the threshold and into the monument. Wind echoed through the halls, the rustle of their clothing was amplified in the sparse setting, and every tiny footstep was transformed into a heavy thump. The hallway wound in a circle, Lorcan hadn't a clue how far they'd gone, or how far they would have to go to find what they were looking for. What if there was some secret entrance that they hadn't located, and they just ended up right back where they'd started? What then?

As they wordlessly drew deeper into the bowels of the burial mound, they caught glimpses of carved murals and writings that began to appear on the walls in greater density.

Decorative swirls and knots came together alongside warriors standing proud over scenes of battle. This looked promising. The corridor took a sharp turn and, as they followed, the ceiling began to dip. Lorcan would soon have to duck his head if it continued, but the narrowing corridor spread open into a large, dark chamber. He passed his torch over the room, longing for more light to make out its contents better, but their tiny LEDs just weren't powerful enough.

Oisin led the way into the room, almost immediately leaping back out as an intense orange glow flared on both sides of the doorway. Lorcan heard the low, echoing whoosh of igniting fire within the chamber. A trap? Gathering the nerve, they hesitantly investigated further, Oisin inching his head around the corner before giving the all clear for them to come along. The sudden burst of light and sound had come from wooden torches that had kindled to life through unknown means.

Unsure whether this was a good, bad or neutral occurrence, they proceeded. Hugging the walls of the chamber, they observed as the torch furthest from them extinguished and, at the same moment, the torch immediately in front of the group roared into life. It was following their path around the room like some automatic lighting system. As an experiment, Lorcan stopped walking, letting Oisin and Maeve carry on ahead; he had a hunch. The torches closest to him stayed lit, with more igniting as the other two continued. Good, they could see more of the chamber this way. Seeing the value in this, Maeve suggested they split up and spread out along the walls, they could each get a maximum of two to flare up.

The firelight combined with their own battery powered light meant they were able to get a better idea of the layout now. The room was round with a huge, domed ceiling and stone tombs circled a central statue of a man sitting on a throne.

"Fionn mac Cumhaill and his fianna."

Maeve barely whispered, but the acoustics allowed both Lorcan and Oisin to hear her. They edged towards the statue, the flames repositioning themselves accordingly. In this light it looked incredibly lifelike. Though dust covered its surface, the detail on the skin and clothes were insane. The sculptures had even painstakingly modelled individual strands of hair and pores. Lorcan held his light to the face for a closer inspection, his heart skipping a beat when he realised that he wasn't in fact looking at a lifelike statue, this man was very real. They all recoiled in horror.

"Shit." Lorcan said, "Is he -?"

"Yeah. Florence did say he was sleeping but, I had assumed she meant more metaphorically. Like, his spirit was resting or something." Maeve leant in to re-examined Fionn closer, "Creepy."

"Let's look for this red spear and get out of here." Oisin said, impatience and tension apparent in his voice.

They glanced around. Where to start? There were dozens of tombs scattered around the room, each having its own decorative display of trinkets, treasures and, most importantly, weapons. They did the most logical thing they could think of, split up and check them one by one, and hope this trip wasn't about to descend into a horror movie cliché fest. This was just going to be a process of elimination. Starting on opposite ends of the room, they examined each display carefully. Lorcan found rings, necklaces, tunics, shields, swords, slingshots and a whole host of other items caked in dust, but otherwise in pristine condition. He found spears too, however, nothing matching the description of the weapon they were looking for. All the while Lorcan felt like they were being watched from behind by the man frozen on the throne. He wondered if the others buried in here might be slumbering also, and if they'd even let them leave with the spear. First they'd have to find the damned thing.

Lorcan's nose and eyes itched with all the particles floating about, he wanted to get out of here as soon as they could. Tomb after tomb went by and they'd found nothing of importance so far. He hoped they had not made a mistake in coming here, finding another dead end, they didn't have the time to spare. Uncovering another pile of junk, he heard Maeve excitedly calling them over. She had found a tomb that stood out from those surrounding it. There were more etchings on the stone, and the bounty of ornaments on top more ornate, fitting for one of Fionn's greatest protectors.

"I think this is the one." She said.

She held up a piece of paper with some sketches. Using pictures she'd found online, she matched the symbols carved onto the casket. Once again, Maeve had come prepared.

"Good, can you see the Gáe Dearg?" Oisin asked, scanning the items.

In the soft light, Lorcan could see Maeve wince and steel herself for what she was about to say

"That's the thing."

She indicated a spot on the lid. Whilst everything else in the room was coated in a thick layer of dust and grime that had accumulated over the years, this area was clean, as if someone had wiped it down, or something had been perched there until very recently. Lorcan examined it closer, the gap in dust was long and thin, widening to a leaf shape at one end. The shape of a spear. They stood staring at the empty space, like if they looked hard enough the spear might suddenly materialise into existence. It didn't, and now they were out of ideas or things to do.

"Unbelievable." Oisin whispered bitterly, turning on his heels and walking out of the chamber.

Lorcan and Maeve went after him, calling for him to come back. He powered ahead, nearly breaking into a run. When they caught up with him outside, he was pacing back and forth, rubbing at the back of his neck and face.

"Oisin?" Maeve said, holding her hands out, "Oisin, it's okay. Maybe that wasn't the right one we were looking at. We can go back in and -"

"It was! It was the right one, you know it and I know it." He threw his axe down, "They know it!"

"Who knows what?" Lorcan asked.

"Who the hell do you think? Who was there when we were first planning to come here, huh?"

Lorcan shrugged his shoulders, "Florence?"

"Come on." Oisin sneered.

"Lea and Bal? Is that who you mean?" Maeve suggested, edging closer.

"Christ!" Oisin threw his hands over his eyes, "You don't see it do you? Neither of you do! They've got you both wrapped round their little fingers."

"Who?" Maeve and Lorcan said, practically in unison.

"Aiden and Bronach. Your parents." He said, gesturing to Lorcan.

Lorcan was blind sided. Was Oisin really accusing his parents of masterminding this whole operation for them to come to Sligo and *not* find the Gáe Dearg? What purpose would there be in that?

"Why the fuck would they send us here to do… *this*?" He gestured to the tomb.

"I don't know why they'd do something like this. Who knows why they do anything." Oisin began imitating Aiden and Bronach, "We're dead? Sure, we'll just turn up in Droichead Dubh and see our son. Revolution? Sure, why not! Let's get our son and his friends involved. Oisin's been cursed? Let's send them all on a merry adventure, and conveniently have the very thing that'll cure him go missing!" His eyes were wide, and he was gesticulating wildly, he looked crazed, "How are you not seeing this?"

Both Lorcan and Maeve said nothing for a while. They didn't want to get into an argument with someone who was obviously having an episode brought on by stress. Oisin recognised the way they were looking at him, it was a look he'd given many times, he took a breath, making an effort to calm himself.

"Look, I'm just saying, they knew about this. They were one of the few people who did. Don't you think it's a bit coincidental that the only thing we saw missing in there was the very thing we needed?"

His tone was calmer, but that wasn't helping his argument much. It was still a wild accusation.

"I see what you're saying, I do." Maeve said, "But, de Meath was the one who sent the fear gorta. He would be aware that one of us had been cursed, and he could have sent someone, or come here himself, to get the spear."

Oisin considered this and then shook his head dismissively, more to himself than to Maeve. She narrowed her eyes, drawing back.

"You don't think - you don't think Aiden and Bronach sent the fear gorta, do you?" She asked.

Oisin didn't answer but scowled and turned his head. It was as good as saying 'yes'.

"You can't be serious!" Lorcan burst out, "They wouldn't! After everything they've done, they saved your life, remember? Or did you conveniently forget that in amongst all your fucking conspiracies?"

"They're already dead! I doubt a bite on the arm is going to change anything!" He got right into Lorcan's face, "Who's controlling the narrative? Eh? Wake up, mate!"

"Shut up! For all we know they could have become a shade for saving your ungrateful ass!"

Lorcan's hand clenched around the baton in his jacket. Oisin caught the action and tensed for the upcoming fight. Before either of them could make a move, Maeve stepped in between, shoving them apart with surprising force.

"Stop it! Jesus!" She yelled.

They all froze, breathing hard and avoiding each other's eyes. Lorcan hadn't realised he'd been clenching his jaw and let it drop, feeling the tension lift. He understood Oisin's stress, but he couldn't get over the fact that he'd come at his parents with such ferocity. There was just no way they'd do anything like that.

"You don't know them." Lorcan said eventually.

"And you do?" Oisin replied, more composed.

They continued the stand-off, the initial heat of the confrontation wearing off leaving soured emotions, and a bitter, heavy feeling in Lorcan's stomach. The fun of the adventure had worn off and apathy was setting in.

"Let's go back. We need to get off this rock." Oisin said, picking up the axe, walking toward the summit's edge.

"Wait, we should go back in, we don't know if it might still be there." Maeve pleaded.

"We do know." Oisin didn't break his step, "I'm done."

They watched him storm ahead before following a few paces behind, saying nothing. There wasn't much to say now. They'd go back, drive to the B&B and maybe sleep off some of these bad thoughts. Lorcan caught Maeve's eye, and she looked at him as if to communicate, *don't pay Oisin any mind, he's distraught, he doesn't know what he's saying.* He wasn't in the mood to cut anyone any slack. Oisin knew exactly what he'd been saying.

They reached the spot they'd entered from and Lorcan took out the dagger. Like before he did an overhand stab into the air but met with no resistance, his arm swinging loose. He tried it again. Still nothing. He waved the green blade around, seeing if there was any traction to be had, but still nothing was happening. He repeated the process all over the patch of land to no avail. They were stuck.

# 28.

The sun dipped dangerously low on the horizon, the heat of the day fading. They had no desire to be stuck up an Otherworld mountain at night. Two choices lay in front of the group, stay and keep trying the portal method, or climb down. They could see a town nestled close to the bottom of Benbulbin, its lights shimmering in the hazy atmosphere. Maybe there'd be some friendly faces that could help them.

"Why isn't it working?" Oisin said in tired frustration.

"I don't know. Why don't you ask my parents, they're behind everything, right?" Lorcan snapped back.

"I would if they hadn't stranded us here."

They glared at each other.

"Right, we can't just stay here." Maeve said, "I say we go down the mountain."

"Fine." Lorcan put the dagger away, "I agree."

Oisin nodded without speaking.

They hiked their way back along the ridge. The layout of the mountain was roughly analogous to how it had been in the living world, except things were proportionally larger. Rocks and structures that had been knee height before, now reached above their heads. Either they'd been shrunk down, or everything else scaled up. If their hike had taken three and half hours earlier in the day, that would mean it could take over ten to clamber down, given how much taller it appeared to be in the Otherworld. It wasn't a dangerous hike but who knew what fresh challenges awaited them. Florence's words rattled in Lorcan's mind, *do not linger on the mountain.* He didn't intend to.

The sun sank, plunging the world into darkness, forcing them to rely on torches to light their way. They'd already used a lot of the battery power in the burial mound and would have to use their phones' torches soon, which wasn't a long term solution, Lorcan suspected. Then they'd be in real danger.

They came to a slender passage that ran between two rock faces after an eternity of trudging. The ground looked as if it had been carved by hand into something resembling a set of stone steps. They shone their now failing lights into it, unable to see past the sharp turn part way in. There was a brief debate whether they should take such an unknown, sketchy route; but it was headed down, which is where they wanted to go, and the other paths were either heading up or were level. Need won out over fear. Dark and spooky passage it was.

They were swallowed by the shadows of the narrow passage. Sheer black walls rose up to encompass their entire vision, the pathetic light from their torches only served to illuminate a few feet ahead. It was oppressive, and they clung to each other's shoulders as they made their way through. Lorcan could feel Maeve's fingerings digging in at every small disturbance, their breaths and footsteps reverberating around them, obfuscating a sound's origin; the paranoia was real. One sound in particular made them stop.

Something resembling a sustained ragged breathing pattern was coming from ahead. Or was it behind? It was impossible to tell. Lorcan readied the baton, his sweaty hand gripping tight, he could feel the others doing the same with their weapons. They rounded another bend in the passage, their weak lights bringing into relief the outline of a figure blocking their path. It was in the shape of a person, but everything about them looked off, bulging in the wrong places and their mouth opening far too wide. Long arms reached out for them as a pair of dark wings unfurled from behind their back. They would have run but found their escape blocked by another of the same creature from behind. On pure instinct Lorcan spun and lunged forward, aiming a strike at the thing's head with his baton. He felt it connect as the thing reeled, holding its eye. They didn't stop to question or acknowledge his success, they just hoofed it.

They could hear those things behind them, the inhuman gurgling and beating of wings that were now presumably taking flight and prepping to prey on them from the air. They crashed into walls as the route twisted every which way, stumbling on rocks and uneven surfaces. Lorcan heard Oisin grunting followed by a screeching wail from one of the creatures, his axe had connected. Darting along the winding path, they were approaching the end. A slender exit ahead that led back out into the open air. What lay beyond, they didn't know, and they didn't care, it was a way out. They pressed on harder and faster.

Lorcan recalled features of Benbulbin's geography as he feebly tried to mental-map his way out. Flat top, steep ridges and - oh no - sharp, sudden drop-offs. All too late he realised that they'd come to one of said sharp drop-offs. He skidded to a halt, but Maeve's momentum, coupled with Oisin crashing into them both from behind sent them careening over the edge. Skidding and tumbling their way down, Lorcan lost both his torch and baton in the confusion. Fortunately they'd found themselves toppling along one of the grassier sides where the danger of smashing against a boulder was heavily reduced. That didn't stop it from hurting like hell though. They came rolling to a halt, the slope levelling out enough that they were able to get their bearings after the world had stopped spinning.

The creatures hadn't been hindered much by the sudden drop off, in fact they were in the process of dive-bombing them and more were gathering every second. Lorcan started a hard run down the hill, grateful he was used to this kind of terrain. Gracefully hopping from foothold to foothold, picking his placements carefully, he would let gravity do most of the work while he controlled momentum and trajectory. His main job was to remain upright. Maeve doing the same thing, she'd gotten much better at handling herself on their runs.

Oisin, while not quite as graceful, took long, confident and quick strides using the axe as a counterbalance. How had he managed to keep a hold of it throughout the chaos?

The winged creatures were on top of them. Yes, gravity was aiding the trio's descent, but was aiding those things more. Oisin swung his axe as they ran, keeping claw-filled attacks at bay. They were closing in on a pathway below and, in the dim light they could see the trees just beyond. If they could just reach them, the tightly packed branches might be able to provide some cover. That's where they needed to be.

They were nearly there, they were nearly home free when Lorcan heard a familiar sound, hooves, racing towards them at an alarming pace. Maeve heard it too and fumbled in her pockets, she was going for the gold ring. Splitting her attention proved to be a huge mistake. She missed a foot placement and stumbled head over heel, landing awkwardly on her side a few feet from the path, the air leaving her. She looked dazed as Oisin struggled to pick her up while holding the axe at the same time.

Lorcan changed direction in an instant, throwing all his power into one leg. He took Maeve's weight from Oisin, so that he could focus on the distorted limbs reaching from the sky. He swung the axe one-handed, connecting with a leg and forcing it back with a pained screech. They were so close, but it was no use, he was here, the dullahan had arrived, heading right for them. The speed of his black horse was unearthly, no animal could move like that, no living animal. They were out of time

Oisin stepped in front, taking a wide defensive stance. He looked woefully outmatched as de Meath's headless figure glided to a halt in front of them, his steed bucking and rearing beneath. Oisin stood fast, his entire being shaking and tensed for action. This was it, Lorcan thought, this was the end for not just Oisin, but for them all. A strange stillness fell between them as they sized each other up, before de Meath spurred his horse onwards and, instead of attacking, he galloped past them towards the leather-winged creatures. He shot out one of his hands, producing a long whip that looked to be made of bone, a spinal column specifically. He swung it powerfully over his head, lashing at the flock, its sharp barbs ensnaring one and ripping it to shreds with one huge tug on his part. He drove them back up and towards the pass they had fallen from, spurring his steed on as he tore them apart one by one.

Though stunned, they didn't wait around. The three of them ducked into the patch of trees and continued their journey to the bottom. Maeve had recovered enough to run unaided, but it wasn't long until they heard hooves coming back their way. Lorcan threw himself behind a mass of roots, Oisin and Maeve doing the same. Breathing hard, they muffled the sound as best they could with hands over mouths.

The dullahan paused at the entryway to the small woods. The rattle of the harness, the deep thrumming breaths of his horse and the scraping, clanging coming from his armour as its plates collided. All sounds of a dangerous predator. He seemed to consider pursuing them but thought better of it. Instead, he cracked his horse's harness and retraced his path, hoofbeats fading into the distance.

Taking a few minutes to recover, their heart rates returned to an acceptable pace before they set off again. Not wanting to question their luck too much, they focused on getting off this damn mountain. They ducked in and out of cover as they dashed from tree to tree, hiding in grass, behind rocks - anything they could find. Time seemed irrelevant when you were hiding from death itself, and it felt like they'd never get off of Benbulbin. Lorcan halted their onward progress when he felt a quivering from the glass dagger as they entered another small copse of vegetation.

He pointed it in different directions like an impromptu compass, following the strongest vibration. It led them to a rocky circle surrounded by boulders and standing stones. He could have cried with relief as he plunged the dagger into the air and saw it stick. In one swift motion he'd torn a hole in the fabric of the Otherworld and stepped wearily back into their world. They had overshot their target, landing in a field adjacent to Benbulbin but none of them cared, happy to be out.

The dagger disappeared from Lorcan's hand and, not even checking to see if the rear had sealed itself, they trudged through the wet grass and back towards the car park. This trip had been a complete and utter disaster. Fireworks exploded, lighting up the distant sky and bathing them in changing colours, ushering in the New Year.

# 29.

Not much was spoken for the remainder of their getaway. They'd said all they needed to say and had done what they came to do, however badly it had turned out. It wasn't like their previous encounters with danger in the Otherworld, where the thrills and excitement had bonded them, no, their seams were starting to fray.

On their final morning they ate breakfast, made their goodbyes to the B&B owners and began the drive home with minimal chatter. The mountains and scenery of Sligo receded into the distance as motorways overtook their vision. The journey was long and tedious, they didn't even bother changing over from the preset news radio show.

*In an almost biblical scene, swarms of locusts now ravage parts of North Africa and southern parts of Europe. Egypt has been hit the worst, with seasonal crops failing across the region, and many left starving, uncertain of the future.*

More disaster headlines. Lorcan knew the feeling.

*News of a possible pandemic emerging in parts of Europe as weather conditions worsen. How will this affect the stock markets, food supplies, and is there anything to be concerned about where you are? All this and more after the break.*

More death. It was inescapable.

They arrived back at Oisin's, the apocalyptic news following them the entire way. They were greeted by his dad, who held his arms out wide to mark their return.

"Jesus, folks! You look wrecked! Hungover?" There wasn't a note of sympathy in his voice.

"In a manner of speaking." Oisin answered flatly.

"Is your hand better?" He asked, taking Oisin's hand and examining it.

Collectively their breaths hitched. They'd all been so tired and distracted that they'd forgotten about the bandage, he'd been brandishing it in plain sight all day. They waited for the barrage of questions.

"Looks good. Your ma will be happy." He said, letting Oisin's hand drop, "Well, you get sorted, and we'll see you inside."

They exchanged confused glances. He'd looked right at the mark. Didn't he see it? Yet another unanswered question to add to the ever-growing pile of enquiries they would have to make. They had neither the energy nor the inclination to pursue them at the minute.

"I'll sort everything out here, there's not much to do. You two just go on home, and we can talk about it tomorrow, okay?" Oisin handed Lorcan and Maeve their bags.

"Alright." Maeve said, hugging him, "We'll figure it out. We'll think of something, I promise."

"Sure." He replied.

He didn't look so sure, despite the smile he'd plastered on his face as he wriggled out of the embrace. Oisin turned his attention to Lorcan.

"Look, man, about what I said -"

"We'll talk later." Lorcan cut him off.

Whatever it was, he didn't want to hear it now, he just wanted to get home and be alone for a while. They would message later when they'd had some time to mull over the past few days. Oisin was left to unpack. The roads were quiet, people were probably still in bed or nursing a sore head from their New Year's celebrations. To be fair, they both looked like they were recovering from a hard night of drinking as they ambled along.

"He'll come around." Maeve started, "He was just upset, we all were."

"It didn't sound like he was 'just upset', it sounded like

he'd been holding onto those thoughts for a while." Lorcan said as Maeve shot him a reproachful look, "But - we'll talk about it. He probably was just spiralling."

Maeve gave a quick bob of her head. Lorcan was still sore from all the accusations. How the hell could he think they'd do anything so sinister? And for what? They'd set the record straight the next time they met up at Dún Dubh and he'd see how wrong he was.

"You have to admit, though -" Maeve mused out loud, "something's up."

"What do you mean?"

"I mean, *someone* knew that we were after the spear, and they got there first."

"Yeah, but my parents had nothing -"

"I'm not saying that." Maeve stopped him, "You know I'm not saying that."

Lorcan swallowed the sudden influx of anger.

"I'm glad."

Maeve fixed her eyes straight ahead, "We do have to consider the possibility that someone betrayed us, or that we're being watched."

Lorcan remained quiet. He wasn't fuelling this fire of suspicion that was circling around his parents. He wouldn't have it.

"Anyway, we'll message later and meet up. Oisin should have cooled off by then." Maeve knew she wasn't getting much more out of him.

They walked in silence until they came to Maeve's house and waved goodbye. He felt guilty for giving her a hard time, she hadn't openly accused his parents. In fact, she'd defended them.

"Hey!" He called after her.

She turned expectantly.

"Thanks for the shoes. They're great."

Maeve smiled, "Oisin picked them for you."

She vanished inside, leaving Lorcan to walk alone.

Everything had become so complicated so quickly. Part of him wondered what it might have been like if Oisin had never joined in their expeditions. Would they be any better off?

*     *     *     *     *     *

"I don't think it was de Meath." Maeve said through a mouthful of sandwich. She was in full-on research-theorist mode as the previous day's dourness washed away bit by bit.

"Who else would it be?" Lorcan asked.

"I don't know, we couldn't exactly stop and ask his name. But, think about it, there are multiple shapeshifters, and we saw loads of those flying sluagh." She'd identified what had attacked them in Sligo as 'sluagh', demented spirits that sought to steal other's souls, nasty pieces of work, "Why couldn't there be another dullahan in a different part of the Otherworld?"

Maeve rapped her knuckles on the table when she'd finished. A signal that it was time for everyone to contribute.

"Another dullahan, who just happened to show up looking for us?" Lorcan half-laughed.

"He wasn't after us." Oisin corrected, "He never attacked us. He seemed way more interested in those sluagh. I'm not sure if he even registered that we were there really."

"I agree, and his armour looked different; lighter." Maeve added.

"Since when did you become an expert in historical battle armour?" Lorcan asked.

"Hey, I'm only telling you what I saw. We have to consider everything here."

Maeve was getting fed up with Lorcan being defensive. He was so fixated on his assertion that de Meath had set this all up, he was overlooking any other suggestion or possibility that took the spotlight off of the dullahan.

"Not everything we say is pointing to your parents." Oisin said, "We've moved past that, and I've already apologised for what I said, so open your mind, Lorcan."

Their first meeting after their bust of a trip was not going well. They were at each other's throats with Maeve acting as moderator between the hostile parties. After a long negotiation they came to the conclusion they were getting nowhere by arguing or speculating on what might be. They'd have to go to the source to ask Aiden and Bronach directly about their next steps. Perhaps they'd have some suggestions.

"Tomorrow morning then?" She said as the talks came to a close.

"Sure, sounds good." Lorcan got up to leave her house.

"Okay, this meeting is adjourned." She joked, trying to bring some levity into the situation; it totally flew over the boys' heads.

Lorcan made his exit, leaving Maeve and Oisin alone. Something had shifted in Oisin from the moment they'd found the Gáe Dearg to be missing. He'd always been wary about this entire endeavour, and cagey about asking questions, but he'd taken a turn for the dark and morose. It didn't suit him.

"You know it'll be useless asking them any questions, Aiden and Bronach." He began, "They'll just say that they know nothing, and need to ask someone about something, and fob us off until they get their story straight."

Maeve gave him a quizzical look, "Why are you being so hard on them? I don't see what they've done to earn such distrust from you."

"There's just something about them that I don't buy. This whole nicey nice routine they've got going on along with their 'revolution'. It's all so - convenient. It's the only way I can describe it." He turned his nose up while he spoke about them.

"They saved your life." Maeve said, "And they're not the only ones involved in the uprising."

He was looking for someone to blame. She understood the impulse to need a target for anger and grief. He had been through a lot over the past while and was still reeling from the massive disappointment that was Sligo. She put her hand on his cheek and kissed him tenderly.

"Let's just see what happens. I said I was going to get that mark off you and I meant it." She kissed him again, "Maybe lay off Aiden and Bronach a bit, at least while Lorcan's around. It's not helping matters."

He gave a crooked smile and agreed. They cleared the remains of their lunch away and Oisin readied to leave. Before stepping off of the porch he turned to Maeve, a shadow passing over his face.

"Your judgement is as clouded as mine. Maybe I am being too harsh on them. Maybe. But you're so desperate for them to be who they say they are, that you're not questioning anything." He leaned in to give her one last kiss, "Please be careful, Maeve."

He stepped off of the porch and made his way down the path.

"Love you." She said, waving to him.

"Love you too." He called back.

She watched him leave. Tomorrow would bring answers.

# 30.

Lorcan stood waiting with shoulders hiked up to his ears as Maeve approached. He didn't look like he had slept a wink, the dark circles under his eyes were back and his skin had grown a shade paler. She hoped he hadn't been up all night worrying about what Oisin might say to his parents. Oisin was tactful and there wasn't much point fretting if they were indeed innocent. They walked together to the foot of the hillside where he awaited them, seeming altogether less highly strung than he had the past few days. The righteous air of someone who would soon be proven right clung to him. They might get some closure at least. Either way, he greeted them with a grin, and they began their short hike.

It was an unusually warm January morning, Maeve was actually sweating and had to undo her coat as they walked. After their escapades in Sligo, it was a relief to see their regular entryway into the Otherworld, rather than having to stab randomly in the air. Lorcan, who'd been a man of few words this morning, got ready to request his mum and dad's appearance. Before he could, Oisin stopped him.

"Look, I wanted to say - I didn't mean to insult you or your parents. I just want to get to the bottom of this, and find out the truth of what's been going on, regardless of what it might be." He said.

"Thanks. I appreciate that." Lorcan replied.

*Good*, Maeve thought, maybe they'd be able to make some progress today as long as cool heads could prevail.

Lorcan began to call, his voice rang around the chamber, immediately gathering that sense of solidity. They wouldn't have to wait long this time. Maeve felt the temperature drop around them like normal, but then she felt something that she hadn't before. A lightness, an emptiness in one of her hands, the one that had a hold of Oisin. She looked to her side, he was gone, and they remained. It took her a second to process what was happening. She saw Lorcan looking as well, an expression of total confusion on his face.

"Oisin?" Her voice trembled.

Maeve left the circle in a vain hope that he had decided to run out on them. No chance, why would he do that?

"Where is he? Where did he go?" She demanded, rushing back into the ruins.

"I don't know. It felt like normal and then he - I don't know, he just disappeared." Lorcan's voice was in a high panic.

He had been taken across, and they hadn't. Why? Why was it always him?

"Call them again!" She said.

Lorcan began his routine, faster and more frantic. Maeve joined him this time around, pouring everything she had into calling out to Aiden and Bronach. The longer it took, the more she focused. She *would* be going to the Otherworld today, and she'd get Oisin back from whoever, or whatever, had dared separate them.

As she concentrated she felt a rush throughout her body, from her core and through her limbs. It wasn't like the usual wave of cold, this was an electric tingling sensation, and somehow she knew that this was it, they were being pulled through and crossing over. It gave her stomach a floating feeling like she'd missed the last step coming down the stairs, catching herself just in time. That pulse of fear and adrenaline and then - solid ground. She opened her eyes. They had done it, they were in the Otherworld, but no-one was here to welcome them. Maeve had no time for that technicality, Oisin wasn't here either, and she needed to find him.

"Oisin!" She cried, running out of the dark and into daylight.

Blinking, Maeve strained against the sudden change in luminosity and caught sight of three figures a short distance ahead along the ridge. The middle one was Oisin, but who were the other two? She started forward, needing to get a better look and stopping short when they turned to face her.

Was she seeing things? It couldn't be. A boy and a girl. The boy was Lorcan and the girl was - her? The sense of dread sent her into a flying sprint she shouted, begged Oisin to run. He spun to face Maeve, the real one, as she screamed for him. She was too sluggish, her legs just weren't doing the job they were supposed to be doing, she should be there by now. It was all happening in slow motion right in front of her.

She registered the look of bemusement on Oisin's face flicker quickly to fear, but it was all far too late. The doppelgänger Maeve gritted her teeth and thrust her arm forward, straight into and through his back. His body spasmed, tensing as she twisted her hand inside his chest and pulled savagely. There was no blood. Her hand had passed into and out of him like a ghost, but she knew - she knew what it meant. Oisin's shoulders slumped and his head lolled forward, a blank pain etched on his face. His legs crumbled beneath him, and he fell bodily to the ground like a marionette that had its strings severed all at once.

Ice stabbed her heart and a sound began to make its way up through Maeve's body. It didn't seem to simply come from her lungs and throat, but from every fibre of her being. Every cell was screaming out now, screaming out at these fakes to tear them apart. Terror flashed across the fake Maeve's face as the sound reached her, the pair of them turned on their heels and began to run. What had been a bright sunny day only seconds ago had turned black as thunder boomed overhead. The Otherworld itself was crying out in anger, Maeve wanted to direct it straight at them. She watched as their bodies twisted and morphed into the shapes of wolves, and they sped off, making terrified yipping sounds.

She wanted to follow, she wanted to hurt them, but

Oisin was only feet away now. Launching herself next to him on the ground, she cradled his head.

"Oisin? Oisin, you're okay, I'm here." She whispered, "You're fine now. Open your eyes."

He lay motionless and unresponsive. She brushed his hair back, feeling his neck and then his wrist for a pulse. How was he so cold already? She put her ear to his chest, feeling and hearing nothing except his still body beneath her. She had seen this done a million times in movies, she was going to save him. Maeve checked his throat. It was clear. There were no visible injuries anywhere. She placed her hands over his sternum and began to pump rhythmically.

"Please." She said out loud, "Please, please."

She could sense Lorcan standing behind her, having caught up, but she continued on more determined. Oisin's rib cage bent beneath her hands with every pump, and she recoiled as a bone snapped, giving way under the pressure. She started back into it immediately, they said that sometimes happened during these things and he'd be grateful when he woke up. He would wake up.

Maeve might have been at it for ten minutes, she was breathing hard and sweating. A hand came to rest on her shoulder.

"Maeve." Lorcan said softly, "I think he's -"

"No!" She shouted, "He's not!"

Lorcan's hand gripped her shoulder more firmly, stopping the compressions. Maeve fought him, if she stopped now then Oisin would be dead, she had to try. She had to help him. Struggling to free herself from his grasp, Lorcan pulled her closer and held her fast. She pushed against him, but she was weak from exertion.

"I have to - I have to save him!" She wailed, "He's not dead! He's not!"

"I'm sorry. I'm so sorry, Maeve." She could feel Lorcan's body heaving with sobs too, "He's - he's gone."

"No!" She shoved him with everything she had, falling

next to Oisin.

Her hand cupped his cheek, and she dipped her face next to his.

"You're not dead. You can't be." She said into his ear, "Wake up."

She checked his face for a response; it remained still. She took his shoulders and gave him a shake, he was in a deep sleep and just needed a nudge.

"Please. Please, wake up, Oisin."

Her hand ran down his arm, taking his frozen fingers in hers, it almost hurt how cold he was. Then she noticed it. The mark had disappeared from his palm. For some reason this brought it all home.

"Oh god! Please don't leave me!" She buried her head in his chest, "Oisin."

She felt the sky open up then. A few drops and then a deluge of rain poured down, soaking them to the bone in seconds. Maeve didn't care, she would lie here forever. She'd die here too for all anyone cared. But that wasn't to be, Lorcan picked her up, and she didn't have the strength to fight him this time. She lay limp and numb in his arms, letting the rain wash away her hot tears. It all felt like it was happening to someone else.

Aiden and Bronach were there now. When had they appeared? Aiden bent to pick Oisin's body, cradling him like a sleepy child. Lightning flashed overhead, illuminating his tranquil face. It had been so distorted with worry and fear the last while, Maeve forgot how young and lovely he had been. The accompanying thunderclap was so loud it seemed to split the air around them. Did she see Aiden jump at its intensity? Oisin remained still.

When they reached the chamber, Lorcan set Maeve down and Aiden lay Oisin's body next to her. She took his hand once again, pressing it to her cheek. There was talking above her and then coldness as they appeared back in the living world. It was raining here too. Lorcan leant down to say something about phoning someone, but she could barely hear him, she just wanted to be here with Oisin. This would be the last time she'd be able to touch him and hold him properly.

After a while the distant whine of sirens cut through the white noise of the rain. This was it. They'd take him away from her now. Maeve brushed his hair once more and kissed his forehead for the final time. Her body was so cold, her lips so numb she couldn't even feel him.

"I'm sorry I wasn't able to protect you. I love you so much, Oisin."

# 31.

The house was quiet apart from the shifting of Maeve's dad slipping on his dress shoes. Maeve sat on the couch in her black dress, staring out the window. All at once she wanted this moment to last forever and for this day to be over as quickly as possible. It was as if she were moving through a dream that would end if only she could force herself awake, but every time she tried it managed to pull her deeper and deeper into itself. Her dad came into the hallway, his shoes clacking loudly on the wooden floor.

"You ready, sweetheart?" He said.

She wasn't, but that wasn't going to stop the day from happening. Maeve closed her eyes, willing her legs to stand and joined her dad. They got into the car and set off. There was a profuse sense of inevitability about strapping herself in and being driven to his house - Oisin's house - for their goodbyes. As the car rumbled down the road she spotted the crowd gathered outside his house. An urge to open the door, leap out of the car and run away began to overtake her. Her dad's hand wrapped around her own, he must have noticed, and she breathed. She hadn't realised she'd been holding it in. *Just get through today.*

They parked up and joined the procession of other mourners who were here to pay their respects. He'd been well-liked. Gravel crunched under her feet, weakening her gait as the uneven stones rolled beneath her heels. Her dad stuck out his elbow to take and she did so, grateful for the stability. As they approached, Maeve could see Oisin's dad shaking hands and thanking people for coming. Practically the entire town had come to the send-off. He had an easy smile that he gave to everyone he greeted, it reminded her too much of Oisin's crooked little grin she'd seen so often. Reaching him, her dad stuck out his hand and exchanged condolences. Maeve stuck out her hand, but he instead pulled her in for a tight hug.

"I'm sorry." She said.

"There's nothing to be sorry for, love, thanks for coming. You know you'll always be one of the family." He released her, giving her a soft pat on the shoulder.

*Nothing to be sorry for,* that stabbed her in the gut. They shuffled their way into the living room where the coffin was located, and where most of the people were gathered. Oisin's mother was there, handing out tea and biscuits to elderly relatives. Maeve flashed back to the last time she'd seen her, on the floor and inconsolable as the news was broken to her about their only child. The sound still haunted her. That primal, agonizing lament had caused Maeve to retreat into herself, she just couldn't listen to something so pained - so cavernously raw and real. Now she looked more pieced together, but the grief was obvious, palpable behind the mask. Maeve was wearing the same one. Oisin's mum spotted them and made a beeline through the crowd.

"Maeve, darling, it's so nice to see you." She set down the tray, embracing her, "Oisin thought the world of you."

There it was again, that stabbing. They untangled themselves and Maeve made her way into the room after politely refusing offers of refreshments. His casket was lying open, but she didn't look. She could look anywhere else in the room, the floor, the walls, her shoes, the biscuits, but her mind would not allow her to look at him. The guilt of everything that had happened repelled Maeve's gaze from his face. It was her fault.

She was closely examining her fingernails when she felt a hand on her arm, it was Cara. Her eyes were red, and she dabbed at them with a hanky.

"You okay, pet?"

"Yeah, I'm doing fine." Maeve lied.

Behind Cara was Lorcan in a slightly baggy black suit. She imagined that it had fit a little better at his parents' funeral when he hadn't been so thin. He too, failed to look at Oisin's casket, or at Maeve for that matter. He stood with his head down, desperately trying to fade into the background. She knew how he felt.

All too soon it was time for the funeral to get going. The priest came in to bless the body, and they closed the coffin. She wanted to look, she really did, but she couldn't bring herself to give Oisin's body more than an oblique glance as the lid closed. That was it, she would never get that chance again. They followed the hearse to the chapel where the service took place. Maeve was asked to do a reading which she reluctantly agreed to, she could hardly say no. What she really wanted to say was how sorry she was to his parents and to the town for not being able to protect him. For allowing harm to come to him when it should have been her. But she didn't. The words of the reading flowed out of her without any real feeling as she stood in front of everyone, guilty as sin. She retook her seat and put her head in her hands.

Then she was standing at the grave. Oisin's mother was crying silent tears opposite her as the priest gave his final prayers, and the wooden box was lowered into the ground. It all felt numb. The prayers. The offerings. The gentle thud of the coffin coming to rest in the six-foot hollow of earth. It was all insubstantial.

The wake afterwards was a blur. Attendees all agreed that it was *'a lovely funeral'* and *'the family was very brave'* over their soup and sandwiches. Maeve barely talked to anyone except to thank them for their thoughts and prayers, as if that would do Oisin any good. An Irish wake is a time for reminiscing, to celebrate the deceased person's life and laugh at the good times. She just wanted to go home and lock herself away.

Maeve got her wish when she got home after the arduous day. She kicked off her heels in the hallway, making straight for her room.

"Maeve." Her dad said, stopping her in her tracks, "Talk to me for a second."

She twisted her head slowly, "I just want to -"

"I know exactly how you feel, sweetheart." His tone was softer than usual, "I've been through it all before." He beckoned her down the stairs, "If you need someone to talk to, I'm here. You might not want to talk to your old dad, but just know that you can."

"I know. Thanks." Her eyes began to sting, this is why she didn't want to talk, the floodgates were bound to open, "I just - it shouldn't have been him."

Maeve threw her arms around him and let out what she'd been holding in all day. She squeezed him hard and he let her.

"I know." He said, stroking her hair, "I know."

"I couldn't do anything." She cried into his lapel.

"Sshhh, you're okay. None of it was your fault, you couldn't have done anything. Nobody's blaming you." He crooned.

The coroner's report had come back to say that Oisin's death was a case of SDS, or 'sudden death syndrome'. They'd found no structural faults in his heart but, since there were no external or internal injuries, and his toxicology tests came back clean, that's all they could put it down to. There was nothing she could have done. Maeve was totally blameless in his death.

Only she knew that wasn't quite the case.

\*       \*       \*       \*       \*       \*

Maeve was excused from attending the first week back to school after the holidays, she got a personalised note from the principal himself to say so. She wasn't missing much, the first week back was pretty much a bust as people got back into the routine, complaining about having to get up early again. Her dad offered to stay off work and keep her company, but Maeve said it would be fine, that she was fine. She wasn't, but some alone time might be good for her.

She would use this time to do nothing. That was it. She'd been running around planning adventures, going to another world, researching, playing peacemaker, and going to school for the last few months, and it had all come crashing down. It was time to take a break, and to take stock of things. She continued her morning runs, although she waited until the sun had risen before setting off. She didn't so much run as walk because of her low energy. Occasionally she broke into an all out sprint, her body had no idea what it was running from, but her mind knew exactly. Maeve read online that was called 'high intensity training', it felt like the only way she could get around right now. All or nothing.

She tried to read some books she'd been meaning to get to but found herself staring at the first pages, unable to actually read. She watched mindless online video compilations until she felt like she should be doing something productive. Then Maeve would remember she was supposed to be taking a break. She walked into town, maybe a hot chocolate from *A Wee Tea* might make her feel better, make her think of happier times. She stood outside the shop, the beginnings of a panic attack rose to meet her when memories of her trips there with Oisin flared up. She sprinted away from the café and out of the town, not caring about the looks she was receiving.

There was one she could do, something Oisin had been nagging at her for months over, Maeve could fill out a university application. She downloaded the forms and printed them out. Filling out her name, address and all the other relevant information in the boxes, it was now time to make some decisions. Maeve had been considering what she wanted to do with her life during their Otherworld trips, and she thought she might have some ideas. With pen hovering over paper, however, those ideas didn't seem to matter much, nothing came to mind. What was the point? For a solid hour she sat with those forms until giving up and chucking them in the bin.

The rub was, Oisin had been needlessly killed, and she felt endless guilt for ever having involved him in it all. He knew it was dangerous, he'd said so, and she hadn't listened. If she had, would he still be alive? There was no end goal to these questions, she was torturing herself, blaming herself for everything. She thought of what Oisin had said about Lorcan's parents, about being taken in by their lies. She didn't want to believe she could be so stupid, and she didn't see why they would lie, or what for. To kill him? Hardly.

If only they had been there to take them *all* over, instead of those doppelgängers kidnapping him. If Maeve saw them again she would do everything in her power to end their miserable afterlives. They were shapeshifters though, weren't they? She wouldn't even know what they looked like if they walked right up to her and said 'hello'. She couldn't even have a good revenge storyline. There would be no resolution to this tale.

She sat in a daze, watching shite daytime TV when her phone buzzed. It was Lorcan. They hadn't talked much since it all happened, but equally she hadn't been avoiding his messages. They'd mostly just said 'hi' to each other and that was it, probably just checking she hadn't thrown herself off of the mountain yet. She opened the chat.

> **Hi.**
> *Hey.*
> **How are you?**
> *Fine. Just watching TV.*
> **I'm in politics class.**
> *Fun.*
> **Yeah.**

She didn't reply to the last message. There wasn't much to add. Her phone buzzed again.

*Can I call by after school?*

*What for? The teachers are emailing me my homework if that's what you mean.*

**It's something else. Something important.**

*What?*

**Better if I tell you in person.**

This was intriguing. Maeve didn't much feel like talking, but Lorcan had given her space, and it sounded like he had something to say. She left the reply hanging for a few minutes before typing.

*OK.*

At least it would break up her marathon of talk shows and reruns of old sitcoms.

# 32.

Maeve had a good guess when Lorcan would drop by, after all she knew how long it took to walk from school to her house, giving her time to wash and change her clothes, wanting to appear semi-presentable. What was so urgent that he couldn't just message her or chat on the phone? Right on cue she clocked him walking down the road towards her house. Her nerves rose as he stepped onto the porch and rapped the door, suddenly wishing she hadn't invited him over.

Taking a deep breath, she turned the snib to let him in. They made light chat for a few minutes. How had she been? How was her dad? How was Cara? Were the people at school saying anything? She offered him tea, he accepted; plain of course. Boring. When the pleasantries were dispensed with, Lorcan shifted in his seat and started in on what he had come to say.

"So, I wanted to give you time." He began, "I didn't want to bombard you with anything. I mean, I needed some time too. To process, y'know?"

"Yeah, I know. Thanks."

"But, I wanted to know what happened on that day and I thought you might as well."

Oh god, she didn't want to deal with this right now. Did he really think that this was the best time to bring this up?

"Lorcan, I don't want to talk about -"

"Just hear me out." He said quickly, "It's important, and I think you'll want to hear this."

She took her head out of her hands and waved him to continue. She'd let him speak, for now, but this was exactly why she hadn't wanted to talk to him.

"So I went to Dún Dubh alone, after it all happened -"

"You what!? That was so fucking stupid, after what happened to Oisin?" She couldn't believe him sometimes.

"I get that, but I'm fine, nothing happened. I knew you wouldn't want to go, but I wanted to see if I could help in some way. So, I managed to get talking to my parents."

Maeve put her head back in her hands. Yes, Aiden and Bronach, the arbiters of everything truthful and good in the world. She never wanted to deal with them again, even if they had done nothing wrong. They and the Otherworld had been nothing but a catastrophe. Lorcan was ploughing ahead with his story regardless of whether she was sending clear signals for him to stop or not.

"They have sources that say it was William de Meath that sent those assassins to break us apart, but the rebels are currently hunting them down. So, maybe we'll get some justice." He looked at her expectantly.

"Great. Is that it?" She wanted to be left alone.

"Well, I thought you might like to hear that." He broke eye contact, "There's something else."

"What?" He still couldn't look at her and was obviously choosing his words very carefully, "For fuck's sake, Lorcan, what is this big piece of news?"

"They found Oisin." He blurted out.

Her head felt light. What did he mean they *found* Oisin? She'd been there for his last moments, she'd seen him go into the dirt. He was nowhere to be found. The confusion must have been clearly readable on her face because Lorcan went on to explain himself.

"I don't know if you considered it, I know I hadn't, but if my parents could survive the transition. Why not Oisin?" He smiled, like this was supposed to be good news, "They've spoken to him, Maeve, he's in the Otherworld. You can still see him." He put his hand on hers.

She withdrew it slowly, "And you believe them?" She

said.

He turned the corners of his mouth up, "Why wouldn't I?"

This was a lot to take in, and she couldn't think right now, whether this was what she'd been hoping to hear, or if it all seemed too good to be true. A cruel joke. Was Oisin really waiting for her? If he was, what was her next move?

"Okay, I need to think." She said, taking Lorcan by the arm and escorting him out.

"Maeve, we need to talk about this. You can still be with him if you want."

Be with him? How would he know what she wanted? Or how would Aiden and Bronach know? He needed to leave - now. He didn't struggle but did protest as she closed the door in his face. She couldn't breathe. The ceiling was spinning, steadying herself as she made her way up the stairs, Maeve flopping on her bed. Closing her eyes, she allowed the raging sea of thoughts and emotions to crash together.

Why had she never considered it? If anyone was going to will themselves to stay in the Otherworld it was Oisin, but the thought had never crossed her mind. To her, he was dead. She'd mourned, she was *still* mourning, and she'd buried him along with everyone else who'd been there. But - she could still be with him. What if he was waiting for her? Would he be the same? Would she even want to see him again in that form?

She was asking herself all of these questions as if she was wrestling with the decision to go to the Otherworld again, but she knew that there was ultimately only ever one choice to make.

# 33.

Maeve creaked her eyes open. She didn't spring out of bed with joyful eagerness. She didn't perform her morning ablutions with gusto. She didn't hum gleefully to herself while she packed. All of these things were done in a trance. Maeve would see Oisin today, and she didn't know how to feel about it. Part of her felt that she should be overjoyed, excited to see him again. The other part felt trepidation at meeting him, like the whole scenario was unnatural in the truest possible sense, that the living and dead should not mix - not like this. However, that didn't stop curiosity from getting the better of her, nor did it dull the ache of longing to see him.

Maeve waited for Lorcan, blowing feathery streams of breath and watching them float on the wind. He was right on time as usual, and they set off. She could barely speak, there was a pressure building right at the front of her head that threatened to explode if things went south today. Lorcan wasn't pressing her for conversation this morning. She was aware that he knew exactly how she was feeling, he'd been through this scenario not so long ago himself.

"What's it like?" Maeve asked.

"You're going to need to be more specific."

"Seeing them again, someone who's died. Is it weird?"

He stopped walking and thought for a moment.

"Yeah, obviously." He laughed, "It's really weird. You've said goodbye to them, maybe not literally, but, in your head at least. I remember thinking that it might have been easier if they'd stayed dead so that I could *move on*, or whatever." He used air quotes as he said 'move on', "But once I considered it, there was nothing I wanted more than to keep seeing them. It's like they never left."

"I see."

Maeve allowed his words to sink in. She had already said goodbye to her mother years ago but, back then, she hadn't known about the Otherworld, or the possibility of life after death. This had recontextualised her grieving process in a way she didn't understand, and had no clue whatsoever how to process. Her thoughts continued to rattle around in her brain as they started walking again. Before she knew it they'd come to Dún Dubh.

"Ready?" Lorcan asked as they stood in the central chamber.

"No, but historically that hasn't stopped us." She smiled nervously.

He let out a *ha!*, and set about booking passage to the Otherworld. As an experiment, Maeve attempted to concentrate like she had when Oisin had been pulled over on his own. She focused on Lorcan's words as he called, inwardly willing the veil to drop and felt the same electric tingling sensation she had before. Her fingertips buzzed as if she were touching a plasma ball, the air itself grew thicker. She moved her hand side to side feeling the resistance and closed her eyes. Maeve raised her hand in imitation of how she'd seen Lorcan's parents do when they were preparing to send them home. Seeing light shift from behind her eyelids, she opened them again, they had crossed over. She hadn't felt anything like ice that time, only the tingling.

Aiden and Bronach stood in front of them, their mouths slightly agape, like they'd been surprised by something, but quickly they composed themselves. Expressions of sympathy and sorrow spreading across their faces instead. Maeve lowered her arm.

"Awk, love, it's good to see you again. How're you doing?" Bronach said, hand over heart.

"It's been rough." Maeve replied honestly.

"I'm sure. Has Lorcan told you about -?" She trailed off.

"Yes, he has. Is it - is it true?" Out of nowhere, Maeve's eyes began to sting, realising just how badly she wanted it to be true.

Bronach smiled, "Come on, see for yourself."

It must have been some trick of the light. When she'd initially caught sight of them in the chamber, Lorcan's parents had looked more gaunt and sinuous. Now that they were out in daylight though, on their way to see Oisin, they appeared more or less normal to Maeve, perhaps a little paler. It could have been the overcast weather playing with her vision. Her heart began to pound as they made their way towards the Otherworld's equivalent of Droichead Dubh, de Meath's town. Aiden told her how they'd had a good idea that Oisin would appear again in the Otherworld, it was just a matter of where and when. Coming to the edge of the treeline, they were about to step out onto the road when Aiden produced a few hooded cloaks from the pack he'd brought along. These were their 'disguises' then.

They followed the winding road, hoods obscuring their features. There was something familiar about the path that they were taking, and then it hit Maeve, this was the way to Oisin's house. The Otherworld had twisted and corrupted the geography, and houses may have been plonked where they weren't before, but they were definitely heading in that direction. Sure enough, they came to a row of houses and huts where Oisin's should have been.

"Here we are." Aiden said, pointing to the buildings in front of them.

To Maeve, it looked like the houses were almost stacked on top of each other and competing to occupy the same space as other buildings she'd observed here. The wooden and concrete frames merged into one another, the thatched roof fought for dominance over the slated roof, a struggle frozen in time. Neither of the structures looked like Oisin's home, however.

"Here?" Maeve said, confused.

Aiden had her eyes follow his gesture, "Right there."

He pointed to a zigzagging line between the buildings, no more than a couple of feet across which Maeve had mistaken for the transition between the warring homesteads. Refocusing, she now saw that it was indeed the light colour of Oisin's house. It had wedged itself in between the buildings in a fashion that reminded Maeve of an unpleasant memory from her childhood, when she'd been trapped between two very overfed adults on a plane. It looked uncomfortable. Maeve swallowed hard.

"Is this where - is he -?"

She couldn't formulate a full sentence, but they nodded. Oisin was indeed inside that squashed little building.

"We'll wait outside and find somewhere to lie low, but we'll be nearby if you need us." Aiden said.

"You're not coming in?" Maeve asked.

"This is your moment with him, we wouldn't want to intrude." Bronach's eyes exuded kindness.

Maeve thought they'd be hovering, watching over every move she made. She wasn't expecting to be left alone with Oisin.

"You coming?"

Lorcan looked shocked, "Um - yeah, if you want. I would've thought you might want to see him on your own."

"He was your friend too." She could see Lorcan brighten internally at this.

Aiden and Bronach went off in one direction, and she began a slow walk to the door with Lorcan in tow. Maeve stood on the miniscule porch, having no idea what she would even say to him. Her hand hesitated and then gave a soft knock. They stood, waiting as nothing happened, and she knocked again. Still nothing. She eyed Lorcan, who shrugged and pushed the door. It opened, scraping groan as its hinges worked themselves against the frame. Maeve stuck her head in to get a sense of the place. It was dim, there wasn't much room for windows in a structure like this, and the few that existed were but thin slits.

"Hello?" She half-whispered.

A shuffling came from within.

"Oisin?" She said, opening the door a little more.

As she entered, the door caught on something, a small hallway table. She stuck her head and body around it to properly inspect the house. It looked even more bizarre from inside. It was certainly his house, but everything had been miniaturised and stretched as if space itself had been warped. I looked like it had all been aged about fifty years, stripped of its colour and bleached by sunlight. Except the sun was most likely never a factor given how dull the place was. She could make out a shadowy figure sitting towards the back of the structure at a spindly kitchen table.

"Oisin?" She repeated, a little louder this time.

The figure inclined its head, its torso turning towards the sound.

"Yes?" She heard it say.

It sounded like his voice. Her heart stopped, and she could feel those hot tears stab at her eyes again, "Oisin? It's me, Maeve, is it okay to come in?"

"Maeve? Is it you? Really?" He stood, "Maeve?"

She shoved her way roughly past the door, stumbling fully into the hall. She had to scooch awkwardly past the rickety looking staircase that took up a good portion of the ground floor as she neared the kitchen. Her chest welled with excitement, but pulled up short when she saw Oisin clearly for the first time.

"Maeve, you came." He said thinly, supporting himself on the table.

It wasn't that he looked fragile, that wasn't the case, all the components that made up Oisin seemed to be there. His hair, his arms and legs, his eyes, his nose and even his crooked smirk. But there was something intangible about his presence, he was less than the sum of his parts.

"I did." She said.

"Well, come here." He stuck his arms out for a hug.

Wrapping her arms around him, she shivered. He didn't drain heat like Bronach had done, it just creeped her out. He felt impalpable and that she could fall right through him at any moment. What had happened to him?

"I stayed for you." He whispered.

They released from their embrace and sat at the table. Lorcan clumsily made his way into the kitchen, with Oisin not seeming to notice until he banged a knee painfully on the table.

"Lorcan!" he said with a surprised gasp, "You came!" Getting up to give him a big hug too, Maeve saw on Lorcan's face a similar reaction to what she'd had. He sensed it too. "Look, Maeve came." Oisin indicated to her.

"I know, I came with her." Lorcan laughed, unsure how to react.

"Oh, is that so? Very good." He plopped himself back down, staring at them placidly.

An odd quietude floated through the kitchen. Neither Maeve nor Lorcan knew what to say, and Oisin appeared content to remain gawking at them. He reminded her of a wind-up toy, or a character in a video game who required prompting before they'd do anything.

"So, how are you?" Maeve had to start somewhere.

"Oh yeah, can't complain."

This was not normal behaviour for him. Where was the sarcasm? Where was his scolding her for being stupid enough to set foot in this world after everything?

"Oisin, are you - do you know what happened?"

"Hmm?" He honestly appeared to have no idea what she was talking about.

Maeve looked to Lorcan who shared her concerned expression, "You - you died, Oisin, this is the Otherworld. You know that, right?" It felt blunt to state it outright, but she needed to know that he knew.

"Of course I know that." He continued smiling gormlessly, but a switch flicked in his head, "I remember. Yes, I remember. I'm glad you're okay."

"Was it painful?" Lorcan asked.

Oisin screwed up his face, thinking, "I don't know. It was cold. I'm not sure how it even happened, but I do remember the last thing I saw was Maeve." He reached out and took her hand.

Maeve had to suppress a cringe at the feeling of his grasp, "I'm sorry I couldn't do anything." She said, "I'm so sorry."

"Please, Maeve, it wasn't your fault."

"It was! If I'd never gotten you wrapped up in all this, none of it would've happened, you wouldn't be here and -"

"Hey, hey , hey!" Oisin cut her off, "I'm a big boy, or I *was* anyway, and I made my own decisions. I don't need you going around feeling sorry for yourself, or blaming yourself for what I did willingly. Yes, I came here because of you initially." There it was, he'd said it. He'd never have come if not for her. "But, I also came because it was fascinating and wonderful... and bloody terrifying. You were just a good excuse. We knew it was dangerous, and I'm thankful you haven't been hurt - yet. So, shut up and stop your whining. I'm here now aren't I?" And he was back, at least a part of him was.

"God, you're still annoying." Maeve said.

"Some things never change." He laughed.

They talked about his experience crossing over and about the choice he made to stay. Oisin echoed Aiden and Bronach's sentiments about the empty whiteness of death and there being a choice to make. Should he stay or go?

"It's difficult for me to identify any changes that have happened to me. My memories are already a bit hazy, although talking with you both is helping." He drifted then.

Every so often, however, his attention would waver, and his gaze would focus on the mid-distance before snapping back to the conversation at hand like nothing had happened. The more they spoke, the more it seemed to occur.

"Yeah, the house surprised me too, it's weird -" He drifted again and then looked at Lorcan with surprise, "You - when did - Lorcan? Did you just get here?"

Lorcan was the model of confusion, "No, Oisin, I've been here the whole time - we were literally just talking, remember?"

"Were we? Weird." The gawk was back, "I'm so glad you came, Maeve. I stayed for you, y'know."

Maeve held her voice together as best she could, "And I'm so glad to see you, Oisin. I think we've taken enough of your time today. Lorcan's parents are probably waiting for us."

"Oh, are you leaving already? It's like you just got here."

"Time flies, eh?" She said pleasantly.

They squeezed their way out of the spaghetti thin house. Was it this narrow when she had come in? The house might have shaved an inch or two off of its width in an attempt to trap them. Oisin stopped at the door and bid them goodbye.

"Will you come back soon to visit?" He asked with puppy dog eyes.

"I'll be back before you know it." She gave him a kiss on his frozen indistinct lips.

He shot a weak smile and then indicated to the figures of Aiden and Bronach behind her.

"Who're they?"

"Huh?" Had he lost so much already? He didn't remember? "They're Lorcan's parents."

"No they're not." His eyebrows knitted.

Maeve bit her lip, "I'll be back soon, okay? You'll never even know I'm gone." She rubbed his cheek, turning around to walk away.

"That's not them!" She heard him calling from the doorway.

She threw him one of their classic big waves which snapped him back to himself, and he waved back. She was glad he couldn't see her tears now. They walked back to the fort mostly in silence. Aiden and Bronach asked a few questions ,but Maeve was not in the mood for talking, she couldn't - not after what she'd just witnessed. Reaching the chamber she handed the hood back before speaking.

"How long does he have?"

They were taken aback by the question, "What do you mean?" Bronach said.

"Please don't bullshit me." It came out more pleading than demanding.

Aiden looked serious, "We don't know, there's no set time."

"How long for what? Set time?" Lorcan said, obviously not following.

"You noticed it too, Lorcan, the way he looked, how he was slipping up and forgetting things. He's - he's fading." She choked out the last past, "He's going to be one of those things."

"A shade?" He said, realising.

"We don't know that, he might -"

"Oh you know!" Maeve said, interrupting Bronach before she could spout any more of her platitudes, "You fucking know! If you'd been there to take us *all* through he'd still be alive! He wouldn't be turning into one of those things!" Her voice was amplified by the hard stone around them, "Where the hell were you? Huh? It was very convenient to turn up when you did! Where were you that day?" Aiden and Bronach said nothing, their placid features warping in the gloomy light, "You abandoned him!"

The echoes died down, and they remained quietly standing, letting the wind whistle through the stoney windows above. Maeve wouldn't be the first one to talk. They had to answer for their negligence.

"We're sorry." Aiden said, "It's our fault for getting you involved in this war."

"Fuck you." Maeve said, she wasn't accepting their half-arsed apology, she wanted retribution, "What are you going to do to fix it?"

Once again, silence reigned, leaving nothing but the

wind to fill in the gaps.

"I'm coming back one last time to see Oisin and say a proper goodbye. I never want to set foot in this place again. It's poison." She said with finality.

"Maeve -" Lorcan began.

"No! That's it. I'm done. Send me back. We'll say our goodbyes next time."

Bronach reached out her hand, "We're sorry to hear that."

Unlike their trip to the Otherworld earlier in the day, the trip out of it was full of pain and ice. Maeve didn't care, she'd be rid of it all soon enough. Propping herself against the crumbling wall, hugging and rubbing her arms to regain some feeling.

"You didn't mean that, did you?" Lorcan was alarmed.

Maeve took a steadying breath, "You bet I did."

He began to protest, she put up a hand, there'd be no discussion. Next time would be her last, and she was going to make it count.

# 34.

No time to waste. Maeve understood that Oisin didn't have long left, even though Aiden and Bronach were failing to be specific. She just knew. Parts of him were already missing, and it was an ongoing process. Even sitting with him in that warped house she'd seen him shed his former self like a snake shed its skin, only to be replaced by something new and unrecognisable. She prayed he'd be able to hold out for another week while she organised herself, and got ready to say a proper goodbye to him, something Maeve had been robbed of before.

Wanting to remind them of their time together, she would give him a worthwhile day out. A picnic was in order. Yes, she understood that was riffing on an idea Oisin already had for her, but she loved that solstice date together, and she knew he did too. It was unoriginal, although he might benefit from something familiar. Throughout the week she gathered all of his favourite foods and drinks that she could think of (or was capable of carrying to the for), printed out photos of them at parties, at school and generally goofing around. A treasure trove of memories. By mid-week, everything was pretty much ready to go, she'd make the sandwiches the morning of the trip. Oisin might not actually be able to eat anything from the living world, but they'd be there in case. It would be the perfect send off. The perfect goodbye.

Planning the route of their picnic, she realised something important. She was being completely selfish. Maeve wasn't the only one who'd never gotten to say goodbye to Oisin, and was of a very exclusive club consisting of two people who actually knew how he had died. What if his mum or dad had some final words, or sentiments that they'd never been able to express? She wasn't alone in her grief, and maybe they could help give him a more well-rounded farewell. Maeve dreaded discussing Oisin with his parents, especially his mother, but it was the right thing to do. They deserved some closure, even if they didn't know just how she was going to give it to them.

After school on Thursday Maeve called to their house, she'd rung the night before, not wanting to ambush them. Only his mum was home, she was still on leave from work. His dad apparently had to keep himself busy during his time of grief. Maeve understood that compulsion well. Tea was poured, biscuits laid out and they exchanged their pleasantries between pregnant pauses. The house had fallen quiet in a way that can only happen after the death of a loved one. It stood still, like a dog awaiting its owner - a room awaiting its long-term occupant. She noticed new smells too. No, that wasn't right, those smells had always been there, it's just that *his* smells were fading, with others rising to take their place. Oisin had always been out doing something, dragging the outdoors inside along with him. Mud, wet grass, cold, fresh air. That's what was missing now, the earth. Maeve chose to concentrate on the steaming cup in front of her and shoved the lump in her throat down.

"So, you said on the phone that you're doing some sort of ceremony?" His mum asked.

Maeve set her saucer on the table, "Yeah, I read about it online. You gather friends and loved ones last words or wishes for the person, and write them down, and you burn them. Those wishes send out energy into the universe, and it'll reach them in the afterlife."

"Where'd you hear about that?"

"Online."

"You young ones and the internet." Oisin's mum wasn't exactly old, but she looked like she'd aged a decade in the last few weeks. Her shoulders fought with an invisible force that weighed her entire body down.

"It's kind of like when we burn our hopes for the year on pieces of paper during spring for Brigid of Imbolc." Maeve was trying to sound casual about the whole affair.

"Ah, I suppose you're right - so you want a message from me in there?"

"Of course, as long as you're happy to do it."

She looked at Maeve with those heavy eyes, "I pray to him every night, y'know. I didn't pray before this, and I'm still not sure if I even believe in it, or ever did. So, if there's a chance of something reaching him, however wacky or froo-froo it might sound, I'll do it." There was steel in her voice.

"I'm glad to hear that, I appreciate it." Maeve reached into her school bag and pulled out a notepad and pen.

"Oh, you don't need that." His mum said, waving her to put them back, "I've already written mine down." She lent over the armchair and produced a photo album with a piece of A4 paper sticking out of the top. Opening the album, she whipped the bit of paper out and unfolded it, "I sat down this morning to do it."

She stared at the piece of paper. Maeve listened to the ticking of the wooden clock on the mantelpiece as she sipped her tea, waiting for the conversation to resume.

"Do you - want to hear it?" She finally said.

"If you want me to. I was thinking it was more between you and Oisin." Maeve replied.

"You and I both know he's probably never going to get it. At least one person will hear it this way."

Maeve said nothing and indicated for her to begin.

Oisin's mum settled into the seat, clearing her throat, "Dear Oisin, first of all, I want to say that you left your room in an absolute tip. I hope wherever you are you learn to pick up after yourself. Your dad and I haven't had the heart to go through it yet, we keep expecting you to walk through the door and tell us you got lost, or it was all some big joke. But, we know that isn't going to happen. We know that you're gone, and we know that it's just wishful thinking. I do wish you were here." She took out a tissue and dabbed at her nose, "I suppose that's why we haven't touched your room. We want to keep it how you remember, so that you'll feel at home. Someday though, we'll have to face up to the fact that our wee boy is gone and move on with our lives. But how do I move on when you *were* my life? If someone could tell me that I'd be very grateful, I know that's what you'd want, for us all to just get on with things. You were always like that, weren't you? Maeve has prompted me to think about my hopes for you. That's a difficult one because I had so many hopes for you. I'd hoped you'd do well in school and go to university. I'd hoped you'd be able to do something that you loved for the rest of your life. I'd hoped you'd be with someone who'd love you as much as I did, I'm glad that hope at least came true for you." She smiled at Maeve at that part, "What do I hope now? I want you to know that you were, and are, loved. I want you to find peace and happiness. Most of all, I want you to know that you will always be our wee boy who brought light and meaning into our lives and, even when we get around to cleaning your room, it will always be ready if you want to come home. Love, your mammy." She sniffed and finished reading, folding the letter in her lap.

Maeve wiped her eyes with the back of her hands and tried speaking, letting out only a breathy sob. They finished their tea and biscuits, neither able to say much for the remainder of the meeting. When it was time to go, she handed the letter to Maeve.

"Make sure he gets it." She grinned.

"I will. What about his dad? Does he have anything to send?"

"Everything in that letter comes from the both of us. Oisin was his wee man too and his best friend."

Maeve nodded and gave her a long hug.

"Oh." His mum said, "I have this." She reached into the hallway table and pulled out a photo, "It's Oisin and us after his exam results, he had brains to burn. We have another copy if you want to burn it - or maybe you'd like to keep it?"

Maeve gazed at his smile in the photo and bit her lip, "Thank you. I think I might keep this one."

"That's no bother. It was lovely to see you, darling, call by anytime okay? You're family too."

"I will." With that, she set off home.

She was glad she had done that. Even if Oisin's mum didn't know it, her words would reach her son in the afterlife. When she got back to her house, she saw her dad's car parked up already. Home early?

"Hey, dad, what's up?" She asked.

"You alright, sweetheart? Just had a half day. I know it's a weekday but do you want a chippy tonight?" He was lazing with his feet up on the couch, not a care in the world.

"Sure, I'll be down in a sec." Maeve went to print off her university application forms again.

Something Oisin's mum had said struck her. He would have wanted everyone to get on with their lives. That's what she was going to do. She filled out all the relevant information, and now it was time to make some choices. Over the past while, Maeve had developed a keen interest in history, particularly ancient history, and there were plenty of options to choose from. With that in mind she put her first, second and third choices on the form - all as far from Droichead Dubh as possible, a break from this town would do her some good - and then she went to order some takeaway with her dad.

"You seem in a better mood." He said over his fish supper, "School going alright?"

"It's going better, yeah. I made my choices for uni."

"Oh yeah? Happy with them?"

"Yeah. I think I'm actually excited about going."

She could see him try and fail to suppress a little proud smirk, "Good girl. I'm glad to see you getting on with things."

Maeve had to agree, she was glad too.

\*       \*       \*       \*       \*       \*

Lorcan fumbled with his phone, it was Maeve. Was he ready for their final trip into the Otherworld together? She emphasised 'final' in bold. He quickly typed his reply before Cara could spin around and catch him.

"Here!" Too late, "What'd I say about phones at the table?" She waved a dangerous looking chef's knife in his direction.

"I know, I was just texting Maeve about tomorrow." He sighed.

"Ah yes, your wee hikes. It's nice that you're still doing that after... everything. You're lucky to have a friend like that, let me tell you."

"Yeah, sure." He didn't sound so thankful for her.

His thankless tone flew over Cara's head as she continued cutting whatever cured meat they were having with tonight's tapas. She'd gotten really into Mexican inspired food ever since the burrito ratings fiasco, when Maeve had dared to give her cooking below a ten. She *would* get that perfect rating eventually by immersing herself in the culinary culture. She set the plate down, pushing another out of the way to make room. The table was overflowing with bowls and cutting boards.

"You do realise it's just the two of us tonight?" Lorcan said.

"Whatever, if we don't finish it we can have some sandwiches or wraps tomorrow with the leftovers." She heaped a helping of stuffed olives and patatas bravas onto her plate, "Dig in."

"We'll be eating this for a week." Lorcan stabbing some calamari rings onto his fork.

"Saves me cooking. It's clever when you think about it."

"Mmhmm." He mumbled through a mouthful of squid.

They picked over the various bits and pieces she had

sliced, diced and cooked, choosing their favourites, and the best candidates for the inevitable dinner party they'd be having. Maeve would be the guest of honour seeing as they needed that previous score rounded up to something more acceptable. To give Cara her dues, it was some pretty tasty tapas. Maybe he'd conspire with Maeve to rig the ratings so that the experimental cooking could continue. They washed up after stuffing their faces and Lorcan started up the stairs to his room.

"Hold on a minute." Cara called after him, "Don't be abandoning me. It's a Friday night."

"What? You want to go clubbing? I don't think they'd let you in unfortunately."

"You watch it!" She waggled a finger, "No, I was just thinking we could have a fun night in."

Lorcan rolled his eyes, lord knew what she was going to suggest, "Okay, what have you in mind?"

Cara had obviously planned this out because she just so happened to have a casino game set to hand. They played blackjack, Texas hold 'em, roulette (the set had a mini wheel with a mini metal ball), and then they moved onto Monopoly before finishing out their game night with some Scrabble.

"Y'know, I don't think they have board games in casinos." Lorcan said, shuffling his letters around.

It was difficult to properly concentrate when she'd also made cocktails to go along with their night of fun, but he played the word 'position' along the top of the board on the triple word score and a double letter score for 'n'.

"Not bad." Cara said, "that's thirty-three for that. You've taken a good lead late in the game."

Cara rearranged her five letters and rubbed her chin. Unless she made a great play here, Lorcan had defeated her in a hard won game. He only had one letter left and knew where he was going to place it.

"So, tell me," She started, "why'd you act weird when I mentioned Maeve earlier?"

"Hmm?"

Where was this coming from?

"You think I can't tell when you're being a strange boy?" She didn't take her eyes off of her pieces.

Ugh, she could be annoyingly perceptive, "She said she might not want to go anymore and that this would be the last time." He admitted. He might as well tell a half-truth.

"Aw, that's a shame. Is it to do with Oisin?"

"Yeah, I guess." She didn't know just how close she was to the crux of the issue.

"Does she like your hikes and hanging out?"

Lorcan nodded

"Well then, just get her to remember why you started hanging out again in the first place. It's done you the world of good and I'm sure she could use some company right now. Both of you."

He tilted his head, "What do you mean?"

"I mean, you were sad for a while, weren't you? Having some friends to talk to helped, and I could see you improving. You've come a long way since then. She might just be retreating the same way you did."

Lorcan thought about this for a second while Cara set out her letters.

"And, there we have it, 'juxtaposition'. Triple word score and double letter score on 'a'. That gives me an extra ninety and the game."

He gawked at the board, "Are you serious? You were so lucky I played 'position'!"

"What makes you think I didn't plant that in your head?" She said tapping her temple, "All my talking was a distraction. Winning the game and giving life advice? You've got one smart aunt."

"Crafty, *evil* aunt is more like it." He took a defeated sip of his fruity cocktail.

Cara laughed and they clinked glasses. Lorcan gave her a hard time, but tonight had been fun, he'd needed a reprieve from all the heavy goings-on and was infinitely grateful to her for sensing that. Plus, her advice wasn't half bad. If he could get Maeve to rethink her position, maybe they could keep hanging out, and he could convince her to keep going to the Otherworld. That way he'd keep her as a friend and have his family. Lorcan could have it all if he played his cards just right.

"Another drink?" Cara said.

He held out his glass. A little craftiness could go a long way.

# 35.

Sunlight broke over the horizon as Maeve made one last check of her supplies. Ensuring nothing was amiss, today was going to go according to plan, and nothing would take away from her time with Oisin. Lorcan texted to say that he was close. Tie to go. Stepping out into the morning, she breathed in cool, refreshing air and noted her stomach turning, twisting itself in knots with anticipation. She lent on the wall, taking this time to reflect. She felt good about her decision to leave the Otherworld behind, she wasn't saying forever, but for now it was time to get on with her actual life, there was enough in this world to keep her busy. This wasn't the *Narnia* type of adventure she'd wanted it to be. It actually turned out that getting mixed up in mythical worlds and revolutions was a dangerous thing to do. Oisin had been right from the very beginning.

Lorcan appeared over the hill, he was jogging.

"Morning!" He waved, coming to a huffing stop.

"Morning. Eager are we?" Maeve said.

"Hungover. I'm trying to run off the alcohol."

"Freak! When I'm hungover I usually just spend the day in bed."

"I find getting up and doing things helps." He did look a little greyer than usual.

"You're psychotic." She said, her eyebrows arched.

"Shall we?"

They began the short hike to Dún Dubh. Lorcan was handling the notion that this would be their final trip together better than she'd expected. She thought there might have been some guilt trip laid on, but he was positively chipper during their walk. Maybe he was finally exercising some empathy. As they reached the foot of the steepest part, he stopped them, looking stern all of a sudden.

"Hey, look - I just wanted to say that I understand not wanting to go back, I do."

"Okay." She was sure there was more.

"I've decided that this'll be my last time too."

*That* she wasn't expecting him to say, "What? Really?"

"Yes. I think it might be time I started to move on, kinda like you're doing."

"But, Lorcan, your parents are not like Oisin. They're - they're whole."

"I know, but they've found something to fight for in the Otherworld, and maybe it's time they started to focus more on that. We're just a liability and I don't want anyone else to get hurt. I feel so bad about what happened and about dragging you both into it." He hung his head.

Maeve looked Lorcan over. He was serious, he really was going to let his parents go, "What about them? What if they want to see you?"

He raised his head, "Maybe they should learn to let go too." Lorcan meant it, "And I don't want to lose you as a friend. We can still hang out and go for runs - I mean, if you want."

"Of course we can." Maeve didn't think he'd want much to do with her if she wasn't actively furthering his relationship with his parents. She'd misjudged him. "Do your parents know about this?"

"No, I'm going to tell them today." He said, cringing, "I'm not sure how they'll take the surprise."

Maeve thought about that. It would be a lot to swallow, having your child ripped away like that.

"We'll talk about this later, but maybe hold on telling them, okay?" She said.

"Why?"

"Just, for me."

Lorcan shrugged, agreeing, and they began the climb. She didn't want to be the one responsible for breaking up a family unit, she'd already done enough damage to one family. Even if she was souring on this particular unit She'd think about that later though, now she prepared herself for the transfer to the Otherworld. They were ten minutes ahead of schedule by the time they reached the chamber, Lorcan had been pushing the pace hard. He lent against a wall while Maeve adjusted her pack.

"What were you doing last time?" He said casually.

"With what?"

"Your hand, you held it out when we were about to go through."

Maeve had to think, "Oh yeah, I was concentrating to see if I could mitigate the cold that we usually feel. It was just an experiment."

"And?" He pushed himself off the wall.

"And it worked."

He seemed to take this in, "Show me."

Maeve walked him through what she'd been thinking and doing the last time, wondering why he wanted to know. As she told him to funnel his entire concentration on feeling the veil and pushing through, like sweeping aside a tangle of webs, a familiar tingling buzzed about her fingertips.

"Do you feel that?" Lorcan said, his eyes closed and face full of strained focus.

"Yeah." She closed her eyes too.

Lorcan reached out and took her hand. The circuit completed itself as she felt the tingling transforming into a surge of energy throughout her body and, just like that, they were in the Otherworld. She looked to see Aiden and Bronach making their way quickly through the doorway of the inner sanctum, their smiles forced - slightly manic, askew.

"Folks! Good to see you." Aiden said in a higher pitch than usual.

"And you." Maeve said.

The whole exchange was strained, like they'd been caught doing something and were desperately deflecting. They offered to accompany Maeve to Oisin's house. She refused. She'd have her day with him in peace, and Lorcan would have his day with his parents, then meet up and go back home. The less time she spent around those two right now, the better. Maeve's fingertips still buzzed from their crossing over, both she and Lorcan were on the cusp of something, but it all felt too little too late. They gave each other a conspiratorial glance as they hugged and said their goodbyes.

"We'll talk later." She said as they parted.

"We will." He nodded.

Aiden and Bronach watched from the sidelines. Their faces seemed drawn again, like they hadn't eaten in days, and their bodies were somehow more angular. Maybe they weren't so untouched by this realm's effects. Maeve had bigger things to think about than those two right now. Pulling the hood over her head, she set off to Oisin's, stomping at pace.

She arrived, red-cheeked and puffing, and froze. Maeve stood rooted to the spot outside Oisin's thin strip of house. Had it gotten even smaller and more insubstantial than the last time she'd seen it? There wasn't a second to lose. Checking no-one was around, she knocked on the door. No answer. Opening the door, she peeked her head inside. There he was. Oisin sat at the table, silhouetted against a crack of light the window allowed in. He was motionless until she approached, drawing his attention. When he raised his head to look at her Maeve was brought up short. That intangible, unfocused feeling she'd got from him before had become more pronounced. There was some large part of her brain that told her to run. That told her this was not the Oisin she knew as she looked into his wide, saucer eyes.

"Oisin?" She said, reaching her hand to his, "Oisin, it's me."

There was a look of unrecognition. His face a blank slate as he took in her features, and then a few muscles began to work, twitching his mouth and eyes until a soft twinkle became apparent.

"Maeve?" He said quietly, "You came back to see me?"

"I said I would, didn't I?" She held his hand, her nerve endings screaming for her to let go, but she held on.

"You did." He said after thinking about that for a time.

"I've got a nice day planned for us. Do you want to get out of here?"

Oisin pulled back, reticent at the thoughts of leaving his den. Maeve held his gaze and let him process the request. It was like he was working in slow motion, or every thought had to go through ten times the channels as it had before until it reached the correct neuron. Perhaps he had a limited number of channels to work with now. Decision reached, he gave a slow bob of his head, allowing her to help him up. Maeve couldn't help but notice how fragile he felt. As they stepped outside he shielded his eyes. It wasn't an especially bright day, but she suspected he hadn't been getting much sun as of late.

He shrugged her off, not wanting the help, however it was slow-going. He shuffled along like someone five times his age. Maeve rethought her timeline for the day, things might get a little protracted. She had to prompt him every so often, as he would suddenly stop or walk off in another direction entirely, his attention span was shot to pieces. After some wrangling and a lot of encouragement they made it to where Maeve had been aiming for, the same spot Oisin had brought them to see that spectacular solstice event. He paused as he looked out on the landscape. His head swivelled from the spot where the tattooed man had once stood to the horizon, following the golden spear with his mind's eye.

"I - I remember. We came here?" He'd lost that glazed-over quality, "I brought you here, didn't I?"

Good. She'd been right, something familiar for him to latch onto.

"You did." She bade him sit as she lay out a blanket and began unpacking.

He eased himself into a crossed-legged position and basked in the sun. It reminded her of the sun worshippers they'd seen that day, renewing themselves in the first light of dawn. She rustled around in her bulging backpack, pulling out sandwiches and two brown bottles.

"Here." She handed him one of the plastic wrapped sandwiches, "I don't know if you can eat, but -"

"I suppose we'll find out." He said, taking the package and undoing the wrapping.

Oisin sniffed at the ham and cheese sandwich, shrugged and took a bite. He chewed slowly, shifting the food from side to side in his mouth, swallowing thoughtfully. Looking at Maeve, he grinned.

"Buttered them properly this time, did you?" Some colour returned to his face as he ate, clearly relishing the sensation.

Maeve beamed, watching as he came back to himself before her eyes, and then painted a look of exaggerated annoyance on her face, "Jeez, I'll never live that down."

"I'm holding onto that one for eternity." He said, taking another mouthful.

Maeve uncapped the beers, and they clinked their bottles, taking a big swig each. She was glad there was still enough of the real him left in there to say goodbye to, she hadn't been too late after all. They sat for a while, enjoying each other's company and watched the gargantuan branches of that magnificent, impossible tree flit in and out of the clouds, swirling about on an imperceptible wind.

"What do you think it is?" Maeve asked, craning her neck.

"A tree."

"Oh, shut up." She threw her crust at him.

"I'm saying what I see!" He said, trying to bat it away but reacting too slow, "It sure is fucking massive though."

"Sure is."

He became transfixed by the sight of the tree, that

glassy look overtaking his vision, his body slumping. The liquid in his beer bottle tipped at a dangerous angle as she rubbed his shoulder.

"I guess I'll never know what it really is." He said dreamily.

"You might, you've got all the time in the world now." She lied.

"No I don't." There was no intonation, "I'm pretty sure I don't have long."

"Come on -"

"Please don't bullshit me." He interrupted in a soft voice, "Not today."

Maeve watched the remnants of Oisin flare up again as he faced her, "Okay."

"You know it too, don't you?" He asked, and she nodded, not wanting to lie again, "Damn." He hung his head, "I tried."

"Tried what?"

He slumped further, "To hold on - for you. I thought I was strong enough to come back. I thought I could do it." His body began to heave with heavy sobs.

Maeve pulled him closer, holding back an involuntary shiver, "You're okay, I know you did - I know you did. You'll be okay." She sounded like a mother consoling her child as they rocked back and forth together.

"I'm scared." He whispered, "I don't want to go."

"You'll be fine."

Maeve hadn't convinced Oisin, nor had she convinced herself with that. Continuing to stroke his back and hair, his lack of weight felt unnerving against her, like a hollow mannequin, "Y'know, I thought I might see my mum when we first came here, to the Otherworld." She'd never actually verbalised that before, not fully.

"Oh, I didn't think. Did you... want to?" Oisin squirmed.

"I don't know." The answer came more reflexively than she'd intended, "I mean, yes. But also no."

She shrugged as Oisin tried to comprehend her non-answer. Sighing, Maeve centred herself, wading through miasma of buried emotions, collecting and stacking them into coherent thoughts - however unsuccessfully.

"She was one of the first things I thought of when I came here, after I got over the initial shock of being flung into another world." She began, "I saw Lorcan and how happy he seemed with his parents, and I said to myself, 'Wow, what if -'... I couldn't finish the sentence. I stopped myself. I couldn't even say, 'What if I get to see my mum again', because somehow I just knew that wasn't going to happen." As she spoke, Maeve's gaze fixed on the horizon, "I don't really remember much from when mum was sick. Late nights, hospitals, watching my dad looking after her, and wishing I could do something. It's all a bit of a blur. Like a dream I can't quite get a hold of, it's all mushy. But I do remember one thing that's really solid. It was one of mum's good days. We were out for a walk - believe it or not, I did actually walk places before Lorcan started dragging me up mountains - and she just looked up to the sky, took a big breath and said 'I think I'm ready'. I didn't get what she meant, but thought it was odd. After that she seemed to relax. I didn't catch her crying as much, and she laughed more often, even when it got really bad, she always managed to smile. I'm glad I remember her being that way."

Maeve could feel Oisin's eyes peering up at her, "What did she mean about being 'ready'?"

"Well, I think mum meant she was ready to die. We all have to accept it eventually... she just got there quicker. So, I kind of knew I'd never see her here. She'd already made the choice to move on."

"Brave choice." Oisin's eyes returned to the ground.

"Yeah, maybe."

They breathed, their chest rising and falling in unison as a gentle breeze brushed its fingers along the swaying grassy expanse.

"What if I disappear, Maeve? What if it's like I was never even here?" Oisin said, interrupting their brief reverie.

"You'll never disappear, Oisin, never. I can promise you that."

"How?"

"Because none of us will let you. We'll always remember you."

He let out a weak laugh, "That's so cheesy."

"Yeah it is, but it's true. Here." She released him, pulling out a piece of paper, "I was waiting for the right time and this seems like it."

He took it from her, unfolding it carefully, "Mum."

They fell quiet as he read the letter. She saw him finish and restart it at least twice, alternately chuckling and sniffling as he read his mother's final message to him. He finished and tried handing it back to Maeve.

"No, keep it." She said, "She wrote it for you."

"Thanks." He wiped his nose, "God, even in death she can't let go of my messy room."

"You were a pig at times."

"That I was. They do say geniuses are slobs."

She raised her eyebrow, "Who says that?"

"I don't know... people."

They spent the remainder of the afternoon finishing up their picnic. As the sun made its journey across the sky a growing sense of melancholy gripped Maeve, which she hid it as best she could. This was Oisin's day, better to focus on the good aspects. Every time he drifted, or forgot what they were talking about, or how they'd gotten there, she saw another small piece of him shed itself from this world, never to return. Bit by bit, he was fading and there was nothing she could do to stop it. Like the ruins of Dún Dubh, time chipped away at him. She could only watch as he became something lesser than he'd been before, feeling the weight of her guilt bury her further into the ground.

The sky glowed a brilliant, fiery orange with streaks of red-pink clouds cutting across the horizon like wild paint strokes haphazardly strewn on a canvas. Maeve looked at Oisin.

He was intently gazing at the scene, soaking in every detail for posterity. She wished the universe would just stop, just give them this one break and let him be in this moment forever, frozen and at peace.

"I suppose it's time." He said, shattering the fantasy without taking his eyes off of the blazing tableau.

"We can stay as long as you like." Maeve offered.

He took a deep, controlled breath, ever the pragmatist, "We can't. I can feel it. It's time."

Packing up the remains of their food and drink, the backpack was significantly lighter now, they set off back to his house. He was even slower than he had been before, and she helped him with the trickier bits of terrain. As they drew nearer to their final destination Maeve's stomach became a tangled pit of anxiety, and a pressure was building in her chest. She'd told herself what she was going to do, she'd run through it in her head dozens of times this week, but now that it was here, her resolve weakened. Maybe she could come back another time? He'd seemed pretty cognisant at points today, what if her being here helped to strengthen him? They hadn't given that theory a fair shake. How could she possibly leave him after everything she'd done to put him here?

"Okay." He said, abruptly turning, "I don't know if I'm going to get another moment where my mind is so clear."

"What?" Maeve said dumbly.

"I want us to say our goodbyes, that's why you came, right?"

Maeve stuttered out her reply, "But we're not - your house is -"

"Articulate as ever." He said, his eyes sharp again.

"I just wanted us to have as much time as possible."

"So did I." There was his crooked little smirk, "But I don't think we get to choose how long we have with someone. I'm glad we had today. I'm glad for our time together."

"Me too." She said shakily, "There's so much I want to say. I - we didn't get the chance before."

"Now's our chance. What is it?"

Maeve laughed, "I can't think. I had this whole speech prepared, and now it's gone."

They both stood, staring at each other like idiots. The best laid plans.

"You're going to have to hurry." He prodded.

Maeve fumbled in her jacket pocket, "Here. I almost forgot." She pulled out two pictures. The one his mum had given her, and another of herself and Oisin at the beach, "If you feel like you're losing yourself, look at these. The people who love you and will always think about you. Keep them with you. You'll never be gone."

Oisin took the pictures, running a finger over each of the faces, "Thank you for being with me until the end. There's nobody else I would want here."

"There's nowhere I'd rather be."

He reached out his hand and she took it. Pulses of unpleasant cold ran through her arm, but she savoured them. These were their last moments, it was her turn to soak in every painful detail.

"Be careful, Maeve." His face was starting to lose its light, "Around Aiden and Bronach. I don't know what they want, but they're not what they seem." He gripped tighter, fighting to stay lucid.

"I will, I know that now. Thank you for always looking out for me. I love you, Oisin, I always will."

"And I love you."

They kissed for the last time. When she pulled away she saw his expression dim. He was gone. She walked him the rest of the way and watched as he tottered back inside his house, the door closing behind him. She stood gaping at the building before ripping herself away and walking. That walk turned into a jog, which became an all out sprint, she had to get out of here. There was too much hurt.

She bounded along the lanes, not caring who saw her, not anymore. Maeve was done, and she'd never be coming back. Tears blurred her vision, but she knew the way, moving on instinct. So focused was she on removing herself from this world that she didn't notice what, or who, was gaining on her. All too late, the low rumbling of hooves filled her ears and she felt the cold metal grip of an armoured hand plucking her from the earth. William de Meath had found her.

# 36.

The world moved around Maeve, heaving up and down as she came to, finding herself tied up and laid across the back of a jet black horse. No wonder she was struggling to breath, all of her weight rested on her rib cage. The black beast panted and whinnied as its master spurred it along. She tried to speak and cry for help. No good. There was nothing wrapped around her face as far as she could tell, but she just couldn't command her body to make a sound. The particular wires between her brain and her mouth had been disconnected by some unknown means. If de Meath knew she was awake, he wasn't letting on. Straining against her bonds, Maeve wrenched her head up and to the side to get a better view of where they were, and where exactly they were going. Had she been capable of making a sound she would have gasped audibly.

Ahead of them in the distance was the castle. The castle that Maeve had been drooling over since first setting foot in the Otherworld. How far had they come, and how long had they been travelling? The horse didn't seem to be galloping that hard, but the scenery flew by in a blur, the black mist at its feet whisking them along.

Up close the castle was absolutely the most impressive structure she had ever beheld. It encompassed her entire frontal field of her vision. With the sun set, the moon gleamed off of it and the surrounding land. Its sheer white walls erupted at right angles from the ground with no obvious disturbance of the earth - they were seamless - and no visible joins existed between the stones that she presumed had to make up the castle. It gave the impression that it was one giant monolithic chess piece, planted here by deistic hands, rather than a building designed and built brick by brick. Like everything else she'd seen in the Otherworld, it was unnatural in its beauty and magnitude.

The horse stopped a dozen or so metres from the front wall. There were no obvious doors or entrances that Maeve could see. The hell horse settled whilst de Meath raised one of his hands in a fluid, practised motion. The earth vibrated beneath them and a thin vertical line materialised, unbroken from top to bottom, on the wall. The line became wider as she caught on to what was happening. It was a pair of mammoth doors, and they were swinging outwards towards them. The mechanisms would be unfathomably big for something on this scale. It was practically a geological feature.

She felt him shake the reins, and they began moving again. The walls came to tower over them until there was no top to be seen, becoming endless. Travelling between the gates was like entering a smooth, geometric valley, and they emerged out of the other end into a bustling, fortress settlement. People and creatures ran to and fro as they passed, staring at them, particularly in Maeve's direction with wildly unfamiliar sets of features. Mixed into the general expressions of curiosity were faces of fury, triumph, and guises that were altogether far too difficult for her human brain to read. They were preparing for something, weapons were passed from hand to hand, wooden stakes driven into the ground, pointed at vicious angles that were meant to maim, and battalions of soldiers stood at the ready for some as yet unseen threat.

She turned her attention forward, they were still a distance away from the great, shimmering tree, but it spread out so that it became the backdrop to the whole castle. It must have been tens of kilometres wide. How was something like that possible? Even in the Otherworld, how could anyone conceive of something so unreal? She wanted to ask, but doubted de Meath was the talking type. Besides, she still couldn't make a sound. Through the chaos of the preparations happening around them, she saw what looked to be their destination, a central castle with a spire that overlooked the rest of the grounds. Maeve imagined it to be the hub where the overseer might look out onto his troops, and where de Meath ruled with an iron fist. What was going to happen when they got there?

As they neared the castle security began to beef up. They passed row after row of sword and lance wielding guard that eyed them as they breezed on by into the depths of the structure. Obviously de Meath had the highest clearance given his vice grip on the land. They came to a halt when they reached a small interior courtyard, de Meath dismounting from his steed in one quick motion. Plucking her off of its hind quarters effortlessly, he slung her over one jagged shoulder. His armour bit into her abdomen and she let out a muffled, pained groan. To her surprise, de Meath noticed this and shifted her to a more comfortable position between his shoulders, and began walking towards the door. Maeve tried not to think of his grotesque neck stump beneath her, she had enough to worry about without being grossed out. With a flick of his wrist he dismissed the horse, it melting into a shadowy mist, dissipating into the ether.

They entered a sparsely decorated, stone-walled section of the building and climbed a winding staircase that went on forever. Maeve's headless kidnapper didn't struggle with the climb, he didn't even seem to breathe, he kept a steady pace until he finally came to the desired floor. Passing one of the narrow windows, she saw that they must have been at least two-hundred feet up, a small fraction of the castle's actual height. He swung open a heavy door and planted her firmly down on a chair in a windowless room. The only light source was a flickering torch casting deep shifting shadows from high up on the wall. Closing the door, de Meath took his spot on the opposite side of the rough wooden table between them, settling into his seat.

Maeve was able to take him in fully now that they

were only feet apart. This was the man - the creature that had ordered the death of Oisin. His asymmetric mail armour glinted in the firelight with one broad shoulder left exposed, showing off his sage green tunic. He was huge. His girth took up a significant portion of the room, and he clanked with every movement as his armour shifted. She wasn't sure where to rest her eyes, he had no face to focus on, and she didn't want to focus on his half-neck, so she kept her eyes fixed on the centre of his barrel chest. That was probably the most polite location. He waved a gauntlet in her direction, whatever was keeping her from speaking or opening her mouth was lifted. She took deep, appreciative breaths, stretching her stiff jaw muscles.

"There." He said.

His voice seemed to emanate from every corner of the tiny room.

"What do you want?" Maeve's voice, by contrast, was insubstantial.

"The truth."

His hand slid from the table, reaching for something beneath his flowing tunic. She tried not to react, but she couldn't help sharply inhaling through her teeth when he revealed a head. His head. Its eyes were closed, as was its mouth. Its sallow skin stretched against the underlying bone, creating pits and shadows that accentuated its already monstrously wasted appearance. He placed it carefully, balancing it on the neck stump, turning it to face her.

"Now, let's begin."

Fear ran its fingers down Maeve's spine as she stared at the decapitated head in front of her. There were clicks as tendons stretched and bubbles popped between long disused cartilage, its mouth and eyes slowly opening in a grotesque silent scream.

"Lies." de Meath said in a measured voice.

"I told you, I came here alone. I don't know what else you want me to say." Maeve said shakily.

"I want you to tell me who aided you in infiltrating this

world, and why."

"And if I don't?"

If his head were attached, Maeve imagined that he might have appeared smug as he leant back, "Your friend already told us everything we need to know. Lorcan, was it?"

She fought the urge to react, seeing enough true crime dramas to know he was most likely bluffing. If he knew where to find her then he probably knew their names too, so he may have just been trying to get under her skin by mentioning him. Lorcan wasn't here, she was sure.

"Yeah, like I'd believe that." She said with an indignant snort.

"Believe it or not, it's true." de Meath inclined his body towards the head, it returned to its resting expression, "Since you're being cagey, I'll ask you some simple 'yes' or 'no' questions."

Maeve shrugged, "Do whatever you like." She was acting terribly brave for someone whose clothes were soaked through with nervous sweat.

"Did you knowingly pass through to our world from yours?"

"Yes. Though not initially." She didn't see much point lying there.

"Have you been to our world multiple times?"

"Yes." Or there.

"Did you have help getting here?"

She thought about this one, "Yes."

"Who helped you?" He leant forward.

"I thought these were supposed to be yes or no questions."

"Very well."

It became a barrage of questions upon questions. He'd gotten her baseline with those yes or no questions, now it was time to probe. Had she been here during Samhain? Had she spoken to anyone from here? Did she have knowledge of the enemy's plan? Maeve felt like it had been going on for hours and, though she'd entered the ring strong and defiant, her head was starting to reel with all the blows. Her emotions were becoming ever more fragile under fire from the dullahan, the events of the day beginning to take their toll. Thoughts of Oisin alone in that house pervaded her mind. He was wasting away. Losing himself completely. She felt her eyes begin to blur and the whole scene became a watery mess in her vision. She'd missed his last question.

"What?" She said, rubbing the moisture from her cheeks.

"I said, what is your association with Alice Kyteler and William Outlaw?"

"Who? I don't know who you're talking about."

She watched as the head opened its eyes, but its mouth remained closed. What did that mean? She looked back to de Meath whose attention was still on the head.

"Interesting." He said, shifting his weight back to her, "What do you know about Alice Kyteler and William Outlaw?"

"I don't know." She threw her head back, exasperated.

She just wanted to go home. Although, the names rang a bell. Where had she heard them? Maeve closed her eyes and searched her memory, if she could find where she recognised those names from, maybe that could be the key to getting the dullahan to leave her in peace. Then it hit. Of course, Alice was the name of the woman who'd supposedly framed de Meath's mother, Petronilla, for being a witch, and William Outlaw was her son. But, what, if anything, did they have to do with their current predicament? And how was Maeve supposed to know anything beyond the basic historical details?

"Okay, yes I remember hearing about them, but that's it. I don't know them or anything. How would I?" She looked at the head. Its eyes wide open.

"You think you're telling the truth." He said slowly.

Think? How could Maeve *think* she was telling the truth about people she didn't know? This wasn't making any sense, it only made her long for home all the more. This was supposed to be her last trip to the Otherworld.

"Who are the two who've been aiding you in crossing into our world? What are their names?" He pressed on.

Maeve went quiet, she was done performing for him. Instead, she put her head in her hands, letting her eyes drift closed. She imagined that she was back on that hill with Oisin, they were alone and watching the solstice. Music filled her ears as the spear raced across the land and a flash of light expanded, engulfing the sky and everything it touched. That was nice. The table shook violently as a giant hand slammed onto it. He was growing impatient.

"Wake up!" His voice boomed in her ears, "It's imperative you tell me everything you know."

"Why?" She raised her head, "Why is it so important that I answer your questions? Why the hell should I care about helping you when all you've done is torture us?"

"I'm trying to help you." He actually forced sincerity into his voice.

"Help us?" Maeve was furious, "Was it 'helping us' when you sent your fear gorta to curse us, or when you murdered Oisin?" She stood, throwing the chair aside with surprising force, "Was that fucking help?"

Leaning over the table, the light in the room seemed to dim, and she could swear she heard the stone itself creak. She had been in a stupor since first arriving but was wide awake now, adrenaline pumping, feeling ready to stand her ground, no matter the size differential. Even de Meath was taken aback by the sudden explosion of anger that emanated from the tiny person in front of him.

"Now, I don't know what *you're* talking about." He said, raising an armoured palm to her.

"Like hell you don't." She noted a wave of static beginning to build in her fingertips and held onto the sensation. It felt empowering.

"Indulge me." He said, beckoning her to sit, "Tell me what you think happened to Oisin."

Maeve didn't sit. She remained standing as she recounted what had happened to Oisin in graphic, minute detail. How he'd been pulled through on his own, how there'd been doppelgängers sent my de Meath, and how she'd watched him die right in front of her. Fresh tears flowed as she relived the moment for the first time out loud since it happened. Her voice shook as she hung onto the table, but she never wavered in relaying the story directly to the person responsible. More and more she felt that electricity building, it was like a pure energy inside of her that, if she could only release it, she could harm him with it. She spat her last words viciously at him as she finished, breathing heavily and steadying herself. His abominable head still had its eyes wide open with its interminable gaze.

He remained still, unreadable, "Oisin, that's who you were visiting today?"

"Yes." She snapped, insulted he had the audacity to even utter Oisin's name.

"I see. If you believe I did all that, then you might not like to hear this, but I'm sorry that happened to him. I truly am."

Maeve screwed her face. Who the fuck did he think he was?

"How dare you." She said dangerously.

"Careful." He replied, "I don't think you know what you're doing, or who you're dealing with. Either of you." His tone was soothing.

"We know exactly who you are."

"I don't mean me." He said, "And it's good to see you finally opening up. It took Lorcan a while too, but he seems even more confused about things than you do."

Damn it, he'd got her riled up and then she'd let slip that there was indeed a 'we'.

"I apologise for the interrogation, but I have to be sure that your stories are consistent. Now, please, who are those two that are facilitating your crossing over?" His voice was measured, kind even.

She'd gone over it in her mind, not seeing why that information was relevant if he'd already spied on them, and she was tired, so tired, "They're Lorcan's parents, Aiden and Bronach Delaney, but you already knew that. You've been hunting them, haven't you?"

He sat there and twisted his body towards the head again, its eyes stubbornly frozen open. If the signal for her telling the truth was for it to relax its features, why was it stuck like that?

His shoulders slumped, "Hunting them? You could say that. Those names are new to me, though. Sit." He gestured with his hand again.

He waited patiently as the anger drained from her and became a rotten pit in her stomach, a hangover. All of that electricity that had been fuelling her was gone. When she took her place he shifted in his chair, it was his turn to do some explaining.

"You seem to know a little bit about me, but you know nothing of the pair who claim to be Lorcan's parents, or what they're involved in. Nor are you aware of your place in all this." He began in earnest.

"Wait, my place?" She asked.

"Yes. Now, tell me, what have you learned about your 'perception' of this world?"

Maeve looked at him blankly.

"I'm not surprised that you've been kept in the dark, but I thought you might have been clever enough to figure it out on your own. Even a little." There was disappointment in that tone.

Maeve prepared to listen. Oisin had said they needed to hear the other side of the story, this was her opportunity.

# 37.

Sounds of the castle and its surroundings entered Lorcan's cell from every conceivable direction. Scraping from unknown implements outside as denizens ran about, preparing for battle. Soldiers giving and receiving orders, scuttling frantically while he remained stuck in his own small room, replete with an uncomfortable bed to sleep on, and a bucket for - well he didn't want to think about that for now. The air was damp, thick with musty odours, and of stuff that made his nose itch. He wondered when they would let him go free, or if they would let him go at all, and if they were just keeping him around as a bargaining chip - or to kill at a later date. He lay down for another nap, best to deal with that eventuality when necessary, when he noticed shuffling footsteps approaching from further down the corridor accompanied by voices. Mixed in was one that he recognised. Maeve!

She had been captured too. The door to the adjacent cell creaked open, metallic clicking and clacking reverberating in the stone around them. She was being ushered in, no struggling or screaming to be heard. Quite unlike how Lorcan's imprisonment had gone. In fact, it all seemed rather amicable and calm, like she was a willing guest of de Meath and not a prisoner of war. He wasn't happy that she'd been apprehended, but on some level it was comforting knowing she was here too. The clack of the turning lock sounded, clattering around the barren hall, and he waited until the footsteps had faded before he dared to speak.

"Maeve?" He said, his face pressed to the small barred window of his cell door.

"Who - Lorcan?" He couldn't see her face, but the surprise was evident in her voice.

"Yeah, it's me. He got you too then?"

"I guess he did. What happened to you?"

Lorcan told her how he'd been on the way to the bog town when de Meath struck, managing to separate him from his parents. After a tense game of hide-and-seek in the small patch of forest, he was caught and brought to the castle to be interrogated, just like Maeve.

"And your parents?" Maeve asked.

"They got away."

"Of course."

There was something in the way she said that. Hostility? Sarcasm?

"Anyway, they said they'd come for me, but I haven't heard anything yet."

Nothing. The mention of his parents had shut her down. What had de Meath said or done to her? That the intimidating headless bastard had tried to turn Lorcan against them, but that wasn't happening. Never. He'd given up and thrown Lorcan in this cell when he'd refused to speak any more. Had he succeeded in getting to Maeve?

"Is everything alright?" He said.

He could hear her sigh before answering, "You really think they're coming?"

"Why wouldn't they?" There was no hint of hesitation in his answer, although a feeling in his gut was trying to tell him another story.

"I think you know why, you just don't want to believe it."

"Believe what?" She didn't answer, "That they're tricking us or something? That I've been an idiot this entire time? Is that what de Meath was telling you?"

Still no answer.

"You think I wouldn't know it was them? You think I'm so desperate that I'd latch onto the nearest fucking pair of things that called themselves my parents?" His voice trembled as he said these words aloud, and his hands shook, rattling the cell door.

No way. No way had de Meath been right. He couldn't be and Lorcan would prove it. His parents *would* come for him.

"I'm not saying you're an idiot." Maeve said over the racket he was making, "Far from it. I'm just saying -"

"That you believe him? That's it." His tone was venom, "That they're parasites just using us? You're the one who sounds like an idiot, not me! So you can go and fuck yourself if you think I'm going to listen to that piece of shite instead of my parents. I can't believe you'd side with a murderer over my family."

His words hung in the air, creating a barrier between them. He was astonished that she'd broken so easily under the little pressure that the dullahan had applied. Perhaps she wasn't as loyal as she made herself out to be. Still that stirring sensation remained in his gut when he thought of his parents, but he made a conscious effort to shove it down back into the depths.

"You need to change the way you're thinking about things Lorcan." She said simply, her voice cutting through the atmosphere, "We'll both see soon enough."

There were little scuffles as she backed away from her door and sat on the bed.

He stood resting his head against the cool metal of the bars, letting them drain the excess heat from his sweating forehead. It was never his intention to hurt her, it was hard to restrain himself when it came to his parents. First Oisin had suspected them, and now it was Maeve. Couldn't either of them see that they were all being manipulated by de Meath? Everything was his fault. It had to be. He went to lay on his back, the hard mattress digging uncomfortably at his body, and rested his eyes. His mind ruminated in circles as the long hours of the day took their toll, and he began to drift. The assassination attempts. The curse. Oisin's death. It was all de

Meath's fault. She'd see.

*　　　*　　　*　　　*　　　*　　　*

The hairs on Lorcan's arms stood on end, feeling a charge all around him that jolted him upright. He hadn't been out for too long, the sky was still dark. There was a flash of light accompanied by a crackling sound like electricity outside his cell. He leapt off of his bed to see what could possibly be the source, but he only heard laughter coming from Maeve.

"Hey!" he called, "What was that? Are you okay?"

Although the anger towards her was still raw, he wanted her to be safe. He wasn't a complete monster.

"I'm fine." He heard her say after more laughter, "Lorcan! You have no idea."

"About what?" Had she cracked?

"He was right... de Meath was right."

This again. He was about to restart the argument when the main corridor entrance darkened as an imposing figure began its journey to their cells. He had come for them. Maeve's cell was first. He heard a muffled exchange, they were speaking in low, quick tones, probably so that Lorcan couldn't hear them, then it was his turn. What were they up to? Had she turned a traitor and was now conspiring against him? He readied himself for whatever was about to happen. The metallic scratch of a key and then the clicking of the ancient lock, the door swung open to reveal them both. What struck him most heavily was Maeve's appearance. She looked exhausted with dark bags under her eyes, her hair in complete disarray. She really was in need of some serious rest. He saw in her body the weariness of everything they'd been through, and his suspicion softened. Although, her expression didn't reflect that weariness. She looked hyperactive, like she'd been up all night on one of her researching binges, on the verge of something big.

"Come on." de Meath's voice was as booming as ever.

Lorcan sat, unmoving.

"Lorcan." It was Maeve's this time, "Come on, I think we can trust him." She said with her wide-eyed stare.

The dullahan *had* gotten to her. Well, whatever the case was, he couldn't do much at the minute, he was outnumbered two to one. He complied and went with them. As a unit they followed a series of hallways that zigzagged in every direction; there obviously hadn't been a floor plan in place before the castle was built or, if there was, the contractors were probably off designing confounding labyrinths with Minotaur running around them. There was no rhyme nor reason to how the building twisted in on itself. They had to jog every other step, de Meath's striding gait carried him much further much faster. By the time they'd reached their destination both Lorcan and Maeve were red-faced, keeping pace with the dullahan. They stood in front of a pair of tall, steel-reinforced, wooden doors, and he placed one of his humongous hands on either door and paused.

"Your parents have come to see you, Lorcan." With that, de Meath shoved his way through, like all that wood and metal weighed nothing.

The doors opened on what looked to be a long banquet hall, minus the oversized dining tables. Gaps in the roof that were allowing in moonbeams to supplement the dancing torchlight that plunged out of reach corners into heavy shadow. Further down were two figures, he assumed them to be his parents. Lorcan didn't react, not knowing what games were being played here, but he wasn't about to make any rash moves. Internally he sighed with relief, he knew they'd come for him as promised. Maeve must have felt pretty stupid right about now. There was a rustling of armour and cloth as de Meath started forward, and they followed.

His mum smiled as they approached, but his dad's face remained stoney and firm, no doubt he was hatching some plan under de Meath's nose to whisk them away. Whatever it might have been, Lorcan was ready to join in. They stopped just out of touching distance. None of them spoke, they just stood.

"Can you see?" de Meath said.

Who was he talking to?

"See what?" Maeve answered.

"Look closely at the two in front of you." He indicated to Lorcan's parents, "See past the deception."

He saw Maeve intensify her gaze, her eyes narrowed and brow furrowed in concentration. What in the hell was she supposed to be looking for? He didn't get what was going on. Then she let out a yelp.

"I can see!" She said excitedly.

"Good, and you?" His headless torso twisted in Lorcan's direction.

"See what?" He wasn't playing along.

A metal gauntlet went to an armoured hip in dismay, "You'll have to do better than that if you're going to survive."

Survive? What was this thing on about? He was the dangerous one.

"Mum, dad, what's going on?"

"Lorcan!" Maeve said, "They're not -"

"Please." de Meath held up a hand for her to stop, "Let him get there himself."

She shut her mouth like a child who'd been chastised for speaking out of turn in class.

"Not everything in this world is as it seems on the surface, sometimes we have to look deeper to see the truth. Now, I told you before we entered this room that your parents would be here, yes?"

"Yes." It didn't seem like he would continue the lecture if Lorcan didn't provide some sort of response.

"And then you saw two people standing at the other end of the room. Who were they?"

He was pretty sick of these inane questions, but the sooner he answered them, the sooner they could move on, "My parents, obviously."

"Wrong." The huge man bent down on his hunkers so

that the space where his head should have been was level with Lorcan, "That's what I told you, and that's who you *assumed* or *believed* them to be."

Lorcan's stomach sank, "What, are they transformed? Shapeshifters? Like those wolf things you sent to attack us?"

Waving that last comment away, de Meath continued, "No, but they're not who you perceive them to be either."

"I don't get it."

He was lost. They looked exactly like his parents had when he'd last seen them. If they weren't shapeshifters or illusions, what were they? This was probably another one of de Meath's tricks to poison his mind.

"They're not your parents." He said, standing to his full height again, a touch of impatience in his thick voice, "I want you to look at them, and tell yourself that until you know it in your heart. The rest will make itself clear."

Throughout this exchange his parents had remained quiet, maybe there was something afoot. Fine. Even so, if this is what it took to shut him up, he'd do it. Lorcan focused like Maeve had, he furrowed his brow, repeating in his head that the people before him were not his parents. There was a small surge of energy that flickered in his body, like a gentle wave lapping at the shore of possibility - it startled him. He was reminded of when they'd crossed over, that hot electric charge in his fingertips, and what he'd felt only minutes ago in his cell. His vision lit up, whiting out for a split second and then returning to normal. Well, that wasn't quite true. He could see again, but everything was more vivid somehow and the sepia filter that he found was usually present in the Otherworld was less pronounced. It was like he'd removed a pair of stained glasses, finally able to see his surroundings in full definition. Lorcan waved his hand in front of his face, his fingers left little trails in the air, and when he refocused on his parents they were no longer there. In their place were two people that he didn't recognise. He took a cautious step back.

"Well done." de Meath said.

"Who are they? Where did my mam and dad go?"

"They were never here. You only thought they were, or rather, it's what you absolutely believed was true." He spread his arms, "This world is built on belief you might say. From the earth to the sky, and everything, and everyone in between. It only exists because people made it so. People like you and me... once."

He was talking in riddles and Lorcan wasn't following along. He looked to Maeve, who didn't seem half as confused. Was she really buying this, or had she figured out something he hadn't?

"I can see I've lost you, but we don't have time." He stepped towards them with his long stride, "In fact, we're out of time."

A horn sounded from somewhere in the grounds, its baritone sending a swell of dread with it. The two people formerly known as Lorcan's parents whirled to de Meath, who ordered them out with a swift motion, and they set off running. He put an arm on both of their shoulders. Lorcan expected it to feel uncomfortably cold, but it felt relatively normal, despite being dwarfed by his elephant-like proportions.

"My soldiers and I will do everything to protect you. I wish I had more time to teach you, but I don't, perhaps later if all plays out like it should. Maeve," He nodded his torso at her, "fill him in on all you can. Lorcan," He paused and sighed a deep, rumbling sigh, "my advice... don't take *anything* at face value. Question everything, no matter who's asking you to believe them. Don't just look, perceive." He quickly stood and whistled, "Sí!"

They heard a high meowing, and turned to see a black cat with white spots adorning its chest casually sitting in one of the windowsills. It eyed them in a way that suggested a sharper mind than that of a normal cat.

"Sí, they're here. Get these two to safety and if all hell breaks loose, you're the best one to protect them." The cat nodded and de Meath made his way to the exit, "Take care."

With that, it was the two of them left in the large empty room - plus the cat. It took them in with one long, lingering inspection from top to bottom, blinked once and turned purposely on its heels, heading towards a different door.

"Do we follow?" Lorcan asked.

Maeve was already off. She was way ahead of him.

They wound through a new set of confusing corridors, sidling past soldiers struggling with stacks of weaponry and armour. Preparations for battle had ramped up. Lorcan hoped they'd be long gone before arrows and other projectiles started flying in their general direction. It was even more difficult to keep up with Sí than it had been de Meath, because of its small size the cat was able to weave effortlessly in and out of the commotion surrounding them without slowing down. Neither he nor Maeve had that luxury. In an attempt to hop over a bundle of wooden shields, Maeve stumbled and fell hard to the floor. Lorcan noticed her ragged breathing as he gave her a hand up, she was worn out. Had she managed to get any sleep at all?

"Hey, can we slow down just a bit?" He called to Sí, who didn't acknowledge him but did seem to reduce the frenetic pace it'd set.

"Thanks." She said, getting to her feet, "But let's keep going, we need to get out of here."

They continued dodging weaving through the throngs of soldiers until they found themselves outside on an open rooftop. High up, they overlooked the grounds where thousands of combatants with various levels of protection stood ready to fight, each of them picked out in faint highlights courtesy of the moon. They looked like toy soldiers. From beyond the wall they heard what sounded like thousands more footsteps marching in unison, partnered with war cries carrying up and over its immense height. This wasn't good. When they had talked of rebellion, Lorcan never imagined ever becoming embroiled in a battle on this scale. A few town meetings and putting up posters, maybe even a march or two, but never this, he didn't want it.

"My god." Maeve puffed, stopping to stare out over the soon-to-be battlefield and catching her breath.

She wasn't going to last much longer at this pace.

"Are we nearly there?" Lorcan asked the cat, as it looked dispassionately at the pair.

It indicated a stone bridge a few flights up that connected the castle to a nearby mountain. Already there were people on it, forming a disorderly queue that was moving with slow urgency into the bowels of the jagged rock. A hideout?

"I'm okay to keep going." She said, "It's not too far."

They set off again at speed. As they ran, Lorcan became aware of strong, evenly spaced tremors that shook the very foundations of the castle. He guessed them to be footsteps, but what could possibly be that massive? He kept his mind on the task at hand, there was no point in thinking about that until he had to. With any luck, he'd never have to find out. Their priority was getting out of Dodge and finding his parents. They'd know what to do.

Maeve lugged herself up the last few steps with a bit of help, and they got in line, she looked grateful for the respite. Sí gazed ahead while they waited, shuffling forward, never once turning to check on them, the perfect countenance of indifference.

"Okay, we'll wait this out, and then we'll find my mum and dad to see what our next steps are." Lorcan said, half to himself, half to Maeve.

"Seriously?" She shot him a disbelieving look, "After everything that's happened tonight?"

"Come on, Maeve, you can't tell me you trust de Meath. That was a trick, back there in the hall, it had to be."

She shook her head at him, "You saw it for yourself. They've kept you in the dark. They kept all of us in the dark this whole time, you have to know that now."

"He killed Oisin." He could see her face fall, that had

struck a raw nerve, "You're going to trust the *thing* that did that?"

Maeve closed her eyes briefly, centering herself, "I'm pretty sure now that it wasn't him... and he's helped us understand this world better in a short amount of time than they have."

"Maybe they didn't know about 'perception'! It's not like they've been here that long." He retorted.

"Come off it, Lorcan, they knew everything. We've been lied to."

He couldn't accept this, they were his parents and wouldn't do that to him, "What did de Meath say that made you think all this shite?"

"He told me the truth."

They took a few small, awkward steps forward as the line of people continued to move amidst the growing panic. If Sí was listening in on their conversation, it didn't let on. There was a rising, angry heat up the back of Lorcan's neck as he mulled over Maeve's accusations. He didn't want to hear it, but a part of him had to know what untruths she'd been fed.

"So, what is this 'truth' anyway?" He said without looking at her.

"Are you going to listen, or just argue with me?" She shot back.

He shrugged his shoulders non-committally, "First of all, they're not your parents." He whirled to say something, Maeve held her finger to him, and he backed down, "I know this is difficult for you, but you're going to have to be quiet for once. You saw for yourself back there, the way your perception can be altered with just a few choice words. You came to this world believing those two spirits were your dead parents. That's what they wanted you to believe, and you bought it, we all did. They had been gathering information to be used against you. All those shadows you saw in your house? All those dreams? They were following you, learning about you, and they've continued to do so."

He couldn't believe what he was hearing. Some random spirits were gathering intel on him? For what purpose? He had the urge to let out a deriding laugh, but he bit his tongue, letting her continue. Letting her dig her own grave. Maeve would probably realise the ridiculousness of what she was saying at some point.

"They've acted as our gatekeepers to the Otherworld, controlling when we crossed, telling us where we could go, curating our interactions. They've had a hand in everything that's happened to us; Oisin was right about everything, he could sense it. He wasn't as wrapped up in the fantasy of this place as we were. He was able to step back and grasp it for what it really was... is." She looked wistful for a second before continuing, "We don't even need them to cross over from our world. I know you already suspect that."

Lorcan did. He'd felt the veil for himself earlier. But that had been a fluke, she couldn't prove anything she was saying. However, there were needles in his mind, needles that had been pricking at him for a while.

"That cold we felt every time we came here? That was them." She sighed, knowing that there was going to be pushback for what was coming up next, "They have been feeding off of us ever since we got here, off of our life energy. That was the cold. The price for coming here."

"Fuck off." He blurted out, "My mum and dad are vampires, or some shite, now?"

"No, well, not like *Dracula* vampires anyway. Do you remember that guy that got up and spoke at the town meeting, Abar?" Lorcan saw Sí's ears prick at the mention of that name.

"Yeah, the thin guy."

"Exactly. They're similar to him. They feed off of the living, weakening them and learning about them until they can -" She looked uncomfortable.

"Until?"

"Until they can possess them, and take over their body. Permanently."

This time Lorcan couldn't hold in his laughter. He let it out in one loud *ha!*, right in her face. He knew it would hurt her, he knew everyone in the vicinity would turn to look at the two strange teens arguing in the back, but he wanted it to hurt. He wanted people to see. Did she realise how stupid she was being? William de Meath, the creature who'd been hounding them for months, and who'd practically murdered one of them, just told her a bunch of ludicrous lies and she'd bought into it. She deserved to be laughed at.

"I knew you'd react like this." She said, looking away, "You're so gaslit you can't even see past the lies and consider the possibility."

"I'm sorry, *I'm* the one who's been gaslit? Okay." He said contemptuously.

He was being vile, but he couldn't help himself. It was actually refreshing to have her be the idiot for once, she was always so well researched and prepared, but it seemed her smarts had failed her now. What did she know of this world? Or his parents for that matter? *Everyone* they'd met had been lying to them? He gave her a look of scornful pity.

She stared straight ahead, "I just hope for your sake that your blind faith doesn't backfire when the time comes."

That was the end of the conversation, but he didn't feel like giving her the last word, "Oisin doubted them. It didn't seem to serve him well in the end."

Her shoulders tensed. He wasn't able to react to the hand that rose quickly to his face with a sharp slap. Her eyes blazed with icy fire, and she was shaking with anger. He was sure that he felt his hair stand on end again with some stored static but, before either of them could continue, a small voice sounded from their feet.

"You can't be that dense, boy." It was Sí, "You're going to get yourself killed, you know that?" Its voice was silky and high with just a hint of disdain. It really was the quintessential example of what Lorcan imagined a talking cat to be. He was about to respond when a huge tremor rocked the grounds. He felt the castle shift and jump underneath his feet, everyone on the bridge fell to the floor. Screams of terror sounded from below, both from within and without the castle, and from inside the mountain. He hadn't yet righted himself when the world exploded around him.

A powerful, blinding beam of light cut a vertical slice in the bridge ahead, decimating the stone like it was nothing, reducing those caught in it to atoms. A pure streak of sunlight cutting into the night. He brought his hands up, shielding his face from its brightness and felt his skin blister on the softer parts. The acrid smell of burning flesh and hair filled his nostrils; the moans of the injured rose above the rumbling, as those unfortunate enough to have been closer were scorched. He felt lucky the line had been so slow, they'd avoided the worst of it. Lorcan blinked away the sun spots clouding his vision and managed to see where that attack had come from, blinking once more to make sure his flashed vision wasn't playing tricks on him. It was a man. The man, however, was colossal in the most literal sense. Easily as tall as the bridge that they were standing on, which was in imminent danger of collapsing, with thick, hide-like skin, and he had a singular oversized eye that sat in the middle of his forehead. His heavy lid glowed as it closed over the offending eye. There was a team of people on either shoulder with a system of levers, hooks and pulleys that seemed to be opening and closing the lid. Was it so heavy that he couldn't lift it himself? They were gearing up for another round, but had pivoted and weren't pointing in their direction - for now.

"Get up!" Sí said quickly, "We'll have to find another way." A couple of its whiskers were smoking, but it looked relatively untouched.

Maeve groaned, pulling herself to her feet and wincing. She hadn't reacted in time to shield herself, one half of her face was painfully pink. He went to help her, his hands hovering over her arm and not wanting to dig into tender skin. She waved him away in a signal that meant, *it's fine,* and they followed Sí, leaving behind their crumbling escape route.

# 38.

The stone floor heaved as another part of the castle was obliterated. Though nowhere near them this time, chunks of debris rained in every direction, spreading the destruction further. Lorcan caught himself against a wall, managing to stay on his feet, Maeve did the same. They both sharply inhaled through their teeth in shared pain as raw skin impacted the hard surface. Sí's pace had slowed to a trot as it decided where to go. There was no clear route to safety.

"Does it know where to take us?" Lorcan whispered.

"It has a name." Maeve whispered back, dusting off her clothes.

"And *it* is a *she*." Sí said, her head tilting back towards them.

"Oh, sorry." Lorcan said, feeling slightly ridiculous apologising to a cat.

Sí was a she. That wouldn't be confusing at all. They set off again, hoping that giant eye wasn't looking at their section of the castle.

"I have an idea about where to take you." Sí, called back to them, "It'll just take us awfully close to where the fighting will be, but if we can get there quickly, we might have a chance of missing it. So hurry up!"

That was all the prompting they needed. Their jog quickened to an all out run through the obstacle courses that were the castle corridors. All of them nearly ended up on the wrong end of a spear more than once as nervy soldiers jumped at their sudden appearance through the acrid, haze of smoke filling the air. From what he was able to garner through the window, the front wall of the complex had a massive gouge in it presently, no doubt caused by the one-eyed big boy. He and the army were still a ways off from the main building, but he had the advantage of a devastating ranged attack. It didn't seem like de Meath's side had any response to that. Not that they'd shown anyway. Which meant the invading forces would probably be able to cut a path straight to the castle with ease. Lorcan's mum and dad might be a part of that charging party, and they'd be looking for him. Though that thought didn't fill him with the same warmth or confidence as it might have awhile ago, he pushed those feelings down. His parents would take care of him. They'd know exactly what to do. They weren't lying to him. End of.

Turning a corner, the group skidded to a halt. A section of the structure had been sliced away, exposing the floors of the castle, like a knife through the layers of a cake. The structure audibly cracked under their weight, forcing them to take a hasty step back. One-eye's handiwork. Sí cursed and spun to find a set of stairs. Every second they spent wandering around the hallways was a second closer to all out warfare that they definitely did not want to partake in. They raced down the stairs, skipping every few steps and coming close to falling flat on their asses more than once.

"I'm glad you encouraged me to run!" Maeve wheezed out, "Otherwise I'd be fucked!"

"Glad I'm good for something! Don't get too cocky, we're not done yet." He replied, hopping the last few steps to the bottom floor.

Flying past more soldiers, they came to a wide open yard that spanned hundreds of metres in every direction, with an inner wall that gave the illusion of safety from the oncoming horde. Between them and their destination on the opposite side lay hundreds, no, thousands of men and women awaiting what would inevitably burst through the massive wooden gate.

"Can we go around?" Maeve asked.

"That would take longer. It's okay, they're on our side, and they all know me, so you'll be safe too. Let's go!" Sí took off running again.

Lorcan always preferred running on grass, it was softer and didn't rattle his bones quite as much. The soldiers mostly ignored them as they huffed by, their faces and figures rushing past in his peripheral vision. He could see people and creatures of all shapes and sizes preparing for battle. Some of their claws and teeth meant that they weren't holding any sharp implements, they would be using themselves as weapons. It was going to get bloody. He was glad they wouldn't have to see that, flashbacks of the wolf creature that had mangled his dad's arm raced into his mind. They had to keep going.

Nearing halfway point, a voice sounded across the battlefield. Lorcan thought he recognised its distinct thinness.

"Abar." Sí said under her breath, coming to a halting stop along with everybody else around them.

"Your reckoning is nigh, lay down your weapons, hand over the prisoners, and we can settle this peacefully." It hissed out.

The sensation was similar to de Meath speaking, it sounded like the voice was coming from within Lorcan's own skull, but without being able to pinpoint the source. He rubbed at his temple, a gesture mimicked by a few of the soldiers, they too were experiencing the same discomfort of something else commandeering their thoughts.

"For too long have you corrupted our ancient ways. We, the Formóire, seek to take back what is ours, and unite the living and dead once again. This is your final warning, William de Meath, surrender, or face your end." There was a certain smugness in his tone, like his victory was assured.

"Maybe you should surrender us. Let me go back to my parents." Lorcan suggested to Sí, "It might stop the fighting."

She turned to face him, her cat eyes about as disdainful as cat eyes could be, and said, "You have no idea how bad that would be. We would fight one-hundred wars to prevent that from happening."

"I don't understand. What's so bad about it?"

"You heard what Maeve said, your parents -"

She was interrupted by de Meath's vocals crashing over Abar's, sending a visible ripple of surprise throughout the crowd.

"You dare speak of corruption to me? You are naught but poison to this land and every other land." The dullahan sounded incensed, "Attack this fort all you want, we'll repel you as we always have. Like water from stone. You won't set foot in the living world as long as we can help it. You will not spread your filth! As for the prisoners, they're long gone into hiding, out of your reach. Your key from the Otherworld is long gone."

Sí cringed at that. What did he mean by *key from the Otherworld*?

"I see you put too much faith in your servants as ever." Abar laughed, "My sources tell me they're closer than you'd think. Yes, they're very near indeed."

No sooner had he finished that sentence than a section of the thick wall blew into fiery pieces, and scores of warriors broke through. Arrows flew past their heads, and they dove into a huddle on the ground in an attempt to avoid being skewered by a stray shaft meant for another's torso. Lorcan tried to crawl along the ground on his elbows like he had seen in countless war movies, but it was harder than it looked, he quickly gave up and opted for a hands-and-knees crawl.

"What do we do?" Maeve shouted to both of them.

"We just need to get to the other side." Sí said, narrowly twisting out of the way of a stomping foot.

"What's the plan then?"

"There is none. Run!" Her hind legs sprung her lithe body forward into the thick of the action, "Keep close you two, I can protect you."

He didn't know exactly how something so small was going to do anything to one of those shapeshifting monstrosities he dreaded meeting, but he was proven wrong in an instant. A huge man, twice as tall and maybe five times as wide as Lorcan, swung for her. Her tiny body easily dodged his thick arm, scratched him lightly as she did so. That wouldn't have been much except her claw caught on something, a pale blue substance, it stretched and pulled from his body as she fell away from him. He howled as she tugged, whatever it might be, the result was definitely painful. With one sharp jerk of Sí's neck, masses of the blue substance rushed from every pore of his body and towards her. She opened her mouth, inhaling it like a vapour, leaving his lifeless, limp body to fall with a sickening thud. Maeve and Lorcan exchanged looks of astonishment. That was... unexpected. They were sorry to have doubted the diminutive cat.

"Come on!" She shouted, rushing onwards, repeating the process on another unfortunate victim.

As he passed the body, Lorcan noticed sprouts and vines consuming it, growing up from different orifices. It was rapidly becoming one with the landscape. He suspected that a new forest might be in the process of springing up soon if proceedings continued. He ducked around people charging in from his side, but was clipped with the front end of a shield as he hopped over another sprouting body. He fell hard, seeing a flash to his front, where Maeve was, as he righted himself. Lorcan worried the worst had happened, feeling relief when she appeared to be making her way past a stunned looking man-wolf. Someone must have tagged the thing as it was approaching her. Nice one!

They were making good progress across the field, most of the soldiers ignored them in favour of a recognisable enemy, and they only occasionally had to tussle with someone or navigate around contained skirmishes. Sí was doing her job and leading them to safety.

The rest of the wall came down then.

"Balor!" de Meath sounded to his army, "Bring him down!"

The hulking giant from before shouldered his way through the already compromised wall, showering friend and foe alike with tons of rubble as clouds of vision-obscuring dust enveloped the battlefield. Immediately, volleys of arrows were lobbed his way but did nothing other than bounce off of his thick skin. The operators on his shoulders repelled the arrows mid-flight by means of an invisible shield. It seemed futile to attack that thing. Its eye was being wrenched open by the pulley systems again, this time he was aiming right for the towering spire that de Meath was presumably overlooking the battle and issuing orders from. The angry glow built beneath the lid when Balor wrenched violently to the side. A shining spear had found its way deep into one of his biceps, returning to its owner's hand like a homing missile. The owner of the spear spurred his horse on furiously. A tall, muscular man with a series of tattoos intersecting over his body. Bounding along at his side was a fierce looking hound that Lorcan did not want anywhere near him, it looked nearly as big as the horse. There was a collective intake of breath from both armies as the man charged, all eyes on him.

"That's the guy who was at the solstice!" Maeve said, pointing excitedly.

He raised the spear once more, it shot from his hand with incredible speed and accuracy, this time burying itself into one of the operators on Balor's shoulder. The shields didn't mean much against this man's power. The interlude had ended, the tide of battle was yet to swing either way, and the armies got back to slashing and clawing at one another. Their trio got back to running. The metallic scent of blood was thick now, along with all the other bitter earthy smells that come with death.

A strong hand pulled Lorcan roughly to the ground. A

woman with only half of one of her legs still intact slashed at him, her fingers were razor-tipped and her head was warping into that of a bear. Her eyes mad with bloodlust as he kicked at her face, frantically trying to free himself, but her paw kept him pinned as her jaws snapped for his thigh. Sí was just in time to claw out the bear's essence, it went limp. Little flowers sprouted from its dull eyes as its tongue lolled numbly out of its mouth. He swallowed.

"Thanks." He managed.

"You're going to have to learn how to handle yourself." Sí said, trotting lightly along the bear's neck, "She can."

She nodded to Maeve who was glancing alertly around her, ready for danger. What did she mean? When had Maeve "handled" herself? It didn't make any sense, he'd been with them both the whole time. He then thought back to the flash he'd seen out of the corner of his eye a little earlier, and the flash he'd seen in their cells. Is that what Sí meant? But surely that hadn't come from Maeve. He was going to protest, but the cat was being picked up by some invisible force now. She let out a piercing *meow* as she struggled against whatever it was that had a hold of her.

"You really ought not encourage the boy, he might hurt himself, poor thing." He recognised her, it was Lea, the woman who'd accompanied them to Florence's hut, "Your parents are very eager to see you, Lorcan." She said, her long glowing hand outstretched to Sí.

He didn't reply. How had she found them in the middle of this chaos? It couldn't have been mere coincidence.

"Run! The pair of you! Just keep heading underground!" Sí yelled, flailing her small paws every which way.

"Quiet you." Lea said calmly as she flicked her wrist, sending the cat to the ground with a cracking thump, "Stay. Both of you. They'll be here soon."

He was in a state of pure indecision. He wanted to see his parents. He wanted to stay. But something about it felt dangerous, and his instincts were begging him to get out of there. Maeve tugged on his arm.

"Come on, Lorcan. We have to go!" She said desperately, "It's a trick!"

Lea looked disapprovingly, pinching her thin forefinger and thumb together, shutting Maeve's mouth from a distance. Calmly she pointed to her side at two figures approaching through the fire and fog of battle. It was his mum and dad. They weaved through the mess of people, easily dodging attacks aimed squarely at them without responding, moving relentlessly forward. Maeve pulled at his arm while he stared, transfixed, as if in a dream.

"Enough!"

He heard Sí say as her little limbs began to stretch out before her, fur turning to pale skin. Golden hair sprouted from her head and she raised a slender human hand to her captor, sending Lea flying into a large boulder, shattering the surface

"Enough of this, Leanan, or are you going by *Lea* these days? You won't harm these two." In place of the tiny cat Sí stood a wiry, majestic sorceress.

"If you really wanted to stop us, you would have just killed them and been done with it." Lea snarled, picking herself up from the rubble.

"That's something only you and your cohorts would do, besides it wouldn't make a difference. You'd just latch onto some other unfortunate pair."

She flung a jet of purple energy at Lea who deflected it in Lorcan's direction. Maeve stepped in front of it in an attempt to shield him but Sí had already stopped it with a flick. She was lightning quick, her hands working fast whilst her lips whispered powerful, sharp words under her breath, building the next projectile. She fired it off with a quick slicing motion, five golden arrows that rocketed through the air. Lea outright blocked these and responded with a conjured arctic jet stream. Sí's hand rose to meet it, glowing red-hot, creating a bubble of warmth around the three and sending steam swirling upwards. Lorcan got the distinct impression she would have been doing much better in this fight had there not been two useless humans to protect on the sidelines - or one useless human, at least. He was quickly realising that he may have been the dead weight around here.

"When we get the chance, we need to move." Maeve said, the effects of whatever Lea had done to her voice had ceased when she'd come under fire, "Give us an opening if you can." Sí twitched her head in affirmation, too busy building arcane energies to talk, "Lorcan, are you ready?"

He looked at Maeve's face, snapping out of the daze he'd been in, her burned, tired, filthy face, and saw everything clearly for the first time in - ever. She wasn't trying to hurt him or trick him, whether right or not, she believed that fleeing was in their best interest. He'd put his trust in her for now. He nodded.

"Okay... now!" Sí shouted, clicking her fingers and sending a torrent of blue fire in Lea's direction. In a fluid motion she had the fire transform into a bird and pursue the lanky, grey-skinned woman. There was no time to take in the spectacle, they had to go. Kicking off of the ground, they sprinted to what they hoped was the safety of the inner castle. Lorcan looked over his shoulder at his parents, who had been held up by opposition but were now making a beeline for them. He didn't know how to feel about that, hoping that this would resolve itself into some big misunderstanding on everyone's part, and they could go back to how things were. The knot in his stomach spoke to the foolishness of such a wish.

They bolted into the building, throwing themselves down corridor after corridor until they were completely lost within the labyrinthine structure. Sounds of the battle raged on outside, although thick stone dulled the impacts and made it all seem more distant than it was. They slowed to a walk as occasional booms vibrated the surrounding walls. Lorcan was tired, and he didn't know if Maeve was good for another sprint, her skin coated in a slick layer of salty sweat. She was exhausted.

"Where to?" he asked.

"Sí said underground, so we'll look for some steps I guess." She puffed.

The castle leaped under them, knocking them both to the ground, another one of Balor's blasts. Dust fell from between cracked stone, and he had visions of it collapsing right on top of them. It didn't, but they needed to keep moving. Lorcan hauled himself up and helped Maeve get to her feet, her hands clammy against his. They rounded a few more corners until they were forced to stop. Part of the roof had caved in, there was no going this way, they'd have to retrace their steps. There was one problem with that plan. Amongst the noises from outside and the unnerving rumbling from within the castle, footsteps approached. There was no other path to take, they were trapped.

The footsteps neared and soon two figures emerged from around the corner. The woman spread her arms.

"Lorcan, love, where are you running off to? Your father and I have missed you so."

They had been found.

Lorcan forced a smile, playing the role he was expected to. A couple of hours ago he would have been genuinely happy to see them, but now he didn't know how to react. He had run from them, so something in his gut was telling him this situation was askew.

"Mam, dad." The words felt hollow, "We need to get back to our world."

"I know you do, that's what we're here for. To help take you back, we only want to help. Why are you so afraid?" His mum advanced slowly, taking care with every step.

Her eyes glued to the two spirits, Maeve murmured, "*Perceive*, Lorcan, don't just look. See them for what they really are."

Reluctantly he focused. He so wanted everything his parents had said to be true, he wanted his family back. If they were telling the truth, there'd be nothing to fear. As he commanded his mind to look past any deception that might be taking place, any hope of he and his family living happily ever after faded. It wasn't like the shapeshifters transformation, their bodies didn't distort and twist and crack. Rather, it was like a fog lifted from his brain, and he was waking up from a half-sleep he'd been in ever since coming to the Otherworld. Their gaunt faces made themselves apparent, as did their gruesomely long limbs and appendages. Their skin dulled and lost the deeper fleshy tones of live human complexions, replaced with the translucent paleness he'd seen before on Abar. The placid smile that had been plastered on their faces dropped along with the pretence. They were not his parents.

"Who are you?" Lorcan said in a heave. He wanted to cry and throw up and run away all at once.

The woman smirked, her inhuman eyes narrowing, "You don't recognise us, love?" 'Love' was emphasised mockingly, "Awk, I suppose it doesn't matter. What matters is that we know who *you* are. We know all about both of you."

What did that mean? His mind may have been clear, but his vision stung with the smoke that was filling the hallway. Coupled with his seething anger, it was hard to breathe.

"I think it's a little premature to be saying that, *Alice*." Maeve retorted, "I think you would've liked to spend a little more time grooming us. Am I right?" There was a knowing in her voice that gave her the confidence to stand her ground, even in the state she was in.

"Alice?" Lorcan was confused.

"Alice Keytler and William Outlaw. Yes?" She directed at the grotesque pair in front of them.

"Oooh, Maeve, always so knowledgeable and well-informed, aren't you? Tell me, where was all that brainpower when Oisin was telling you both to open your eyes, hmmm?" This thing, Alice, knew how to hurt, "Did all your reading help him? It was a shame to do what we did, but *he* was the smart one, not you, he needed to go. You were just as fooled as wee Lorcan here. So wrapped up in your own fairytale. So blind to the danger in front of you. It's your fault he's dead, you know." He could see Maeve clench her jaw, "Don't pretend at being clever now, girl."

"You'll pay, you fucking bitch." Maeve said shakily, her face flushing red.

"Oh, I very much doubt that." Alice stretched her neck from side to side, "Before we do this, I just want to say what a displeasure it was to know you. Both of you are utterly pathetic specimens unworthy to be our hosts, but we'll have to make do." She crouched, as did William who had been silent thus far. They were ready to make their move, poised to strike like wild animals.

Maeve readied herself too but, before anything could happen, Lorcan needed some answers.

"Wait!" He shouted. To his surprise, they did wait. They seemed more amused than anything else, "Why now? Why didn't you make your move much earlier when we didn't suspect anything? Surely that would've been easier than this."

She shook her head wryly, it seemed she wasn't about to have an elaborate villainous monologue, and they were cutting straight to the action. He wasn't going to get his answers. Alice made a quick diving motion towards Maeve while William came straight for Lorcan. He didn't know what he could possibly hope to do against them, would he be able to put up any fight? He'd almost died back on the battlefield, always having to be rescued by those around him. Maybe he was pathetic. He stood, motionless and accepting. This was it.

"No!" Maeve raised her hand, producing a blinding yellow light that shot forward, impacting Alice hard and grazing William, knocking him aside. Alice flew back, slamming into the wall, taking a chunk of the stone with her.

Maeve fell to one knee, panting hard, while Alice shrieked and clutched at her side where the projectile had connected most painfully. William crawled to her side.

"Mother!" He cried, tending to her.

Lorcan bent and tended to Maeve in a similar fashion,

finding that he couldn't touch her, she sparked with an energy that repelled him. Her hair stuck out at odd, spiky angles, rigid with static. It would have been comedic if it hadn't been a life or death situation. She looked like she was about to pass out.

"How did you do that?" He asked, astonished.

She eyed him wearily but urgently, "Not the time - go."

Alice was still incapacitated and howling in agony as William, fraught with worry, comforted her, ignoring his own pain. Lorcan put his arm around Maeve, swearing as he received at least a dozen electric shocks, and hauled her into a standing position. He adjusted his grip so that she was supported, and they squeezed past the stunned pair at a brisk walking pace. It was about all he could manage with both of their weights to account for. If they could make it back to the battle, maybe they'd be able to get lost in the crowd, but at the risk of getting killed there too. He didn't know his way around the castle, so they'd only get more lost, plus he was certain they had some tracking capabilities. Abar had implied that before Balor knocked down the wall, and they'd been found easily afterwards. There were no good options here.

"We'll both get caught if you keep dragging me along." Maeve groaned.

"You want me to leave you then?" He replied between ragged breaths.

"No."

"Then shut up and come up with a plan." He couldn't think *and* be the muscle, "How did you do that?" He repeated his earlier question.

"Perception. I thought about it and it happened." She was struggling to get the words out, whatever it was it had clearly taken a lot out of her, "We're still living creatures, so we can alter things here. You can do it too."

"Really? And where did you learn this."

"From de Meath."

"Of course."

It was turning out that their sworn enemy wasn't such

an enemy after all. He'd deal with this revelation when they found some semblance of safety. The sounds of an intensifying battle became louder as they approached the exit. Out of the frying pan. Maeve indicated that she could carry herself, and he let her go. She took a few unsteady steps and began walking at a less than optimal pace, but it allowed Lorcan to catch his breath.

"So when you say 'you thought about it' what do you mean?" He continued.

Maeve swallowed, it was an effort to exist at the moment, "I mean just that. It's an intense concentration. You've felt it before."

"At Dún Dubh."

"Yes." She sighed out, "Exactly. Like de Meath said, the Otherworld is made up of conscious and unconscious thoughts. If we try hard enough, we can make our desires manifest."

He tried to remember the feeling but nothing was springing forth. You'd think now that he had knowledge of his supposed capabilities, he'd be able to do something, but it wasn't so. He was useless as ever.

"Intense concentration, you say? Not my strong suit." He tried to laugh it off.

"Oh, I don't know. You've always seemed pretty narrow-minded and bullish to me."

"I think you mean 'single-minded'."

"I said what I said."

It was good to see she could still make jokes at his expense. He tried to imagine his hands crackling with energy like hers had done, but all he got was a slightly warm pinky finger. Even then he couldn't be sure that it wasn't just his imagination. What was he going to do if they caught up? He thought of what they would have done to him had Maeve not stopped them. Again, she was way ahead of him when it came to this stuff. Conscious and unconscious? Manifesting thoughts? He didn't have long to mull this over before he noticed shuffling coming up behind them, something they definitely didn't want to hear. It seemed she'd hurt Alice, but the pair were not out of commission yet.

"Go!" He said, grabbing Maeve's hand and pulling her along as fast as he could.

The end was in sight, but it was no good, he could tell they were closing in, they must have been lightning quick with those long limbs, with insane recovery time. He would have to muster what power he could, this was his moment and he felt a charge build in his chest. Their primal snarls were right behind them, and he turned to see William's eyes wild with hunger, set on Lorcan. That charge dissipated into nothing. He wasn't stopping them, he just didn't have it in him. He'd failed again. He braced for the worst and, instead of feeling fangs or claws, he felt a rush of something else past his ear. A bone whip. It wrapped itself around the creature's waist and yanked him bodily over their heads and into the open. Alice lunged after William, holding her side, evidently still hurt.

"Finally." The headless figure of de Meath proclaimed, "I've been looking for you."

He reeled in the whip as William struggled wildly, digging his heels into the ground and shrieking like a trapped animal. The inexorable force of the dullahan's grip pulled steadily until Alice slashed at the precise spot where he kept his head under his tunic. He spun away just in time, the jagged spikes of bone loosening and allowing William to free himself. It was two against one, but the horseman kept his weapon moving and undulating around him, allowing for no openings or flanking manoeuvres. The vicious barbed tip struck at the pair as they danced around him.

"This is your chance!" He pointed to Lorcan and Maeve, "I've got them. You find a way out, and I'll finish these two once and for all."

"Still pining over that whore mother of yours are you?" William sniped at his son, "You're going to have to grow up boy."

Lorcan suspected that this confrontation had been a long time coming for all parties involved, it was best to stay out of it. He tugged Maeve's arm, she was gearing up to help, but he shot her a warning look, and she relented. This was not their fight, and she'd done enough already. They sped off in the opposite direction, de Meath had given them a chance, and they'd take it.

In the distance, Balor was still wreaking havoc, his eye was open and disintegrating what was left of the castle tower, leaving deep gouges in the bark of the mammoth tree in the process. The gouges glowed a brilliant gold as thick sap bled from within. He thought it may have been a trick of the light at first, but Lorcan saw a vast serpent dipping from the clouds above and gazing down on the proceedings without intervening. Utter chaos. His attention was brought back to ground level as he saw the tattooed warrior's golden spear darting to and fro, unable to find its target. Abar was using some sort of charm to deflect it off its path, flitting about and casting spells as Sí had, the great hound nipping at his heels. It wasn't looking good for de Meath's side, they were being pushed further and further back into the depth of the fortress which looked in real danger of collapsing altogether, entombing them. The battle had moved far enough away from the gigantic hole in the wall, leaving a clear path for them to flee.

"Leanan!" They heard the voice in their head, Abar was calling across the battlefield for her, "The children!"

They'd been spotted. How acute were Abar's senses to see them in the middle of all this pandemonium? They made an effort to hurry, but the ground had been torn to shreds, and rubble was strewn everywhere like an obstacle course. Stumbling over a large ditch, Lorcan saw the air warp in front of him like a mirage, Leanan stepping into existence. She held out a hand in the same manner she'd used to quieten Maeve, but stopped mid-motion. Her face strained with effort as she struggled in place.

"You two! Praise Danu you're safe" It was Sí, "I'm not going to be able to keep this up. Here!" She made a circular motion with her hand and a distortion appeared a few feet in front of her, similar to the one Leanan had just stepped out of, "It's not a precise spell, but I'll get you as close to the place of power as possible. You should be strong enough to cross yourselves."

She could teleport them? "Why the hell didn't you do this before?" Lorcan asked, furiously.

"I was a bloody cat! And a 'thank you' would be nice, now go!" She waved them through.

He didn't see what being a cat had to do with anything in the Otherworld, but he was relieved that this ordeal was nearly over, "Thank you." He said, stepping through with Maeve in tow.

The scene shifted around them, light and colour refracting, shimmering like they had physically entered a prism, and they stepped out onto a new location far away from the battle. The sudden quiet was shocking as their heavy breathing became very apparent, along with their pumping hearts. Lorcan wanted nothing more than to rest, but that was not on the cards right now. They had to get to Dún Dubh. He spun his head in search of the fort through the darkness, and there it was, her teleportation spell had been accurate enough. A short hike over a ridge and they'd be home. He hoped that they could repeat their success of crossing over by themselves. It mattered this time.

"Come on, let's go, we can have a breather when we get home." He said, but Maeve held him back, "What is it?"

Her hand raised she pointed a trembling finger to the middle distance at another prismatic flickering in the air. It couldn't be, they were so close.

"Move!" He yelled, gripping her hand even tighter and forcing them both into a sprint as Alice and William strode through their portal in pursuit.

# 39.

His lungs burned, his legs burned, his mind was on fire. They were nearly there. All they had to do was keep running, and they'd have a chance of making it. Alice and William were worn out from their fight with de Meath, their movements were less smooth, less precise; they too had slowed significantly. This was their opportunity to put some distance between them. Maeve was struggling, however, her breathing was harsh, and she looked like she could go at any second. If she could just hang on for a minute, they'd be home free, and then she could rest. Lorcan held her fast, he would run for them both. He pumped his legs as hard as he could. The fort was in sight, he was going to do it, he was going to save them. A slender hand grabbed at the back of his neck. No! He was good at running, he could do this. Another tightened around his free arm, pinning it. If he could just keep going. Maeve's hand was torn from his grasp, sending him tumbling forward. He needed to get her back.

The powerful, sinuous arms twisted him around to face his attacker and pinned his other arm with a painfully placed knee. Lorcan tried to shout but all the breath had left him when he'd been slammed. He managed little snuffles and grunts as he struggled and kicked at the wet grass, his feet slipping. He became acutely aware that Maeve was going through the exact same struggle only feet from him, her whines high and desperate. He couldn't see William's face, he was but a shadow against the slowly lightening sky, but Lorcan sensed the triumph. The predator had caught its prey, and it would feast. He tried to calm his mind, Maeve had said he needed to concentrate to do what she had done. It was difficult when someone had their hand around your throat and were about to enact some unknown horror. He felt the beginnings of a spark in his chest as he focused, but that was quickly replaced with a white-hot agony in his hand.

He looked down to see what was causing that pain, but he couldn't make sense of it. William manoeuvred his hand so that his fingers interlocked with Lorcan's, and it was - moving into him. It was like the creature had become a liquid and was somehow diffusing itself like a dye into water, Lorcan's body being the water. The feeling spread its way up his arm as William pushed further and further. Lorcan couldn't scream even if he wanted to, it was the kind of pain that struck a person silent because the mind couldn't begin to comprehend what was happening. His airway cleared as the hand was lifted from his throat, the process repeating itself in his other arm. Time became irrelevant. Lorcan felt like all he had ever known was this moment, the profound pain encompassed his entire being, past, present and future. William lay his body fully on top of him so that he contoured to the form of the writhing figure beneath and pressed their faces together. Every cell lit up from the tips of his toes to the very hair on his head, William was seizing his body. It wasn't about the agony anymore, that had long passed, it was the unbelievable pressure of having another person occupying the same space as him that was the most unbearable part of the whole ordeal. As the creature wormed his way inside, it left less and less room for Lorcan, he had nowhere to go. He ceased breathing when their faces unified. He could smell the sour breath. He could taste William. He could feel his heart and every heave of the thing's body as it crushed itself into Lorcan's comparatively smaller frame. He wanted to die rather than experience this. At least it would be over soon, he could take comfort in that.

In the darkness he heard Maeve's whimpering. He was sorry. He was so sorry that he had ever brought her here. That he had ever coerced her into coming to the Otherworld in the first place. He had wreaked such destruction on her life because - what? He couldn't let go of his parents? What kind of person did that to another human being? Used them for their own means and couldn't care less if they were broken in doing so? He did. He deserved this fate, but she didn't. As he felt himself succumb to the black void, he was greeted with images. He didn't know what they were or who they belonged to. Feelings that weren't his own began to strike out at him. They were recognisable, however. Inadequacy, jealousy, cowardice, fear. He knew intimately how each of these things felt, however, it wasn't he who was feeling them, these were William's. This merging was a two-way transaction.

Lorcan let himself drift through these new sensations, these memories, taking comfort in the distraction. Running from the pain. He watched himself arriving at Cara's house for the first time after his parents had died, but through William's eyes. He felt sorrow palpably emanating from his past self, he was so vulnerable. He felt hunger. Skipping forward, now in the Otherworld with Alice, relaying this information to her, she smiled. He found himself walking through Cara's house in the darkness, looking at old photos, at his parents, studying them. He listened in on conversations and watched as he walked to school. William had studied him for months, like a recon mission, they must have done the same to Maeve. Gathering every ounce of information that could be used against him, against his grief. They'd picked him because they thought he would be an easy target to manipulate, their ticket to the living world where they could - do what? He dug deeper, finding a thread of related memories, he knew these were the answers he'd been seeking earlier.

*     *     *     *     *     *

"And you're sure the boy is a suitable vessel?" Abar's wispy voice inquired.

"Yes, he'll be ideal for William." Alice crooned, setting

a bony hand on William's shoulder, "A little push, and he'll be ours."

"And what about you, my dear?" Abar said, inclining his head to her, "Have you found your host?"

Alice gave him a knowing smirk, "Ah yes, well, our little Lorcan has some friends and I have my sights set on one in particular, a girl. It's all a matter of time. My William has done brilliantly, haven't you?"

William looked to his mother, pride swelling in his chest. Praise was a rare thing to come by, so he took it when he could, "Yes. Thank you mother."

"It's settled then," Abar rose from his seat, "you'll be the first among our kind to walk in human form in over a century. See to it that the children are unaware of what you really are."

"You needn't worry, we'll put on some very familiar faces."

The image swirled and faded as new ones emerged from the recesses of William's mind. They were in a familiar building now, the town hall. The crowd of monstrous entities whooped and hollered as they learned of Abar's plan to infiltrate the living world with his sleeper agents.

"Why do this now?" A member of the congregation shouted over the noise.

"A fine question." Abar responded, holding his hands out to quell the ruckus, "Too long have we been denied what is rightfully ours. Too long have we been at de Meath's mercy. He will soon be named steward of Ireland, and we will suffer under another age of repression. We will break the barrier between worlds, and rid ourselves of this dictatorship. Who are he and his king to enforce their will on us? We will make the living world ours once more, inverting this cycle of loss that we've been playing out for millennia, finally the Formoire will triumph over the Tuatha Dé Danann. Now is the time to begin a new cycle. One in which the dead rule over the living. Ireland will be the epicentre for the new world order, we'll spread our message far and wide. Now is our time!"

There was an explosion of thunderous applause that died as the memory dimmed and metastasized into another. A fire-lit hut in the middle of the night. Spices and strange aromas hung thickly in the air. A red haired woman held a glassy dagger aloft, inviting William to examine it for himself.

"It will guide them, knowingly or otherwise, to the correct doorway." Florence said, handing the dagger to him, "The tear will further weaken the veil, but it can only be done from the living world. A fracture that will spread outwards, shattering it into countless pieces. The old gods will be unable to repair it, and we will have our day." She smiled deliciously, William felt old desires reawaken in himself.

"You're sure they'll be able to find the doorway?" Alice asked, giving her son a reproachful sideways glance.

"I can't guarantee it, these things have a way of working themselves out. Quests bestowed upon mortals are never easy, they must suffer pain, confusion and loss, but I have faith they'll carry out their task to the letter." Florence leaned back in her chair, "One of them has been cursed you say?"

William nodded, "By a fear gorta."

"Very nasty." She winced, "Bring them to me. I'll point them in the right direction."

"Thank you, Florence."

"Anything for an old friend."

The light in the cabin became distant and remote. More images flashed by. The trio of Lorcan, Maeve and Oisin being ushered through the mountain pass. Receiving the dagger for themselves. A dark room, Fionn mac Cumhaill's burial chamber. William plucked the red spear from its resting place and scarpered off. Oisin had been right. He'd been right all along. More and more memories whirled by as Lorcan dove deeper. He'd been followed for months, groomed to be this thing's perfect host, manipulated from day one, and he'd dragged his friends down with him. He'd gotten Oisin killed, and now both he and Maeve were dying as well. Except, there was still a chance. A faint glimmer of hope that they might yet win. He sensed that the plan had been launched prematurely, and that they hadn't quite beaten them down enough to make the transfer of souls an easy process. Oisin's death was meant to break them, only Maeve hadn't reacted how they'd planned, she'd seen through it in a way Lorcan hadn't. She'd opened her eyes and forced their hand, now it was his turn. Maeve was the clever one, and she'd be their downfall yet.

*       *       *       *       *       *

The spark within Lorcan reignited itself and this time he used the pain. This was his body and he wouldn't make it so easy for the bastard. He dove into those memories, raiding them for anything he could use. He would weaponise William's thoughts against him, like he and Alice had done to their group. Images of Ireland, long ago. William's home. His father. Alice, standing over his father's body, a dark foam pouring from his mouth. He felt intense sadness. Good, there was some ammunition. A young woman, Petronilla. He felt love, passion. Petronilla was holding a bundle, a baby de Meath. Happiness. He saw Petronilla and Alice on trial. They were accused of something. The word "witchcraft" rang throughout the makeshift courtroom. A choice had to be made. His mother or his lover. Fear. Petronilla was burning at the stake, her flesh blackened and thick smoke filling the air. His choice had been made. Alice stood by his side, dispassionate. Inadequacy. Constantly at her feet, constantly berated and constantly envious. William had been the same in life as he had in death, an easily manipulated pawn that fed off of others. He held onto these thoughts, wringing them out for all they were worth.

"You need to grow up." Lorcan choked out, the smothering sensation lifted, "You fucking mammy's boy."

He forced himself onto his hands and knees, chest heaving and straining to keep control. Maeve's head turned towards him, her eyes streamed tears. He couldn't physically shout out, but screamed with his eyes. *Fight!* Her face hardened, if he could resist, she definitely could. Her arm reached out and gripped the grass. Pulling herself to lie on her front, she gasped, crying out in anguish. Alice was doing a number on her. Lorcan wished he could help, but felt like his chest would explode there was so much pressure from his invader. William was not giving up without a struggle. His arms buckled underneath, sending him into a face-plant.

"No way." Lorcan muffled into the dewy grass, "No way, am I giving you my body. I'm not going to let you use me anymore."

For all the times they had impersonated his dead parents. For all the times they'd lied to his face, and told him they loved him. For all the times they'd put his friends in danger. For Oisin. He'd get this vile thing out of him. It wasn't focus he needed, it was rage. Pure hot rage to burn William out of him like the infection he was. Control was returning to him as he peeled his face off the ground. It felt almost good to let go like this, he'd been cultivating a cold numbness for so long.

"Fuck you!" He said, it was time to get rid of him.

Lorcan closed his eyes, fanning the flames of that spark within, but a harrowing sounded disrupted this inner focus. It was Maeve, she was on her side screaming, clawing at her face. Red streaks lined her skin, blood trailing into her mouth. What was Alice doing to her? That momentary distraction was the chance William needed to regain dominance. His body dropped and lay as if pressed to the ground from behind, but he barely noticed. Maeve's scream continued as she contorted into impossibly unsettling positions, her throat sounding like it was tearing itself apart. She hacked and coughed up blood, retching with the effort, panting like a dying animal.

"I can't." She rasped, "I can't do it." She looked to Lorcan.

Again he wanted to shout out, to say, *you can do it! You can fight, Maeve!* but he wasn't the one operating his mouth right now. He blankly stared, body rigidly held in place. Maeve met his gaze. At that moment they were each other's anchor in the middle of the storm, something to hold onto. *Fight!*

She was back in control. Nodding once, Maeve closed her eyes, that look of intense concentration falling over her face. He was amazed she could do that even now, in this situation, in her state. Her hand began to crackle and glow with the same yellow energy she'd mustered before, now she was holding it like a ball in her palm. Before he could grasp what she was planning, her hand had shot towards her chest, stopping only millimetres from her skin as the two vied for dominion.

"You can't have me." She said through a clenched jaw, "You can't have my body or my world, you psycho bitch!"

Lorcan stared agape, powerless to stop her, as Maeve's hand broke free of Alice's control, laying itself flat on her chest. The area lit up with violent energy. Her body convulsing as if she'd been zapped with high voltage electricity, and an ascending note escaping her lungs until it faded, along with the light from her hand. She collapsed in a heap with smoke hissing from her chest. She wasn't breathing.

"Mother?" He heard himself say, watching his hand reach for the body.

Mother? That wasn't him, he'd been distracted and now was in danger of being deleted from his own flesh and blood. He was being smothered again, but he knew how to resist this time. Drawing on those red-hot emotions, he twitched his arm back, regaining a semblance of autonomy. Maeve's body jolted awake, letting a huge intake of air fill her lungs with a rasp, and she lay gulping for a few seconds. He grinned triumphantly, hoping she'd done Alice some serious damage. It was a tug of war now between Lorcan and William for who would hold sway over this form. He rolled and spasmed like someone in the throes of a powerful hallucination. He ached profusely, tiring, but so was the parasite, it was a question of stamina. In amongst his struggles, he watched Maeve get to her feet and stretch out her back casually. Her hands rose to meet her face, examining her palms closely. She let out a small laugh as she walked, coming to stand over him.

"Maeve?" He managed to stutter out.

It couldn't be.

She tutted, "Poor boy. You were never strong enough, were you?" She bent down and planted a kiss on his forehead.

He could see her face clearly. Her wounds healing right before his eyes as the sun broke the horizon, and a cruel look that had never been present was rooted in her countenance. It just couldn't be. She turned and strode to the fort.

"No." He muttered, "Maeve!"

Shooting him a dismissive wave with the back of her hand, she disappeared inside.

*Get up!*

He had to get up.

Who knew what that thing was planning to do with Maeve's body while he was stuck here fighting his own battle. How had this happened? Maeve was way stronger than him, there was no way she could lose. She had been exhausted and wiped out by everything that had gone on, Alice couldn't have defeated her otherwise. Lorcan, however, had the chance to get some rest while he was playing at being prisoner in de Meath's castle. It should've been him. He was sure that Maeve would be able to think of something if she were in his position, she would come up with some plan to rescue him, while he botched everything. That wasn't the case this time. This time he had to do it all on his own, but first, he'd have to get a hold of himself, quite literally.

"Let me go." He growled.

Nobody was coming to help, they would all be lying low because of the battle Huge plumes of smoke rose from the castle's direction, they'd know danger was afoot. It wasn't the time to look to others, it was time to eradicate this virus all by himself. Lorcan dug his fingers into his thigh, squeezing as hard as he could.

"Let me go!"

"No." He heard the reply come from within him, "You think I'll just give up now? I almost have you."

Lorcan sneered, "And you call *me* pathetic?" He forced

himself into a kneeling position, "All your planning, all your preparation, and you still can't seal the deal. Sneaking around in the shadows is more your style, I can tell you're shite scared now. Remember, I can feel what you feel."

It was true. It wasn't just his own fear and desperation that was sky-high, William was petrified. Lorcan centred himself, this was a battle of wills. That meant nothing in the living world, but here willpower meant something, and he was going to eke out every last drop that he had. The real him was going back to Dún Dubh, not some abomination. He clarified his goal, getting to Maeve, he let that thought consume him. He felt it like a heat in his chest, and it filled him with renewed energy. That heat went from being a spark, to a flame that erupted into an inferno, expanding and filling him so that William had to make room for it. It was that thing's turn to feel the pressure.

"You've been following your mother around for all these years like a lapdog. You think you're strong, but you're nothing without her," He was speaking calmly, "and you know it. Don't you?"

He felt the panic building in William's voice, "Who are you to talk to me? You were so grossly desperate to have your mammy and daddy back, that you clung to us like a leech - you're a feeble little weakling that brought the rest of your friends down. *You* killed them." He was aiming to destroy.

"I know." Lorcan said simply, letting the words wash over him, "I know what I did, and I accept that. What I need to do… is right that wrong, whatever way I can. Starting with getting you the hell out of me."

He clenched his fists. He would stand up. He would be leaving here alone. Lorcan would find Maeve.

"No." William's voice was getting weaker.

"How does it feel, dickhead? You're about to be beaten by a 'feeble little weakling'?"

There was a fresh eruption of pain throughout his entire body as he made a huge effort, letting the inferno detonate in his chest. The shockwave spread from his core to the outer edges of his body and William was purged from his hiding spot. He felt that invasive sensation again but in reverse, like tearing off the world's most painful plaster. It was a massive release, his body was lighter than air as he fell flat backwards, letting the gentle rays of morning sun caress his cheeks. He basked in this reverie for no more than a few seconds before he realised that the vampire was probably planning some counterattack. Pulling himself upright with his stomach muscles, Lorcan came face to face with what used to be William Outlaw - at least, that's what it looked like. It had his features, but they were faded, insubstantial, and he had a confused expression on his face. His big, glassy eyes fixed on Lorcan.

"How?" He said, reaching out one of his long hands.

He reminded Lorcan of one of those scáthanna, the shades, they'd seen in the bog, what Oisin was in the process of becoming. This possession had carried risks, whoever lost the war, lost a lot more than their pride, or their life. He felt pity forming in him, it was a hard task not to feel sorry for something, so vulnerable, but he swallowed that emotion. William deserved his fate, he needed to suffer for what he and his mother had done. Without a word, he got to his feet and left the creature behind as it grabbed at him with decrepit fingers, kicking him off and breaking into a run. Lorcan was surprised to find his body ready for action as he bounded into the fort, none the worse for wear. He summoned that fire in him forth, making a grabbing motion, as if to tear the veil away and found himself back in the living world. He exhaled a breath he'd been holding for the longest time.

"Thank you." He said to no-one in particular and set his mind to the task at hand.

As he formulated his next move, Lorcan noticed his senses were on high alert. He could see every detail on the stone around him despite the dull, diffuse light, and his ears picked up the minute sounds of shifting gravel beneath his feet. He shoved these observations aside, Maeve was his priority. Where would Alice have gone? He'd gathered at least part of their plan from William's memories. She sought to sow the seeds of chaos in the living world by fracturing the veil in different locations. Where would she begin? He calmed his mind, thinking only of her. Narrowing his thoughts into a bottleneck, he felt something, a small tingle in one particular direction. Lorcan couldn't say what it might be, but he knew on some instinctive level that was where she had fled. It pointed straight to his house. To Cara's.

He flew. His legs worked as fast as they could to take him from the hilltop to Cara's. He may have been in a state of heightened terror, but his body was working better than ever, it felt effortless to leap from point to point. Rocks and trees and grass whizzed by in a blur of colours and motion. If he hadn't been worried about the fate of the two most important people in his life, this would have been exhilarating. It was amazing what the people could do when people were pushed to their limits, he mused. Cara would be out of her mind with worry about where he'd been the past twenty-four hours, especially in light of Oisin's death. This was going to be rather difficult to explain, but he'd deal with Alice first and explain later. Rain pricked at his skin as he darted along the empty, early morning roads, arriving at Cara's barely out of breath. The front door was wide open. Alice was here alright.

He crept up the driveway, his eyes darting back and forth, examining every shadow and every window of the house. He saw nothing. He didn't expect to see anything out of place because he could sense exactly where that creature was. Lorcan stepped carefully into the house, the smell of fresh coffee and toast filling the morning air along with - something else. He tried not to make a sound, but every small noise was amplified by the silence, and by his heightened awareness. He could practically hear the blood rushing through his veins in this quiet, and the irregular shuffling coming from the kitchen. Poking his head around the corner the tableau resolved itself, and he froze. There Maeve stood, or what was masquerading as Maeve, with Cara crumpled at her feet, bending casually to pick his aunt up by the hair. Cara's eyes were wide open, she was still alive but unable to speak. The creature hadn't killed her then, that was something. Its eyes became suspicious slits.

"Which one are you?" She asked.

"Maeve, I know you're still there. Just fight her." Lorcan pleaded.

"Ah, it's you." She said, the disappointment evident, "He was too weak then." She spoke more to herself now than to him.

"Maeve!" He continued, "Listen to me -"

"Do shut up, boy." Alice snapped, "She's gone, or are you too moronic to realise that?"

He gestured to Cara. "What have you done to her?"

She looked down and smiled, "Nothing, just stunned her for now, but she's very much aware of what's going on, don't worry about that."

"Okay, then just let her go. What are you doing here anyway?" He edged closer to them, attempting to keep his voice even.

Alice sighed, she looked bored, but it came across more as an affectation, "Well, I thought my son was a little too soft, I'd hoped for the better, but alas. I figured in the event that he lost, you'd want to come here to check in on your dear aunt Cara and let her know you were doing okay. I was right," She arched an eyebrow, "but you're just full of surprises."

What did she mean? What was surprising about wanting to rescue someone?

"You don't realise what you've done, do you, boy?" She said, seeing the questioning look creep across his face, "As slow as ever."

"What are you talking about?"

He was done with all of this cryptic bullshit, he needed to come up with a way of getting through to Maeve, she could still fight. She had to.

"Here, I'll give you a demonstration."

She wrapped her hand tighter around Cara's hair, hauling her up until she was almost standing, it didn't seem to require much effort on Alice's part. Lorcan stepped forward to stop her, but she put a hand around Cara's throat, giving a warning look. He backed off.

"Are you hungry?" She asked, "I'm starving myself and was thinking of having breakfast." He didn't know where she was going with this, "But, seeing as you don't even understand what's happened to your body, I'll let you have the first bite. Your first time is always so special."

"What the hell are you talking about?" He rushed forward, she wouldn't have her way.

"Stay." She said firmly.

Lorcan froze. Not voluntarily, his body had just stopped, and was now awkwardly posing mid-step. Alice looked back to the limp figure in her hand.

"I suppose I'll be kind and allow you some last words." She rubbed a finger over Cara's lips.

"Lorcan!" She said frantically, "What's happening? Maeve, stop this! Please!"

"Last words, dear, you need to choose them more carefully."

Realisation dawned on Cara what was coming. It dawned on Lorcan too, he could see it in Alice's eyes. He begged his body to move, searching for that fire that had been there before, but there was only an icy grip that held him fast. All he could do was exhale madly through his nose, making small, panicked, closed-mouth bleats.

"Lorcan, love," Cara began, "I -"

With a quick motion, Alice's hands twisted in opposite directions and wrenched her head until there was a loud, popping crack. Lorcan screamed, his mouth still shut. He had failed. Her body slumped to the floor as long hair slipped from between the thing's hand.

"She's not dead." Alice said, "I mean, she's *dying, but* she's not dead."

He moaned profanities at her, straining with all his might to move as Cara lay on the cold floor, motionless, except for her dancing eyes.

"Don't worry, I'll free you in a second, I'm just allowing her to - decant, if you will. Plus, I need to explain a little something to you before you're overcome by desire."

He could tell that she was getting an immense amount of pleasure from this, from torturing him. Why was she doing any of this? Why was any of this happening? It didn't make sense.

"You messed up everything, I hope you know that. Plans that had been in place long before you arrived on the scene. We were going to go with another pair, but then you came along." She looked up, remembering something glorious, "You were so weak, so vulnerable, we wouldn't even have to hurt you that much, the work was already done. You were perfect! What happened, Lorcan? When did my little helpless baby boy develop a backbone?" She stuck out her bottom lip like a mother talking to her toddler, "Certainly not alone, you had help, didn't you? You'd never have got this far without your friends, you're not that strong or clever. What will you do now that they're gone, hmmm?" She eyed him contemptuously.

While Alice was pontificating, a scent began to fill Lorcan's nostrils that replaced the dark, smoky aroma of coffee. It was lighter, more fragrant, he couldn't pinpoint exactly what, but it was the most delectable thing he'd ever come across. It made it impossible to focus on what Alice was saying or doing, or care about her for that matter. He wanted to know what that smell was, and he needed a taste of it.

"Oh." Alice said, "Drooling already?" She tilted her head towards him to get a better look, "I'd better be quick before I lose you completely."

She bent down and turned Cara so that she was facing upwards, her eyes wide with terror, completely at Alice's mercy. He knew how she felt, but found it increasingly difficult to care about anything right now as he swallowed the river of saliva his mouth was producing.

"You see, my dear, you're in a rather unique situation right now. When you first walked in I didn't know what had happened, but I think I'm starting to get it." She paused for effect, "You've got a little bit of me in you."

This caught his attention. What did she mean by that?

"Now, now, don't be giving me those eyes. I don't mean me specifically, but when you somehow forced my William out of you, he left something behind, I can see it. That's why I wasn't quite sure who I was talking to earlier. You read like someone from the Otherworld." She took Cara's forearm and gave it a long, lingering sniff, "Someone of my kind."

Her mouth hovered over Cara's wrist, open and ready to bite down. Lorcan made some noises, protesting through the haze of whatever drug was attempting to carry his thoughts away on the wind.

"Don't worry, I said I'd let you have the first bite. Smells good, doesn't it?" She said, laying the arm down, "I - rather we - feed on life energy. That's what you're smelling at this moment. It's just pouring out of your sweet aunt here."

What? It was Cara? He wanted to eat her? Impossible! The more the aroma swirled around in his head, the more he realised it to be true. He could almost see the aura around her. In that case, he'd resist, there was no way that was happening. Alice clicked her fingers and Lorcan's body lunged forward. He'd meant to attack her, but he found himself grabbing Cara's other wrist, pulling it roughly to his mouth. He stopped dead, forcibly gaining control back. He saw Cara's eyes fixed on him, her skin brushing his teeth tantalisingly. Slobber flowed from his mouth, onto her arm, dripping on the floor as he knelt, shaking. Resisting.

"Aren't we the paragon of self-control?" Alice said in mock congratulations, "How long will you last though? You're nearly there, it just takes one little nibble and that'll be you.

Don't worry, you're not going to *eat* her, you'll just drain her life. Much less gruesome."

"I won't." Lorcan said rigidly, her wrist still between his teeth. As he formed the words his tongue came into contact with some of that aura, sending urgent feeding signals to his brain. He was losing.

Maeve's face contorted in a way he'd never seen, a sadistic smile broke out and her eyes widened manically, "You will."

She took his head and slowly forced it down until his incisors pressed hard against Cara's warm, pulsing artery. His heart pounded in his chest. It was everything he could do not to bite, but his jaw was working of its own accord, like a pair of oxygen-starved lungs pulling water into a drowning man's body. He didn't want to do it. He didn't want to hurt her. But he was going to. He knew that with all the will in the world he wouldn't be able to stop himself, it overwhelmed every sense he had. He wasn't the one in control.

With a final tiny nudge his tooth broke her skin, like a needle popping the membrane of a balloon. Warm liquid filled his mouth and the metallic flavour of blood coated his tongue, quickly replaced by a torrent of the most delicious substance he'd ever tasted. It rushed into him, triggering every pleasure centre he had. His spine tingled with heat and his brain lit up in pure unadulterated ecstasy. Colours around him intensified, the crimson red of Cara's blood looked almost like neon paint. He moaned involuntarily as he bit down harder, snapping tendons and crushing bone, he had to have more, he needed more. Somewhere in the back of his mind he knew that he shouldn't, and that this was exactly what that parasite wanted from him. But did he really want to listen to that voice right now? This was too good. He inhaled more, his body quivering as every neuron and nerve ending was erupting in delight. He was all instincts. In a brief second of lucidity, he saw Cara's mouth spasm in pain and her bloodshot eyes glistening. Why was she crying? Should she not be happy that he was having such an experience? Why wasn't everybody as happy as he? It didn't compute for him, he just took hit after hit, crying tears of joyful gratefulness that he could feel so utterly complete.

Morning turned to noon, turned to afternoon. The winter sun was setting, bathing the house in a pale golden light. Lorcan felt a hand pull the cold mangled wrist from his mouth and stroke his cheek, rubbing some of the cracked, dried blood from his lips. He turned his head to see Maeve and smiled blearily at her. It was so nice to see her again. Why had he ever been concerned for her? She smiled back and took his face in her hands, forcing his attention on her.

"Well done, I'll see you again soon, son." He heard her say through the thick afterglow of his first meal.

Son? He wasn't Maeve's son, he thought, giggling. Who cared anyway? He felt her shadow leave his side. He was alone. Throwing back his head, Lorcan let the rapture run through him as his mouth hung open, continuing to giggle softly in the dying light, wondering why he couldn't be like this constantly. The feeling whisked him away, far away from his troubles. He was unburdened, free. He wanted to stay like this forever, right here, in this moment. Bliss.

# 40.

It was pitch dark when his trance was interrupted by lights from outside. They flashed, blue, red, and spun around the room with a long high whine accompanying them. Who would be rude enough to do such a thing? Lorcan descended from the heights of pleasure and began the long touchdown back to reality. Swinging his head loosely, he scanned the room as lights created funny looking shadows that danced off of the walls and furniture scattered about, making it look like the household items had come to life. He laughed. It was all so ridiculous. His floating gaze eventually settled on the sight in front of him. A woman. She was laying on her back, unmoving. Her grey skin was utterly drained of colour, a hand hanging loose on one of her wrists. Cara.

Memories bubbled to the surface, bringing with them waves of shame that slowly trickled their way into his groggy, awakening conscious mind. He was remembering what had transpired. No. He didn't want to remember. It was too much to handle, it must have been a dream. It had to be. That couldn't have been him.

It had been him though.

He tried desperately to cling onto that dull, heady buzz that was quickly turning venomous. There was a commotion around him, pairs of legs rushed past, things were pointed at him, voices shouted, and hands grabbed him roughly from behind. He let it all happen. Something had to distract him from the knowledge that was creeping its way into the forefront of his mind, and the bitter, metallic taste that coated his tongue. The frigid night air hit him as he was escorted out of the house towards the harsh flashing lights. He turned away, imagining he saw a petite figure watching him from the bushes, a black cat. It slinked from view as he was shoved into the back seat of a waiting car. Lorcan buried his head into the cold leather of the seat, trying and failing to block out everything around him.

Alice had won. He'd been used.

# EPILOGUE.

Darkness encompassed Maeve's vision between flashes of horrific scenes. Scenes over which she had no control. Cara's neck was in her hands, she broke it. Lorcan was - he was biting her? Why? She wanted to scream out. To stop him. But she couldn't, she could only watch as his life was torn apart. Again.

She got the distinct impression that she was being permitted to see these events at the whim of the demon within her, as she felt it suppressing her again. For that was all it could do. Hurt her. Suppress her. Alice couldn't obliterate Maeve, and she would regain her strength.

For now, she would rest.

Printed in Great Britain
by Amazon

27776443R00185